THE SILENT AND THE LOST

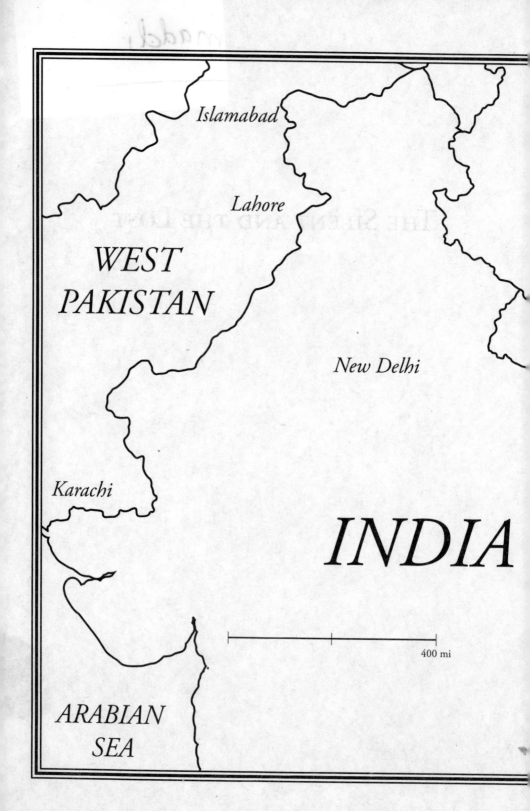

Islamabad

Lahore

**WEST
PAKISTAN**

New Delhi

Karachi

INDIA

*ARABIAN
SEA*

400 mi

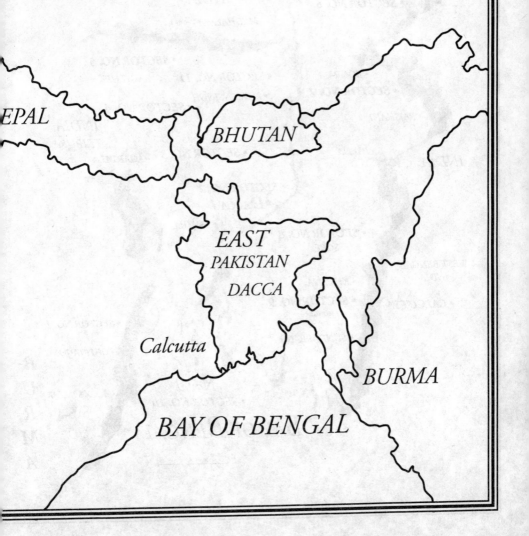

CHINA

MARCH 25, 1971

NEPAL

BHUTAN

EAST
PAKISTAN
DACCA

Calcutta

BURMA

BAY OF BENGAL

1971 BANGLADESH
WAR OF INDEPENDENCE SECTORS

The 12th Ethereal Sector
Radio Free Bangladesh
SWADHIN BANGLA BIPLOBI BETAR

INDIA

MEGHALAYA

• RANGPUR
SECTOR NO. 6

SECTOR NO. 5

SECTOR NO. 11   • SYLHET

• BOGRA
SECTOR NO. 7

• MYMENSINGH

SECTOR NO. 4

• RAJSHAHI

INDIA
TRIPURA

• PABNA

SECTOR NO. 3   •AGARTALA

INDIA

SECTOR NO. 2
•DACCA

• COMILLA

SECTOR NO. 8
• JESSORE

WEST BENGAL
INDIA

• KHULNA

• CALCUTTA   **SECTOR NO. 9**
• MONGLA

SECTOR NO. 1

• SUNDARBANS

• CHITTAGONG

Naval
SECTOR NO. 10

•COX'S BAZAR

BAY OF BENGAL

B U R M A

60 mi

THE SILENT
AND
THE LOST

❧

A. ZUBAIR

Pacific Breeze Publishers LLC
P.O. Box 3651
Costa Mesa, CA 92628
USA

email: info@pbreezep.com

www.zubair.com

www.pbreezep.com

2 4 6 8 10 1 3 5 7 9

Zubair, Abu Bin Mohammed.

The Silent and the Lost: a novel / by A. Zubair - 2nd printing

Library of Congress Control Number: 2010923075

ISBN 978-0-9825939-6-7

Bangladesh Price Tk. 1,495

Dedicated

To
The Bironganas,
The Mukti Juddhas, The Martyrs
and
The Wounded

To
The Silent and the Lost
of 1971

Acknowledgements

"No man is an Iland, intire of it selfe"
[John Donne, 1624]
And neither am I.

This work would not be possible without the enthusiastic
encouragement and invaluable assistance of my wife,
Zebunnesa Zeba Zubair.

In memory eternal to
Brother James Talarovic (1915-1987),
Headmaster of St. Gregory's High School, Dhaka for
lighting "the fire of searing lightning[1]" seeking out emotion
in the translation of literature early in my life.

---

[1] *Show yourself to my soul* / Rabindranath Tagore; a new translation
of the *Gitanjali* by James Talarovic.

Land of Rivers

1971's Red Rivers of Blood and Bodies

Riparian View

1971
Freedom
This earth
This Bangladesh
My blood, this water
My flesh, this soil
My breath, this Freedom
In the gentle caress
In the soft embrace of the Kash phool
In these waters my soul you touch
Rivers of my blood, thy flow is Freedom
In the Bulbuli's sweet song
My heart flows
In the Krishnachura's fiery red flames
In the fragrance of the
Shiuli and the Kamini
In the deep of green
In the heart of Bangladesh
In this watery grave
I became your soil
My blood, my breath, my flesh
This earth, this Bangladesh
Freedom
1971

Contents

Book One: The Sinuous Path

The Sinuous Path... 1

The Road Taken... 13

Last Letter Home... 25

Dacca or Dachau?... 31

Book Two: 1971

Joy Bangla... 41

Viva Bengal... 55

Operation Searchlight... 63

Curfew... 79

Exodus... 91

Tears in the Heart... 105

Razakars, Traitors Within... 115

A Short Farewell, a Long Goodbye... 127

Of Guerrillas and Refugees... 143

Mukti Bahini... 165

Rhythm of the Rumble... 181

Refugee... 195

While My Guitar Gently Weeps... 201

Bell-bottom Guerrillas... 219

No Tomorrow Like Today... 241

Enemy Within 259

Eye of the Storm 267

Beyond All Borders 273

Silent Screams 285

One World 291

Intelligentsia Genocide 303

Red Sun of Freedom 315

On Wings of Freedom 323

War Within 331

Bironganas 341

Tarred Road 353

Into a Thousand Rainbows 359

Book Three: Journey into the Heart

Winging Over the Bay of Bengal 367

The Riaspora 373

Mother Teresa's 381

Silently They Come 395

Rebirth 401

Phantoms of the Soul 407

Afterwords 411

Acknowledgements 425

Glossary 431

Book One

The Sinuous Path

The Sinuous Path

"FROM TODAY TO FOREVERMORE, I, Alex Salim McKensie, take you, Sangeeta Rai, to be my lawfully wedded wife. To love, to cherish, to honor and to support. To be a true friend in happiness and in sorrow. To be a constant companion in sickness and in health."

Alex disappears into Sangeeta's enchanting black eyes set in the perfection of her tawny oval face. In the filtered Southern California sunlight, Sangeeta's slender frame sparkles in ornate rubies and emeralds. She is exquisitely wrapped in a silver-embroidered crimson *Banarasi* wedding sari, her shoulder length silky black hair coiled on the nape of her neck.

This is the first time Alex sees Sangeeta in a sari. Mesmerized, lost in the subtle timelessness of grace, Alex wonders about his birth mother.

Looking at him with eyes of love, Sangeeta stands in front of him—his today and tomorrow—reminding him of the enigmas of his yesterdays. Lingering on his breath today is one syllable encompassing everything,

Ma.

Sangeeta tiptoes up and kisses Alex, her soul caressing his through soft parted lips, in a moment full of promises, in an intimation of eternity.

Guests clap. Friends cheer.

Surreptitiously Sangeeta glances at a late arriving couple, hoping it is her parents, and through a smile planted on her crimson lips, she swallows a lump lodged in her throat all day. She slowly breathes a sigh of dejection and pain, as she looks across a small crowd of friends and family gathered on the lush, manicured backyard of the sprawling Brentwood house on Sycamore Drive.

Missing today are the two most important people in Sangeeta's life—her parents.

It was Sangeeta's wish to have a small wedding and reception at the McKensies'. A white rose lined walkway on green grass skirted by white chairs leads up to the tuberose decorated wedding arch on a raised floral platform. The fragrance enamors the bride and groom, the guests, in an exotic oriental attar. To the right of the platform is the jazz band, and the riffs waft over the guests, the bejeweled women in bright designer dresses of red, gold, and silver, the men in handsomely tailored dark suits.

Rachael, Jack and Laura McKensie, seated in the front row, are beaming in pride. As his mother, Laura, looks at Alex, she thinks about her son's miraculous life. Joy lights the time-traced lines of her face.

Alongside the wedding platform, on the tennis court next to the pool, a grand silver canopy is set up for the reception. Floating in the warm fragrant air, a lost butterfly circles then lands gently on the nectar of a newfound pink Ranunculus in a floral arrangement. In the tall pines on the sloping hill behind the wedding platform the melodious warbling of a Song Sparrow on a high bow and the skittering of a baby squirrel in the pine cones below add to the splendor of the day.

It is an afternoon like many afternoons, yet perfect for Sangeeta and Alex.

With the vows over, Alex's niece, Melissa, prances on twelve-year-old legs up onto the wedding platform holding the rings on a muslin pillow tied with a silver ribbon.

Sangeeta beams, holding out her hand in front of Alex. He turns the flawless diamond solitaire set in platinum over in his hand and then slips it into place on her ring finger. She tosses her head, holds her finger up, a twinkle in her eyes, a burst of happiness eclipsing thoughts about her parents. Sangeeta puts the thick gold band on Alex's finger, twisting it in, the ring a bit tight.

They kiss deeply.

With the ring exchange over, Mrs. Priti Kumar and Rachael approach. Mrs. Kumar with the vermilion pot in her hands, glows in a green *Kanchipuram* sari. Rachael carries on her arm two garlands of white and deep red fragrant roses. She kisses Alex and Sangeeta and squeezes her brother's hand as she hands him a garland, her blonde hair perfectly complemented by her stunning cerulean blue Dior dress.

Alex and Sangeeta garland each other, and happiness reflects in Rachael's blue eyes.

Twenty-five years ago, Rachael remembers her infant brother Alex at the airport in the arms of a caring nurse. How frail he was. "You are an angel bringing us another angel," she told the nurse. What has this tiny baby gone through? He felt so light—a mere ten pounds, barely alive at four months. Like the touch of a tendril, he wrapped his little hand around Rachael's index finger as if he was searching for someone, someone familiar. Was the baby looking for his mother in her touch, wrapping his tiny fingers around hers? This afternoon she squeezes the same hand, the hand of a successful engineer, a valedictorian, and Sangeeta's proud husband. Alex's Ma would be proud. If she is no more, she must be in heaven smiling at him, rejoicing in his happiness.

Alex turns to Mrs. Kumar and takes a pinch of vermilion powder, gently puts the red *shindoor* dot on Sangeeta's forehead. With an anointed forehead, and the velvety touch of roses around her neck, Sangeeta feels she is truly a married woman today. A modern woman on the wedding altar, Sangeeta reaches back a millennia to drape herself in an identity adorned in tradition, ratified in rituals. She smiles at Mrs. Kumar and Rachael, embracing them both, seeking warmth, feeling loved.

The wedding ceremony over, Alex and Sangeeta kiss again amid the cheering of friends and family. A long kiss, an electric touch, the moment eternal.

An April afternoon breeze is filled with voices exuberant with congratulations and warm wishes.

Sangeeta signs on the dotted line of a new life as Sangeeta Salim McKensie. She drops the Rai. A change she hopes will be the start of a new, happy life with Alex. As Sangeeta looks on, Alex signs his name, noting his fictitious birth date of April 27, 1972. He was born twice: first as Salim in Bangladesh, then four months later in America as Alex Salim McKensie. In his life many things are not what they seem, but in front of him Sangeeta, Rachael, Laura and Jack are true. But over the years, the sketchy silhouettes, the deep shadows of his birth in the war-ravaged country of Bangladesh have haunted him.

Today Alex overcomes the sharp anguish of these memories, standing tall, smiling warmly.

Alex and Sangeeta wave and step down from the wedding platform into a life together. Jack McKensie stands up tall, runs his fingers through his thin, gray hair; a loving, content look spreads across his face. After losing his son Frank, only twenty, in Vietnam, he has traveled down an anguished hard road. The emptiness, that haunting, that maimed feeling is exorcised today. Looking at Alex, suave and handsome, Jack experiences a peace of mind he has not known in a long time.

"Congratulations newlyweds," Jack says as he and Laura embrace and kiss Sangeeta and Alex.

The jazz band plays Coltrane's "I'm Old Fashioned" and textured riffs of the tenor saxophone can be heard over the giggling of small children, the laughter and sounds of guests. In this moment made magical, Sangeeta and Alex are walking on a dream carpet of music, with intricate backdrops of piano and thrumming drums, with repetitive flowery inlays filling in the edges.

Mrs. Priti Kumar and her daughter Janaki sit together in the front row. In a gold-embroidered orange swirling skirted *lehenga choli*, wearing her mother's wedding gold, Janaki smiles, her face radiant. But her face darkens when she overhears someone in the back row say, "Where are her parents?" Janaki tries to ignore these comments, hoping Sangeeta does not hear.

Janaki remembers how enraged Sangeeta's mother, Mrs. Shobha Rai was, pointing the finger at her. "Janaki, you were always jealous of Sangeeta, bringing us down introducing her to a bastard! Why are you not marrying Alex yourself! Don't you look at yourself in the mirror? You're getting past marriageable age!"

Janaki had forced herself to gain control of her seething anger. Her face burning, she replied, "Aunti, Sangeeta is a grown up girl. You raised her as an American. Now you are imposing values she has not grown up with. You expect your American daughter to act like she is behind the veil in Mumbai or Kolkata or Delhi in the last century? Where you are, where you grow up, that is who you are more than the color of your skin, your ethnic roots. And Alex is a fine man. A gentleman. More so than many of your horn-tooting Deshis with a lineage that supposedly goes back to the Moguls."

Looking at Sangeeta, Janaki thinks what have I not sacrificed for your daughter's happiness? She had grown up with Alex, liked him since childhood, but could never express her feelings as she saw him in her teenage years only in bits and spurts.

What would it be like to be standing next to Alex today? She, Janaki, might be wearing that garland, anointed in *shindoor*, wrapped in a red *Banarasi*, if she had not left for Exeter and Yale, far removed from Alex. And then, how would her mother find Alex as a son-in-law? Her mother would be happy; there was that difference between Mrs. Rai and her mother. Could she blame Mrs. Rai? No—her mother was more open-minded, tolerant and thought of Alex as her own son.

Floating on cloud nine, a cold crystal glass of Bruno Paillard in his hand, Alex looks with love at Sangeeta as they walk over to greet Janaki.

"Alex, not only did you pick up Sangeeta's purse, but today you have picked her for life!" Janaki says laughing, hugging Sangeeta. "Sangeeta, look at you, you are just drop-dead gorgeous in that sari! Alex, you got a real *Devi* here!"

"Yes, I know! A real *Devi* Diva Cat!" Alex says grinning from ear to ear. "And you, you are to blame, Janaki!"

"If you had not asked Alex to give me a ride that evening from your home, Janaki, we might not be here today!" Sangeeta says as her face brightens, her cheeks glow once more at the thought of that night at the Kumar's.

Two years ago, Sangeeta turned around to look into the eyes of a broad-shouldered handsome man, sharp-featured with soft, brown eyes sitting cross-legged on the carpet behind her at the sitar recital at Mrs. Kumar's in Westwood. At the end of the performance, when she got up, Janaki had pulled her over and whispered, "I want you to meet someone."

Nervous, Sangeeta remembers dropping her purse while being introduced by Janaki. Alex had jumped to pick it up for her.

Sangeeta rearranged her *dupatta*, fidgeted in her intricately embroidered off-white silk *salwar kameez*, and said, "Thank you." Fingering the white flowers in her hair, she stood there for an embarrassing moment as Alex gazed at her. Finally she said,

"What are you looking at?"

"You."

"Me?"

"Yes, you. Is it a crime to look at the moon, so beautiful?"

"Yeaaaaaah," Sangeeta said, releasing a long breath she'd been holding unconsciously. She had heard so many lines—but this was new. And poetic even. She blushed self-consciously, but she desired to know more about this man, this poet.

After the sitar recital, Janaki and Sangeeta chatted, Janaki filling her in about Alex.

"He's an engineering student at UCLA," Janaki said.

"Oh?" Sangeeta said trying not to sound too interested.

"EE, I've known him all my life, grew up with him. He's nice Sangeeta, you should get to know him."

"Maybe."

"Maybe? Maybe I see that gleam in your eyes, Sangeeta!" Janaki said laughing into Sangeeta's blushing face, her cheeks burning and turning red below black slashes of mascara.

Sangeeta's eyes had searched him out in the crowd, over in the corner by the drinks. And later in the evening, when Sangeeta needed a ride home to Malibu, Janaki suggested Alex drop her home.

"You sure it's OK, Janaki?"

"Yes, I know him from birth Sangeeta. A perfect gentleman."

Sangeeta, a bit hesitant at first, agreed, only to find that Alex's ride was a silver and black exotic Ducati café racer.

"Wow!" Sangeeta said as her jaw dropped, filled at once with excitement and anxiety.

Alex flashed a wide smile, proud of the upturned expansion chrome muffler, drilled out disc brakes, speed screen and smooth oversized rear tire. He handed his only helmet to Sangeeta and said, "I don't need one."

"Sure?" she asked, tightly knotting her *dupatta* around her waist.

With a pounding heart, Sangeeta climbed on. As Alex gunned the bike, she grabbed on to him, holding on for dear life. "Slow down," she screamed as she gripped harder onto his rib cage.

Alex turned back, grinned and shouted over the roar of the bike, "Tighter! Hold on tighter or you will fall!"

"Why are you going so fast Alex? Slow down!" Sangeeta screamed, as Alex released the throttle, tense in his hand. As she found herself wrapped around the civilized brutality of the Ducati, she wrapped herself around Alex's gallant manners, his enigmatic, inviting smile.

Once Sangeeta was swaying and rocking with the bike, Alex drove her into him, dancing a wild twist with her on asphalt. Sangeeta smiled, hugging onto Alex, moving to the rhythms of the purring bike.

"You sure don't ride in a straight line," Sangeeta yelled into Alex's ear.

"Straight lines are no fun!" Alex screamed back.

"Curves are so dangerous." Sangeeta said in a high-pitched yell over the sound of the engine.

Alex turned his head, looked at Sangeeta and laughed out loud. "But so much fun. You only live once!"

The road ended at Sangeeta's parents' in Malibu, with Alex wishing he could keep her on his bike till the end of the world and then some. He said goodbye, wind-blasted tears streaking down the side of his face.

"Crying for me the first time out, Alex?" Sangeeta said, as they broke out together into laughter, the humor lifting the tension of the night.

"What makes you such a speed daemon, Alex? Are you running away from something? Seems like you will fly off the planet. Don't you like being here?"

"Sure," said Alex his face breaking out in an ear-to-ear grin, still warm from Sangeeta's tight embrace on the ride. "Want to go to Mars?"

That summer of '95, Sangeeta held on to Alex on the winding Pacific Coast Highway, as he cut through traffic and twisted and turned up canyon and coastal roads. As she held on tighter to this wild man, floated on top of the large smooth rear tire, as Alex twisted the bike with precision from one banking turn to another, sending her into him, Sangeeta found herself getting lost in Alex. In Alex, in his asphalt scrapping turns on canyon roads at a hundred miles an hour, as she cut acute angles hanging on to him, the world took on blurry streaking images. The known became unknown, the unknown, Alex Salim McKensie, her own.

In kissing Sangeeta, Alex kissed something deep in his own soul. He wanted to be in the blood pulsating through her very veins, in the breath that she took in, in deep, in everywhere, in every moment and yes, for all of his life.

Alex wanted Sangeeta.

One warm July afternoon on the beach, Sangeeta cradled Alex's head in her lap, gently caressing his face and running her fingers through his thick wet hair.

"Sangeeta."

"Hmmm...," Sangeeta said, her voice drifting off into a soft sensual contentment.

"Wish we could spend the rest of our lives like this."

Sangeeta kissed him, and said, "I want to go to Mars with you." For a moment their eyes met, and they broke out into laughter.

Into that sultry summer, like a vine rooting deep into the crevices and cracks left by time, embracing the sweetness of a moist wall, Alex and Sangeeta secured tendrils into each other's heart strings.

Today, Alex also thinks back to two years ago, sitting behind Sangeeta at the Kumar's. She had turned around and looked at him, drawing him into her soul through the portal of her enchantress *Devi* eyes, her hair curled in little ringlets around her ears and neck and touching the small of her earlobe.

Alex at that moment had wished to reach out and kiss her just there. And just now he does.

The wedding afternoon draws into the evening as the spring sun recedes; the bright hue of a dusty orange disperses through the pine trees. The day's last long shadows linger as waiters serve appetizers: lamb kabobs, fried baby artichoke hearts, chocolate dipped baby eggplant, champagne and sparkling cider. Children run up the slope and parents are quick to call to them to be careful. Diamond-shaped floral petal arrangements decorate the inlaid red bull nose tiles around the swimming pool, a candle burning inside each. With the candles reflecting in the braided ripples, Alex and Sangeeta pose in red *Banarasi* and black Ralph Lauren for their wedding portraits.

In the silver canopy, overhead chandeliers glitter throwing sparkles on the guests seated around the dinner tables. Laura and Rachael together have decided on the menu, catering to everyone's palate. The food ranges from baked Macadamia nut crusted Mahi Mahi to Filet mignon and vegetarian dishes to chicken curries.

At the rectangular head table, Alex and Sangeeta are seated together facing the guests. Across from them are Janaki and Mrs. Kumar, Laura, Jack and Rachael.

"What Laura, no vegetarian Irish Stew for me today?" Priti says jokingly.

"Oh sure, Priti," Laura says smiling.

"Vegetarian Irish Stew?" Janaki asks, her eyebrows raised.

"When your mother first came to our house, I made it even before you were born, Janaki," Laura says as Jack's eyes light up thinking back to 1971.

"And you still remember that, Priti?" Jack asks.

"Of course, Jack. I will always remember those days. Laura was so considerate when I was by myself," Priti adds.

The smooth sound of the jazz band stops, then Jack steps up, takes the microphone, and his voice fills the canopy. "Good evening, ladies and gentleman. It is a great pleasure and honor to have you here on this auspicious occasion. Today I would like to propose a toast to the newlyweds, my beautiful daughter-in-law Sangeeta and my son, Alex. May their days be blessed and prosperous, may they live in peace and happiness." Jack's blue eyes twinkle as he turns to Alex and Sangeeta and says, "May I hear the pitter-patter of little feet soon! Life, a sinuous path, is never as you plan it, but today our hopes have come true." He squeezes Laura. "Alex and Sangeeta, along this path, I hope you find many a flower to smell, many a heart to touch. Here's to the happy couple!" Jack raises his glass, the guests clap, forks tap, and glasses are raised up high in a toast. Jack turns back to Laura, whose face is flushed with emotion.

"Now Laura has a toast."

Alex and Sangeeta look up at Laura, elegant in her black Oscar de la Renta evening gown, her bob-cut brown hair shimmering in auburn highlights. She holds up her champagne glass towards the newlyweds, the color rising to her face.

"Today I feel blessed. Alex and Sangeeta, you are meant for each other. Alex, in Sangeeta, you have a beautiful wife. You have touched our hearts in so many ways, in so many miraculous moments. Now as you continue down that path I wish you a happy, peaceful life."

Laura's eyes well up with tears, and Jack is quick to anchor an arm around her. Alex goes up to hug her and Laura hugs him back, kissing him on the cheek and clinging to him for a moment. Composing herself, she takes out a note from her purse and starts to read, her voice cracking, filled with emotion.

"I take this wonderful opportunity to wish from a family member his best to the bride and groom. If Frank were here today, he most likely would have pulled a silly prank because that was Frank. And then he would have wished you from the bottom of his heart, as I do today, a happy and peaceful and prosperous life! I want to read a line Frank wrote, '*I have heard that two of the greatest things in life are to love and be loved. I know both because of you.*' You Sangeeta and Alex, you have the greatest things in life—you are loved and you have someone to love. How wonderful is that?"

Alex hugs Laura again as she kisses him on the forehead, and blesses him.

Toasts over, the piano strikes up. Alex takes Sangeeta's hand, leading her onto the dance floor. His arm encircles her waist, his hand finds the small of her back.

Sangeeta follows Alex's lead. The singer's rich voice finally encircles her, and the words slowly penetrate through her anxiety. It's a special song that Alex has chosen, a slow tempo Michael Bolton song for the first dance:

"Oh I will always be in your arms
And you will always be the flame within my heart."

Alex and Sangeeta dance this first dance by the pool, their reflection on the candle-lit ripples of the water, as the sound of the music mingles with the conversations of the guests. As the notes proclaim Alex's enduring love, as they sway to the music on the dance floor, she feels the notes undulate through her nerves, the words pulsating in her veins. Sangeeta wonders about the unending love her parents are supposed to feel about her.

"You OK?" Alex whispers into Sangeeta's ear.

"It's nothing," Sangeeta says, turning her face away. She squeezes him tighter, holding him close as Alex whispers, "There's no tomorrow like today."

Jack cuts in, and gathers her in his arms, his face flush with joy. Sangeeta remembers as a little girl how she danced with her own father, her bare feet on top of his shoes. That feeling of soft leather under her toes, the gentle swaying.

And her mother? What was her mother feeling today? A day her mother had dreamt about, planned for all her life. Sangeeta exhales a dispirited sigh thinking about how today could have been her mother's finest moment. Sangeeta's mother should be dancing with Alex. In her place Mrs. Kumar steps up and dances with Alex, whispers into his ear, "Take care of Sangeeta. She is so torn up, Alex."

"Yes, yes," Alex says in a voice full of concern. He looks towards

Sangeeta.

In the bosom of the only family Alex has ever known, on his wedding day his thoughts drift to the one who gave him up.

Ma.

❧

The Road Taken

Late April, 1997, California.

STANDING ON THEIR VERANDA, SANGEETA traces with her
fingertips the crimson and cadmium hues brushed in layers
in the kiss between sea and sky at the distant horizon. Alex
stands behind her, embraces her, kisses the faint fragrance of Coco
Mademoiselle lingering on the nape of her neck.

In the secluded serenity of their condo perched on a hill
overlooking Pacific Coast Highway, Sangeeta and Alex have
unwrapped the gifts from their wedding and slowly wrapped their
lives around a certain daily rhythm.

Since their early April wedding, they spend weekends trying
to find furniture, squeeze it into the back of Alex's olive green Jeep
Wrangler, then wrestle their treasures up the stairs into their nest.
They have filled the rooms: Tiffany lamps, a light brown leather
sectional sofa, a soothing Indigo Persian carpet bought at the endless
going-out-of-business Oriental carpet store down the street at 80%
off. In the airy living room with a wedge of Southern California sun
filtering in through the skylight, Alex's framed motorcycle pictures
have been replaced by miniature prints of Mogul art where the Raja
and his Queen are in a timeless, ever-endearing embrace.

Sometimes on weekends, they get up early to buy fish at the
pier from the fishing boats coming back to Newport harbor, and

Sangeeta prepares a sweet and sour fish *Korma* curry with yogurt, garlic and ginger paste, sugar and lemon sauce.

— ❧ —

IT'S A SATURDAY AFTERNOON WHEN they go for a bike ride on Alex's Ducati to Cerritos for brunch at the Zaffron, piling their plates with lamb curry, tandoori chicken, kabobs and *daal*. Accented by the smells of tandoori chicken, the occasional loud laugh above the sounds of excited conversations, the clinking of spoons and knives, Alex and Sangeeta enjoy a delicious brunch. Alex glances at the garlanded Krishna and the incense sticks in front, unlit yet infusing the air with a sweet scent.

"The lamb curry melts in your mouth," Alex mumbles, his mouth full, as he bites on a sliced green chile that kicks up the flavor a notch.

"Alo Gobi, mmm, try it Alex," Sangeeta says licking from her lips a taste of the *garam masala*.

Alex reaches for the glass of *lassi*, trying to put out the fire in his mouth.

He overhears the Indian couple in the leather booth next to them argue about an in-law problem of a common kind. As he struggles with a pile of lamb curry on his plate, he struggles with thoughts about Sangeeta, her estrangement from her parents, his inabilities to close the chasm between Sangeeta and her parents.

Looking up past the water condensing on the carafe, Alex notices an elderly Indian woman in the far left corner staring at Sangeeta. She gets up, excuses herself from the two other women with her.

"You know her?" Alex asks.

"Who?"

"Don't turn around. That lady over there."

"Where?" Sangeeta says.

"In the corner. Behind you."

Alex watches the blue-and-white-*salwar-kameez*-wearing Indian woman in her mid-fifties as she slowly saunters over like a baby elephant, her face the dimpled roundness of a waxing moon. Tall, she stands at the edge of their table.

Sangeeta looks up, puts her fork down, swallows hard, takes a sip of Alex's mango *lassi*.

"Sangeeta? Hi! Thought it was you. How are you?" the woman says, eyes wide and brows raised.

To Alex, it sounds more like a statement than a question.

"Mrs. Shah. How are you?" Sangeeta says as she looks at Alex helplessly and rolls her eyes.

"Sangeeta, let me take a look at you! What happened?" Mrs. Shah says peering at Alex from the corner of her eye. She pulls on the middle of her embroidered *dupatta*, recreating the 'v' of the fabric on her chest and continues, "Don't see you in the parties or shows anymore. How is your mom? Everything OK?" Mrs. Shah touches the edge of the table slightly, then turns to look at Alex, scrutinizing him from head to toe. Alex flinches, digging his toe into the sole of his shoe, keeping his eyes on the irritated look that has veiled Sangeeta's just-a-moment-ago laughing face.

Sangeeta clears her throat, hesitates.

"You are looking great Mrs. Shah," Sangeeta finally says, composing herself. She turns to Alex, continues, "Alex meet Mrs. Shah, a long time family friend."

Mrs. Shah, through furrowed brows says, "Really, Sangeeta. I talked to your mother last week. She's sick. In bed."

Sangeeta looks away, past the waiters, past the curtained glass windows, wishes she was on the Ducati flying away at a million miles an hour.

"How is Uncle doing?" Sangeeta finally utters dispiritedly.

"Sangeeta, they raised you, you should take care…" Mrs. Shah says as she turns her gaze towards Alex. Mrs. Shah sizes him up and down, looks directly at his face, says bluntly, "And this is your husband? *Maine suna hai tumharay Pita Pakistan me rehetay hain?* I heard your father lives in Pakistan?"

"I need some air. Alex, let's go." Sangeeta says, as she gets up, furious, her fork rattling to the floor, leaving her unfinished lunch, her untouched garlic *naan*.

Sangeeta storms out of the restaurant. Leaving crumpled bills on the front desk, Alex scampers behind her, runs to catch up.

"You OK?" Alex asks, hesitation in his voice.

"Yes," Sangeeta says, looking away, her face flushed. "That lady is a bitch...a real bitch."

Walking briskly past the sari, jewelry and Indian grocery stores squeezed next to each other, bursting forth onto the pavement with 220 Volt hair-dryers, shaving kits and extra large zippered expanding suitcases, Sangeeta wipes a tear from her eye, looks across the street, away from Alex.

Slowly, like tea leaves settling to the bottom of a cup of hot water, Sangeeta regains her composure and brightens to Alex and his many verbal concoctions and jokes.

"How many engineers does it take to change a light bulb?" Sangeeta asks.

"None, this engineer is in bed with the architect, and who needs lights?" Alex replies with a mischievous smile.

"Shut up, Alex," Sangeeta laughs as a thin smile appears on her lips.

Alex and Sangeeta quip and jab at each other as they walk towards the Indian grocery store they like to haunt. There they shop for Tulsi Masala Chai that Sangeeta loves, and a few spices that need replenishing.

The inevitable "How's your mother doing? We have not seen her in a long time," asked with a side glance towards Alex by shopkeepers who know Sangeeta from childhood brings an uneasy look on Sangeeta's face.

Alex does not interject. Trying to be as nonchalant as he can be, he stands smiling, the tension growing in his neck, moving down between his shoulder blades.

Sangeeta pays for the tea, and they walk out, headed for the bike.

—❧—

THEY JUMP ON THE DUCATI and as Alex guns the throbbing engine and snaps the clutch like a tightly strung bow, they turn out of Pioneer Boulevard onto the highway.

"Alex, I love you!" Sangeeta shrieks into his ear over the roar of the bike as they skirt the oversized side mirrors of an F-350 dually. The streaking red brake lights of the cars come towards them like flying bullets under Alex's revving palm.

Under Alex Salim McKensie's feet, only inches away, the world is a flashed blur, yet far in the distance everything is crisp and clear.

The Ducati purrs and growls under Alex's iron grip, then swerves, sways, dances and burns rubber in a sinuous path, slicing in between the tight lanes of stalled cars on the 405, cutting through the Saturday traffic like a slithering cobra through thick underbrush. As Sangeeta looks on, at the back of Alex's Bell helmet is a small hand-painted red thunderbolt: he is her superman, and in rhythm with the vibrating bike, Sangeeta's heart thrums against Alex's leather wrapped California sun baked back. As she holds onto Alex with an even tighter grip, her thrill-seeking arms lock around his chest, her black five inch stiletto boot heels wrapped around the passenger foot post. Riding high, Sangeeta breathes in the fresh air, her rose-pink heart dotted panty line jostles up and down with the surges of the roaring bike, her shoulder length silky raven hair blasts back in the dry air.

"I love you too!" Alex screams glancing back at Sangeeta.

Sangeeta's breasts press into the small of Alex's arched back as she hugs him. Alex finds open road and sends the Ducati flying into a bullet blur of speed.

Now late in the afternoon, twisting and turning on Pacific Coast Highway, bordered by beautiful costal homes, the Southern California Mediterranean life of sun and water that paints Spanish style houses in swaths of soothing white and terra-cotta red, they make their way South towards Newport Beach. The bougainvilleas are in full bloom on the hills above the road, and below, spots of pink chaparral honeysuckle carpet the bluff.

The ocean is braided in a million uncut *Polki* diamonds in the glittering afternoon sun. Overhead a band of gulls squawk, below at the edge of the spume Sand pipers chirp, pecking into the sand.

Alex kicks the stand out and parks his bike by their condo. Unstraddling the bike, Alex and Sangeeta take off their helmets. Alex runs his fingers through his wind blasted hair, straightening it out, and Sangeeta shakes out her long mane. The afternoon sun streaks through the dense bougainvillea bushes on the side of the Spanish style hacienda next to their condo. A hyper group of wild parrots, green and red, welcome them with eager and excited squawks as one shows off its acrobatics on a branch. Sangeeta laughs at Alex, then kisses him. In the midst of her heartbreak with her parents, she finds her new married life with Alex evoking deep feelings of love and strength.

On the living room coffee table, fresh-rolled architectural blueprints sit atop "EE Design" and "American Motorcyclist" magazines. Alex and Sangeeta have both brought home work that is yet to be touched. The salty sea breeze blends with the sweet potpourri, and with the summer tide come the sounds of weekend beach life and laughter floating into their love nest.

Sangeeta walks into their mauve bedroom and falls on the bed exhausted. As she lays there, tears start in her eyes. The day has pushed too many of her buttons, is too much a reminder of one earlier in the year. She remembers it just like this beautiful afternoon, the day she decided to tell her parents about her decision to marry Alex.

Sangeeta has seen many movies, sitting in the comfort of their Malibu home. Movies in black and white of Jinnah, Gandhi, Nehru. She knows the stories, but feels no connection to her mother's feelings about Alex.

She cannot relive the pain her mother felt in 1947 when she lost everything in Lahore and had to escape with only the breath in her body. Sangeeta keeps trying to argue that Alex had nothing to do with the pain her mother went through in 1947, that he is an American, far removed from the social and racial tensions of India. But it is Shobha's deep and unflinching anger against Alex's birth father who she believes is a Pakistani soldier that is driving this wedge.

In 1947, during the birth of Pakistan and India, Shobha's home in Lahore was burnt by a murderous riotous crowd. Rivers of blood flowed down gutters as knives and *daow* machetes hacked into innocent men, women and children.

Shobha Rai had told Sangeeta how at only six she saw women being dragged away, how she had escaped with her parents, her mother and grandmother hidden under burqas. Shobha's parents and grandparents had fled to Lahore Cantonment Railway Station on August 11, days before the curfew, with the aid of a Sikh family friend. The Sikh soldiers in the Cantonment area had given her mother and her family, along with other Hindus, protection and they were the lucky few to arrive alive on the trains to the Indian side of the border at Ferozepore. Sangeeta had seen movies, pictures telling the story of the hundreds of thousands, maybe close to two million Muslim and Hindu refugees who had died in this mass exodus. Over twelve million refugees had moved from one country to the other: Hindus moving from now Muslim East and West Pakistan to India, and Muslims moving from now Hindu India to Muslim Pakistan.

All of Sangeeta's mother's relatives, originally from Jammu Kashmir, who had migrated to Lahore at the turn of the century had been burned alive, shot and hacked to death in the buildings set aflame in Anarkali and on the Mall in Old Lahore during the August 13th curfew.

And now, fifty years later, the fear of 1947 resurfaces. Resurfaces to engulf Sangeeta in rekindled flames of hatred. In California, a continent away, a lifetime past.

Sangeeta looks at her tears as they wet the cotton pillow covers of her bed.

"Will Ma not give up her blind hate?" Sangeeta says, crushing the edge of the pillow, wishing it was the hate in her mother's mind.

IN THE CRISP COOL OF that February afternoon six months ago, they rode into Sangeeta's parents driveway in Malibu.

She remembers calling her mother, "Ma, I have something important to talk to you about."

"Come, come for dinner Saturday and we will talk," Shobha Rai had said.

"Alex is coming with me."

"Why?"

"Because, Ma, it involves him. You know, so I don't know why you pretend you don't."

She had heard a deafening silence on the other end, then a click as the phone went dead.

Alex parked the bike, followed Sangeeta into the Rais' Malibu home, sat alone in the living room listening to Sangeeta fight with her mother in the kitchen.

A frigid dinner, Sangeeta said little, exchanging glances with her mother as her father tried to make small talk with Alex. Shobha Rai could say nothing, but sat there silently trying in vain to eat dinner, pushing her food around on her plate, from time to time looking at her husband, then at Alex and then Sangeeta.

After dinner, Alex retired to the living room while Sangeeta went upstairs.

"This is how you honor my sacrifices? This is how you respect your family, your *Khandan*?" Mrs. Shobha Rai had said in response to Sangeeta telling her about her plans to marry Alex. Her father, a prominent doctor originally from Kolkata, spoke little.

During the Bangladesh War of Independence, Arjun, Shobha's only younger brother, a Major in the Indian Army, had died fighting on the border of then East Pakistan, fighting to liberate it into Bangladesh. Mrs. Rai had suffered in 1947 and again in 1971. First her relatives in Anarkali, Lahore in '47 then Arjun in '71. Arjun's death by a West Pakistani bullet crushed Shobha Rai and her family.

When Sangeeta wanted to marry a war baby of Bangladesh, Mrs. Shobha Rai could not believe it. "*Haramzada*. Bastard. This is wrong Sangeeta. You have no sense? No. Not even close. We struggled so hard to get here. And because of this guy you want to throw it all away." She cried out, "Is this what I sacrificed for? We brought you up to understand the difference between right and wrong. You are out of your mind Sangeeta. We let you have everything."

Wiping her tears, Shobha added, "Everything!"

Sangeeta tried in vain to reason, but nothing she said made any difference to her mother. Her words fell on deaf ears. At the top of her lungs, Sangeeta yelled, "Being born a war baby is not Alex's fault. NOT HIS FAULT!"

"No, but that's what he is, regardless. You just can't brush that away. That's what he is. A bastard." After a long painful minute, Shobha Rai stared into Sangeeta's tear-flooded eyes and uttered bitterly, "To have my daughter marry a *haramzada* bastard, is that why you think I came to America. Is this what I deserve in my life?"

Shobha Rai's face was contorted in pain, her eyes tinged with sadness. She took the end of her *dupatta*, wiped her face, her nose.

"Hindu and Muslim are two different religions!" Mrs. Rai said, collapsing on the couch.

"Alex is Catholic, Ma, not Muslim," Sangeeta replied.

Furious, Mrs. Rai spoke out, "*Iska Pita* is a Pakistani soldier. His father is a Pakistani soldier. If Alex is not the *haramzada*, you are the *haramzadi*."

Then she stood up and tried to push Sangeeta away, "Get out from here! I never want to see your face again!"

Sangeeta screamed at her mother, "Mom, stop it!"

"Over and over again, I've told you, Sangeeta, that we don't approve of this relationship. But you don't want to listen, ever," Dr. Subash Rai, her father insisted. "I don't want to argue anymore with you, enough is enough."

"No, Baba. You can't decide my life. It's my life! My decision! And I have decided to marry Alex. And Ma, did you not tell me once that Anwar Khan secretly loved your mother, and it was Anwar Khan who had helped your family escape Lahore? He was Muslim. He gave your mother that burqa that bloody August in Lahore," Sangeeta said, her voice filling the expanse of the room, her eyes glaring at her mother.

"Sangeeta!" her father said as he slapped her hard.

Sangeeta had stormed downstairs that day to find Alex standing in the center of the living room, his face ashen with rage.

Following Sangeeta, Shobha Rai came down the stairs and said, "*Beti*, listen, you are naive, this marriage is a mistake!"

Sangeeta took the vase on top of the glass center table and smashed it down hard on the plate glass. It shattered into a hundred thick shards and as Alex jumped to stop her, his right index finger was cut deeply.

Alex had looked at his index finger bleeding profusely, the blood that the Rais never want mixed with theirs. The blood, red and fresh, flowing in Alex's veins so vile and despicable. Shobha stood between Sangeeta and Alex as Alex stormed out of the Rais' living room. A single droplet of Alex's blood splattered on Shobha Rai's Muslin *dupatta*. One dark red spot stained her dreams.

"Alex, wait, Alex!" Sangeeta said running after him.

"Just stop it, Sangeeta! Just leave me alone! I have had it up to here!" Alex said as he mounted his bike and kick started the angry engine alive.

Sangeeta ran behind him, screaming.

"Alex! Stop!"

She jumped on the back of Alex's motorcycle as it took a long wheel-spinning arc across the well-manicured lawn and sped away from the Malibu Estates towards Newport Beach. Halfway down the street, they came to a screaming stop and a sobbing Sangeeta put on her helmet, her face streaked in tears. Alex was quiet, squeezing his finger to stop the bleeding, his throttle now covered in blood.

That was the last time that Sangeeta had seen her parents. Her parents never spoke to her again, slipping into an abysmal silence. Sangeeta had been prepared to field angry rebuttals, protests and arguments, but not utter silence. What did they want her to do, leave Alex and go running back to Malibu; she reflected today with a wry inward grimace, her face contorted in anger, sadness and frustration.

Sangeeta, torn between her parents and her love for Alex, feels as if she is the orphan, the abandoned, the war baby.

It is the most difficult and yet the most wonderful of times for Sangeeta.

—❧—

ALEX WONDERS WHY SANGEETA IS so quiet. Curious he peeks into the bedroom. Sangeeta is sprawled on the bed, the pillow case stained with tears rolling down her cheeks.

"Sangeeta, what's wrong?"

"Nothing..."

Alex sits on the edge of the bed, bends over, kisses Sangeeta, tasting the salty moistness of her tears on his lips.

"Sangeeta, you know how much I love you."

Sangeeta is reticent. Quiet. A distant detached look in her eyes.

"Are you finding yourself in me, Alex?" Sangeeta says, crushing the bed sheet in her hand.

Alex looks away.

"I love you Alex. Don't you know?"

"I know that Sangeet." And then Alex adds, "Yes, I did want to find out things about myself. You know that. But that burnt away like morning mist." Alex bends over and kisses Sangeeta again, biting her ear lobes, running his fingers over her hair. He whispers, "You know how much I love you Sang..."

Sangeeta, gets up from the bed, takes a hairbrush and starts slowly to brush out the wind blasted kinks in her hair. She looks at herself in the full-length mirror, as Alex admires her slender figure. She unbuttons her pink and turquoise Thai silk top, and Alex gently slides it off her shoulders. He touches a strand of her hair running down her back, wraps it in his finger and kisses it.

"Sangeet, Sangeet..." Alex says slowly as he leans down, wraps his arms around her, kisses the nape of her neck.

Quivering, she turns around. Alex buries his face in the softness of her cleavage, lost in her arousing musk. He unhooks Sangeeta's bra, the color of her upturned perky breasts.

Alex caresses Sangeeta's breasts and squeezes as she gives out a moan. "Alex," Sangeeta whispers as he caresses the tiny blue and red butterfly tattoo just over her taut left nipple. He puts his mouth to one of her nipples, tasting her there. Locked in a tight embrace they fall into the folds of the sheets.

Alex forgets all his worries as he gently glides into Sangeeta, as he holds her close and then closer and she and he no longer exist, lost in a perfect embrace of them. He loses himself in the nape of her neck, her long legs wrap and lock around his back. He traces the concaves and the cups of her body with his fingertips, as he kisses every velvety smooth curve, her ankles rubbing against the small of his back, her tongue deep in his mouth, as she digs her nails into the sinewy muscles of his back, moaning in pleasure, yearning, never wanting these feelings to end.

In this embrace, they fall asleep.

❧

Last Letter Home

❧   ❧   ❧

Tuesday, May 13, 1997, Newport Beach

ALEX WAKES UP IN THE near dark with the early scattered sounds of surfers on the beach, the squawk of seagulls and pounding surf. On the sky to the east the sun has drawn a pale swath of crimson. He looks at Sangeeta sleeping, curled up next to him like a nuzzling cat, breathes in the tiniest hint of floral perfume as she stretches out her slender yoga body into perfect form, the lavender silk nightgown clinging to the soft curves of her breasts, her flat stomach. Covering her with the down comforter that she's kicked off, Alex heads to the kitchen. He brews a cup of coffee, wanders into the living room. The smell of rich Colombian dark roast flavored with French vanilla creamer fills the living room, walls the color of Moroccan sand.

Alex's eyes rest on two pictures on the living room table that tell the story of two lifetimes. One is of Alex in Laura's lap when he was only a baby of one in 1973. He grips Rachael's thumb as Jack towers behind them, beaming. Next to it is another family picture. One taken seven years earlier in 1966. In Alex's place is Frank standing next to Laura.

Alex is still. Quiet.

He looks into the eyes of Frank McKensie, Private First Class,

25

U.S. Marines.

Frank stands tall with a glint of mischievousness in his blue eyes, a warm, contagious smile on his lips. Those eyes speak volumes: of love, of sacrifice, of heroism. Alex smiles back at his brother.

"To a cause unknown," Alex says. "To a brother unknown. Thirty years. Exactly thirty. To give your all to save a buddy in the elephant grass swamps of 'Nam. To you brother!"

He puts down his coffee cup and salutes Frank, something he has done for his fallen brother in private moments like this since he was a child.

Today is May 13, 1997, the thirtieth anniversary of Frank's death. A day Alex has taken off work to spend alone. In the evening he'll see family.

Alex walks closer to Frank's picture. Frank is dressed in a new marine-blue uniform with polished brass buttons, a crisp white hat on his crew-cut sandy brown hair. A bright red marine flag with the globe, anchor and eagle insignia hangs behind. A flag Frank died for.

He runs his fingers through his short-cropped hair, exhales a long breath as he stares into the semi-darkness of the room. An emptiness fills him. *And you had to come back in a body bag, Frank. Only twenty years old. A son, a brother, lost in the endless tears, lost in blood spilled far from home. To a cause unknown.*

Alex picks up a family photo album, a wedding gift from Laura, opens the sliding glass door to the veranda and steps out into the stiff Pacific breeze as the sound of the crashing waves washes over him. The salty air fills his lungs as he sits down on the patio chair, places the album on the side table. Clasping his hands together, resting his forehead on folded hands, he says a prayer for Frank, his words whispered into the wind.

He raises his head, breathes into his tightly clutched hands. Finally he opens the album. Inside is the last letter from Frank. The wind tearing at it, Alex holds onto the letter with both hands like holding onto a dear friend's hands.

Slowly, deliberately, he reads between faded lines, bringing back a place distant, a time long ago.

Alex's chronic pain for a fallen brother is like a bullet embedded

26

inside—too deadly to take out, too painful to ignore. A tearing pain felt through his mother's quiet tears, his father's slow long exhalations of sorrow, his sister's flowers on Frank's grave, his baby salutes, so sagacious, so profound.

Alex looks out across the breaking blue Pacific pounding out frothy spume on the sandy shore. Over the years, he has felt the waves of time from distant shores, across the mighty Pacific, pounding at his heart, pounding at questions unanswered.

Frank said so much in his letters about fighting for a cause he did not understand, in a body-count war with no clear victory in sight. About watching buddies die in his arms as they bled to death eight thousand five hundred miles from home.

Thursday,
May 11, 1967

Dear Mom and Dad,

I just got the care package. Thanks! The home baked brownies were great and I devoured most of them, then spread the wealth around to Ryan, Mark and Bill. Good thing I ate some first!

Things sometimes get lonely, even when your buddies surround you. Sitting here by this muddy paddy field, I wish I could be a million miles away from here right now, or at least that's how far home feels.

Dad, learned a new trick. Put insect repellent into a can of peanut butter and you can use it as sterno. Peanut butter burns real well. You can heat the canned grub for a whole bunch of guys—little tricks that make life bearable around here. But heated or not, canned turkey loaf, canned peaches and crackers are getting a little old. Mom, I miss your Irish stew. A heaping helping would hit the spot right about now. I can smell it all the way from here.

Tell Rachael I send her my love. I got her letter yesterday. Will finish writing to her as soon I get done with this mission coming up.

I sure want to see Sarah. I wrote to her but haven't heard from her lately. I still have her Christmas card.

Mom, I live for your letters, in the minutest of details. Through your words I am not in this snake and mosquito infested hell, but back home. Sitting here with my back on a muddy tank, mosquitoes the size of grenades dive bombing my face, arms and neck, it seems to me those little everyday things are what life is about.

Hanging out in the den. Eating ice cream with Rachael. Doing the laundry. Waking up late on a Sunday morning. What I wouldn't do to be back in Brentwood with you guys for just a day.

Mom, you don't know just how much importance these "trivial" events take on out here. Helps keep me from going crazy. I love to read anything about what you or Rachael or Dad are doing. As I read your letters, I am a normal person again. I'm not killing people, or worried about being killed. While I read your letters, I'm not shooting into the night or throwing grenades into the dark.

What war does not take from me seems to be burnt to a crisp in these hooches we have been torching. Lord knows, I have been on my knees in too many paddy fields praying for sanity. Like Mark said yesterday, he can't figure out the why's of Vietnam.

We are on the edge of this jungle we're going into tomorrow. The canopy is so dense it defeats sunlight. When we are loaded down with gear, it feels like these quagmires are going to suck us in. They come alive with tentacles pulling us down.

Been dreaming about coming home, California sunshine. It's going to be a year soon. I have heard that two of the greatest things in life are to love and be loved. I know both because of you.

I'm doing great. Don't you guys worry about me.

> *Love,*
> *Frank*

Holding the creased letter, blue ball point on lined white paper, the ink faded by time and weather, Alex carefully folds and puts it back into the album. Written two days before Frank was killed in action on Saturday May 13, 1967. Saving a friend. Alex takes a sip of coffee, murmurs, "Friend."

In the folds of the album is a slightly discolored picture of Alex, a newborn in a blue blanket, only four months old. And with it another piece of paper—a name, a birth date, a mother's name, in a place distant, Bangladesh.

Alex touches the words, imagines a time, a place that haunts him. He closes the album, feels blessed finding the two greatest things—someone to love and yes, he is loved back, loved back by his family and Sangeeta.

Slowly he walks back into the living room, his eyebrows furrowed, an enigmatic expression on his face, and turns on the radio; an old George Harrison tune plays.

"Little darling ... here comes the sun, and I say it's alright."

Specks of small clouds start to flame in the eastern sky. Dawn comes quickly over the Pacific—first a wash, a glimmer, a lightness, then a burst of color as the sun rises up out of the gray and blue.

Alex turns off the radio. His thoughts racing through his mind, he steps out onto the veranda to get a breath of fresh air.

Sangeeta calls out from the kitchen,

"Alex, you want some breakfast?"

"Yes, in a minute, Sang."

Sangeeta puts on a *Shakti* CD, the percussive thrumming of the tabla in the hands of Zakir Hussain rides and ripples on the wind pulling at him.

⌘

Dacca or Dachau?
✷   ✷   ✷

The fruit from the graveyard is sweetest,
The flowers on blood deepest.

August 1997, Newport Beach

UNDER TRAINED GUNS, A GROUP of men pile bodies upon bodies. Transfixed in silent horror, Alex leans forward, watches a gruesome story unfold on the screen, taking him back to 1971, Bangladesh, his birthplace, and the Genocide that created him.

"Reporting Ron Nessen, NBC news," is overlaid on the screen at the start of the grainy, black and white, home video. Men are lined up to the right. From the extreme right of the screen, a group of soldiers opens fire.

The men crumble backwards on top of the pile of dead bodies.

Alex stares blankly at the screen, hoping he might cleanse his eyes of an hallucination, ejects the tape and slowly pulls it out of the VCR. He sits back on the leather sofa, holds the videotape in his hands. For long moments he sits still. The archival copy of the NBC news broadcast is stamped January 7, 1972.

Through the living room skylight the sun filters in illuminating the coffee table cluttered with Alex's research into 1971—articles,

31

photocopies of old newspapers, and an open white legal-size envelope. Sangeeta has gone to her yoga class. Here alone in this large airy living room, Alex's mind feels empty like that last desperate contorted ignored plea of a human being before being killed. Holding his breath taut in a kind of incredulity, he puts the tape down on the coffee table, on top of the envelope.

Images well up in Alex's mind, images of a Vietnamese man in checkered shirt, dark pants, his hands tied behind his back, his face wrenched in anguish, his last desperate plea pulling the lines of his cheek in a demented contortion just before being shot point blank with a snub nosed revolver above the right ear. Man killing man. The blunt reality of war. The soldier in the background unphased by the cold-blooded execution. He has seen it many times. Death common place in this setting of Vietnam in the 1960s.

Alex gets up, stares at the twirling patterns on the edge of the Indigo Persian carpet. Images of Dhaka, 1971, the plea before death, the desperation fill his mind. Under his feet, the borders of the carpet turn crimson, blood stained like the killing fields of Dhaka University.

Outside on a busy August Saturday morning is the scattered sounds of surfers on the beach, the squawk of seagulls rising and circling on air currents.

Alex puts the tape back into the VCR. He holds the remote tightly. The screen starts to roll, wiping away twenty-six years. Adjusting the vertical hold, Alex sits back on the sofa, leans forward, his eyes

---

THE HISTORICAL FLAVOR OF SPELLINGS. Spellings are subtle but undeniable etches of time that hold rich historical texture. Dhaka was spelled Dacca in 1971 and for the feel and flavor of 1971, I have kept its spelling Dacca in the 1971 chapters and subsequently changed it to Dhaka in the 1997 chapters. Kolkata was spelled Calcutta in 1971, and Myanmar was Burma. In the chapter "While My Guitar Gently Weeps," Bangladesh is spelled Bangla Desh as it was on the *Concert for Bangla Desh* signs. History is encapsulated in these inflections of syllables; their metamorphosis over time inks the transformation from the callousness of colonialism to the present indigenous phonetic culture.

The video described here is viewable at the moment if you follow this URL. http://www.youtube.com/watch?v=sMg9Ly9nK0g (URL note: zero, not O.)

narrowed, his face sculpted in tense lines.

"One of the reasons there is a Bangladesh today is the fact that troops from West Pakistan savagely terrorized the Bengali population of East Pakistan. Perhaps a million people died," John Chancellor states in introducing the video shown on NBC Evening News just after the birth of Bangladesh. On the screen is a video heroically shot ten months before by a Dhaka University Engineering Professor from the roof of his apartment building on the morning of March 26, 1971.

"Here is some blurry videotape taken ten months ago, hidden since then, of how the terror began," Chancellor says as the video starts to roll.

Standing in front of Jagannath Hall, Dhaka University, I looked down at the cemented plaque, knee high, sticking out of the broad leaf grass.
Etched on the plaque, in black lettering on a white background, these words:

**Specific Charge: Genocide & Crimes Against Humanity of Murder
Main culprit: Pakistan Army, 57th Brigade, 18 Punjab, 22 Beluch, 32 Punjab
Brigadier JahanJeb Arbab, Lt. Colonel Taj. Dates of Murder: 25th March–26th March, 1971 War Crimes Facts Finding Committee.
Professor A. A. M. S. Arafin Shiddique, Vice Chancellor, Dhaka University, Dhaka-1000, 2nd April 2009. On behalf of Dhaka University.**

I looked across the killing fields of '71 where uncounted innocent lives were extinguished in a heinous execution.

Kneeling on the green blades of grass nourished on the blood of martyrs, I felt the dark earth, moist on my fingertips.

Young blood lost.
When your dream disintegrates into dust,
When screams shriek red in the blue sky,
Hold the dust in your hands,
And plant a seed of sorrow,
Water it with your tears.
Flowers will bloom,
The earth will rejoice.
Again.
The fruit from the graveyard is sweetest,
The flowers on blood deepest.

It is a bright clear early morning. From the roof of the Professor's apartment building, the video covers the open field with the dead piled up in the middle.

"Dacca," is overlaid on the upper left of the screen.

The grainy video shows five or six soldiers standing with guns to the right of the bodies. Beyond the pile of bodies and in front of the eucalyptus-like tall trees and a building that looks like a student dormitory, more soldiers quickly march by.

"Reporting Ron Nessen, NBC News," is on the bottom of the screen.

There is a soccer goal on the left side of the field, a field on which on a normal day students would play. There are some birds flying by in the foreground, a few unconcerned cows lazily grazing on the grass.

"The slightly blurry amateur videotape which has been kept secret, hidden for the past nine months, shows Pakistani soldiers executing students, professors and workers at the University of Dacca last March 26th. The first sequence shows the soldiers forcing students to carry and pile up bodies of victims already killed. The tape was made secretly by a Professor of Engineering on a portable tape machine hidden on the roof of a building about three hundred yards from the killings," reports Ron Nessen.

The first videotape ends and a second sequence, shot a few minutes later starts.

Alex closes his eyes, buries his head in his clasped hands.

"A Pakistani execution squad lined up slightly to the right of the center of the screen. About twenty people were herded on to the killing grounds from the right corner of the picture. One man dressed in black dropped to his knees and begged for mercy," Ron Nessen continues.

The soldiers raise their machine guns, the men stand still, holding that last breath, an eerie stillness, an eternity of anguish preserved forever on celluloid.

Kluthunk. Kluthunk. Kluthunk.

A palpable flesh and bone and soft tissue penetrating thud. In panic a white cow grazing on the field by the boundary wall careens left while a few others scamper to the right.

Ripped apart by the bullets, the students and staff fall backward like a line of cards, crumpling on top of the bodies they just piled, a massacred mound.

Point blank execution. Like a Nazi Lt. General Tikka Khan killing Bangladeshis.

Echoes of Dachau. Images of Auschwitz.

A man in black is left standing.

A soldier marches up close to him. Raises his rifle. Unloads into the man's chest. The bullets pierce through him and a cloud of dust comes off the field. The man collapses in slow motion folding like an accordion, first his knees, then his body into a small pile at the booted feet of General Yahya's finest.

Alex runs his fingers through his hair, exhales a long breath.

"Then the Pakistanis went amongst the bodies shooting close up to make sure their victims were dead. This is just one small episode of the Pakistan massacre. The killings were the beginning of a reign of terror by Pakistan, which set off a revolt by the Bengalis and ended in the liberation of Bangladesh," Nessen concludes.

In a fast-forward blur, more than fifty students, staff, faculty are dead. This is how history swallows young innocent lives in old festering hate. And this is how dreams are torn to shreds in the killing fields.

Alex turns off the TV, his shoulders tense against his body, his fists curled up tight.

Am I like one of them? Is that who Sangeeta's mother thinks I am? The son of one of those soldiers?

His mind spinning, Alex gets up and walks to the picture of Frank, to the smile held in a silver frame. He puts out a hand to steady himself on the edge of the table.

In Vietnam Frank tried so hard to grasp the meaning of war, reasons lost in buddies dead, war as meaningless as your best buddy's body dragged through the muck and mud.

"I was never so scared in my life last night with Charlie snipping at us from everywhere in the dark. I just can't understand this senseless killing, this war. Any war. Period." Alex remembers Frank's words in his diary.

If you give a soldier a gun, his buddy dead next to him, and the permission to shoot anyone without question, how long before he takes it out on the first moving object? Animal, human.

Alex buries his head in his hands, pulls at his hair.

The sheer madness of war. Men drunk mad on power ordering the slaughter of innocent men like animals. He tosses the remote on top of the documents fanned out on the table and picks up the envelope.

He puts his feet up on top of the papers, holds the envelope open. Takes out the ticket slowly, inspects the Singapore Airlines golden yellow stylized pale bird insignia on the dark blue background. Unfolding the itinerary, he looks at his planned journey next month, unfolds a map for lost souls.

His trip back.

Los Angeles. Tokyo. Singapore. Dhaka.

Bangladesh.

Alex turns the envelope over. With a blue ball point pen, the movements of his hand deliberate, forceful, he writes Bangladesh on the envelope.

He gets up and walks out through the sliding glass door to the veranda. The salt air fills his lungs. He gazes at the small twisting path that Sangeeta and he walk down the bluff to the beach. Floating like the sea gulls to a distant, precious place, fighting the wind, Alex struggles to overcome some great emotion, a sacred silence of the decades inside him, echoing like the cry of the gulls carried on currents.

Alex looks to the east, to the Land of the Rising Sun, over Vietnam, South East Asia, then farther east past Burma. There, cupped by the foothills of the Himalayas, is Bangladesh, the mighty Ganges delta. His birthplace.

His lips silently move forming a word.

Bangladesh.

Syllables holding secret his tenuous faded past.

Silent enigmas of 1971.

❦

THE SILENT AND THE LOST

Book Two

1971

Joy Bangla

March 7, 1971: Ramna Race Course Maidan, Dacca, East Pakistan

"*BIR BANGALI ASRO DHORO!*
Bangladesh shadhin koro!
Joyyy Banglaaaaa! Joyyyyyy Banglaaaa!
Brave Bengalis, take up arms!
Fight for your motherland!
Victory to Bengal, Viva Bengal."

This resonating, thunderous slogan rang out in chorus from an ocean of aching voices, broke like a tidal wave of freedom over the crowd gathered at Ramna Race Course Maidan on March 7, 1971.

A pilgrimage to freedom.

They carried banners of hope, they carried bamboo sticks shining with revenge, and in their combined screaming voices they carried their aching hearts' desire.

Freedom.

Lung bursting shrieks of "Joy Bangla!" from a million plus Bangladeshis moved the crowd. Sound had fury. Ear-shattering voices rocked the air, moved, swayed the crowd.

"Brave Bangladeshis, arm yourself! Free Bangladesh! Joy Bangla!"

41

Shaking their clenched fists, punching the air, waving placards, the surging processions headed towards the Race Course to hear Bangabandhu, Friend of Bangladesh. Today Sheikh Mujibur Rahman was going to give his historic speech.

Nahar Sultana came with her husband Rafique from Sheetalpur and like millions of others headed to Ramna Race Course.

The atmosphere was expectant and tense. In the March sun, approaching Ramna Race course, she was now part of a revolution in the making, powerful and complete.

Nahar had started walking from in front of Dacca University Ruqayyah Hall in a women's procession, the women mostly students living on campus, carrying banners they had stayed up all night making.

In her tight grip, Nahar carried a banner she waved as she yelled out,

"*Ma bonera asro dhoro, Bangladesh moktoo koro!*
"Mothers and sisters, Arm yourself, Free Bangladesh!"

She felt herself swelling with pride at being part of the Dacca University women students' procession—Dacca University where she was planning to apply soon and attend.

There was, in Nahar's mind, a feeling of firsts to this day, this procession, a freedom of her own she had never experienced. A period in life—hers and Rafique's—was coming, if not to a full close, then at least toward some transforming twist. She, Nahar Sultana, had become part of something infinitely bigger than anything she had known in her life.

The women around her screamed with bursting lungs, with voices cracking with rage, fists clenched in the air. Nahar joined in as loud as she had ever done in her twenty-year-old life, her voice cracking, erupting in emotion. On this route from Dacca University to the Ramna Race Course, Nahar could feel the scorching heat of the sun on the skin of her face, her nose, throat full of dust.

She reached for the *áchol* of her black-bordered white sari and dabbed at the sweat on her forehead. In her big brown eyes twinkled thousands, yes a million marchers today. Slender and long-limbed,

Nahar had braided her hip-long hair, prepared for this march. A smile rose to her face, and she screamed "Joy Bangla," as she thought about her husband, Rafique, a student leader, leading his own procession. In unison, the women and the girls yelled out, their voices now shrill and cracking,

"Kick the dogs in their mongrel faces,
Independence for Bangladesh now!
Joy Bangla! Joy Bangla!"

Walking backwards, leading their student procession, Rafique Chowdhury and Nazmul Islam, in bell-bottom cotton pants, their shirt sleeves rolled up, yelled out slogan after slogan at the top of their voices. Picking up fervent students in a magnetic force, they marched the several miles from in front of Iqbal Hall on the Dacca University Campus to the Race Maidan.

Rafique clenched his fist, put back his head, screamed into the sky,

"Padma, Meghna, Jamuna!"

"*Tomar amar thikana,* your and our address," Nazmul yelled out and in unison with thousands of students, created a oneness of voice, a venting of common frustrations.

Rafique was sweaty, his voice hoarse, his face mottled with dark black stubble around his handlebar moustache, eyes blood-shot from being up all night organizing, painting slogans. Beside him marched Nazmul in his sandaled feet, a slight, smaller man with sharp features. On his face also a weary, exhausted smile, in his brown eyes the hope for freedom that Bangabandhu was promising today.

"*Bir Bangali asro dhoro!*
Bangladesh *shadhin koro*!!!!
Joy Bangla!" echoed back the voices, joining in the contagious fray.

From every corner of East Pakistan, on trains, trucks, vans, cars, rickshaws, and on foot, Bangladeshis marched, surged forth into the center of Dacca. From every distant corner of East Pakistan came the supporters.

Today all roads led to the green grass and hoofed dirt of the huge, sprawling Ramna Race Course in the middle of Dacca. The white wooden fence that encircled the entire ground for horse races was now encircling an ocean of people on a foot race in their bare and sandaled feet, in a lung-bursting, surging race to freedom.

From the South: Chittagong, Barisal, Khulna; from the West: Jessore; from the East: Comilla and from the North: Rajshahi, Rangpur, Mymensingh, Sylhet. Like a torrential flood they flowed unabated, flowed onto the hundreds of acres of open space of the Maidan. And they came from every walk of life: farmers, day laborers, rickshaw-wallahs, cart-wallahs, students, shopkeepers, beggars, businessmen, teachers, government officials, even members of EPR and police in civilian clothes. The handicapped, the old, children—everyone joined in.

In the bright afternoon sun, in the humid March air, the new flag with the bright mustard yellow Bangladeshi map in the center of a blood red sun in a field of deep green fluttered tall on bamboo poles, fluttered like the hopes of freedom of a million thrumming, throbbing Bangladeshi hearts.

Exhilaration. Anticipation. Rage. Anger.
A million strong. And more.
Undeniable. United. Unending.

Inside the bamboo corral specially set up for women, sitting on the Ramna green, Nahar looked up into the sky. Further down, halfway to the Kalibari Mandir, Rafique, his face turned into the mid-afternoon brilliance of the sun, a slogan in his mouth, looked up into the same sky.

Rafique stood up. And he stood with the ocean of Bangladeshis holding long bamboo staves and waving them menacingly in the air. The crowd pressed on all sides of Nahar, Rafique and Nazmul. Currents of emotions swayed the crowd like the waves on the Padma, Meghna and Jamuna. Pressed together, in one breath, in one pressed soul, they looked skyward.

And high above, circling in the clear afternoon Dacca sky, were the Pakistani military helicopters. Like hungry white-rumped vultures swooping in looking for dead carrion, General Yahya's choppers came in for a close look to report on the ocean of placard-wielding Bangladeshis. From above, the surging humanity looked like a swarm, like a bulging ocean of swarming angry black bees buzzing on the field, waving bamboo staves at the green military helicopters, trying to sting the foreign intruders.

From the North, the West Pakistani helicopters took off from Tejgoan Airport and Cantonment and flew South over Dhanmondi into the Dacca University area and the Ramna Race Course grounds. The helicopters circled to Dacca's south boundary, the Buriganga river, over Shadarghat and Old Dacca into the Gulistan and Motijheel Commercial areas, and over Baitul Mukarram Mosque, finally over Dacca University, and today, over the protesting humanity at Ramna Race Course. Human heads like pins dotted all of Ramna as far as the eye could see, interspersed by the new Bangladeshi flags, snapping in defiance of oppression.

In the crowd all discussions centered on freedom and whether Mujib would declare outright independence from West Pakistan.

Exhausted, never having experienced anything like this, Nahar sat on the brown, thirsty Ramna grass, her legs crossed under her sari. She dabbed her forehead again, felt the dusty heat, pulled her *áchol* over her head. A few women were chewing *paan*, trying to squeeze out a little red juice into their parched dry throats. Many had walked all morning, carrying packed meals. Many came with four-layer aluminum tiffin carriers, *daal,* fish curry and rice stacked separately in their own containers. Exhausted and hungry, throats parched, voices broken, some were now digging into their lunches with their hands, *shootki, daal, Koi bajhee,* biting into green hot chilis and sliced red onions for the taste uniquely Bengali—gathering strength to fight for freedom. Freedom to speak, to live, to flourish, to enjoy the fruits of their labor in a free land.

The sun passed its zenith and Nahar eagerly awaited the Bangabandhu in the women's section. In front of her, only a few hundred yards away, she could see the tall bamboo and cloth-draped podium where the Bangabandhu, Sheikh Mujibur Rahman, the leader of the Awami league, would deliver his speech. In the hot sun, Nahar felt the breeze come up and the unfurled new Bangladeshi flags snapped in the wind and the women wearing white saris, black ribbons pinned on for the recent martyrs, covered their heads from the afternoon heat. Scores of reporters sat on the wooden podium, many foreign, holding cameras, pencils and pads.

Nahar enthusiastically waved her placard, "Mothers and sisters, arm yourselves. Free Bangladesh!"

Like the fluttering Bangladeshi flags, her emotions surged and Nahar felt the urgency of the fight. She felt the throbbing in her heart for a better future. Sheetalpur and Joydebpur were the place where her very own, very particular story had its origin, but the thought of going back there today somehow unsettled her, stirring up thoughts of arguments with her in-laws about coming to Dacca.

"*Bou Maa*, you could get lost, or hurt in the crowd. The military could fire or explode tear gas," Jahanara Chowdhury, her mother-in-law had pleaded with her. Her father-in-law, Mustafa Chowdhury, was brooding, not saying much, completely opposed to Nahar coming to Dacca.

Right now, sitting on the Ramna grass, Sheetalpur seemed far, and the cry for boycott, more marches, a new nation, a free Bangladesh very near, pressing. Raising her placard high in the air, looking at the podium, Nahar screamed with the women around her.

"*Ma bonera asro dhoro, Bangladesh moktoo koro!*

"Mothers and sisters, arm yourself. Free Bangladesh!"

"Is he going to declare an independent Bangladesh and freedom from the colonial rule under Yahya Khan and Bhutto?" This was the question on a million lips, everyone expecting Bangabandhu to spell out the future course of action. The crowd erupted, their blood pulsating and throbbing in their enraged veins.

"Kick Bhutto, Yahya in the face,
Bangladesh independence now!"

It was now, it was today, it was the instant of truth. Freedom or more tyranny?

About 3:00 P.M.

As far as eye could see stretched placards-waving slogan-screaming supporters all the way to the far off high Minar on the left and the water tank to the right, several miles away. A million bamboo staves, well oiled, glinted in the Ramna air.

"Joy Bangla, Joy Bangabandhu!" the crowd called out, buoyed by the sight of Bangabandhu. Nahar screamed as everyone stood up, excited, reenergized.

Bangabandhu, Sheikh Mujibur Rahman, got out wearing his signature black Mujib waistcoat with high collar over his white cotton Panjabi. He climbed up to the raised bamboo podium; behind him stood the Awami League leaders, including Tajuddin Ahmad, Syed Nazrul Islam.

Bangabandhu took off his black-rimmed glasses and put them down on the wooden podium. Standing tall and determined, towering over the surging crowd, Sheikh Mujibur Rahman embodied that iconic centrality of Bangladeshi politics. That unique voice that comes along in a nation's lifetime. That unique compassion that embraced Bangladeshis from the very destitute to the highest intelligentsia.

With a raised right hand, his index finger pointed up, Bangabandhu started to speak in a thunderous voice,

---

Date with Destiny: Fury, Rage and Seventy Million Bangladeshis

In the annals of human history few speeches have moved so many to do so much as Bangabandhu Sheikh Mujibur Rahman's speech *"Ebarer songram muktir songram, ebarer songram shadhinotar songram!* This time the struggle is for freedom, this time the struggle is for independence" did that defining historic afternoon of March 7, 1971.

The world's eyes were focused on Ramna that day. Many hoped Bangabandhu would declare independence from West Pakistan. And many have speculated why he did not declare outright independence. Was it because of the recent history of failed declarations of independence: the 1965 failure of Ian Smith's declaration of independence in Rhodesia and the 1967 failure of the Biafra struggle in Nigeria? This was then, has been, and is still today the topic of heated discussions—possibly Bangabandhu did not want to instigate further bloodshed.

Included in my translation from Bengali is the full text of the fiery speech as it so

"My Brothers,

Today I stand before you in anguish and heartache.

You know and understand everything. We have tried our utmost, but it is heart wrenching that in Dacca, Chittagong, Khulna, Rajshahi and Rangpur the streets are awash in my brothers' blood.

Today the Bengali people cry out for our freedom. The Bengali people want to live. The Bengali people want our rights.

What crime did we commit?"

Bangabandhu's emotion-driven voice, loud with determination, brought to a crescendo the boiling blood of revolution and the crowd broke into loud slogans, surged forth screaming "Joy Bangla, Joy Bangla, Joy Bangla!"

Bangabandhu continued,

"In the elections the people of Bangladesh voted for me and the Awami league so that a National Assembly could convene and there we could formulate a constitution. There we could build up this nation so that this country's people can gain their economic, political and cultural freedom.

But it is a deplorable matter, and it is with a heavy heart I have to say that 23 years of this country's dark history is a history of bloodshed and of oppression of the people of Bangladesh.

---

eloquently presents what preceded one of the most pre-planned genocides in history. Mujib's speech ranks with those of King, Kennedy, Gandhi, and great leaders of men; this speech moved seventy million people to action and served as the master plan that created a free Bangladesh out of the ashes of President Yahya Khan's East Pakistan.

Preludes to genocides have eerie resemblances in the eagerness on the part of the assassins to make promises, and under those pretenses blitzkrieg a nation and its people into the ground. It was in the face of cunning and cloying on the part of General Yahya Khan that Mujib defined what turned out to be a prophetic course of action for the people of Bangladesh, and ultimately the road map to freedom through one of history's worst genocides.

Where do you find one man addressing millions and within ten countable minutes unifying them into one fighting nation?

Sheikh Mujibur Rahman did just that on March 7, 1971.

48

Our history is a history written in tears.

The history of Bangladesh is the history of bloodshed.

We shed our blood in 1952. Then in 1954 we won the election but we were not allowed to rule. In 1958 Ayub Khan declared martial law and enslaved us for another ten long years. On 7th June, 1966, during the Six-point Movement, Bangladesh's sons and daughters were gunned down unmercifully in the streets. After our 1969 uprising, and Ayub Khan's downfall, General Yahya Khan took over the reins of power with the promise to restore constitutional rule and democracy and return power to the people. We agreed. So much has happened since then, and finally the election took place."

With focus, force, fortitude Bangabandhu's voice drove the millions into frenzied cries of "Joy Bangla!"

They cried out,

"Stop Military barbarity!

Brave Bangladeshis, Arm Yourself!

Free Bangladesh!"

Bangabandhu's voice rose above the cries for freedom.

"I have met with President Yahya Khan. I requested him, not only as the leader of East Pakistan, but also the majority political leader of all of Pakistan, that you set February 15 for the opening session. He did not keep my word, but he kept Mr. Bhutto's word. He said it would be the first week of March. I said, we agree to sit in the Assembly. I also said, that even though we are the majority we would have discussions in the Assembly and we would agree to reason—even if the statement is made by just one person.

Mr. Bhutto came here and we met. He left stating the door to further conferences was not shut, and we would discuss matters further. Then I had meetings with other West Pakistani political leaders—please come, sit and together we will through communication and discussion make an agreement on a constitutional framework.

Mr. Bhutto stated firmly that if West Pakistani members of Parliament came to Dacca, then the Assembly would turn into a slaughterhouse. He said whoever would come would be murdered. If anyone came to the Assembly from West Pakistan, then West

Pakistan would be shut down from Peshawar to Karachi. I restated that the Assembly would convene. Then without warning on the first, the Assembly was shut down.

Yahya Khan as President had called the Assembly.

I stated that I would go. Mr. Bhutto said he was not going to attend. Thirty-five members came here from West Pakistan. All of a sudden the Assembly was called off, and the blame was placed on the shoulders of the people of Bangladesh.

I was blamed.

After the calling off of the Assembly, the people of Bangladesh cried out in protest. I asked that the people protest through strikes in a peaceful manner. I said, close down the factories, close down everything. The people rose to the call. Spontaneously, the people came out on the streets, and they joined ranks in peaceful protests and strikes.

What did we get in return?

We bought arms with our money to protect our people from external enemies. But sadly today those arms are pointed at the poor and downtrodden unarmed people—today the bullets are finding their vindictive mark on our innocent brave chests.

We are the majority population of Pakistan.

Whenever we have yearned for our rights and power, they have crushed our dreams.

I spoke to him on the telephone. I told him, Mr. Yahya Khan, you are the President of Pakistan, come see how your bullets are being aimed and fired into the chests of the poor and the people of this land. Come see how my mothers' laps are being robbed of their sons and daughters, how the people are being murdered. Please come, see with your own eyes. We demand justice from you.

He stated that I supposedly agreed to a round table conference on the 10th of March. I had stated a long time ago, what round table? And with whom will we sit down? Sit down with the same people who tore the life out of the brave chests of our citizens? Out of the blue, after a five-hour secret meeting and without discussing anything with me, in the speech that he gave, he has squarely put all the blame on my shoulders. He has put all the blame on the innocent people of Bangladesh.

Brothers, they have called the Assembly on the 25th of March.

The blood has not dried on the streets of this country. I strongly stated on the 10th that I will not tread on the sacred blood of our martyrs and join this round table conference.

You have called the Assembly, but first you must agree to my demands. You have to withdraw martial law. All the army personnel must return to the barracks. I demand an investigation into the murders of my people. And you must relegate power to the rightfully elected leaders. Then and only then will we even consider if we can sit in the Assembly or not.

Before these demands are met, we will not sit in the Assembly.

I do not want your position of Prime Minister. We demand the rights of the people of this country.

I want to be crystal clear in stating that from today the courts and legal system of this country, government offices, schools and universities will be closed for an indefinite time.

So that the poor do not suffer, so that our people do not suffer, those institutions that they need will be kept open. Rickshaws, cars, rail lines will operate, launches will operate. Only the Secretariat, Supreme court, High court, Judge court and semi-government offices, and WAPDA will not be running.

On the 28th the employees will draw their salary. If the salary is not paid, if one bullet is fired, and if our people are murdered, I am requesting you to fortify each home into a fortress.

We have to fight the enemy with whatever we have on hand. And even if I am not around to give orders, then you must barricade all the streets. We will starve them and we will not quench their thirst."

The crowd erupted into wild applause and a chorus of "Joy Bangla! Joy Bangla! Joy Bangla!"

"You are my brothers. I say to you, stay in your barracks and no one will harm you. But do not try to fire on us anymore. You cannot suppress 70 million people. We have learned to die.

No one can stop us now.

We from the Awami League will try our best to help the people who have become martyrs and the wounded as much as we can. Those of you who can help, please donate to our relief committee. In this seven-day strike, all of the employers must make sure the laborer brothers who have joined us are paid.

Government officers must follow what I say. Till this land is free, no taxes will be collected or paid.

Remember, the enemy has penetrated our ranks and will try to create division among us, and through looting create derisions in our ranks. Hindus or Muslims, Bengalis or non-Bengalis, all are our brothers. It is our duty to ensure everyone's safety.

Remember, radio-television employees, if they don't listen to our orders in the radio station then not one Bangladeshi will go to work. If the television does not broadcast our news, then no Bangladeshi will go to the TV station.

The banks will be open for two hours every day so that the people can get their paychecks cashed. Not one penny will be transferred from East Bengal to West Pakistan. Telephone and telegram will work and news from this East Bengal will be let to travel to the world.

But if the people of this country are going to be massacred, then Bangladeshis work understanding their motives.

In every village, in every neighborhood I ask that under Awami League you set up committees to carry on our struggle.

With whatever you have, prepare for the struggle ahead. Since we have shed blood, we will shed more blood. Insha'Allah, we will free the people of this country."

At the end, Bangabandhu, in a voice that filled all of Ramna with resolve said,

"*Ebarer songram muktir songram, ebarer songram shadhinotar songram!* This struggle is for our freedom, this struggle is for our independence. Joy Bangla."

By the strength of his voice, by the processions, by strikes and speeches, by sweat and by blood, Bangabandhu raised the spirit of the crowd into a crescendo of applause and riveting slogans of "*Ebarer songram muktir songram, ebarer songram shadhinotar songram!* This struggle is for our freedom, this struggle is for our independence!"

The sound of a dusty chorus of erupting voices screamed out new strength as they joined in loud, then louder. Clenched fists in the air, they wanted rights of their own. Rights to a free life, rights to dignity, to honor, to a life unshackled, to the colonial rule of the West Pakistani Junta.

Today Nahar could taste a free Bangladesh. She stood cheering with the women, her chin held high, collectively undefeatable. The thoughts of sharing her experience this afternoon, her part in this march, filled her with a sudden sense of urgency, with satisfaction. Thoughts of describing Bangabandhu's forceful manner, his ardent determination, to her in-laws, Amina and Halim and others in Sheetalpur made her swell up with pride.

Nahar's blood was thrumming with new resolve. Part of Bangabandhu's movement, finally she could do something for her people. Now she could do something for her country.

"Ebarer songram muktir songram, ebarer songram shadhinotar songram" she loudly exclaimed, her voice swelled with the desire to move this struggle forward, rising in an emotional crescendo, reaching the pinnacle of *songram*. "This struggle is for our freedom, this struggle is for our independence!" Nahar shouted with the crowd, the very mingling of her voice with the loud chanting, yelling, the screaming created a harmony in unison, a wondrous strength in numbers, in a chorus, a oneness she never felt before.

Thrust into a sea of history,
Nahar was one with millions just then.

❦

Viva Bengal

Monday, March 22, 1971, Modhur Canteen, Dacca University

*I*F A UNIVERSITY HAS A heart, Modhur's Canteen was Dacca
University's soul. Ancient, built at the turn of the century as
an open dance hall on a concrete slab, sporting high Victorian
arches painted in an aging yellow going mildewy black, Modhur
Canteen was the womb of Dacca University student politics.
Born here on unfinished wooden tables were protests, revolts and
revolutions.

Fists banging on the wooden tables here drummed into every
corner of the country; the political vibrations here reverberated a
thousand times over in the boatman's song, in the anticipated gossip
of the village chai stall and in the farmer's coconut-shell hookahs at
the village gatherings.

Here, under a corrugated tin roof, plastered walls covered almost
completely in posters and loud banners, surrounded by a high
shaded canopy of variegated green and banana plants, the student
organizations gathered all day, planning, deliberating, designing
posters and painting banners. Alam, Shazu, Monir, and a dozen
others were already clustered around a table, drinking tea and
wrestling over political points and procession plots. They looked
bohemian, pony-tailed, bearded, scrawny, dressed in *kurtas* or un-

tucked shirts, faded cotton bell-bottom pants, carrying artist's satchels. There were a few women, braided hair and pronounced *teeps* on their forehead, in white saris with prominent black ribbons for the recent martyrs. Over cups of tea, they carried on conversations working on a pamphlet or just plain arguing politics. The black metal bars on the windows reverberated with passion and politics.

Walking towards Modhur Canteen from a student gathering at Iqbal Hall, Rafique and Nazmul were lost in a deep argument.

"My throat feels like sandpaper. A cup of chai would hit the spot," Rafique said.

"But Bangabandhu disappointed everybody. He did not declare outright independence from Pakistan," said Nazmul.

"Bangabandhu did the right thing. It's too dangerous to declare Independence. If he had, the artillery might have fired on us. Those choppers in the air could have given the command to fire."

"Impossible!" Nazmul said.

"Absolutely!" Rafique replied.

Rafique and Nazmul walked through the doors of Modhur Canteen late in the afternoon. The place was humming. Rafique scratched at his day-old beard nervously. Nazmul clenched his teeth, focusing on the activities for tomorrow—March 23rd, Resistance Day, a day to show Yahya's Junta total defiance. The Bangladeshi flag and a black flag mourning the martyrs were flying on top of every building today.

Snippets of the conversation greeted the men.

"Even the foreign missions are flying the new flag."

"Did you see Qamrul Hasan's poster? Made Yahya's eyebrows into Satan's horns. They are posted all over the Shaheed Minar. Looks great!"

"Yahya's Satan."

As Rafique and Nazmul joined in, the gathered students shifted and made space for them.

Nazmul looked around the table and said, "The so-called Bangalee heroes armed with bamboo staves are marching to Bangabandhu's house to salute him. After returning home they will have a feast of rice and fish and take a siesta with the satisfaction of having done their duty." Breathing in the palpable tension filling every corner of Modhur's Canteen, he continued in a low voice, "At the Paltan grounds, they are parading with dummy rifles. Are we still living in a land of fairy tales? We will fight them with dummy rifles? There must be a limit to this stupidity."

"And in the meantime thousands of Pakistani troops are landing in plain clothes at the airport, and ships loaded with weapons are anchoring at Chittagong port," Rafique added, his voice calm.

"Don't you guys feel we will have to face a lot of bloodshed? The students have accumulated some machetes and knives, .22 rabbit hunting rifles, maybe even some arms, but so little to fight this West Pakistani army," Nazmul said.

"We can make Molotov cocktails, bottle bombs" said Alam.

"Yeah, and that's going to destroy a tank?" a wild-eyed student quipped.

Rafique, clutching a handful of his hair, said, "What is everyone thinking? Do you think they will give us independence on a silver platter? We will have to win it—fight for it."

Nazmul shrugged his shoulders and added, "The Pakistani army has the latest weapons. What would you fight them with? Damned bamboo sticks?"

"We are going to need machine guns and grenades and real bombs," said Rafique.

"Pakistan is ruled by twenty-two families. You think these West Pakistani families want freedom for Bangladesh? We don't want this country ruled by families. We need a nation for citizens," said Nazmul strongly.

"What's the plan for tomorrow, for Resistance Day?" Rafique said.

"Be alert, we might need to barricade Fuller road," Nazmul said.

"With what?" asked one of the students.

"Anything. Water tanks, trees. Whatever we have. Didn't you hear Bangabandhu?" said Rafique.

"The Bhashani Party has been holding street corner meetings every day, calling people to declare March 23rd as Independence Day of East Bengal," said Nazmul.

"We will lead a procession out of Iqbal Hall," said Rafique.

"Do we have a large Bangladeshi flag?" asked Nazmul.

"Yes," replied a young student.

"Make sure you tell Asad, Alam and Rehana to be there," said Rafique.

"Do the girls in Ruqayyah Hall know?" asked Nazmul.

"Yes," answered one of the girls.

"How many placards do we have?" asked Rafique.

"Hundred."

"Make sure we get at least seventy more made. And don't forget the large banners that Salaam was going to make," said Rafique.

"I'll check on it right now," said another student.

The planning and the pathos reached a pinnacle as East Pakistan was peacefully demanding freedom from the West Pakistani military Junta's slavery. From Dacca University was flowing the red of revolt into every hidden village, every home, every street corner gathering.

Rafique and Nazmul left, in their heads plans for Resistance day activities, in their hearts overwhelming anger. Twenty-three years of West Pakistani colonialism had to end. Two hundred years of British colonialism extended by the Generals of Pakistan from 1947 to March, 1971 had to end.

It had to end.

Now.

They felt their seething anger and their steely determination take concrete shape in posters and placards and signs and clenched fists and lung bursting shrieks of "Joy Bangla!" And today at Modhur's Canteen they stood elated, stamping their sandaled feet on the cement floor. If dancers entertained in this hall seventy years ago, today in 1971, on this March afternoon, a war dance was afoot and an ocean of blood was thrumming in the veins of these students deep in the heart of Dacca University to be let out in a bloody revolution.

— ⚜ —

March 23, 1971, Dacca University Club

THE MARCH AFTERNOON SUN SLICED by the metal bars on the windows threw light and shadow into the large empty room usually full of faculty and staff. Like a sitar string twisted to a tautness before breaking, in the air there was a strained tension just waiting to snap. Sitting alone, Professor Rahman took a sip of tea and he gazed far away, past the green lawn and past the tennis courts of Dacca University Club. Badminton nets had been tied on bamboo poles on the tennis court, but the University was closed. Noticeably missing were the usual boisterous badminton players jumping up and down with a racket, following the shuttlecock.

Professor Rahman felt the emptiness of the usually crowded Club, looked across to the stacked empty chairs as the waiter placed the white china teacups and the plate with the samosas on his table.

Taking one more sip of tea, Professor Sen said quietly, "The trap was set and baited long time ago. Hindus and Muslims were living together, but the British made the Hindus the official workers and the Muslims the down trodden scapegoats." Sen scratched at something fictitious on his face, rattled his tea cup on the saucer for a while, and in the echoing emptiness of the room said, "How, how could it ever have worked? Only in the divide and conquer minds of the British!"

Rahman held onto his cup, stared into the miniscule black tea leaf bits at the bottom. "Not even in the minds of the British!" he continued in a raw voice. "'East Pakistan won't last for more than 25 years in Pakistan,' exiting British Governor General Mount batten told his Indian successor C Rajgopalachary during his farewell Banquet in June 1948."

"In 1947, redefinition by religion was the arch triumph of Jinnah and Muslim League," Rahman said.

"Two people, divided by over a thousand miles! Two disparate lands, one mountainous and one the Ganges plains, tied together by the Gordian knot of Islam," Sen said, then got up, put his teacup down and fidgeted with the cap of his fountain pen.

"Pegging Germans against Jews was Hitler's way," continued Sen.

"And pegging Hindus against Muslims, divide and conquer, was the British way," Rahman replied, and then added, "Pegging us against Hindus, making us a lower echelon, faulting the Hindus for siding with India, was the same search for a scapegoat tactic that Hitler used by blaming German economic woes on the Jews!"

Sen got up and excused himself to say hello to Professor Gosh as he entered. Rahman took a last sip of tea, called to the waiter and ordered some fried *puris* that the Dacca University club was so famous for.

Professor Gosh sat down, and asked, "Are you staying Sen?"

"Yes," Sen replied.

"How about you Rahman?" Gosh asked.

"Same as Sen. Selina is pregnant. Moving to the village right now is difficult. Rafique's wife, Nahar, is here helping Selina. She is taking care of the children,"

"Rafique's wife? Oh, yes I saw her," Gosh said, and then he continued, changing the subject. "Maulana Bhashani, I heard, is going to go beyond Sheikh Mujibur Rahman and declare outright independence."

"Really? When is this going to happen?" asked Rahman.

"It's so easy to forget the Red Maulana," said Sen. "Since 1969 his favorite slogans were *Swadhin Bangla Zindabad* and *Azad Bangla Zindabad*. Maulana Bhasani was the first among the politicians to conceive of an independent East Pakistan."

Gosh nodded. "As early as 1950, Bhashani, said that an integrated Pakistan was no longer possible. He declined to participate in last year's national election, saying that it would only help perpetuate the rule by West Pakistan."

"I just hope we can come to a peaceful conclusion. Everything is shut down as Mujib wants it, but what now? You think Yahya is just going to let us have our freedom on a platter?" Rahman asked, an undertone of uncertainty in his voice.

"*Allah-u Akbar, Ash-hadu an la ilaha illallah...*" The *muezzin* called the faithful to the Maghrib evening prayer on the loudspeaker from the Dacca University Mosque.

Professor Rahman got up, said his good-byes, an uneasiness knotting up in the pit of his stomach as he walked towards his apartment in the University Quarters. No, no freedom on a silver platter for Bangladeshis.

Fearful for his family, in the stillness of the dusk Campus he silently prayed.

Operation Searchlight

❧ ❧ ❧

March 25, 1971, Dacca University Campus, East Pakistan

JOLTED OUT OF SLEEP BY gunfire in the fourth floor bedroom overlooking Nilkhet, Nahar screams out, "Bhabi!" With little Tia hanging on, she tries to scramble away from the windows, away from the shooting. As the sound of her voice fades, she hears rapid footsteps coming up the stairs. She cries out again "Bhabi"— the sound catching, dying in her dry, terror-filled throat.

Awakened by ear-piercing explosions, human shrieks and the sharp stammer of machine guns from the Nilkhet slum, in the master bedroom a pregnant Mrs. Selina Rahman wakes up startled, confused, shocked. Amidst the sound of soldiers barking out orders in Urdu, heavy troop trucks, metallic clanking of tank treads, Professor Rahman runs in from the living room, scoops up Tia from Nahar's arms, crawls to Selina's bedside. In a tracer shot-up darkness, Professor Rahman scrambles to protect his children. Crouching between Nahar and Selina, Tia, Babul, and Moina whimper, petrified in terror.

Over the barrage of gunfire, Rahman says to Selina cowering on the floor, "Nilkhet Police Barracks." His eyes are hollow, his expression cold.

"Nilkhet ..." is all Selina hears as an explosion rocks the room.

Huddled together, they lay in a numb, cold sweat. When Selina looks out across the hallway to the outside windows, she hears screams, more gunfire, explosions. Wincing as another glass pane shatters, sending flying shards of sharp daggers everywhere, Rahman hunches by his family, his whole body curls in tension as every muscle tightens, his mottled face now twisting into a grimace.

"Allah, help us!" Selina says. Her voice fades, drops below a whisper as she repeats "Allah" a few more times to herself. "Pray everything will be OK," she says to her eldest daughter, Tia, only six. Tia quivers, her gentle, heart shaped face now streaked with tears.

In a lull in the shooting, Nahar says to Professor Rahman, "They are killing everyone in Nilkhet." Then taking her *dupatta*, Nahar ties it tight around her waist, prepares for running out of the fourth-floor apartment, escaping down the long flight of stairs with Moina, the children, and for whatever comes their way this darkest of nights. With the power and phone lines cut, the flashes of tracers light up the dark apartment. Nahar looks up; the hands of the large wall clock have not yet quite closed in prayer. Hunched on a cold concrete floor, breathing in short raspy spurts, Nahar clasps her hands in prayer.

Crawling on all fours, Professor Rahman curses his way to his flashlight lodged in the far corner of the bed. Gnawing in his mind is the new Bangladeshi flag he raised on the roof just two days ago.

He cowers down, covers the women and children with his body, as another explosion rocks the whole building, shattering all the remaining windowpanes. Like translucent daggers of death the shards burst and scatter all over the floor of the living room, the hallway, all the rooms facing Nilkhet Road.

"The flag. I forgot the flag on the roof," Rahman says to Selina, his words muffled by the loud explosions. "The Bangladeshi flag! I must take it down, or we are all dead."

Selina pulls hard on his Panjabi sleeve and says, "They will shoot you." Beside her, the faces of Nahar, Tia, Babul and Moina are ashen in horror.

"I have to do this Selina. No way out, no way," he says, his voice sure, determined. "If they see the Bangladeshi flag we are all dead!" Swallowing hard, breathing in harsh gasps, Rahman tells Selina, "You take care of the children."

Rahman looks for his shoes. Quickly, he pulls on his pumps. Under the bed, he finds a pair of Selina's sandals and says, "Nahar, put these on. Come with me."

With trembling hands Nahar puts on her sandals. Glass crackles under their feet as Nahar and Rahman tip-toe down the hall towards the entrance door and stairwell.

"BOOM…swisssh…BOOM…ratatatata…shwisssh…BOOM."

A tracer explodes in the sky. Covering their heads with their hands, they fall to the floor. Minutes later, edging by the wall, they stoop and inch towards the door. Tracers reflect in Nahar's eyes, flooded with tears. She shudders as any noise outside sounds like heavy boots coming up the stairwell. Her thoughts of a certain, impending death are marked by her breath—raspy, ragged.

Rahman's hands shake as he unbolts the door, his face now glazed with sweat. Any moment now the military could come up the stairs. Any moment they could be all dead.

"Bolt the door Nahar. No one. No one. Don't let anyone in. No one!" Rahman says in a strained voice. Nahar tries in vain to put on a brave face, then nods, wipes off tears and cold sweat from her face. Across Nilkhet road, an inferno blazes out of control. She crouches down by the base of the door, her hands and legs shake uncontrollably, prays Rafique and Nazmul are safe in these killing fields that now surround her.

Tightly gripping the torchlight, Professor Rahman crawls out of the apartment into the stairwell. Nahar slides the top and bottom metal latches shut and places the heavy bar across the door.

"We are all dead!" Professor Rahman says, as he crawls up the concrete stairs to the roof. Then he recites the *Ayatul Kursi* verse from the Koran, "*Allahu la ilaha illa Huwa, Al-Haiyul-Qaiyum …,*" getting strength in the *Surah*. His attempts at a prayer sink into silence; his heart is in the dry tomb of his mouth. In his nostrils, his eyes, his throat is the acrid smell of smoke; in his ears erupts a crescendo of intense sounds of tanks and machine guns and death shrieks, echoing and reverberating in the long stairwell.

Barely making out the faded white and yellow floral patterns painted on the concrete steps, Rahman grips the flashlight in his sweating palms, too scared to turn it on—a soldier might see him through the small slits of the stairwell. Caught inside this net of death, Rahman feels his way up to the roof, his back pushed up against the cold wall.

He pulls back the sliding metal latch and opens the door to the roof. His head buzzes from the deafening sound, the nauseous smoke. On the roof, he crawls on his hands and knees on the flat concrete, past the large earthen pots holding the snake plants, rose bushes and arrowhead plants, under the clotheslines overhead. He scampers forward towards one of the little circular rainwater drainage holes on the side of the roof's mildew-stained retaining wall and peers out at Nilkhet road. An eerie vision unfolds in front of Rahman—the slum and the East Pakistan Police barracks ablaze through the dense Dev-daru canopy.

A military flamethrower tank burns up the bamboo shacks like matchsticks, the shanties spewing dark sooty smoke. The low, semi-circular plaited huts, square tin sheds, gunny sack curtains, all makeshift, have become a flaming holocaust. People flee out of the burning slum. Satanic soldiers, dark black silhouettes against the flames shooting tongues of death, swallow the men, women and children alive. Fleeing victims are picked off one-by-one by machine-gunners on waiting trucks.

In the heart of the roaring incinerator, a figure, another silhouette against the flames, a woman with a child in her arms, races out of the slum into the street, her sari aflame. Turning his rifle sight into her, a soldier mows her down like an animal. The baby, falling under her, squirms in agony.

In disbelief Rahman utters, *"Inna lillahi wa inna ilayhi raji'un,* Surely we belong to Allah and to Him shall we return."

MASTERMINDING A GENOCIDE

With slow, deliberate and stately cadence, on February 22, 1971, President and General Yahya Khan said, "Kill three million of them and the rest will eat out of our hands." [Robert Payne, *Massacre, The Tragedy of Bangladesh and the Phenomenon of Mass Slaughter Throughout History*; p. 50; New York, Macmillan, 1973] Military dictator Yahya Khan stated this to the four other hand selected Generals who sat around the table in the opulent glass and teak conference room in the capital, Islamabad, West Pakistan. The four other military men were Lt. General Tikka Khan, who commanded an army corps; General Pirzada, who was Chief of Staff; General Umar Khan, the

At that instant the gas tank of a car explodes, shooting flames high into the air and bits and pieces of metal fly in every direction.

As Rahman creeps towards the metal grounding rod from where the Bangladeshi flag snaps in the wind, he keeps praying. In a mad rush, he rips down the symbol of resistance from the rod, along with the black flag flying below it. He shoves the Bangladeshi flag under his Panjabi, next to his thrumming heart. The blood races in his arteries and veins, races in fear of death for his family.

Gripped by terror, little Moina, two, shivers and cries as Selina tries to calm her down. Four-year-old Babul, wisps of his curls over his big brown eyes, the usual boisterous leader of the Rahman children, acts brave but just for a moment. Clutching Nahar, Tia, at six the eldest, is shaking and neither Selina nor Nahar can console them.

"Where is Baba? Tia asks.

"Baba, Baba," Monia whimpers, starts to shake violently, going into convulsions as her teeth clamp together. Nahar runs to the dining room to get a spoon and water jug. Returning, she wedges the spoon in between Moina's teeth and splashes water on her face. Soaking the end of her *dupatta* in water, Nahar wipes Moina's face, and then she tries to put some water into her mouth.

"Moina, Moina," Nahar whispers into her ears, gently caressing her forehead. Slowly, whimpering, Moina regains consciousness.

Exhausted, Nahar pours water into the mouths of Babul and Tia as she and Selina also take a drink. Crushing Moina against her chest, Nahar anguishes about Rafique and Nazmul. Did they even have a chance? All around Dacca University's sacrosanct fields of

---

Chairman of the National Security Commission; and General Akbar Khan, the Chief of Intelligence.

Over twelve hundred miles from East Pakistan—the target of the massacre—the military Generals, with their polished medals and spit-shine boots, raised their glasses and drank a toast to genocide.

Absent from the meeting was the sixth co-conspirator, the West Pakistani People's Party Chief, Zulfikar Ali Bhutto, who was informed immediately of this meeting.

General Tikka Khan, "the Butcher of Baluchistan," already had won his medals razing to the ground parts of Baluchistan, and he went to the front of the line and immediately headed to Dacca to earn a new badge of dishonor, "the Butcher of Ban-

dreams are now devilbroweddrunkfatjawed General Yahya Khan's blood-soaked killing fields.

Nahar looks up through the metal bars of the outside window. A vindictive searching tracer spews into the night sky, first red then blue. Immediately afterward is the long 'swissssssh' and then the ear-shattering BOOM of the shells as they explode, tearing up the mortar and concrete of the dormitories.

Time stands still. The gunfire and the screams grow louder. Bursts of "dat-a-dat-dat" automatic rifle-fire sounds like it's next door. Another burst of rifle-fire, and somebody screams—a scream abruptly cut off. A moment's silence, and then more shots, thundering, echoing through the high-ceilinged rooms. Nuzzling against Selina and Nahar's ribs, the children cringe. To calm the children and for their own sanity, Nahar and Selina keep repeating the *Ayat al Kursi*, "*Allahu la ilaha illa huwa Al-Haiyul-Qaiym ...*" over and over again.

On the roof, Rahman crouches on the stairwell landing.

"Allah *bachow*, Allah save me," men cry out. The 'wheeee' of a few bullets whistle by just above his head, a wind of death, and the sound ricochets down the long concrete stairwell.

"Where is Baba?" asks Babul, the question repeated in the minds of Selina and Nahar. They pray, listen and wait for his knock on the door. Nahar checks the clock. It is quarter past one. Pregnant and nauseous, Selina vomits.

Feeling the rough walls in the darkness, Rahman finds his way downstairs to the two doors to the apartment. One he has locked from the outside. On the other paint-chipped yellow door, he pounds,

---

gladesh." Oh, and least we forget Bhutto, he would eventually reward Tikka after the war with the leadership of the People's Party of Pakistan. You scratch my back and I will carry you on mine tomorrow.

General Yahya Khan rapidly removed all West Pakistani officials and military personnel who had a conscience and were against his massacre. In came the crack genocide team.

First we must not forget the grunts on the ground, the nefarious Pathan-Baluch-Punjabi well oiled machine of war of 80,000 men armed to the teeth with modern Chinese and U.S. made weapons, and least we forget, the collaborators: the Al Badr, Al Shams and Razakars, eager Islamic right wing fanatics who beheaded with a ven-

"Nahar open the door!"

He knocks repeatedly. No answer.

"Nahar, Selina, open the door," he repeats, his face glazed with anxious sweat. Rahman listens to his wife's tortured breaths on the other side.

"Selina, Nahar open up!"

A metallic click. The vertical metal latch is pulled down. The wooden metal slat raised. The door opens.

Selina reaches out and embraces him. Just a moment later, a twin explosion, followed by machine gunfire, shakes the apartment and signals the beginning of one more barrage. As the last shards of unbroken glass shatter, Rahman crumples to the floor, covering Selina with his body.

"How are we going to escape? The children are terrified," says Selina. "What if they come up the stairs?"

"No, no they won't..." Rahman says, cursing himself, not believing a single word. Big mistake! We should have left a long time ago!

The tall heavenly arching Dev-daru trees lining Nilkhet Road are now burning, with tongues of flames lashing out at the canopy. Through shattered windows, the flames flash across the walls and as the flames rise higher and higher, panic-stricken, Selina screams, "The apartment is going to catch fire!"

Rahman and Nahar run through the living and dining rooms, dodging chairs in the darkness. At each window they rip down the cotton print.

Time is marked by the sounds of bullets and gunfire. Minutes seem like hours, as death ticks faster and faster around Nahar.

---

geance not seen from the time of Timurlane. Make Bangladesh a monolithic society, the hell with Hindus, kill them all, and murder all the Muslims who prayed to an Allah who viewed all men as equals.

Soon thereafter, on a bright morning of March 18th, 1971, on a light blue office pad, with a lead pencil, Major General Rao Farman Ali etched on five pages and in sixteen paragraphs Operation Searchlight: the start of the massacre of millions of Bangladeshis and the rape of hundreds of thousands of women. Working side by side with Major General Rao Farman Ali, in Governor Tikka Khan's Dacca office, was General Raza.

Just a day before, on March 17th, Lt. General Tikka Khan had become the Gover-

Laying on the cold cement floor, she feels nausea and fear knot up in her stomach. "Rafique," she murmurs. Under the bed Nahar holds onto the floor, suffocating, as if someone is drowning her in icy cold water. As she comes up for air, a dark black hand pushes her down into the depths, pushes her face in again and again. She gasps for air, breathes in smoke as she hears the machine guns fire away incessantly from the dormitories where Rafique was last night. The sound of every ricocheting bullet makes her shudder, ripping into her. *Is life over so quickly?*

Suddenly bullets fly through the living room window and hit the ceiling, raining down plaster. Babul, Tia and Moina scream. Heavy caliber machine gun bullets pepper the building. The wind presses down the black shroud of smoke over the buildings, and their noses fill up with acrid smoke. They pray they are not in the direct path of a direct tank shell.

Dazed, Nahar smells something strange in the air. Sticking to the back of her throat is this sweet sickening smoke. Nahar crawls to a corner and vomits. Laying on the cold floor, in darkness, Selina, Nahar and Rahman taste fear like shards of glass in their mouths.

Surrounded, they wait for death.

In the eerie darkness of the March Dacca night, the machine gun bullets cut titanium white slashes in the night sky. Nahar looks up at the clock: 3:30 a.m.; the only sound in the room is their breathing, in spurts, in quick short bursts, as if they are out of breath from running a long race. In the distance the sound of more explosions and gunfire.

Rahman makes preparations for survival, and a confrontation with the military, gets out the Koran and puts it by the door.

---

nor of East Pakistan. General Hamid, Chief of Staff of the Pakistan Army called over the phone from West Pakistan to give General Raza the green light to go ahead with Operation Searchlight. With the planning in high gear, General Yahya Khan was in Dacca with Bhutto putting on a fervent false façade, meeting with the Awami League Leader Sheikh Mujibur Rahman, under the pretenses of working towards handing over power. Quite a game of masquerades!

To achieve this military high command's plan was simple. Kill indiscriminately the following targets:

     1) Awami league members

     2) Students who supported the Awami league

     3) Intellectuals who supported the East Pakistan autonomy program.

"Selina, I have to go downstairs to the Sens'. We are dead if a tank fires up here," says Rahman.

"We can't stay here," says Selina looking into the terror-filled eyes of the children and Nahar.

"Wait until I check out the situation downstairs," says Rahman.

From a corner table of the bedroom where he says his prayers, he picks up the Koran and a prayer mat, wraps the Koran in a cotton cloth and says,

"Selina, lock the door. Don't open it until I come back!"

Rahman edges down the stairs, creeps along the side of the wall away from the windows. As he steps over the fading white and yellow floral wedding patterns painted on the steps, over shards of glass, outside the guns and flames paint a scene of total satanic destruction, of heinous murder.

Rahman waits. Takes another step, clutches the Koran, prays *"Bismaillah Hey a Rahmaner ar Rahim,"* takes another step and waits on the third floor landing.

He stares at the large lock on the door of Professor Salaam. Professor Salaam left over a week ago after Mujibur's rebel rousing speeches at Ramna and Paltan Maidan. Everyone is gone.

With his back to the wall, edging down, he makes it to Professor Sen's.

"Sen, Professor Sen, it's me Rahman," Rahman says, knocks again. Then again. He puts his ear to the door. The only sound a quiet silent fear pounding in his chest. Again he yells into the door, this time louder, his voice cracking, "Sen, it's me, Professor Rahman."

Minutes go by. Unable to stand anymore, Rahman puts the

---

4) All Hindus, in an ethnic cleansing action, to create a monolithic East Pakistan only for Muslims, devoid of any other religion.

5) Kill, massacre, rape and pillage whole sections of the land to terrorize the general population into submission.

The rape of Bangladeshi women was a planned cornerstone of this genocide. Rape immediately demoralizes a society and was aimed to bring terror into every Bangladeshi's heart, and to destroy the moral fiber and fighting spirit of the men. Furthermore, following Himmler's Lebensborn, "well spring of life", the impregnating of Bangladeshi women by West Pakistani soldiers was to create a 'more pure' Muslim race. A son would never go against a father, not even a bastard one! So rape

Koran on his lap and collapses to the floor, catching his breath. He knocks a third time, "Sen, it's me, Rahman."

Rahman puts his ear to the door, senses another heart beating, another ear on the other side of the door. "Professor Sen, it's Rahman! Rahman! Rahman!" he screams.

Finally the latch, bolt and a lock open.

Professor Sen looks pale, all color and blood drained out of his face, his lips dry and cracked, his eyes bloodshot.

Rahman walks in and gives Sen a hug and says, "Are you OK? *Boudi* and the kids are they OK?"

"Rahman!" Sen says collapsing against him. "Yes, yes," Sen says in a voice broken and frail, as cold sweat beads on his forehead, his eyes watering, his knees trembling. He locks the door behind them, padlocks it, latches it and recreates the fortress that he has made of his home.

Professor Sen's wife, Indubala, and his two daughters, Rani, four, and Priya, two, come out of hiding from the bedroom. Indubala begins to sob uncontrollably. Her hands cover her face, and Rani and Priya hide behind her, cringing. Her vermilion *shindoor* on her forehead is gone and Professor Sen is wearing a Muslim cap and a Panjabi.

Rahman turns to Sen, hands him the Koran and prayer mat. "Put it by the door," Rahman says. Then looking at Indubala, he says, "Wipe off the *shindoor,* a little is still showing."

"Yes, Yes," Sen says, his voice harsh and hollow.

"Anything Hindu is death," Rahman says. In tracer flashes he catches sight of some Hindu books in Sen's bookcase.

---

away, commanded the Generals to the grunts on the ground.

To create a monolithic society, the plan called for the ethnic cleansing of all non-Muslims, particularly Hindus. Push out the Bangladeshi Muslims and in their place induct "loyal" Pakistanis so as to reduce the Bangladeshis to a minority, thus rendering Bangladeshi nationalism powerless. Destroy the finest cultural renaissance to appear in the Muslim world, and entomb secularism deep in the graves of Bangladeshi patriots.

These top military men were well versed in Nazi torture and atrocities and torture techniques; they were battle hardened men, most of them having fought in World War II, cutting their teeth in the Royal British forces, having fought against the

"Put those books away right now," Rahman says.

"OK, OK," is all that Professor Sen can say, his hands trembling by his side. Rahman stands gasping, while Sen regains some color in his face.

"Is everyone in the dormitories..." Sen says, his voice dry choked.

"I don't know," is the inevitable answer Rahman has. "I just don't know."

"Sen you have the lock for the front gate?" Rahman asks.

"Yes I do, I do, I have a lock..." Sen goes to the store room. A few long minutes later, Sen brings out a lock and key. Immediately they go out and lock the gate, hanging the lock outside to give the impression that the gate was locked as the owners vacated.

"I'm going upstairs to bring everyone down," Rahman says, a little relief in his voice now. "Not safe up there."

When Rahman gets to the top of the stairs, he knocks. Selina is waiting, her ear to the door. She lets him in, and Rahman squats on the floor. Exhausted. Selina stays quiet, many questions in her mind.

"We will be safer downstairs on the first floor with Sen's family. We have no way to run from here, but on the ground floor..." Rahman says trying to believe his own words.

Selina clutches at her belly, protruding with a six-month-old fetus. She feels it move.

While Nahar, Rahman and Selina prepare to go down the stairs, Babul starts to crawl on all fours, too ashamed to say he has wet his pants. Shards of glass glitter on the floor and the furniture. As he makes for the bathroom, a sharp shard of glass slices into his

---

Japanese Army in Burma. More importantly they knew how to implement psychologically crushing techniques of warfare, how to demoralize a nation and inject fear in the general masses. Murder, rape, torture and the bribing of local collaborators with the windfalls of war were their tools.

General Yahya Khan served in the British Indian 4th Division during WWII, and saw action in Iraq, Italy and North Africa. In June of 1942 he was captured by the Axis forces in North Africa and was sent to a war camp in Italy. Here he was hardened in a prisoner of war camp, and after three attempts he escaped. The basis for the inhuman torture his soldiers inflicted on the people of Bangladesh and on the Mukti Bahini prisoners was based on the Axis of Evil torture techniques.

right palm. On the cement floor he leaves behind a trail of bloody handprints.

In the corner of the next room he pees, makes his way back to his Ma, shows her his deep cut. "It doesn't hurt." Using a safety pin from her *kameez*, Nahar takes out the small piece of glass. tears an end-piece of her *dupatta* and bandages Babul's hand.

"We must go now!" Professor Rahman says, helping Selina who is slow to move. Rahman leads the way down the stairs, as they move silently into the dark stairwell, holding each other's hands. Selina carries Monia, and Nahar helps in the rear with Babul and Tia. Rahman's eyes are trained on the steps. Nahar's eyes, like a cat's, dart around in the flashed darkness, her heart pounds in her chest. She prays with each step.

At the bottom landing, they pause as one, and Professor Rahman bangs on Sen's door. Immediately Sen lets them in and latches and locks the door.

Now both families are together, two pregnant wives, two worried fathers, five children and Nahar. In the Sens' apartment they all seek shelter in the farthest corner, in the master bedroom, away from the broken glass and debris covering the floors. Quickly pulling the cotton mattress to the ground, they cling to each other. Nahar closes her eyes, clutches Moina and Babul to her sides, and musters all her strength through prayer: prayer for the lives of the children, for Rafique, for Nazmul, for the Rahmans and the Sens.

Having the women and children huddled in one space gives the men a feeling of comfort, a sense of security.

"We have to make like we are not in here," Rahman says. After a long minute, he asks Professor Sen, "You have any pliers?"

1971 was only twenty-six years after Hitler's fall in 1945 and as such, the demented doctrines of the Third Reich were very well known and practiced by the new SS of Pakistan.

Behind Operation Searchlight was the idea of blitzkrieg, a total burning to the ground of the opposition and obliteration of the enemy. The idea, at least in the high command's mind, was to eliminate the opposition in a few days. However the operation dragged on and the fierce resistance by the East Pakistani troops in all sectors thwarted the desires of Lt. General Tikka Khan, and, of course, General Yahya Khan, for a quick, decisive dominance of the land.

Out of March 25, out of the ashes of the phoenix, rose the fighting spirit of all

Sen nods and he and Rahman head to the storeroom cabinet where Sen digs up a rusty pair of pliers and a screwdriver. Rahman puts them into his Panjabi pocket, heads down the hallway to the entrance doors.

"Take out the bolt from one of the hasps holding the padlocks. We will lock both doors from the outside, put the nut on from the inside into one of the hasps. With both doors padlocked from outside, they will think the apartment is empty."

Rahman and Sen padlock one of the two doors from outside. Using the pliers, Sen unscrews the nut of the hasp. Rahman points the flashlight at the hasp. Through shaking hands, Sen drops the nut. Finally after two attempts they succeed. Both doors now padlocked from the outside.

Professor Rahman grips the flashlight, wipes the sweat dripping on his face on the cuff of his Panjabi. Through a parched, cracked voice, he utters, "I just hope they don't come into the building."

Frantically, in the corner room, Nahar tries to break Indubala's *Shaakha Pola* bangles symbolizing her Hindu married status. After many years of marriage, the bangles are just too tight.

As Nahar tries to break the bangles on the mortar, the hammering "cluthunk, cluthunk" sound of the heavy stone pestle fills Indubala's ears. Indubala feels her heart being crushed; her whole life ground up into small fragments, disappearing in front of her very eyes— becoming a widow.

Sen comes in from the hallway, wets the end of his Panjabi and tries to rub off what is left of the *shindoor* on Indubala's forehead, the symbol of a married woman. She looks up at her husband's face, tears blurring her vision of a life that once was.

Bangladeshis. And it was this courage—irrefutable, undeniable, relentless—of the Bangladeshi spirit that became the March 25 to December 16 two hundred sixty-seven day struggle and ultimate victory by the people of Bangladesh over tyranny and genocide.

Yahya Khan calculated that by this blitzkrieg massacre of East Pakistanis, when a man sees his village in flames, and his wife raped, his children butchered, the fight in him will be gone. Yet, exactly the opposite played out in East Pakistan. This, friend, is the land of Tagore, where when you scratch a Bengali, you find the red of a poet, and hope burns eternally in the heart of the Bangladeshi rebel. The worse the atrocities, the more tenacious the freedom fighters, the *Mukti Bahini*, became.

Suddenly, a loud sound in front of the building. Then sounds outside the front metal gate.

"*Darwaja kholo*," barks a loud voice in Urdu. "Open this gate!" The voice piercing, commanding, angry. Moina, Babul and Tia cringe, clasp each other in horror. Next to them, Sen, Indubala, Rani, and Priya reach for each other as Nahar embraces Monia tightly in her arms.

A boot kicks the metal door. The sound grows louder, filling every suffocating inch of the room in a compressed clanging. Another kick. Then one more.

"Open this bloody door," a man barks in Urdu.

Rahman feels his blood stop. Everything goes blank as he holds on to the floor. Selina and Rahman lock eyes for a moment.

Tia whispers as she faints.

"Baba! I don't want to die."

❧

For that one last flower, the land gave its all.

The Bangladesh Genocide grew out of Yahya Khan's arrogance, bigotry and the sheer lust for power. And it ended because of the hunger for freedom, the courage to sacrifice all for country, and the perseverance and ultimate sacrifice by millions of brave Bangladeshis to earn the cherished freedom.

Freedom to be a human being.

A human being.

Never give in to tyrants, never give up, never say die, never.

This was the slogan of the *Mukti Bahini*. Peasant farmers, students, teachers, laborers, feisty fighting women united into victory. Bhutto flew out of East Pakistan on March 26 and arriving in West Pakistan went on the radio to claim, "Pakistan was saved." This was an ironic death knell cry. The fires that Yahya Khan started on March 25, 1971 ultimately burned Jinnah's 1947 Pakistan into the ground and fired the cries of 'Joy Bangla!' on Victory Day for Bangladesh on December 16, 1971.

THE SILENT AND THE LOST

Curfew

March 26, 1971, East Pakistan

"TATHAANK, BANG, BANG, CRASH, BANG." A fierce, furious, frantic pounding. Possessed daemons were hammering on the front metal gate, beating with their fists on the closed shutters so hard they will come off their hinges any moment. Then boot kicks. "Tathaank, tathank, tathaank."

Hysterically, Selina crushes Moina to her chest, while Indubala embraces Priya tighter. Shaking in fear, Moina and Priya start to cry as Selina and Indubala clamp hands over the mouths of their terrified children.

As every excruciating second goes by, Nahar breathes in short spurts, her lungs about to explode. Indubala and Selina's palms are wet with the muffled breath of their children, children whose faces are turning blue.

Rahman clasps his hands over Tia and Babul's mouths and Sen presses his over Rani's mouth. "Tathank, tathank, taathaaank," the violent pounding jars the insides of everyone.

Nahar keeps silently repeating to herself, "Allah, Allah, Allah, Allah, Allah."

Unbearable minutes tick on as Rahman, Selina, Nahar, Tia, Babul, Moina, Sen, Indubala, Rani, Priya hold their breath in the far corner of the bedroom, counting their last seconds.

"*Bangali kutta bhag gaya*," the soldiers bark in Urdu. "The Bengali dogs have escaped. Search the next building."

Slowly, down the concrete path, the sound of the heavy killers' boots disappear.

Spent, exhausted and crying, everyone collapses with the sound of boots leaving. Nahar tries to sooth Tia and Rani, now crying uncontrollably. Exhausted and dizzy, Moina, Priya and Babul all collapse on the floor. Violently shaking, Selina becomes nauseous, vomits, and faints. Sen runs to the bathroom to get some water. While Rahman tries to rub her hands and feet, Indubala fans Selina with a newspaper. Sen comes back and pours some water on Selina's head.

Half an hour has passed. A lifetime to Nahar. Groggy and coughing, Selina regains consciousness. Indubala puts Selina's head on her lap and runs her fingers through Selina's hair, tries to dry it.

In this bedroom, the fetid odor of sweat clings to the damp closed air, the demonic sounds of the metal gate rattle in their oxygen-deprived brains, a bitter taste clings to their mouths, the sight of blood-spattered Nilkhet Road wells up before their eyes, the distant gunfire from Old Dacca, from the middle of the University echoes in their ears.

Using wet cloths, Nahar, Selina and Indu Bala clean their sweat covered faces as Sen wipes the children's faces with water, trying to revive them.

March sunlight cutting through smoldering fires and smoke paints a deadly crimson dawn. Tension lingers as minutes slowly pass. There is an eerie calm, the smell of pungent cordite replacing the morning breeze. Birds quiet in a mournful silence.

"Curfew has been imposed. Anyone on the streets will be shot," an army truck announces in Urdu over a microphone on Nilkhet road.

Nahar looks across to the wall clock. It is 6:30 in the morning.

"Shot on sight," Nahar repeats, her soft rhythmic voice, now broken, raspy like a cracked bamboo flute. What has happened to the world she knew? In one night, everything has changed. Everything.

Crouched in the dark corner, Professor Rahman cradles the

radio like a child against his chest, turning the knob between his index and thumb. The radio, his lifeline to the world. The Dacca radio station is dead. Dead like Dacca. Only static. Hiss.

Rahman switches to Calcutta. The only news is that Yahya has left Dacca after final talks with Mujib. Fiddling with the tuning knob once more, through static he finds Karachi. There is the news. Yahya Khan was going to make a special announcement. Several minutes later, a slurred and drunk Yahya says, "Mujib's act is an act of treason. He will not go unpunished."

"Have they killed Bangabandhu?" Sen asks.

"I pray not. I don't know," Rahman replies.

Indubala dares not light the kerosene stove in fear of the smoke. Rahman, Sen and Nahar crunch on dry puffed rice and the children eat some Nabisco biscuits, drink powdered milk. Nothing cooked has passed their lips all day. In silence Indubala pours some water into four glasses from the saved water in the bathroom and hands each one a glass. Starved, they struggle to swallow the puffed rice.

Rahman still fiddles with the radio trying to get any news. Around noon, All India Radio announces that there is an indefinite curfew in Dacca.

"Indefinite," Rahman says to Sen. "What now?"

Sen, his voice dropping off into a feeble, lifeless murmur, repeats,

"Indefinite."

WAS ANYONE ALIVE INSIDE DACCA University today?

Dacca University Campus had gone mad. A kill the sleeping students in their beds mad, a murder the Professors in their apartments mad, a burn the children mad, a burn Dacca city mad. A West Pakistani Army killing field mad, a Tikka Khan butchery mad, a murderous red river of Bangladeshi blood mad. A pull the women by their hair out of the girl's hostels and kick them into military trucks mad. A kill the police, burn Nilkhet slum mad. A blackest of black nights in human history mad.

All the military personnel have left the area. No sound of gunfire, no sound of army trucks.

Nazmul and Rafique, covered from head to foot in mud, feces and urine, slowly crawl out from under the broken concrete slab covering the sewer hole on the side of Ahsanullah Hall at the East Pakistan University Engineering and Training center.

They look across a ghostly valley of death. There is an eerie silence all around the campus. No crows are cawing. Nothing left alive. They are the only two in this valley of death that was Dacca University.

A University.

Once.

"Now, now's our chance," Rafique whispers to Nazmul.

"Where to?" Nazmul asks.

"Rahmans'."

"How? Isn't that way certain death? " Nazmul asks, his face pale and weary. "How about Azimpur?"

"We can go on the back road," Rafique says. "The back road, Nazmul."

"I should have not brought Nahar into the middle of this. She wanted to hear Bangabandhu's speech. I should have listened to Abba and Amma and not brought her to Dacca. She insisted on staying and helping Selina Bhabi," Rafique says.

They crouch down at the sound of approaching trucks. After a few minutes, Rafique murmurs in despair, "We should have helped Rahman Bhai leave the campus. Now they are all dead. All dead, because of me. Dead!"

"No, no, we are alive, maybe they are, too!" Nazmul says, his words barely audible, as he tries to console Rafique. Nazmul peers over the wall trying to see if any military trucks are around.

Rafique says in a broken voice to Nazmul, "Whole campus is a slaughterhouse now. Our poet friend—he is no more. Our friend who hoisted the flag of Bangladesh on the Hall-top ... maybe he is no more. Our friends who put the barricade on Fuller Road ... may be dead, too. No, no!"

"Rafique, get hold of yourself!" Nazmul says, patting him on the back. "Calm down or we're dead!"

Slowly, Rafique comes to his senses.

"It's my fault, too," Nazmul says, "I should have told Rahman Bhai to leave after the 7th."

Nazmul and Rafique had gotten word of the impending attack last night and had gone to Nilkhet road around eight in the evening to help build barricades. Then Rafique, a student of Architecture, went to the Engineering University Campus dorm. Nazmul, who usually stayed at Iqbal Hall, went with him as the news was all over that the army was going to attack the Halls. They were pouring gasoline into glass bottles to make Molotov cocktail bombs to throw at the West Pakistani military tanks and trucks when all hell broke loose.

They ran to hide in the back of the Ahsanullah Hall. The shooting reached a crescendo around 12:30am, then in a few hours it ebbed.

There is no sun. The smoke, the stench of burnt human bodies weighs down the air.

"We need to go to the Rahmans'," Rafique insists, agitated, his fists clenched.

"Now? Better stay here until dark. It's suicidal to go right now," says Nazmul.

They whisper, planning an escape route. If they can cross the road and climb into the Eden College, then jump into the Home Economics College grounds, then from the Home Economics College cross the railroad and slum, they can enter the Rahmans' Nilkhet quarters. If they can avoid the patrolling West Pakistani army jeeps and convoys. If they are lucky. Very lucky.

Late afternoon, March 26th

RAFIQUE AND NAZMUL DASH STRAIGHT across the field and take to the road running for their lives, hiding behind trees and walls.

On the road lie dead rickshaw-wallahs, shot sleeping on their rickshaws, the twisted bodies on the rickshaw's metal boards. Blood drips down in pools under the rickshaw and coagulates into a dark glob. The sunburnt stick men, the rickshaw-wallahs were some of the first to die.

Rafique looks down the side of the road, hiding behind the wall around the open garbage dump.

Street dogs scavenge close by, tearing at the body of a rickshaw-wallah. Shading his eyes, Rafique peers into the shadows; there is no one in sight expect for an old man crunched against the wall. He is dead, shot through the abdomen against the brick façade of the whitewashed, mildew-stained wall now stained a dark crimson.

Past the heaps of broken bricks and bottles, scattered among the piles of turds along the sewage drain, are more twisted bodies. Dead.

Rafique flattens himself against the wall. He hears footsteps approaching at a run, on the other side. They stop, recede into the side of the craggy mango tree trunk, and come back out again. Rafique and Nazmul hear the *lungi*-wearing old man insanely muttering to himself, "All gone, all gone," as he runs off hurriedly in the other direction.

Adrenaline pumping, Rafique signals Nazmul and they jump over the high wall of Eden College, make a wild dash for the pond. In the pond they clean their grimy clothes and clean their body of the filth of the sewer. They quench their thirst, filling their stomachs with water, the water like liquid life, cleansing, refreshing.

Nature in an ashen sickness is shedding white acrid tears. A sooty nightmarish veil of death is all over the plants and on the dahlias, on the loam, grass, bushes, trees.

"Eden College!" Rafique says. Then in a sad low voice he says, "A Garden of Eden but only two men alive in this—a strange Eden."

"Rafique, I hope, only hope..." Nazmul says, an anguished expression on his face, as he thinks about what is going on in the Campus and what has happened in the last twelve hours. His mind draws a blank. He tries again, "Rafique, do you think..." but his voice fades looking at Rafique's colorless face in the dim light.

Rafique is silent, collapses after running all the way to Eden College—that after an unbelievable night of murder and mayhem. They hide behind a building, trying to regain some strength.

Minutes pass before Rafique breaks the silence. "Nazmul, from the Rahmans' veranda you can see Home Economics College pond and the garden and bushes. We can hide behind the bushes. Look into the apartment."

Nazmul looks up and says, "Yes. Yes, I think we can see into the back of the apartment, Rafique."

LATE AFTERNOON FINDS SEN AND Rahman planning to go up to the fourth floor for food, clothes.

"Children's powder milk, cookies, some warm clothes. I'll arrange to bring the food down," Rahman says to Selina.

"Biscuits, *muri*, water," Selina adds softly, her face now colorless from throwing up all night.

Professor Rahman and Sen sidestep the shards of glass up to the fourth floor to get the supplies. As they are going up the stairs, through the small slatted windows of the stairwell Professor Sen and Rahman look out into the main street.

As they peer out onto what was once Nilkhet slum and the Police Barracks, they can see the heaped burnt bodies of the dead. Rahman looks away, covers his eyes, unable to bear it anymore. Sen, kneels and convulses in dry heaves.

"Sen, Sen, you've got to get hold of yourself," Rahman says as he helps him get up. Sen holds on to Rahman for a moment, steadies himself. He regains some composure, grabs the cemented railing and slowly continues up the stairs.

After half an hour, loaded down with biscuits, puffed rice, milk, a large clay jug of water, Sen and Rahman descend the stairs.

The day drags on in cries and shouts outside on Nilkhet Road and in murmurs and in tears inside the apartment.

NOW IN THE BACK OF the Home Economics College, across Nilkhet road, Nazmul and Rafique peer from behind a tree towards the Rahmans' fourth floor apartment. Across the road, these yellow and black mildew-stained apartments are silent standing witnesses of the horror of the last twenty-four hours. This burnt wasteland of blackened eucalyptus and Dev-daru trees lower their heads, ashamed of what they have witnessed. The smoke and smell of gasoline and burnt bodies mix together in a sickening, sweetish, greasy smell that fills the lungs, nostrils and mouth of Rafique and Nazmul. Wind borne drifting ash falls on them, covering them in a ghostly veil.

Through a hoarse voice, sooty and dry, eyelashes covered in particles of massacre, Rafique says, "Nazmul can you see anything?" Then in a softer tone he says, "Hope Allah keeps them safe."

"I feel like screaming my lungs out. I just pray they are OK. They are OK, right?" says Nazmul.

"Nazmul I don't know. We will find out soon," Rafique says. He can see the Rahmans' corner room. Just a few nights ago, in that corner "honeymoon room" of the apartment, he last held Nahar.

His Nahar. Just a few nights ago. Now it seems a lifetime ago.

He can still remember her smell, her breath, her soft voice now distant in a time past, in a place not this.

A feeling of complete helplessness washes over him; he grinds his teeth thinking of what the situation might be at the Rahmans'. Like a movie reel that rips, the film thrashing, spinning wildly, the screen blank and white, Rafique's mind is thrashing. Nahar, Rahmans, their children. Rafique holds his head in his trembling fingers. "Tia, Moina, Babul," he murmurs.

The Rahman children. Six-year-old Tia always flitting about like a butterfly, four-year-old Babul always adventurous. And Moina, only two but such a chatter box. Little Moina. Selina Bhabi, always with that great big smile on her lips and like a big brother and a great host, Professor Rahman. And Nahar, only twenty, long silky black hair Nahar, mesmerizing eyes Nahar, voice full of song, full of laughter and innocence Nahar. His Nahar. Alive?

Hiding behind the tree, Rafique and Nazmul search for life at the fourth floor windows.

"*Dost* who else is in the building?" Nazmul asks Rafique.

"Professor Sen."

"They could be down with the Sens," says Nazmul, a wisp of hope now growing in his defeated voice.

Just then a shadowy movement in the Rahmans' storeroom.

"Storeroom door, Nazmul. You notice that?" asks Rafique, his face lit up with a sudden joy. "Somebody. Yes, Nazmul, yes!"

Nazmul and Rafique hug each other, jumping up and down, as tears fill Rafique's eyes.

"*Dosto*, I believe they are safe," Nazmul says in a daze, his voice choked in a suppressed joy.

Rafique starts to move towards the wall, and Nazmul grabs his shoulders, shaking him violently, trying to shake sense into him.

"Rafique, are you crazy? There is a curfew. We will be shot dead! We have to stay put. Wait for our chance."

Rafique stops, looks at Nazmul, his eyes flooded in disbelief and happiness.

An hour then another passes. Like wild cats they scan the area over the wall, waiting for the opportunity to climb across and run to the other side. As Rafique peers down through a small hole in the wall, out onto what was once Nilkhet slum and the Police Barracks, he can see the heaped bodies of the dead where they were set on fire near the rail gate petrol pump to the right, down the street. The rusted corrugated roofs of the Nilkhet slum are twisted up and bend around like a hurricane had made a direct hit. The smell of gunpowder and the stench of the burning corpses lingers in the heavy fetid air as Rafique tries not to cough, his throat full of soot.

Quickly he ducks behind the wall as a submachine gun mounted jeep and a large convoy truck pass by, the soldiers reconnoitering for anyone alive.

Minute after minute in a small, slow, agonizing progression moves on, until darkness falls: interminable hours in breath-holding terror, under curfew, nobody making a sound, hoping not to be found out and killed. The day turns into the ominous night of March 26. Finally, in the cover of darkness, the chance they are waiting for. Nazmul meshes his fingers together, making a ladder for Rafique. Stepping on Nazmul's palms, Rafique climbs up to the top of the wall. He pulls up Nazmul, claws up the wall. Together they fall on the other side of the brick wall, and sprint for their lives across Nilkhet road towards the Rahmans'.

Panting, they help each other over the last wall, the fence around the faculty apartments, and drop to the ground, tip toe behind the apartment's garden, crouching to the back bathroom grill of the Sens' apartment, trying to see something, anything.

— ❧ —

ALREADY RANI AND TIA HAVE cut their hands and feet on broken glass, so Rahman and Sen have moved the children, along with Indubala and Selina, into the storeroom, away from the windows.

Rahman loosens the kitchen window vertical rods—a possible escape route. He props up a chair next to it. Luckily the glass on this side of the bathroom kitchen window did not break, and if need be, they can climb out and flee through it.

The bathroom next to the master bedroom is overused, as everyone is afraid to flush. Nahar gets up, steadies herself by bracing the wall and goes to the second bathroom, next to living room, a dim torch lighting the way. The water in the pail is murky.

She quietly walks to the kitchen to see if there is any clean water in the clay jar to mix with the powdered milk for Moina and Priya before they wake up.

Spying through the window, Rafique sees Nahar. He and Nazmul run up to the kitchen window. Nahar hears someone whispering, "Nahar Nahar." Two silhouettes. She drops the feeding bottle, and at the sound, Sen and Rahman come running into the kitchen.

"Point the flashlight on the window," Rahman says to Sen. Then through bulging eyes, utters in disbelief,

"Rafique! Nazmul!"

Nahar is stunned, speechless. Holding out her hands as if to embrace someone coming back from death, Nahar grips his shoulders and lets out a wail from deep inside, from the very core of her soul. She pulls Rafique into the side bedroom and they hold each other in a tight embrace.

"Rafique, Rafique," is all she can say, her voice cracked and trembling, as she sobs uncontrollably. "Rafique."

Rafique kisses her cheeks, her neck and her salty tears tastes like life itself. Crushed in his hands, he kisses her again and again, feeling her warm and alive next to him, as tears flood her eyes, soak through his shirt, wet against his skin.

"Everything is going to be fine. Fine," Rafique says softly.

Seeing Nazmul and Rafique, ghosts alive, everyone comes back from a distant dead place to fresh life, breathing in a new hope for survival. Indubala hands Rafique and Nazmul glasses of water, a big bowl of moist puffed rice and some biscuits. Rafique and Nazmul empty the glasses, quenching their parched throats. They finish the bowl of puffed rice, gulping down more water, and look at each other in amazement.

"*Oi Dost*, you were right!" Rafique says laughing and slapping Nazmul on the back, as a grin spreads onto his face.

Rafique, Nazmul, Sen and Rahman spend the night trying to tune the news on the transistor radio. During the night, BBC reports the crackdown in East Pakistan. Dacca Radio is working again, but playing mostly Urdu patriotic songs and Islamic verses. In the hollow hallway outside the store room, sitting on the concrete floor they listen to each other's breathing. No one dares to utter a word. The children are in deep sleep, while Selina, Indubala and Nahar lay awake, sometimes dozing off into a fitful sleep.

Leaning against the storeroom wall, gripped by exhaustion, Nahar closes her eyes. Iridescent images of a lush Sheetalpur appear. Amina, Halim, Boochu are running towards her down the thin earthen *lail*, calling out to her against the waving windswept paddy fields. "Nahar Appa, Nahar Appa!" She runs towards them, but a dark hand pulls her back. She tries to run, now they fade into the horizon, beyond the lonely palm, the line of indistinguishable trees meshed into one dark line. From downstairs it's her mother-in-law, Jahanara, calling out to her, "*Bou Maa, Bou Maa.*" Suddenly jarred out of her sleep, Nahar opens her eyes into the dark of the storeroom. It's Moina crying out in Selina's arms, "Amma, Amma."

Now that the night and day of shooting have faded, imperceptibly the terror deepens, sinking into Nahar's soul, finding a permanent hold.

2€

Exodus

March 27, 1971, Dacca, East Pakistan

FROM A DISTANT MINARET, FROM a mosque unknown, from the far-reaching throat of the *muezzin* floats in the faint call to the faithful for the morning *Fajr* prayer, *"Allah-u Akbar, Ash-hadu an la ilaha illallah..."*

Nahar covers her head with her *dupatta*, drained and sleepless in the corner of the Sens' storeroom. She looks at Tia, Priya, Moina and Babul, now an entangled mass of exhausted, sleeping bodies. *Yes, people are still alive. Yes...*

Dacca, City of Mosques, now the city of martyrs, the city of the unburied dead, and on this cold March dawn the city of the survivors: Nahar, Rafique, Nazmul, Selina, Rahman, Sen, Indubala, their sleeping children. Twelve souls entombed alive on the ground floor of the Nilkhet Faculty apartments, surrounded by the dead. Second morning, thirty hours and counting. And still alive.

"Allah," Nahar murmurs, then wipes her tear-streaked face and bloodshot eyes with her *dupatta*.

The cold chill of the night hangs on a smoky gray sky, fires still burning, plumes of smoke rising in the Dacca sky. Sporadic bursts of gun fire.

In the bathroom, Rahman bends over the metal bucket, cups

91

his hands full of precious water, rubs his face, snorting and bubbling the water, feeling the soot, the grime of the last twenty-four hours streak off of his face, down his neck.

In the hallway, he unrolls the *Jai Namaaz*, faces Mecca, raises his hands to his earlobe, and says his *Fajr* prayer—an implored prayer for exodus out of Dacca.

—❦—

THE NIGHT PASSES. WITH THE first faint streaks of an eerily quiet dawn cutting into the apartment, Rahman is still on the *Jai Namaaz*, his hands pressed in prayer. The dawn comes, but no day. A wind cries in the leaves. Smoke hangs over the building, the smell, the taste of greasy smoke in their mouths.

Out of the eastern horizon of a dead, defeated Dacca the sun, a crimson spot rises.

"Listen," Rafique whispers to Nazmul, looks at his wrist around 7:30.

"People on the streets," Nazmul says a moment later. "People!"

Rafique's chest rises and falls, harder, faster. "Let's go Nazmul."

Rafique and Nazmul's eyes sparkle in the semi-darkness, as they crawl and side-step the sleeping children and women in the room.

In the hallway, Rahman is still on the *Jai Namaaz*. Rafique, Nazmul and Rahman's eyes lock in an awakening, an unbelievable realization of a possible escape.

"Sounds," Rahman says.

"*Bangla*," Rafique replies.

"Is it over?" Rahman asks, a stunned disbelief in his voice.

"Maybe this is our chance," Nazmul says as he walks down the hallway towards the front door.

Hands shaking, taking the pliers Rafique removes the bolt on the hasp on the front door, still locked from the outside. Sen unlocks the padlocks on the outside metal shuttered gate at the front landing.

Rafique and Nazmul go out into the open streets.

People.

Human beings still in shock slowly spill out on the streets.

"Where are you going?" Nazmul asks an old man.

"My village."

"Just anywhere away from Dacca," is the echoed answer, repeated over and over again,

"Away from Dacca!"

Desperate in this few-hour window before the curfew is clamped down again, all of Dacca is on the street. People start walking towards the south, to the river.

Anyway possible. Escape. Any path open. Escape.

Rahman and Sen now follow Rafique and Nazmul onto the street.

On the faces of the Daccaites is a weary, dead look. A shocked, unbelieving look.

The sounds outside spill into the inside of the Sens' apartment as a startled Nahar, Selina, Indubala become suddenly aware of a chance to survive.

Rahman fiddles and faddles with the radio, and finally around 8:30, Dacca Radio announces the lifting of the curfew.

Coming back from the street Nazmul and Rafique rush through the front door.

"They are saying the curfew is lifted for six hours," Nazmul says, his excited words penetrating into the closed room, echoing hope in everyone's heart.

"We need to get out of here now, to Demra, to the river and across," Rafique says, breathing hard.

For more than thirty hours, in darkness and in light, this small corner room in the Sens' apartment has been filled full of tension, the odor of fear mixed with sweat.

Rahman looks around the room. Terror is slow in releasing its grip, as thin lines of the hope of survival filigree into the faces of the women, the children. Together they have survived. And become a larger family tied with this tight twine of terror. Rahman exhales into the acrid smoke-filled air, whispering out a drawn out, "Allah."

"Indubala, get ready, quickly," Sen tells his wife. In the far corner, Rahman tends to a nauseous Selina.

Rafique pulls Nazmul aside, points to his dust-covered maroon Honda 90cc motorcycle stored under the stairs. "Take my motorcycle," he says, handing the keys to Nazmul. "Be very careful. Go to Kalabagan. Make sure Samad Uncle is OK. Bring him with you. Head by Demra to the village. Don't take the main roads. Careful... military checkpoints!"

Rahman and Sen follow Rafique out of the apartment, and stand beside him.

"Rahman Bhai, pray if I'm alive, I'll see you in Sheetalpur," Nazmul says, his voice emotion-filled, his glazed eyes watering as he hugs Rahman, then Sen.

"Be careful," Rahman says.

Rafique embraces Nazmul, pats him on the back.

"*Doost*, if we are alive, we will be together again," Nazmul says. Hugging Rafique once more, Nazmul adds, "Wish I was coming with you."

Nazmul rolls the motorcycle off of its stand, out onto the front landing of the building. He kicks the starter, kicks once more. Nothing. Then on the fifth hard try the motorcycle comes to life, comes to life like everyone inside the apartment. In a blue cloud of smoke, Nazmul disappears down Nilkhet, headed towards Dr. Samad's.

Nahar and Rafique run up to the fourth floor to gather up whatever essentials they can carry with them: milk, baby bottles, sugar, tea, cookies, toast biscuits, warm clothes, toothpaste, soap, coconut oil, medicines, detol, cotton, brushes.

The apartment is covered in broken glass, the curtains ripped down, a thick layer of plaster coats every surface. Nahar follows Rafique into the corner bedroom.

In a frenzied hurry Nahar goes through her brown leather suitcase, full of saris, *salwar kameezes*, cosmetics, shoes, gifts from Rahman and Selina and a new picture album, a wedding gift from Nazmul. She grabs a chador for Indubala. Everything else she leaves behind.

Quickly Nahar changes her soiled *salwar kameez*, finding relief in clean clothes. In her suitcase lies the burqa she has bought for Amina, her maid who repeatedly requested her to bring one back from Dacca. She holds it up for a moment—a black veil, hopefully a passageway to Sheetalpur. To hide from murderous eyes, to somehow escape the talons of Tikka and Yahya and the Pakistani soldiers. Nahar pulls the burqa over her head. Straightening the long veil, hot inside the thick fabric, Nahar exhales a deep breath, thinks about the dangers they face on this day, on this journey.

Downstairs in the Sens' apartment, Selina tells Rahman, "Bury the jewelry and deeds in the bottom of the rice sacks." After a moment she adds, "Nahar can carry a few pieces."

"Which ones?" Rahman says.

"My wedding bangles and necklace."

"Selina, get ready. I'll be right back," Rahman says leaving Selina with Indubala.

"We'll manage Rahman Bhai," Indubala reassures him.

Exhausted Rahman climbs back up to their apartment.

"Rafique," Rahman calls out entering the apartment.

"Yes, Rahman Bhai," Rafique says. "I'm in the store room getting food."

"Rafique, hurry."

"I need some clothes Rahman Bhai," Rafique says as he gingerly steps over shards of glass out into the hallway.

Rahman walks to the bedroom, pulls off one of his Panjabis and a pajama from the *alna* and hands it to Rafique. He hands him a Pashmi Kashmiri cap and a shawl from the armoire.

Rafique changes, wraps the shawl around him, and heads to help Nahar in the bedroom. Rahman opens the safe in the back-wall of the armoire, takes out Selina's jewelry.

"Rahman Bhai, we will see you downstairs," Rafique yells heading down the hallway with Nahar.

"Make sure everyone is ready. I will be there in a minute," Rahman cries out heading to the storeroom.

In the storeroom, on his hands and knees, Rahman digs into the burlap sack of rice, buries the folded Bangladeshi flag at the bottom and on top places the rest of Selina's jewelry. What Selina wants, her wedding bangles and necklace, he brings down.

Downstairs, Rahman hands the jewelry to Selina. Selina helps Nahar wrap the bangles and the necklace in a cotton scarf and tie it tightly around her waist, hidden under her *kameez* and burqa.

The little water they have saved they pour into the bottles for the road. With the left over water they clean their faces, their mouths and hands.

Rahman wears his black *sherwani* over his Panjabi pajama and kashmiri cap and Sen wears a Panjabi, pajama and a skull cap.

"This is for you," Nahar says handing Indubala the brown chador, helping her wrap it over her shoulders, her head, covering her forehead still showing a little of the deep stain of *shindoor*.

Desperate to get on the road, Rahman says to Selina, "We need to hurry. Sen and his family are waiting."

Into two small bags they pack food, *chira*, hard palm sugar cones, oil, rice, lentils and some clothes for the road.

— ❧ —

OUT THROUGH THE BACK, THEY climb over a small broken wall. Rahman hands the children one by one over the wall to Rafique and then they help Indubala, Selina and Nahar climb over. Careful to avoid Nilkhet Road, they walk across a destroyed Dacca University, cutting through a deserted, dead campus.

Nahar holds Moina, Rafique carries Babul, a bag on his shoulders, Professor Rahman carries a suitcase and the radio. No buses, no trucks. Hardly, any rickshaws. The streets filled with people fleeing on foot.

"How are we going to reach Demra?" Sen asks Rahman.

"Walk," Rahman replies, his voice drifting off into a whisper. "Our only chance."

"The women. The children," Sen says.

"No other way. We have to try," Rahman says in a broken voice, as he struggles to find something hopeful to say. "We will carry the children."

On the road, people scamper for cover behind walls and trees at the sight of the occasional fierce looking soldiers on machine gun mounted trucks and jeeps. They walk across Iqbal Hall, only a short distance away.

As they walk past Iqbal Hall, over thirty bodies are lined up on the grass for public display. Some are beyond recognition, their faces blown away by bullets.

"Aaahh," Nahar gasps at her first glimpse up close of death, her voice bristling with anger and pain.

"Just to scare us," Rahman says to Selina, trying to calm her. The children wince, trying to see, curious.

"Cover the children's eyes," Rafique says. Nahar covers Moina's eyes with the end of her burqa.

They pass in front of Jagannath Hall. Another battlefield. On the lawn are deep tank tracks, on the walls huge tank shell-holes like gaping wounds.

In front of the Hall is a mass grave.

"Allah!" Selina cries out as she feels her legs going numb under her. Rahman grabs her arm and steadies her. He says in a voice that rises from a calmer, deeper place, "Selina, don't look, keep looking forward, keep walking."

Selina's eyes wander to the mangled bodies. She can only look numbly at a world that was sacred a few days ago, now strewn with the bodies of students. A sacrosanct Dacca University. Now dripping in blood, littered with the bodies of professors, students, workers, children, women and men.

In front of Jagannath Hall, mangled limbs, hands and feet grotesquely protrude from under the freshly compacted soil of a mass grave.

"Aaaah," Indubala moans out, lowering her eyes, her exhausted face wrenched in nausea. Sen grinds his teeth, in an agonizing suffering.

They hurry along, walking towards the central Shaheed Minar, now a heap of rubble. Blown apart by powerful explosives. They approach tentatively, slowing down near the carnage.

A human brush of blood has been pulled across the shiny floor of a razed Shaheed Minar. Nahar notices that there are no bodies; the dead have been dragged across the floor, left their marks in dried dark crimson swaths of blood.

Shaheed Minar. Martyr's Minar.

In '52. Then. Now in '71.

Bengali Language Movement Martyr's Minar.

In a stunned silence, Rafique stands like a statue. Here many an afternoon he has stood by pillars now demolished. Here so many an afternoon he has rallied with other students.

"Rafique, Rafique," Nahar says tugging, pulling him. Dazed he stands, his eyes unblinking, tears flooding his face. Nahar pulls at him again as seething in anger, his clenched fist trembling, Rafique is speechless.

Rahman who is in the front runs back and pulls Rafique's hand, trying to tear him away from a decapitated Shaheed Minar. Rahman says, "Rafique, let's go! We need to go now!"

Martyred blood fills Rafique's brown irises, his pupils aflame as he staggers away, his eyes now narrowed in vengeance.

On the side of the road, a fresh corpse of a rickshaw-wallah, and beside him a little street urchin, a *tookai*. Further out, a sprinkling of corpses on the grass.

Rahman, Sen, Nahar, Rafique, Selina, Indubala, Tia, Moina, Babul, Rani and Priya now walk with thousands, many of them with nothing but the clothes on their back, some in bare feet.

Dacca empties out like death row inmates suddenly released. On foot, hundreds of thousands rush out of the sieged city, without a clear escape route, without any plans, determined to leave devilbrowdeddrunkfatmurderer Yahya Khan's crucible of death.

On the North lies the army Cantonment.

Certain death.

On the South, the moat created by the Buriganga river is now without any launches or ferries to transport people, even the few with private cars and gasoline, to the other side and supposed safety.

The men try to hush the women and crying children. They carry them; they carry their belongings in suitcases, trunks and sacks on their heads. They carry the old on their backs, wrapped around their shoulders on the tarred dusty road out of Dacca. Walking behind the men, the women balance crying babies on their hips, young children in tow, pulling and tugging on the ends of their saris.

They carry hopes of survival from the murderous hands of

Yahya's Pakistani army.

They carry despair. They carry tears. They carry sadness.

They all carry fear.

—⊰⊱—

IN THE AFTERNOON, THEY CLOSE in on Demra when they notice in the distance a military checkpoint. With no path of escape, with thousands of other Daccaites, they trudge into the checkpoint.

Professor Rahman swallows hard and walks up to the glaring West Pakistani officer perched behind a jeep-mounted machine gun.

Under his breath, Rahman prays, *"Lailaha illahu Rusullah"*. All day he has said many prayers.

"Ruk'ye!" the soldier says, glaring at him. "Stop! Where are you going?"

"As-Salāmu 'Alaykum" Rahman says weakly, then adds in Urdu, "Sir, we are going to our village."

"Joy Bangla? You support Mujib?" the soldier barks.

"No sir, my father and I, we are Muslim League. Pakistan Zindabad!" Rahman says, desperate to sound loud and earnest.

Looking back he can see the cold sweat beading on Sen's face.

"This is my brother, and we are two families, sir," Rahman continues in broken Urdu. "We are going to our village home."

The soldiers gesture with their guns for them to come closer.

Fair skinned and tall, heavy moustaches, they stare intently at Nahar. Nahar looks down by the side of the road behind the truck and spies four bodies in a pool of blood, feels nauseous. One of the soldiers stares at her, laughs as he motions to a fellow soldier. He takes a drink from his water bottle and spits it back on Rafique's face.

Nahar shudders. Rafique looks away, tries to control himself, tries to hide the tearing vengeance in his heart.

After looking them over, one of the soldiers approaches Professor Sen. He asks to see Sen's wallet, takes the little cash, and tosses the wallet back in Sen's face. He sneers at the women, spits on the ground. Finally, the soldier releases them.

—⊰⊱—

EXHAUSTED, NOW LATE IN THE afternoon, after the ten mile walk, the two families drag themselves to Demra, to the banks of the Shitalakha river on the southern edge of Dacca, and collapse. Indubala and Selina go off behind a large tree and into the bushes to pee. Nahar joins them with Moina. Constipated, Moina cannot go and cries out, as Nahar relieves herself. Nahar then helps Priya and Rani, as Rahman stands watch by the other side of the tree.

"We need to hurry, hurry," he says, fearful of not getting a boat this late in the afternoon, of being caught in Demra in the approaching deadly curtain of curfew.

Spotting a boat pulling away, Rahman cries out, "Hurry up, we have to catch that boat. Quick!"

"Wait," Rafique screams as he sprints towards the bank.

"*Majhee,* boatman, *Oii majhee,* boatman, wait, wait for us!" Rahman calls out to the small boat leaving.

Rafique wades knee-deep into the water, screams out, "*Majhee, Oi Majhee* Bhai!"

The boatman—sinewy, muscular and short, burnt dark skin, covered in a shortened *lungi* and bamboo *matla* hat—turns his open country boat around and comes back to shore.

"Thank you, Allah," Rahman says when he steps onto the boat.

"Get in Saar, I take you other side. *Meemshaib,* careful. Watch foot."

"Saar. What happened? Saar?" the boatman asks Professor Rahman once they are safely away from the shore. "All day stories I no believe! The birds cryin' cryin' all day. The wind is blowing wrong. Bad wind."

"Dacca is destroyed. Dacca University burnt to the ground," Sen says.

When the *majhee* dips his oars, the boat slips forward easily, with the Shitalakha's dark water frothing around its bow. He pulls at the sail, it catches the wind and they slowly slip away from Dacca.

The boat is an island of escape.

Nahar breathes in a long breath of relief. For a minute, she stands in the breeze. Her black burqa billows outward like a sail, and she, Nahar a mast, tugs the boat towards the far horizon, away from a deadened city, towards the free shore.

"Saar, please, tell what happen, what happen in Dacca?" the boatman asks.

"Many teachers have been murdered, many students and workers at Dacca University," Rahman says.

"Kafirs, Kafirs they call all the Hindus. I can't believe my eyes," says Sen, his voice choked, his eyes watery. "Old Dacca burnt into the ground."

"*Hai Bhagavan*, I am Hindu, poor Hindu. The bad wind is upon me. What will happen to my family?" the boatman cries into the wind.

"If the Pakistani army comes down this river, it's all over. Life is over for everyone in the village," says Rahman as he looks to the other side of Shitalakha and safety.

"*Bhagavan, Bhagavan!* Where I go? My family… All I got this boat. This all I got." Then he adds, "Sheik Mujib, our leader, Saar dead?"

"Maybe arrested…" Rahman replies, wondering himself the fate of Bangabandhu.

On the other side of death, on the Naryanganj side of the Shitalakha, they get off the boat, alive.

"Saar, pronam, good day."

"How much?"

"No Saar…nothing today. Today very bad, bad day."

Rahman gives him a tip, pats him on the back.

In the boatman's face is a pained expression of uncertainty.

Now on the other side of the river, fear still burns in their nostrils. And fear still tastes like shattered glass in their mouths.

Survival is the only thing that Rahman can think of. The vestiges of life, the honor, the courage all fall by the wayside; the burning skies over Dacca left behind.

Sen will go stay at a friend's house in Naryanganj.

"Rahman, spend the night in Naryanganj," he pleads, but Rafique and Rahman are adamant in their wish to reach Sheetalpur.

"Everyone in Sheetalpur is worried sick, we must get there," Rahman tells Sen.

Before parting, the two families eat a quick meal of puffed rice, biscuits and water. There is little talk as they eat, and the food is packed back just as quick. As they go their separate ways, the children's faces draw long. For the last two days they have become one family.

"Take care of yourself," Indubala says embracing Selina.

"Be careful, Boudi," Nahar says to Indubala as Indubala wipes the tears off of Nahar's face.

Tearful good-byes and hugs, and the two families part ways.

Rafique finds a couple of baby taxis off the road, parked next to a bamboo hut. After half an hour of desperate pleading and coaxing, finally the drivers agree to take them.

"Let's get going," Rahman says. Somehow they pile in, the children sitting on laps, everyone squeezed together into a prayer of escape.

The baby taxies, retrofitted scooters made to carry passengers, with unwieldy spring suspensions, bump and bounce on the narrow country road. The city vanishes, and in its place scorched outcroppings of hay pop up in the middle of rice fields recently harvested, beard stubble poking out of the brown wet earth. They pass mud houses with thatched roofs, and along this ribbon of a dusty road are brown sunburnt faces rich in warmth, rich in life—fathomless ink-colored eyes yet untouched by the festering hate and murder of Dacca. Yet. In the courtyards of the mud houses, bamboo lined courtyards of clay, children play. Children laugh.

In the late afternoon, they reach a village. Here the metalled road ends, the dirt road starts. The scenery changes—fewer stalls, less population.

Rahman's throat is parched and his stomach cries out for food.

"Stop over here," Rahman tells the driver.

They get down from the baby taxis. Everyone collapses, as if they have been holding up the world on their shoulders for the last two days and finally the weight comes off. And in this one solitary roadside stall, they have their first meal in peace.

Rice, *daal*, fish and vegetable curry.

"Allah, be praised," Nahar says wearily as she washes her hands in water Rafique pours from an aluminum jug. Her eyes are still holding onto the images of Dacca University, visions of the dead, the agonized expressions on students' faces as they died and the begging-before-death expressions on the bloody bodies strewn all around the Campus of Death.

Slowly, Nahar, Selina, Rafique, Rahman, Tia, Babul, Moina chew, trying to swallow the food as a bitter taste lingers in their mouths. One morsel by one morsel, they try to swallow but the food sticks in their throats.

Still nauseous, Selina runs to the corner, and by the base of the bamboo bush vomits. Nahar holds her hair back and Rahman pours some water on her head. Revived, Selina silently moves far away from the smell of food.

Nahar bows her own head and Rafique pours water from the aluminum jug over her, washing away the smell of smoke still lingering on her hair.

In the cool afternoon breeze, a flock of Shaliks are warbling merrily in the Neem tree. Nahar takes off the burqa, her black coffin, and looks at the fluttering carefree skittering of the birds. Better to be born a bird, just to fly away. The country sweetness of the southern wind caresses the silk of Nahar's hair. Closing her eyes, she takes in a long deep breath, exhales out the stench and smoke of the city.

Never will she go back to Dacca. She remembers Ramna, March 7th. Somehow a different world, a promise crushed in the talons of Tikka. No. She won't talk about March 7th. In her eyes visions of the lush green of Sheetalpur. No, she won't ask her in-laws to let her study at Dacca University. Dacca, now a burnt, dead city, buried behind her forever.

There is an earthy smell in the air, the smell of fresh turned brown clay, of the good earth.

Nahar inhales deeply.

"Allah, be praised," she breathes into this country sweetness.

The last mile, they have to walk, but now villagers appear, help carry the children and the bags.

"Rahman Bhai, is it true?"

"Rafique Bhai, what happened?"

Questions pour out from villagers, who eagerly help with carrying the children and the bags on the last leg of this arduous journey.

Along the dirt road, village people come out like hungry and fearful ants looking for news of Dacca. They scurry, carrying bits and pieces of an unbelievable tale back to their little mud and bamboo and corrugated tin houses. And in these hearths, the waves of rumors and disbelief mix into a wave of uncertainty that now veils the villages.

When the Khan *Shenas* are done beheading Dacca, certainly their little villages are next.

Fear travels fast.

Tears in the Heart

🍂 🍂 🍂

Friday, April 16, 1971, Brentwood, California

LATE ON THIS FRIDAY AFTERNOON, Mrs. Priti Kumar sits in the McKensies' living room in Brentwood, chatting with her faculty adviser, Laura McKensie. Her second year at UCLA's Ph.D. program in Sociology Priti made friends with Laura, who is keenly interested in India, its culture, its many nuances.

"Your husband is on a trip to Calcutta, I heard, Mrs. Kumar?" Jack asks, hovering over the television, adjusting the vertical hold.

"Please call me Priti, Jack," she says, a warm smile on her ruby-red lips. "Yes Alok is in Calcutta for his grandfather's funeral. I have my dissertation to defend, or else I would be with him."

"I'm sorry to hear that," Jack says walking back to the couch. "What does Priti mean, pretty?"

Her smile turns to laughter as Priti answers, "No, it means love. My full name is Priti Lata Kumar."

On her first visit to the McKensies', Priti adjusts the pleats of her dark blue silk sari, her long shiny black hair done up in a bun, as Laura puts a plate of freshly baked chocolate chip cookies on the coffee table. The sweet buttery smell wafts into the far corners of the living room, over the grand piano that shines in the soft light filtering in through the French doors leading out to the backyard.

Outside a spring wind stirs in the trees like the sound of bird wings, a trail of pine needles float down onto the freshly cut grass.

"Have you lived here all your life, Laura?" Priti asks.

"No, we lived in Orange County. That's where Rachael and Frank were born. This was Jack's parents' home, and since they passed away we have been living here," Laura says.

A pained expression washes over Laura's face, as she mentions Frank. Priti, silent for a moment, changes the subject. "Jack, you take great care of your garden back there. It's wonderful to have such a huge backyard in the city."

"Yes, I love gardening. Kinda in my blood. My older brother, Joe, lives up in Hollister on a farm, used to be our family farm. It's wonderful up in the Central Valley. Have you been up North, Priti?" Jack asks.

"No, but I do mean to travel when Alok returns and I get done with this dissertation," Priti says, slowly exhaling a breath of relief. "My father loves to garden, mostly in clay pots on the roof of our house in Calcutta. He loves to see things grow. Says it keeps him alive."

Laura smiles at Priti. "You will get done soon with your thesis," she says, patting her on the back. "I have great confidence in you."

Priti looks out into the lushness of the McKensie backyard, thinking back to the deep monsoon green of Bengal, of the home she now misses dearly, for the first time alone with any family around her.

It's five-thirty, and NBC national news comes on with David Brinkley. Jack gets up to turn up the volume, and on the screen the news begins with the US Ping-Pong team being greeted by China's Premier Chou En-Lai.

"You play ping-pong, Priti?" Jack asks.

"Just a bit. Alok is very good at it. But Pakistan's General Yahya Khan is excellent at ping-pong diplomacy," Priti says.

"Ping-pong diplomacy?" Laura asks, her eyes narrowed in question.

"Yes, Pakistan's dictator General Yahya Khan has a lot to do with this back and forth ping-pong diplomacy between the United States and China topping the news today," Priti says, her eyes locked on the screen.

"General Yahya? Pakistan's dictator?" Jack says inquiringly.

"Yes, that's why Nixon is so cozy with him, not stopping his massacre in East Pakistan. Yahya is great buddies with the Chinese Premier and is setting up some of the meetings with Nixon."

The pictures cut away to B-52 bombers blowing up North Vietnamese bases in the Ashua valley.

"Is there any end to Vietnam?" Priti asks.

"I don't think anytime soon," Jack says through clenched teeth, "Our only son was killed in Vietnam."

"I am so sorry," Priti says.

"What meaning is there to Vietnam?" Jack says, his usually beaming face becoming hard, grim. Priti looks at Laura, who sits quietly, watching intently, one hand tightly wrapped around the other, searching for something lost in the pictures.

In the commercial break, advertisements of New York Life Insurance and Amana Ovens and Del Monte pudding fill the screen.

"I'm curious, Priti. You have clay ovens in your home in Calcutta?" Laura asks.

"No, in India most kitchens don't. Tandoori clay ovens, but those are in restaurants. We mostly fry, don't do that much baking," Priti says, still thinking about Jack and Laura's son lost to Vietnam. She looks at Jack and Laura. Laura is in her late forties, Jack early fifties. But in their faces is a weathered, weary look. In their voices, echoes of loss.

"And your daughter?" Priti asks.

"Rachael is away at Columbia. She's a Junior this year, premed." Laura says, as if convincing herself.

"We felt it was good for her to get a break from home, and after Frank's death, we felt it would be good for her to be away from where all of Frank's memories are," Jack says.

"It was Rachael's decision to leave home. We supported her decision. This place is where they grew up. Being away in New York is doing her good," says Laura.

The commercial break ends, and a special bulletin comes on about the fighting in East Pakistan. Priti's eyes flash back to the

TV screen as Laura leans forward and Jack gets up to turn up the volume again.

India is accusing West Pakistan of systematic genocide in dealing with the East Pakistani autonomy movement. Three weeks after the March 25th massacres, West Pakistan claims to have control over Kushtia, East Pakistan and most major cities. On the screen, in Ghojadanga, India, reporter Frank McGee is showing close-ups of East Pakistani refugees on the road in India. On the border, in a close-up, the East Pakistani refugees look emaciated, their dark faces gaunt, their eyes unfocused, the children in shock. The image cuts to another newscaster, George Montgomery in Bhomphra, East Pakistan, with Bangladeshi rebels and guerrillas who are determined to launch an offensive. The guerrillas are not trained yet, reports George Montgomery. The East Pakistan bulletin only lasts for a few minutes, and when it ends, Laura looks at the now tense face of Priti.

"Do you have any family in Dacca, Priti?" asks Laura in a concerned tone.

"My Aunt and her family are in Dacca. I tried to reach them, but the phone lines are horrible. I can't get through."

"How about your husband?" asks Jack.

"Alok tried from Calcutta, but no luck either. He is worried sick. Hopefully they can come over the border with the refugees flooding into India."

After a moment, Priti continues, "It's really scary. And my aunt lives in Old Dacca. I am praying she got out alive. Hindus are the targets just like the Jews were in Germany. They even painted yellow H's on the walls of their houses in Old Dacca, just like in Nazi Germany they painted swastikas on Jewish houses."

"I'm sure they are fine," Jack says, trying to reassure Priti.

With the news over, the three of them move to the dining area.

"First time Laura's made vegetarian Irish stew," Jack says ladling out the stew, a smile growing in his blue eyes.

"Thank you Laura," Priti says. "So thoughtful of you!"

"Well I had to put in more carrots, potatoes, celery, and spiced it up a bit. What do you think?"

"Delicious! Nothing like home cooking," Priti says. "It reminds me of my mother's cooking."

"And what kind of cooking does your mother do?" Laura asks.

"Lots of curries, eggplant, cauliflower. And during the summer, pickles galore. She pickles mangoes, Indian olives, and the whole house smells of *kashondi*," Priti says.

"Makes my mouth water," Jack says. "I served in World War II. There's nothing like home cooking. Whenever you have a chance, come over Priti; you are always welcome here."

"I tried my hand at chicken curry, but the curry powder here is just not the same," Laura says. "Never tastes like the curry at the local Indian restaurants."

"In Calcutta, we mix our spices. Actually it's everyone's special mix, and I doubt if any two women ever mix the same amounts, so there is your uniqueness in flavor, in the taste of India," Priti says, filling her mouth with more of the stew. "Just the right amount of spices, Laura. Yum!"

After dinner, Priti helps carrying cups and plates back to the sink. Laura stands in front of the purring Frigidaire putting away the remnants of the coffee cake. The frigid light beams on Laura's face, and Priti sees time-stamped lines of pain. She tries to comfort Laura by rubbing the small of her back, by whispering kind words.

"Irish stew was Frank's favorite," Laura says. "I hate seeing footage of Vietnam. Keeps on reminding me..." She inhales a long slow breath. "Sorry Priti, I didn't mean to get upset, but every time I see a body bag, it brings back memories. It will be four years next month that Frank passed away."

Jack walks in loaded down with a tray full of plates and cups and puts them into the sink. Seeing Laura upset, he comes over and tenderly wraps his arms around her.

"I love you so much," he says softly to Laura. She kisses him on the cheek, touches his hand tenderly. They leave the dishes and go to the living room for coffee.

Laura continues, "You know, I have been meaning to tell you all evening, you look like Reita Faria. Especially in that silk sari you are wearing today."

"Reita Faria?" Priti says, her eyes wide with surprise.

"Yes, right around Christmas, when Frank was in Vietnam, Reita Faria, Miss India, and Miss World in 1966 went with Bob Hope to visit them as part of the USO tour," Laura says.

"Reita Faria? In Vietnam? I didn't know she was in Vietnam!" says Priti, glancing at Laura with questioning eyes.

"Yes, it's true. Just a minute, let me get a picture of her that Frank sent us," Laura says. She gets up and goes over to the living room armoire where she brings out a picture of Frank, and with it another blue, red and white air-mail envelope.

Bob Hope and Reita Faria are on stage in Vietnam as part of the USO tour, in front of thousands of cheering GI's. Reita Faria is in a dark blue silk sari, her hair swooped up in an elegant do, on an open stage in front of thousands of US troops with Bob Hope on her right and a freckled faced red-headed GI grinning to her left.

"She looks just like you," Laura says.

"Maybe instead of doing a Ph.D. you should be competing for Miss India," Jack says laughing, trying to lighten up the evening.

"After her Ph.D. she can enter the Mrs. India pageant," Laura adds.

"Sure," Priti says, a smile rising to her face. "After this, anything!"

Scrutinizing the picture of Reita Faria for a long time, Priti asks, "May I see the letter?"

"Sure," Jack says, takes a sip of coffee, gets up and hands it to Priti. She reads the lines written in black ink on ruled paper; a page folded and unfolded many a time. In a spot, a tear-stain water mark.

December 27, 1966

Dear Mom and Dad;
Merry Christmas!
I miss you guys so much. My first Christmas away from home.
Hope you did not forget to hang up my stocking!
Do I have a story for you. I got to see Bob Hope today as part of the USO Christmas tour and wow! Bob Hope and Miss World showed up! Reita Faria, Miss India and Miss World was escorted by Bob Hope.

She looked like a dream come true for every GI. Reita knocked our socks off. She is drop-dead gorgeous in her blue wrap silk dress called a sari, her long, black silky hair done up.

One lucky GI got a chance to kiss Reita and I was dreaming it would be me!

This is the most excitement we've had in a long time. Had Pepsi, hot dogs, and the works. Hopefully, the rest of my stay in 'Nam is going to be as beautiful as this. Reita was great, what a show!

Give Rachael my love! She is next on the list for me to write to. The diary you sent me is wonderful. Been penning my thoughts when I get a spare moment.

We are shipping out today, so I got to run. It was great while it lasted. We have to head out to our base camp tomorrow, and I have a truck to load and then repack my duffle bag.

Guess it's time for the "newbies" to get some experience.

Happy new 1967, guys! Love and kisses, Rachael!

> *Love*
> *Frank*

While Priti reads the letter, Jack finishes his cup of coffee, and Laura studies a family picture of her and Rachael and Frank mounted in a large silver frame hanging over the fireplace. Priti gently refolds the letter, puts the picture with it in the love and remembrance-worn envelope, and quietly hands it back to Jack.

"It tore me up to think I could have stopped him from going over there. But he wanted to go, and I let him. I could have stopped him," Jack says.

"Little boy," Laura says, her words barely audible.

"Little boy?" asks Priti, raising her eyebrows. Laura, who did not think Priti could hear her, exhales and says again, louder, "Yes, a little boy..."

"It was a horrible accident," Jack says. "He threw a grenade. It killed a family hiding in a hut, killed a little boy by mistake. Frank..." Jack looks out through the French doors into the near darkness. "He just couldn't get over holding the dying boy in his arms."

Laura walks back and says, "You know Priti, it's like a big part of him died as he was holding the little kid in his arms."

111

"I'm so sorry," Priti says in a soft whisper, her voice trailing off.

"Frank kept a journal in Vietnam. He wrote in detail about this, trying to make sense of a senseless war," Jack says.

"Frank was so gentle. He died a thousand deaths before he died," Laura says, biting her lips.

"I can't tell you how sorry I feel, Laura. Accidently killing someone. That's so sad," Priti says.

A quiet descends on the living room. Priti pulls her sari tighter around her shoulders.

"It just changed him. He didn't tell us, but we could feel it through his letters," Jack says.

"You know, my father felt really guilty during the India-Pakistan partition of '47," Priti says. "He was sick from it, had a hard time eating for days, weeks after the riots. He could not help neighbors in need. And then he was haunted by the images: children, men, women." Priti bit her lip as she continued, her eyes narrowed, her face contorted in anguish.

"War kills in many ways, Priti. I can understand how your Dad must have felt. Frank was all torn up, holding a young dying baby in his arms. I don't think he ever got over the guilt." Jack pauses, remembering Frank. "He was only a kid, just a kid without anyone to help him in a strange land," Jack says, as he looks away.

For a few minutes no one said anything. Outside the wind grew silent with the setting sun. The Figidaire hummed discordantly in the kitchen.

"You must have been very young in '47, Priti?" Laura asks.

"Three. I don't remember anything, but my father told me many Muslims were killed in my neighborhood in Calcutta, and they had to leave for East Pakistan," Priti says.

"And this, this today is the worst," Jack adds. "A planned Genocide by a General. But here a General with all his army is attacking a country under the guise it's an internal matter, and killing hundreds of thousands as the world looks on doing nothing!"

Jack stands up and walks around the living room. Priti looks at him—tall, blonde, a handsome man, a father in mourning. He pauses at an oil painting hanging in the corner behind the piano. It is an Irish girl on the lush countryside of Ireland looking up at the clouds with her emerald eyes. He continues, "You know Priti, looking at the faces of these East Pakistani refugees, I know some horrible man-made acts are creating a famine of humanity in East Pakistan. My great-grandfather, Patrick McKensie, was a refugee from Ireland's potato famine. He almost died as a boy on the open boat to New York. Ireland was a land of starvation due to the potato blight. An act of nature. But this senseless killing in East Pakistan is entirely man-made. Just as senseless as Vietnam. Senseless as Frank's death."

"Those children suffer the worst. The children are the first to die of starvation," Laura says.

"Children in war are the first victims, always," Priti says.

"I feel so sorry for those sad eyed refugee children of East Pakistan on the news tonight, frozen on the laps of their parents. They seem to have been bombed into some strange numbness. Their eyes so big and empty," Laura says.

"In 1947, the Irish Americans supported Gandhi and his movement for freedom from the British. Today we need to support the East Pakistani freedom movement," Jack says to Priti, his voice expansive, filling the living room. "The East Pakistanis have gotten the short end of the stick for a long time, and now they just have to regroup and fight for their freedom. Freedom is never free, not here, not for the Irish, and certainly not for the people of East Pakistan today," Jack says.

"The Bangladeshis voted in a landslide election for Sheik Mujibur Rahman. They voted him in democratically, and look at this massacre they got," says Priti. "Nixon needs a dictator Yahya to deal diplomacy with his buddy Chou En-Lai more than he needs to support starving refugees."

"You are absolutely right," says Jack.

—⁂—

Late into the night, Priti lays awake in bed, staring at the reflected light on the UCLA graduate student dormitory ceiling, with dinner conversations at the McKensies' weighing on her thoughts.

She thinks about Frank Patrick McKensie, his bright young boyish grin lingering in her mind.

In India, there is a saying, a question, really.

What is the heaviest burden in life?

The weight of your child's coffin on your shoulder.

❧

Razakars, Traitors Within

❧ ❧ ❧

April 1971, Sheetalpur Village, Bangladesh

A BANGLADESHI VILLAGE IS ALIVE. It breathes and vibrates, it thinks, speaks, rejects and accepts, and a Bangladeshi village knows everything about everybody. It has a throbbing pulsating heart, arteries of news, veins of gossip. And here news travels faster than young children's legs, women's tongues.

On this Bazaar Thursday, Sheetalpur was alive, humming. A sleepy farming village perched on the banks of the Sitalakha River, Sheetalpur was still holding onto its innocence, holding on as Dacca bled in the near horizon.

Near the river *ghat*, under the arching banyan tree, here on the edge of the Bazaar, on the periphery of the corrugated tin roof stores lining the hard beaten dirt path, was Munir Mia's chai stall, the heart of the village, where one could find the essentials of life neatly packed into a tiny shack. It's only bench was packed with people, sitting pressed up against each other. Munir Mia could get you a cigarette, a biscuit, a cup of tea, and always the latest hot gossip.

Rafique and Nazmul rode up on his motorcycle on the packed dirt trail to the side of the chai stall and parked. The late spring afternoon rays cast shadows and lights on the two men's faces. A slight wind blew off the Shitalakha's shimmering ripples, and a Doel flitting in the tendrils of the banyan's aerial roots sang a sweet "Sweeeee" and then a harsh "churrrr."

"*Oi*, two cups of cha," Nazmul called out to the chai boy waiting on customers five at a time.

"Saar, one minute, Saar" he said as he jumped to wash out, pour and hand two milky sugar-cane molasses sweetened cups of chai to Nazmul and Rafique.

Leaning back on the motorcycle, Rafique tried to light a cigarette. One try, two tries, on the third the moist match stick bent and broke. He hopped off the bike and held his cigarette to the lit end of Munir Mia's coil of jute rope and puffed. Holding his cupped hand around it, he puffed again, lit the Will's Capstan cigarette, and took a deep, angry breath, blowing thin spirals of cigarette smoke into the damp air that hung there.

Nazmul took the pack of Capstans, tapped it hard against his left palm, and pulled out a cigarette. He took Rafique's lit cigarette, held it against his own. He exhaled into the air, scratched his forehead with his thumb, and looked at Rafique, in bell-bottom pants and a khaki shirt, scratching his day-old mottled stubble.

"*Doost*, we can't ride my bike to Agartala, can we?" Rafique said smiling. He patted his motorcycle seat. "Look at these shiny aluminum spoke wheels, mud guards, chrome front headlights! Hate to leave her behind."

"Not a chance, Rafique," Nazmul sneered and said. "You and your bike. Why didn't you marry it instead of Nahar?"

Rafique laughed at Nazmul, punched him lightly on the shoulder. Like the sooty smoke that billowed out from the small fire under the large aluminum tea pot, the talk, the smell, the chatter rose above the stall, floated over Rafique and Nazmul, drawing them together

---

Razakars:
The definition of hypocrisy.

The single most deadly weapon Yahya and Tikka Khan had in their arsenal was the East Pakistani collaborators known as Razakars, Al-Badars and Al-shams. Through the eyes of these axe-murdering *Jallads* every *mahallah*, every village, every *para*, every corner of East Pakistan was under the surveillance of the occupying Pakistani forces. Before delving into the architecture and heinous engineering of genocide in Bangladesh, let's define Geno-cide. The word genocide didn't exist before 1944 when Richard Lemkin connected the Greek prefix Geno- meaning race and the Latin postfix —cide meaning killing.

Genocide is the systematic deliberate destruction in whole or part of an ethnic,

in a chai chador of closeness.

For a long nerve-racking minute, a voice inside Nazmul's head wrestled with him. Should he? He must. Now or never.

"Rafique What are you going to do about Neezam?" Nazmul finally said, his face taut, a palpable tension in the air.

Rafique ground his teeth, saying nothing, his face deepening into an angry red.

"Just that it's hard to believe. Neezam is the big rat, and Bodor Morol is his right hand man. A fucking shithole. His group are the inside people. People who know us from birth. Without them, how the fuck would they ever get information about our whereabouts?" Nazmul said, anger rising in his voice.

Contorted in rage, shame and frustration etched hard lines on Rafique's face. A vein on his forehead began to enlarge, to pulsate. Rafique held onto the small cup, his grip tightened as he thought of Neezam's neck. The anger Rafique had been containing came welling up.

"Craack!" The chai cup shattered in Rafique's grip, shards cutting into his palm.

"*Oi*, careful Rafique," Nazmul said. "What are you doing!

Jolted out of his murderous grip, Rafique grasped his right wrist to stop the bleeding. Calling out loudly to the stall boy, Nazmul had him pick up the broken chai cup. "Careful Rafique, I didn't mean to poke you. I know he is like a little brother to you, but don't forget the worst enemy, the enemy within."

"No, Nazmul. No more. Not my brother anymore. I'll murder Neezam if he leads the military to Sheetalpur!"

---

racial, religious or national group.

Simply, genocide is the worst crime man can commit against man. And in 1971 General Yahya Khan committed Intelligentsia genocide, Hindu ethnic cleansing genocide as well as the 'plain vanilla' mass genocide, if there is such a thing, against all Bangladeshis. En masse.

Genocide pits neighbor against neighbor; this, in East Pakistan, was the ethnic cleansing strategy of General Yahya Khan.

The art of genocide is nothing new; Hitler used it against the Jews in the Holocaust and Yahya was a good student. The art is to find a scapegoat. For Hitler it was the Jews. For Yahya Khan it was the Hindus. "Kill and rape the Hindus and then their property will be yours," was the offer on the table to the Bangladeshi collaborators and traitors who sided with Yahya's henchmen. By using the property of the Hindus,

Looking at Rafique's bleeding hand, Nazmul thought about Neezam. Rafique was not going to do anything to Neezam Chowdhury, his only cousin.

The chai stall boy picked up the pieces, and straining his neck, peeked in the direction that Rafique had been looking. Self-conscious, Rafique took some water and washed the blood from his palm, the same blood running in Neezam's veins. When he was a child, every summer and winter vacation he eagerly waited for little Neezam's arrival from Dacca to Sheetalpur with his parents, Uncle Masud Chowdhury and Rokeya Auntie. Neezam was such a well-behaved boy.

Nazmul's sharp voice, concerned, broke the silence. "What is *Chacha and Chachi's*, Uncle and Aunt's, reaction about Neezam's activities?"

"Nazmul you know that after Masud Uncle died, Neezam came back from England. In the name off taking care of Masud Uncle's business, he spent all the money on drinking, gambling, hanging out with the wrong crowd. That's when Neezam had the big fight with Abba."

"Fight over what?"

"Neezam was drunk. He accused Abba of selling off his property after Masud Uncle's death. Said Abba was greedy. Taking advantage of him, an orphan. Abba slapped him and Neezam has not spoken to him since. Not a word."

Looking away at the chai stall customers, Rafique continued, "When I told Amma that Neezam and Morol are occupying all the Hindu houses, she did not believe me, her own son. She is in total

---

it was easy to finance the killings. In Shakaripotti, yellow 'H's' were painted on the entrance walls of Hindu houses, eerily repeating the swastikas painted on the Jewish houses and tenements in Nazi Germany.

On the back of the Hindu cleansing, and the degrading of all Bangladeshi Muslims as impure Muslims, Yahya conducted mass genocide on the Bangladeshi people. The stated goal, on February 22, 1971, as reported by British historian Robert Payne in his book *Massacre*, was to kill three million East Pakistanis, terrorizing the other seventy million into a colonial subservience for a generation.

The word Razakar, originating from Persian, literally means, "volunteer." Originally used in Hyderabad, India in the 1940s, Razakar was a term used to describe a private Islamic militia organized to support the oppressive rule of Osman Ali Khan and Asaf Jah VII.

denial of Neezam's crimes. Amma's reply was 'People are jealous, bad mouthing the Chowdhury *Khandan*. We are *Jamindars*. Why should we need other people's property? Our sons are not like that at all.' I told Amma, 'I am not like that, but he is not your son, Amma.'"

Nazmul put his hand on Rafique's shoulder, patted him on the back, and said, "Like *Chachi*, I couldn't believe it either. Love often makes us blind."

Rafique wrapped his handkerchief around his bleeding palm and handed Munir Mia the money for the chai and for the broken cup. With a grinding bitterness in his voice, he said, "I do understand Amma's affection for Neezam. Masud Uncle was like an eldest son to her. After he passed away, Neezam became an orphan and Amma's affection for him grew."

"How about *Chacha*?"

Rafique exhaled a long breath. His voice and face were full of disgust. "He was quiet. Abba knew very well what was going on, but what could he do? You know Abba never told me till the day Amma and I had the argument that Neezam wants a share of our Sheetalpur home. Abba is very frustrated. He did not tell Amma as she will be heartbroken."

"I can't believe this is the same Neezam. Only last year we said our *Eid* prayers together, we embraced each other. Unbelievable!" Nazmul said.

"Abba raised Masud Uncle as his own son. Took care of his education in Calcutta, his marriage. Everything. Even our grandfather's Dacca home in Mitford; our share was given to Masud

---

Razakar is the name given to a paramilitary force organized by the Pakistan Army during the Bangladesh Liberation War in 1971. The Razakar force was composed of mostly pro-Pakistani Bengalis and Urdu-speaking migrants living in East Pakistan. The right wing of the Islamic political parties, Jamaat, who supported the genocide from March were behind the creation of the Razakars.

Ashraf Hossain, a leader of Jamaat's student wing Islami Chhatra Sangha, created the Al-Badr militia in Jamalpur District on April 22, 1971.

In May, 1971, Jamaat leader Mawlana Yusuf created the Razakar Militia in Khulna. The first recruits included 96 Jamaat party members, who started training in an Ansar camp at Shahjahan Ali Road, Khulna.

Initially, the force was under the command of local pro-Pakistani committees, but through the East Pakistan Razakar Ordinance established by Lt. General Tikka Khan

uncle. Abba also sold our Joydebpur property for Neezam's education in England," Rafique said.

Nazmul cupped the cigarette in his hand, hid it behind his back as Professor Rahman, wearing a sweat-stained cotton Panjabi, came walking up from the *ghat*.

"*As-salaam alaikum* Rahman Bhai," Rafique and Nazmul said in unison, as they both quickly crushed the cigarettes and Rafique fanned away the smoke.

"*Walaikum Salam*," Rahman returned the greeting. He looked across towards the base of the Banyan tree where the *napeet*, the village barber, had set up shop. A customer was sitting on a chair looking up at his small hand mirror tied to a low branch. The *napeet* sharpened his razor on a hanging piece of bicycle tubing, running it back and forth, back and forth. With a round brush, he applied the frothing shaving cream to the customer's face.

"Thought I was going to get a shave, but it's getting late," Professor Rahman said, stroking his two-day old beard.

Nazmul gestured with his hand for three cups of tea to the little chai stall boy.

"Rafique, Nazmul, how are you? How is Nahar doing? How is *Chachi*?" asked Professor Rahman.

"Nahar has recovered, but she's still very weak, just quietly sits, lays around. She just started to eat a bit. Amma is doing fine and wanted to visit Selina Bhabi. But she was so busy with Nahar," Rafique replied.

"Give my salaam and thanks to *Chachi* from us, for the food and sari for Selina," Rahman said.

---

on the first of June, 1971 and a Ministry of Defense ordinance established 7 September, 1971, Razakars were recognized as members of the Pakistan Army. Jamaat leader Matiur Rahman Nizami was the supreme commander of this militia. In an editorial published in the Daily Sangram on November 14, 1971, Nizami stated, "We believe that our young members will fight side by side with our army to defeat the Hindu forces, and destroy India, and raise the flag of Islam in the whole world."

The AL-Badar Razakars were a secret killing squad comparable to the SS of the Nazi era, formed with the most dedicated recruits of the student wing of Jamaat.

To Yahya Khan, the East Pakistani version of Islam was not good enough, the people a mixed race from the Hinduinized population, not "pure" Muslims. Not quite human. So easy to kill, subhumans. The Razakar's main function was to arrest and detain nationalist Bengali suspects. Usually, such suspects were tortured to death

"Babul, Tia, Moina? How are they doing now Rahman Bhai?" Nazmul asked.

"Tia is doing much better now. She just recovered from the flu. But Babul and Moina have diarrhea since yesterday. I have not been able to find the right medicine for them. Been giving them molasses saline."

Deep tense lines furrowed Rahman's forehead. He took off his dark rimmed glasses, and ran his fingers through his hair. With the edge of his Panjabi he cleaned the lens of his glasses, deep in thought. The chai boy brought the tea, handing them each a cup.

Rahman took a sip, and tentatively holding the cup in his hand, said in a dejected tone, "Selina is not feeling well. She has been vomiting since yesterday morning. Ran out of her vitamins. I went to Norshindi Town for medicine. Nothing. No flu syrup, not even Detol. No sugar. No soybean oil. Children are just tired of eating molasses. Only thing I could scrounge up was some mustard oil, kerosene, and salt. And the prices? Sky high!"

"On the way home, Rafique and I will stop by your place Rahman Bhai. What else do you need?" Nazmul asked.

"See if you can find some flu syrup and Detol. And how are things with you Nazmul?" Rahman said, looking at him inquiringly.

"OK. But Rahman Bhai, we need to talk. Let's take a walk," Nazmul said, his voice lowering to a whisper, pointing to a padlocked corrugated tin store.

Slowly they drifted off from the chai stall. Behind the store, away from peering eyes and ubiquitous ears, Nazmul continued his

---

in custody.

The Razakars were trained in the conventional army fashion by the Pakistan Army. After the war ended, the Razakars scurried like rats into their holes. On the other end, as time passed, they came out as men in power, subtly changing clothes and identity.

The crimes of the Razakars were forgotten and forgiven by ensuing administrations. Actually, much of the subsequent administrations of Bangladesh were infiltrated by Razakars, while the struggling families of martyrs and the *Birongana* plight has been swept under the carpet, then run over by the steam roller of these criminals.

How does that work? Well, the Razakars were always engrained in power in Bangladeshi society, in the villages and the cities, and when war was over, power eventually went back to these same people. Wealth always wins. And moreover, some

conversation, "Samad Uncle's in-laws are now staying with us. They were trapped in Old Dacca, next to the Shakaripotti massacres. We were worried sick, but somehow with the help of Allah they managed to escape to Norshindi. They got here a week ago," Nazmul said.

Looking at the revenge wrought faces of Nazmul and Rafique, Professor Rahman whispered, "What are your plans?"

"Chittagong's Bangladesh Betar was bombed to bits by the Pakistanis, but some of our friends heard Major Zia declaring freedom on behalf of Bangabandhu before it went down. Even so, we need to join the *Shangram*," Nazmul said.

A throbbing pain in his cut palm, excitement undercutting uncertainty, Rafique said, "We need to fight back and now. We heard that there is a guerrilla training camp in Agartala."

"Rahman Bhai, we must leave for Agartala. A few of the boys from our village have already left," Nazmul said. "We have to join the fight as soon as we can."

"And what are Dr. Samad's plans?" Professor Rahman asked.

"Samad Uncle plans to join us in Agartala in a few weeks," Nazmul said in a whisper.

Rahman said his salaams to two passing villagers; he hesitated for a moment, a dark shadow crossing his face. He turned to Rafique and said, "There is a rumor that Neezam was seen on a Pakistani gun boat? I heard people saw a military gunboat patrol the river, Neezam with them. And Bodor Morol is the head of the Peace Committee and ..."

Rafique interrupted him, "You are right Rahman Bhai, we couldn't make a human out of that Neezam." An angry pall suffused

---

political parties absorbed Razakars in to give them the extra votes they needed to shift the balance of power.

In 1971 Bangladeshi traitors, Razakars, were the killing talons of General Yahya Khan. And these same rapists, murders and traitors today are publicly professing piety. That, my friends, is the definition of hypocrisy.

Rafique's face.

"It's hard to believe that Neezam would became such a collaborator. Hard to believe," said Rahman. "His father Masud Chowdhury was such a wonderful man, always dreamt of Neezam becoming a barrister one day." Rahman continued, "It's Neezam's backing that has made Bodor such a village tyrant."

Drawing a long breath, Professor Rahman said, "Bodor has distributed the Pakistani flag to every house here. He came this morning to our place. I was not home. Selina told him to leave with his Pakistani flag. Morol's excuse for setting up the *Shanti Bahini* Peace Committee's Camp here is it will keep the military away from Sheetalpur. If our own people are against us, how can we free our country?" Looking up, he eyed the Pakistani flags fluttering atop the stores of the Bazaar.

"Are we just going to hold on to our chai? Agartala is where we should head. Only a hundred miles away," said Rafique, his voice rising.

"Hundred miles? Agartala might as well be a thousand miles away. West Pakistani military and collaborators are crawling every inch of the way," said Nazmul.

"Rahman Bhai we may leave in a day or two. Only Samad Uncle knows we are going. We will meet you tonight at your home," Nazmul said.

Rahman wiped his forehead with a handkerchief and said, "Selina and the kids must be worried. I have to go home now. See you tonight." He walked down the slope following a beaten trail and disappeared behind an orchard of jack fruit trees.

Suddenly, two F-86 sabre jets went screaming past overhead, headed towards Narshindhi. Rafique and Nazmul looked up at the sky to see twin vapor trails disappear and within moments, they heard the jets strafing and firing rockets. The noise was unsettling, a distant stuttering growl, followed by booming explosions shaking the tea-stall and rattling its steaming kettle of tea. A short distance away, Narshindhi was in flames.

Shaken out of their dreams of guerrilla training, Rafique and Nazmul ran back to where they had parked Rafique's motorcycle.

Nazmul touched Rafique's arm and motioned with his head.

Bodor Morol and Neezam were coming from the village side approaching the *sheko*, the bamboo balustrade. Rafique and Nazmul stood for a moment watching the precarious bridge bend over the dry canal.

Bunching his *lungi,* Morol scratched his crotch as he walked, jiggled his gluttonous belly, a smirk on his face, a glint in his eyes. Alongside him, Neezam walked wearing an ironed white shirt and cotton pleated pants, expensive brown shoes covered in dust, his hair slicked back. Neezam caught a glimpse of Rafique and Nazmul on the other side of the bamboo bridge through his gold-rimmed aviator sunglasses. A divisive and devious plan had taken root in his brain. And like a bad seed, the evil guile rooted, grew and festered in Neezam's mind.

"Is that not Neezam with the Chairman?"

"Yes," replied Rafique.

"Very cozy, that pig." Nazmul said. His face hardened and his eyes grew cold.

"Yes," Rafique said, his eyebrows furrowed in worry as on the horizon in clear skies storm clouds were gathering.

"Don't say anything," said Nazmul

"No. We should leave," Rafique answered.

Morol and Neezam were placing their feet carefully, one after the other, on the single bamboo pole bridge, hands gripping the sloping rickety railings on either side.

Rafique and Nazmul straddled the motorcycle, kick-started it, and slowly rode on the packed sandy banks of the river towards Nazmul's house in the next town of Joydebpur.

As Rafique's motorcycle faded in the distance, Neezam looked at Morol and said, "Wasn't that Rafique and Nazmul?"

"Yes, sir," Morol said as he stroked his *mehndi* reddened beard, adjusting his white skull cap.

"Those bastards!" Neezam said.

Bodor knew very well what Neezam was up to, knew why Neezam was in Sheetalpur, knew what Neezam needed from him, what he needed from Neezam. With Mustafa Chowdhury gone, Morol would be the village chief.

"Saar this is your one chance in a lifetime. Your Uncle's only heir is Rafique, before Rafique's heir arrives. If Rafique is gone, you will be the sole heir to the Chowdhury property. Don't worry about anything, I am here," Bodor said chewing on a piece of betel nut. Chowdhury had put him to shame in front of the village a year ago for stealing relief blankets. Bodor was going to get even this time. He bit on a particularly hard kernel, thought about Mustafa Chowdhury, then spat out the red juice on the sand.

"Bodor, you can read my mind. I like that," Neezam said as a thin smile crept into his face.

Bodor pulled up his *lungi*, held a corner in his left hand and dug into his Panjabi pocket, taking out a toothpick to clean his teeth, then spat out a morsel of food.

"I have to go to Dacca tomorrow morning for an important meeting. I will come back in two weeks. Can you manage some girls in the meantime," Neezam said.

"Saar, no, no! Not from this village, Neezam Saar. Women, NO! Villagers will kill us both. Managing food is difficult for the military. I promised to villagers that army won't come to this village. Don't touch this village Saar. Also I warn them if anyone from their family joins the *Mukti Fauj* or helps *Mukti*, result won't be good. Look sir how Pakistani flag is flying in the air."

Bodor proudly pointed to the flapping Pakistani flags. The green and white flags fluttered in the wind on bamboo poles stuck atop the stores of Sheetalpur's bazaar, like white flags of surrender to an enemy within.

Bodor whispered, "But I ask Rustom Mian in Narshindi. He snares supplies and grabs girls like chicken." Bodor tittered derisively, his belly jiggled with his snickering.

"Have you been to Rahmans?"

"Yes, Rahman's wife told me to leave, kicked me out."

"How about..." Neezam said.

Even before Neezam could finish his sentence, Bodor interjected, "I don't have guts to step on Chowdhury property. I don't dare face your Uncle Mustafa Chowdhury. He will surely kill me."

Neezam took out a gold cigarette case, pulled out a cigarette, tapped the filter end against his palm, and lit it with a Dunhill lighter. He took a long drag, and blew out a perfect grey ring of smoke that sailed up into the air unbroken.

"Bodor keep your eyes on Rafique and Nazmul," Neezam said, one eyebrow raised.

"I'll keep a close, very close eye," he said leaning close in Neezam's ear. Bodor wiped the folds of his neck with a handkerchief and cursed as he spat out red beetle nut juice on the river bank.

Neezam's face wore a cold, calculated look. He dropped the unfinished cigarette butt and crushed it under the heel of his shoe. "I'll see who has the last laugh!"

Chairman Bodor Morol knows more about his village Sheetalpur than anyone else. He is aware of the delicate political balance between the landowners and dirt poor farmers, between the Hindus and the Muslims and everyone in between. He knows why Chowdhury is giving a *Milad* and who is going to be at the prayer meeting. He is aware of every ripple on the village's surface, the currents below. He knows when there is a *lail* boundary problem brewing and who is starving and who is sleeping with whose wife, and which ripening village girl is secretly running around with whom.

It is how he operated. Sheetalpur was in the palm of his hand.

And so in throat clearing rapport, both men headed to the center of the bazaar as other villagers said their fearful salaams.

❧

A Short Farewell, a Long Goodbye

❧ ❧ ❧

Sheetalpur Village, East Pakistan, late April, 1971

*D*AYS PASSED. FEAR GREW. AND terror spread. Fear grew in Sheetalpur, grew in little villages, grew in big towns. By late April the West Pakistani forces had secured the cities, driven out the rebellious East Pakistani army forces. The few EPR were forced into pockets of resistance, driven and decimated, and the few straggling remnants moved to border areas, remote sites away from the reach of Yahya's killing machine. From Cantonments in the cities, from Dacca, from Jessore, from Khulna, from Chittagong, the West Pakistani military spread like wildfire into the countryside, leaving behind burnt villages, dead bodies, raped women.

People looked away, hurried past, they spoke in hushed tones.

"*Shanti* Peace Committee."

"Collaborator. Careful."

"*Mukti Fauj.*"

Gripping the smooth metal bars of her second floor window, Nahar gazed out into the dying light of gathering dusk. Rafique's grandfather, Mohammed Asgar Chowdhury, had built the grandiose Chowdhury *Bari*, of brick and mortar, lazily spread out on lush green grass, nestled in the variegated greens of lychee, amrool, amlokhi, guava, palm, borooi, betel nut and banana.

127

The distant chatter of Shaliks, the smell of freshly tilled Bhawal earth carried by a soft wind rustled the curtains. On the near distance were hillocks of red Bhawal earth, covered in jack fruit, pineapple and mango orchards. Nahar looked southward over the green water of the large pond, the wide open paddy fields. The breeze blew ripples on the surface of the pond and wonderful memories bubbled to the surface of her mind, memories of time spent by the pond, little cherished words. Sweet memories of a time that now seemed distant and gone. And yet she had been married for just a year.

Nahar closed her eyes. Unsettling, horrific visions of the massacre of Dacca University, of March 25th haunted her.

March 25 had changed everything.

Everything.

Not even a month had passed. After coming back to the village, Nahar had suffered from high fever and flu, bravely and uncomplainingly, convinced that this was the way God wanted it, convinced better days would come. But now that conviction wavered, the flame of hope flickered. Just when she was beginning to recover from shock, Rafique was leaving to fight for his country, to join the *Mukti Bahini*. Now she was living in a recurring nightmare, her world was crumbling about her.

She turned around to look at Rafique's half-packed cotton satchel, clothes, underwear strewn about on the bed. In the morning, Rafique would leave, leave with Nazmul for a guerrilla camp in India. Leave her behind, in a home full of empty rooms. Her face darkened, lips quivered, tears welled up to her eyes. In the unlit room, in the corner, in a jute-twine netted pouch, hung a brightly painted clay vase. On the vase, two colorful parrots sang happily. Nahar thought about Rafique. And herself. She touched a bird, as she thought of Rafique flying far away from her.

These days there was an excitement in Rafique's voice, an obsession about joining the war, fear in Nahar's heart, and much trepidation and anxious worry in Jahanara and Mustafa Chowdhury's minds.

Nahar looked down into the hand-smoothed dirt courtyard, closed on three sides by thatched mud huts.

She sat down on the edge of the large wooden bed, her legs

128

dangling over the edge of a dark chasm. She ran her fingers over Rafique's shirt, as her mind wandered back two years to 1969, *Eid ul Fitar,* the most auspicious day of the year, the day she first met Rafique.

After the morning *Eid ul Fitar* prayers, Nazmul, her neighbor, and his friend Rafique came to visit her at her parents' house on the outskirts of the town of Joydebpur, several miles from Rafique's home in Sheetalpur village. Rafique looked so handsome in his white linen Panjabi, wearing his *Eid* best. From her hiding place behind the door, she stole glances at Rafique.

When he came up to her, he swallowed, cleared his throat nervously. The faint attar of *Eid* hung in the air, and Nahar, blushing, veiled her face in her diaphanous pink *dupatta,* looking down at her toes in her sandaled feet, her heart a fluttering butterfly. Nahar found herself lost in his large brown eyes, in the tilt of his head, his tall stance exuding a certain confidence, a fixed resolve. She smiled, Rafique coughed. Nahar ran upstairs, her heart thrumming in her chest.

Nahar's parents—Shamsher Ali and Sultana—Rafique and Nazmul sat down to a sumptuous *Eid* lunch. At the festive *pilau* rice, goat and beef curries, chicken roasts, sweet vermicelli *shemai* laden *Eid* table, they made small talk as they ate, Nahar's parents inquiring about Rafique's parents, his studies at the University. Rafique was polite, mostly quiet.

Sultana helped serve the *korma, pilau* and goat curry on Rafique's then Nazmul's plates, happiness in her eyes at the sight of the festive *Eid* table set up in front of her, the plates of the men full of food.

Looking at Nahar's mother, Nazmul asked, "Nahar won't eat?"

"Amina," Sultana called out. Amina came at once and she said to her, "Go ask Nahar to come join us." Amina, greatly amused by this lunch, looked at the thin smile on Nazmul's face and scurried off, the tasselled end of her knee length braids swinging like a pendulum behind her. She ran to Nahar's room to tell her that everyone was waiting. Amina found Nahar standing in front of the armoire, applying dark kohl around her eyes. On Amina's words, Nahar sat down on her bed, buried her face in her pillow, crushing it in her hands.

"Go away," she said in a muffled voice. "Tell them I am studying, can't come."

Amina ran back, "Appa said she is studying."

Sultana looked up, amazed that on *Eid* Nahar was studying instead of listening to music or reading a novel. After a moment's hesitation, she said, "OK, don't disturb her. Her exam is soon."

Shamsher Ali, pride in his voice, added, "Nahar is very studious. She placed first in her first-year exams." He continued, "Our wish is that Nahar finish her H.S.C. exam and afterwards attend Dacca University."

Sultana looked at Rafique and said, "After we married off Naila, her older sister, she could not continue her studies. I want Nahar to get an education, stand on her own feet."

Samsher Ali, content, mixed the *korma* and *pilau* on his plate, looked inquiringly at Nazmul, then Rafique, and continued, "Give Nahar some suggestions. What subject would be good for her?"

Nazmul looked up from his plate and said, "Nahar might do well in history; she always loved studying it."

Rafique sat quietly drinking a glass of water. In his mind's eye played the vision of a *dupatta* veiled Nahar, her soft smile, her long lashes fluttering on a blushing face. Carrying a tray of yogurt drink, Amina walked into the dining room and saw Rafique look up, peering into and beyond her face, penetrating into the empty space behind. Amina tried to hide her giggling, covering her lips. Setting down the drinks, she hurried back to Nahar and burst out, "Appa, Appa, Rafique Bhai is looking for you!"

Nahar turned beet red as she looked away beaming. She told Amina to be quiet, her voice suddenly filled with happiness.

That afternoon, walking out of the courtyard, Rafique looked back, gazing into the open windows.

With a sidelong glance at Rafique's face, Nazmul laughed and said, "*Doost*, don't look back, you will fall in love."

"I'm already in love at first sight, Nazmul. Don't worry," Rafique said as his face brightened. Nahar's warm red lips, her deep brown eyes gazing into his, filled his mind.

"Oh that's why you were touching her parent's feet. So many salaams; only a bridegroom-to-be would pay such reverent respects,"

Nazmul said cracking up, as he slapped Rafique on the back. "*Eid Mubarak* Rafique!"

"*Eid Mubarak*," Rafique replied, patting Nazmul on the small of his back, his face colored in embarrassment.

Now, Nahar lay back on the bed, rested the back of her palm on her forehead, let out a breath of held sorrow. Etched into her mind were the months that followed that night, months that were the hardest. Her father died suddenly right after she finished her HSC exam. Nahar's mother became bed-ridden, unable to bear the shock of her husband's sudden death. Rafique's father, Mustafa Chowdhury, came with the proposal of marriage.

Nazmul came with Chowdhury, remembered vividly Samsher Ali's conversation at *Eid* about his wish for Nahar's education. He interjected on behalf of Chowdhury, "*Chachi*, you know after marriage Nahar can continue her studies at the University. I know *Chacha* would have wanted that."

Nahar's sister Naila and brother-in-law Shihab were opposed to her marrying a jobless student leader from the village. They had requested Sultana and Nahar come and stay with them in Chittagong.

"No, it's not right," she had told Naila, not wanting to become the burden of her daughter and son-in-law.

Wiping her tears, Nahar's mother agreed to the proposal, agreed wholeheartedly. Nahar would be safely married, and she could breathe a sigh of relief, their responsibilities now completed, her and Nahar's father's wish for her education fulfilled.

In the shadow of her mother's deteriorating health, Nahar's wedding was arranged in February of 1970. Nahar cried uncontrollably on her mother's neck, holding onto her tightly, full of feelings for a father whom she had dreamt would give her away.

On the palanquin ride from her wedding, she was torn between the past and the future. As the wooden palanquin swayed, carried on the necks of four bearers across the fields, men, women and children stood in front of Sheetalpur village's mud walled thatched homes to view the wedding procession. When the palanquin set down at the Chowdhury *Bari*, Nahar stepped into a new life.

131

Soon after her marriage, her mother died, leaving Nahar completely alone. Rafique was now her world. He was kind and considerate. His parents loving. Nahar became the jewel of her in-law's eyes; they were the shade over her head and Rafique the ground below her feet.

On the edge of the bed, Nahar's feet swung suspended helplessly in space, time stood still. Tears streaming down her cheeks did nothing to soften the hard vicissitudes of her fate.

"Fate," she muttered bitterly.

A stream of tenderness wound through Nahar. The thought of her dead parents, her aloneness in this world flowed through her like a great river without any resistance. She heard herself sob, then she was no longer in control of her tears as they flowed, flooding down her cheeks, wetting the *āchol* of her sari. The tears seemed to dilute something in her, dissolve cysts of sorrow deep within her, cleanse her aching heart. And in the weeping, soft memories swept over her of times sweet, of moments dear.

Nahar looked up to a wedding picture that hung over the bed, the dried wedding rose garland still hanging around it. After her marriage, her cherished memories of Dacca came to her mind.

In March of 1970 Rafique and she had visited the Rahmans, staying at the "honeymoon cottage," a corner bedroom where newlywed students brought their wives for visits to Dacca. Their happiness was infectious; it colored the day and spread to the Rahmans, their children.

Dacca was bigger than life.

Rafique took her to Balaka Cinema Hall, next to New Market, to see *Pitch Dhala Poth, the Tarred Road*. The hard life of Razzak, the hero, an orphan, ends in happiness when he wins Bobita's heart. The whole world and her whole life was in front of Nahar as she stood on those steps of Balaka Hall. Out front of Balaka Cinema was the bazaar. Street hawkers were selling *chanachur, foochka,* and *chotpoti*. The *chanachur* in the newspaper cone, the fried chickpea dough in spices mixed up with mustard oil, puffed rice, peanuts, cilantro, green chiles, onions cut in ever so thin slices. It was spicy, crunchy, tangy, salty and everything tasty.

Happiness came in a used newspaper cone one could hold in the palm of one's hand.

Delicately holding the *foochka* shells, stuffed with a tangy tamarind sauce, Rafique gulped down a few.

The taste bud burning simple pleasures of life.

Now, only a few months later, everything had faded, had become a distant dispersed dream.

Those honeymoon days.

They came back to Sheetalpur together but Rafique had to leave because of his studies. After that Rafique came to visit her for only a few days at a time then left for a month or two.

Alone, newlywed, not quite free with her in-laws, she felt cooped up in the huge Chowdhuri *Bari*. Morning turned into afternoon and dimmed into the still of evening. The light slanted, angled and slanted again from the west on the pages of thick novels and month old newspapers as Nahar sat upstairs, alone in her room, reading, looking longingly out through the bars of her window into an expanse of emptiness.

1971 came. Rafique became busy with politics in Dacca.

Loneliness gnawed inside her every day until finally in the wonderful February of 1971 Rafique returned to Sheetalpur. They rode on Rafique's motorcycle all over the villages and up and down bumpy dirt roads, into and out of deep canals, as she held on tight to Rafique's shoulders. Then came the Sheetalpur *Falgun Mela*, the Fair. Nahar's head spun on the multi-colored wheel, spinning, spinning, the world whirling by. On the way back from the *Mela*, Rafique stopped by the water-lily adorned pond and he blurted out, "Beautiful."

Nahar pushed him from behind. "What's beautiful?" she asked, her eyebrow raised, her offended inquiring gaze fixed on Rafique.

Rafique laughed. "Darling you are my beautiful, you are my beautiful *padma phool*. The first time I saw you, I saw a *padma phool*."

Nahar laughed, bit her lower lip, and said, "What do you feel now?"

"My sweetheart is more beautiful than all the water lilies of the world," Rafique said as he embraced her. "*Padma phool*," he said again and kissed her on the cheek, then on her parted lips.

"Rafique! Stop! What are you doing? People will see. Leave me alone," Nahar said pushing him away, as she ran to sit on the grass at the edge of the pond. The water, the wind rustled in harmony.

"Wait, I want to take a photo of you with those lilies."

She smiled, looked away from his black hair blown back by the wind, his pale blue shirt open at the neck, his chest heaving, his sleeves rolled up.

"Nahar, you want a *padma phool*?" He rolled up his bell-bottom pant legs and waded deep into the pond and picked her a pink water lily.

"Happy anniversary," Rafique had said.

Many an evening they had spent sitting by the pond, idling away the time in conversation.

Then came March of 1971 and Dacca burst out in political upheavals. Rafique wanted to leave alone, but Nahar wouldn't let him. So in the beginning of March, she left with him for Dacca. For Nahar staying at the Rahmans' was a whole new exciting world, a freedom she had never known before.

Surrounded by student politics, in the heart of Dacca University, Nahar came alive. In the afternoons, after helping Selina with the children, she would walk over with Rafique to the women's hall and Modhur Canteen, eagerly listening to the latest news of protests, marches, making posters in night-long parties and savoring the inside scoops of the *Chatra andolon*.

One late afternoon, walking back from Modhur Canteen to the Rahmans' with Rafique and Nazmul, she blurted out, "I want to join politics."

Both Rafique and Nazmul started to joke, to laugh.

Nahar's face reddened. Irritated and agitated, Nahar, her voice rising, added, "You just watch. Don't jeer at me because I am a woman."

"No, no, not that Nahar," Nazmul said, the last light of the day catching a cynical laugh on his lips, "In the procession, tear gas.

Once you swallow some gas you will be choking and running all the way to Sheetalpur!" But Nahar was strong in her convictions, committed to the cause, committed to Bangabandhu.

March 7 came, stirred everyone up. And Nahar joined the women's procession to Ramna.

But March 25th changed everything.

Nahar got up, walked to the window.

"Everything," Nahar said, her lips forming inaudible syllables.

The dying orange hue of dusk disappeared into Nahar's tear-filled eyes. She touched the vase, the painted birds.

"ALLAH BRING MY SON BACK to me safe," Mustafa Chowdhury prayed, his hands clasped together up to the heavens on the green velvet prayer rug pointed towards Mecca. Rubbing his open palms on his peppered beard, slowly, with deliberation, Mustafa Chowdhury sat on the *Jai Namaaz*. His palm rested on the velvet of the prayer worn mat. In the corner hung a painting of his father, Mohammed Asgar Chowdhury, seated, in his fez cap, long black *sherwani*, his right palm resting firmly on an intricately carved wooden walking stick. Mustafa drew a long breath, peered into the eyes of his father, searched for some meaning to the unfolding mayhem of 1971. His younger brother Masud had died in a launch drowning accident four years ago. Now Rafique, his only son, his only child, was leaving for an unknown guerrilla training camp, and Neezam, his only nephew, was his worst enemy. Fighting life's ironies, Mustafa Chowdhury pushed up from the *Jai Namaaz*, walked outside to the veranda and sat on his favorite teak chair.

Broken gray clouds had gathered on the evening horizon. As the wind twirled some leaves on the outer courtyard, as the crickets were starting up a mournful song, a solitary throat-clearing frog joined in.

"Allah," he pronounced slowly, drawn out, reflecting the dilemma he was in. He held onto the long pipe of his unlit hookah made

135

of metal and wood, aquiline and tall. Chowdhury thought about his father, then about his younger brother. He looked across the courtyard into a moonless night, the low banks of fog creeping over the paddy fields.

Jahanara came out of the lantern-lit house and stood by the doorway, her face pale, her eyelids down. She stood quietly.

"Rafique is leaving in the morning," Jahanara finally said, almost in a whisper. Her sari *áchol* looped over her head. Her mouth was dry; she had forgotten to chew on her favorite betel nut.

"Hmm," Chowdhury said gripping onto the pipe.

"Rafique is grown up. He could have left without telling us, but he will not do that."

"Leaving Nahar alone, he wants to go to India. Join the *Mukti Fauj*? But what is there? Right now just a band of kids, no arms. How, Jahanara, do you want me to advise him? Tell me, you are his mother. Tell me." In his heart, if he was young like Rafique, Mustafa too would join the war, fight for a free country.

"It is your responsibility as a father to tell him. Nahar is in pieces. How can we look her in the face? Married for just a year and he will leave her alone, go off to Allah knows where?"

"If you tell him no, he will not even listen to a single word," Chowdhury said.

Both Jahanara and Chowdhury looked out into a dark courtyard. A solitary owl hooted in the distance.

Later in the evening, Rafique came home, exhausted, sweaty from organizing to leave in the morning for Agartala. After finishing a late dinner, he came and stood by his father, leaning against one of the thick *gozari* wooden posts of the veranda.

"You will leave us and fight for whom?" asked his father in a stern voice.

Rafique kept quiet. A bat flitted by, blindly pursuing a bug in the air. "Yes," he finally said.

"You're not going!" Mustafa Chowdhury said in a firm voice, his forehead wrinkled in worry. Mustafa knew his son, knew he would leave, and in his heart he was proud that Rafique was going to join the *Mukti Bahini*.

Rafique did not want to argue with his father. Both men were of their own convictions.

"Well, Abba, I am." Rafique said, his voice sure, loud and rising. He stepped off the veranda, and started to walk out of the courtyard.

Jahanara Chowdhury knew her son well, knew when Rafique had made up his mind to go, he would. She knew it was useless to try to stop him. She thought about Nahar. Nahar who stood inside the door, picking up every word.

Jahanara called out to him, "Rafique."

Rafique stopped, turned his head back, and looked at his mother, her eyes moist. His father sat with a vacant stare on his face, his eyes looking forward, unfocused.

Standing behind her mother-in-law, Nahar watched Rafique pause, turn and slowly walk away, lost in thought.

THE WIND RUSTLED THROUGH THE tops of the palms and twirled the mango leaves by the gnarled roots and the smooth bare earth where in daytime the village children lost themselves hopping to the game of *aka-dootka*. In the lychee tree the night owl called its last and by the *dhenki* hut the raucous rooster crowed its first of the morning.

"Nahar," Rafique whispered, as he held her. "Nahar."

"Hmmm," Nahar replied, in an uneasy sleep.

Rafique hugged her tight and then tighter against his body, squeezing her into him. Her eyes were still closed, her arms twined around him. Rafique crushed Nahar against his chest, kissing her face passionately, her lips, breathing in her sweet musk. Nahar embraced Rafique with longing, longing of that last breath breathed together, of that last warm embrace, frantically fighting that tearing apart of two souls.

"One day, and not too far away, you will see these fields green with the young paddy, and our children will run through them. Free. And we will have our home in Dacca. We will have a family. I will be back Nahar, and we will be together again. I promise."

Nahar held Rafique tighter, said not a word.

"I will come back soon. We will sit next to the pond and I will pick you *padma phool*," Rafique said.

"Sure?"

"Sure."

On the eastern sky, a line of light bloomed. Rafique was now up, getting ready to leave. And Nahar darted about the room like a bird, busy putting some food and clothes into Rafique's satchel.

"Nahar Appa," Amina called out at the door.

"Come in," Nahar said. Amina held some puffed rice and food for Rafique's journey, looked at Nahar's red swollen eyes. Orphaned young, Amina had grown up in Nahar's family since she was only a child. She found a life that she had never dreamt of. When Nahar and Rafique got married, she had come to keep Nahar company at her in-laws. In the love she found first from Nahar's family and now the Chowdhury family, as she comforted Nahar, as she watched Nahar pine for her husband, feelings new and wonderful stirred inside her. She was blossoming from an adolescent girl into a young woman. Amina wondered about what it would be like to be married. To long for someone, to long for someone with every breath. To belong.

Nahar had already sewn a few hundred rupee notes into the folds of the waist of Rafique's brown cotton trousers. He was taking only a small overnight bag with him. In it, he carried two changes of clothes, towels, soap, slippers, two books. Leon Uris's *Mila 18* and Kazi Nazrul Islam's *Sanchayan, Collected Poems*.

Nahar had a brave smile on her face and a lump she could not swallow, tears she could not hide. As he walked out the door, Rafique turned and embraced her, holding her for that last precious moment. Like a river flowing below a tranquil surface, Nahar's pained smile did not betray the currents ripping away at her insides.

She felt her sandaled feet sliding under her on the cold concrete floor as she followed Rafique quietly down wooden stairs.

Rafique stood in the doorway with his bag on his back and with the light of excitement and expectancy in his eyes almost covering the sadness that welled up deep inside. On his mother's smooth cheeks he saw two tears leaving their trail.

Rafique had privately primed himself for a beautiful scene. He had prepared certain sentences, which he thought could be used with touching effect. But his mother's tears destroyed his plans.

"Baba, be careful. Don't think you can win the war by yourself. I know you, Rafique. Use your head and keep clear of trouble."

Rafique bowed down at his mother's feet, touching them lightly. "Rafique, Baba, be very careful," Jahanara said, embracing him, her tear stains on the shoulder of his cotton shirt spreading deep like the pain growing in her heart.

Rafique went out to where his father was sitting on the veranda and touched his feet. Mustafa Chowdhury got up, hugged his son, held him in his arms, his eyes closed in a darkness he could not fathom. "Rafique, Baba, be brave. Allah be with you." Rafique hugged him back, suddenly filled with a feeling of finality.

The April morning sunlight came crimson through the dark clouds, fingering through mango, jack fruit orchards on a red earth hillock in the near horizon. Rafique smelled the good morning wind rippling the green baby paddy, bringing in the odor of damp earth, roots, grass. He stood at the far end of the courtyard and saw his mother holding onto his father, looking lost.

Just then, Nazmul came to the edge of the outer courtyard, and Boochu, Nahar's little brown puppy with yellow spots over his eyes, came and circled him, yelping with pleasure. On a kind word from Nazmul, he wagged his tail excitedly and sat sentry, his tongue dripping with drool.

Halim, the lanky fourteen-year-old who worked for the Chowdhurys, came running.

"Nazmul Bhai, take me with you, please," Halim pleaded.

"Halim, they need you here," Nazmul said, smiled, patted him on the shoulder. "You stay here and take care of them."

"Please Nazmul Bhai, I will do anything, I will carry all your bags, your guns. I can fight. I want to join. Take me with you, Nazmul Bhai," Halim pleaded, his eyes fogged with distant visions of guerrilla camps, of victories, of a road-trip, of unknowns.

Nazmul came up to the veranda where Mustafa and Jahanara Chowdhury stood, bent down and touched both their feet.

"Be safe Baba," Jahanara said gently touching Nazmul on his forehead. "Take care of each other."

"Be brave, but be careful. Keep your eyes open," Chowdhury said and hugged Nazmul.

Rafique choked, emotions now tearing him apart, said, "Let's go, it's getting late," and walked out towards the outer courtyard.

Nahar followed them.

"Don't worry, Nahar, we will be fine," Nazmul said, biting his lower lip, looking away.

Keeping her head down, Nahar looped her sari over her head, hid her face. "Khoda Hafez," Nahar said to Rafique, her voice falling to a whisper.

"Khoda Hafez," Rafique said, as he drew close. He tenderly touched Nahar's hair, reached out to wipe the solitary crystalline tear drop on her cheek that glimmered in the first rays of dawn.

Rafique looked back to see his mother's quivering form. Jahanara raised her tender, luminous tear-filled eyes in a face cast in dark shadows of fear. Rafique, after all the speeches and high talk, bowed his head as Nazmul patted him on his back.

"Halim, take good care of everyone here. Not a word to anyone about us. They will ask. Tell them we went to Dacca," Rafique told Halim.

"Accaha," Halim said, as he carried both Rafique and Nazmul's bags and headed a ways out with them.

Boochu came, and upon a soft word from Rafique wagged his tail and quietly followed behind the three men as they walked into dawn's cold gray horizon. Nahar bit the end of her sari and looked at the painted clay pot swaying ever so slightly. And now only one solitary painted bird showed itself.

Rafique and Nazmul looked back, waved. Nahar stood on the upstairs veranda, a wispy, lonely figure. In her tear glistened eyes, Rafique grew smaller, distant, then disappeared altogether.

Of Guerillas and Refugees

❧ ❧ ❧

April 1971, East Pakistan-India Border

O N THE BORDER, NORTH OF Comilla, a few miles south of Akhaura and Brahamanbaria, lay the sleepy railway station Saldanadi. Quilted by emerald fields, paddy, jute, undulating like a sari hung in a stiff breeze, the Salda river valley cozies up to the gently rising hills of Tripura, India, to the north and east. The Salda cuts through rock and pebble strewn sandy banks, like a writhing snake; it twists and turns, twists and turns cutting into the fertile valleys, finally disappearing in muddy rivulets and vegetation engorged channels.

Parallel rail lines run into Saldanadi rail station, and Rafique and Nazmul followed these tracks, hiding, walking, ears strained, eyes wide open.

"Rafique, you sure? I know we can't take the Akhaura road, but this...this is complete forest. Where does this track lead?" Nazmul asked.

"Ha Noi," Rafique said scratching his week old mottled beard, his rolled-up pant legs now caked in mud, his shirt collar stuck with sweat to the skin of his sunburnt neck.

"Ha Noi?" Nazmul chuckled, plodding beside him.

"Relax, Nazmul. Saldanadi."

"I sure as hell hope the pigs have not set up a checkpoint here.

Every other place is a death trap." On the skin of his face, Nazmul felt the scorching midday heat beating down.

"I hope not. That's what those guys we met told me last night. Best way to cross the border is over to Sonamura, across the jungle, bit south of Agartala. The roads to Agartala are too closely watched. We would never make it on the Akhaura road."

"Fucking bastards would kill us in a second. How far you think Rafique?"

"With luck, another day."

On the road for a week, they passed many refugees and little bits and pieces of information had helped them survive, bypass deadly checkpoints. On their backs swung the satchels once full with food, now only holding a few meager clothes, books, the bare necessities.

Both men were dressed in cotton bell-bottom pants, cotton shirts. Rafique's curly hair was greasy and matted down, Nazmul's face pale and his short hair disheveled after a week of walking, riding on broken down buses, traveling on open country boats, hiding and sleeping under open skies, under the canopy of trees.

"My feet are killing me," Nazmul said, as he touched the blisters on his bare feet. The lower part of his shoe had given in halfway during the journey and now he found himself walking barefoot.

This remote undulating border frontier valley is usually sleepy. Usually, but not today. Today, bypassing the Pakistani army checkpoints, zigzagging over fields and across rivers, thousands of desperate refugees were headed to Agartala and India, for the refugee camps, for safety. And with them a sprinkling of men, young and old, seeking a free Bangladesh, headed into guerrilla country.

"Our lives, our struggle for *Shadhinata*, freedom, seems to be like these parallel rail tracks," Rafique said as he gazed down the tracks disappearing into the distant horizon.

"How?" Nazmul asked. Rafique a little taller, walked in front, quicker of step, eager to get to the guerrilla training camps. Behind him Nazmul followed, and knowing full well Rafique's hot headedness, said little.

"The tracks are so close, yet never meet. Always at the same exact distance. Will our struggle always be so close yet so far from victory?"

144

His happiness seemed always so close, yet far away, happiness left behind in Sheetalpur, left behind with Nahar and his parents.

"We will be victorious Rafique. Certainly. Yahya cannot just kill us like animals and get away with it."

"He is."

"For now. But not for long," Nazmul said.

Approaching the sinuous Salda, Rafique and Nazmul stepped over the rail tracks, down into the open field. It had rained the night before, just a light steady rain before the coming monsoons in the next months, but the fields were muddy. Down the railroad embankment and into the green grass the two men plodded, their muddy bell-bottom pants rolled up to their knees. Long moist grass stems crunched beneath their feet.

On the horizon, on a slight rise, they saw a cement signpost set on two white concrete pillars. Large letters on top declared in Bengali "Saldanadi" and again in smaller type on the bottom line, first in English and then in Urdu.

"Thank Allah, we are on the right path," Nazmul said, reassured by the sign.

"That first line in Bengali is written in the blood of '52. If it was not for the martyrs of the *Bhasha Andolon,* Bengali language movement, then we would not be seeing Bengali on that signboard. Now in '71 we will finish this fight. Wipe that Urdu off the signboard," Rafique said his voice rising, emotion-filled.

"You think if we were in some remote frontier desert town in the Sind in West Pakistan, we would see their village name in Bengali?" Nazmul asked.

Rafique looked at the sign, started to laugh hysterically at the deep colonization of East Pakistan by the West Pakistani Junta.

"We will be free, free," Rafique said confidently. "Like Bangabandhu said, *Ebarer songram shadhinatar songram.* This battle is for freedom."

Exhausted and hungry, Rafique and Nazmul walked with the refugees moving in endless streams towards the Indian border. And this refugee world moved east, west and north, pushed into India, trying to tear away from the talons of Tikka Khan. On the side of the beaten down road were discarded bottles, empty sacks, lives thrown into the dirt, whipped by the wind. Bits of lost lives tangled in the thick underbrush, people perished by the side of rutted roads.

Rafique peered into the tree-shaded darkness of the trail. In a jagged thicket of weeds, under an arching bush of bamboo, he caught a glimpse of dogs tearing at something.

"Nazmul, wait, wait," Rafique said as he edged to the thick underbrush by the trail leading from the tracks towards the river bank. There lay a dead body, an arm stuck out, the torso being pulled and ripped apart by rabid stray dogs, barking and fighting amongst themselves, tearing at the flesh.

"Nazmul, it's a body."

"What?"

"A body."

Rafique strode closer to the body and Nazmul followed fearfully behind him, covering his nose with his hand, trying not to breathe in the stench.

"We need to bury him."

"We can't stop, Rafique. Not now."

"Nazmul, that's a human being."

"We wait around here and next thing someone will come up and shoot us. Look, Rafique. Up the way there are hundreds of people by the river; we need to save the living. We can't wait around here." A cold shiver went through Nazmul as he looked at the bits of torn flesh.

Rafique raised his hands, his helplessness pouring out in anguished prayer. Nazmul joined him. After asking Allah for forgiveness, praying for the lost soul, Nazmul pulled Rafique away down the beaten path. They pounded the dirt trail towards the river bank where hundreds of refugees had already gathered, huddled together, exhausted, hungry.

"Better help the one's still alive," Nazmul said patting Rafique on the back.

Walking alongside the refugees, they found a woman, barely twenty, her husband killed by the military. She was desperately trying to help her father-in-law of eighty hobble along, in her arms a baby not even a year old. When Rafique and Nazmul came upon them, they had collapsed by the side of the river, in the shade of an arching tree. The young woman's face was remote and removed, her eyes inward.

"*Amar shob shahsh, amar shamira maira falshe.* I have lost everything. They killed my husband," she sobbed, her hands covering her face. The old man's wrinkled face was wasted with hunger, gaunt, weary and drawn.

As the other refugees kept on walking by, Rafique took the baby from the mother's arms, put it in a shawl slung like a hammock across his shoulder. The baby gurgled and whimpered, too weak to cry. Nazmul helped the old man up. The man limped heavily with a sprained right ankle. Again they stopped. Nazmul found a bamboo, borrowed a machete, cut and shaped it into a walking stick for him.

"Baba, may Allah grant you a long life," the old man said, his eyes dim and distant, a weary war-worn toothless smile on his sunburnt face.

For the next few hours, Rafique and Nazmul would switch between carrying the baby and the jute sack-wrapped clothes, rice and lentils. The baby whimpered, cried, and then would stop, too tired to continue crying. Exhausted, approaching mid-afternoon, they searched for a little shade. By the base of a large tree that blocked the breeze, Rafique fashioned an earthen stove, digging a small hole into the earth, then cutting a deep groove for branches. Nazmul gathered a few branches and twigs. They lit the twigs, fanning the sooty smoke that billowed as a fire crackled to life. With only one small aluminum pot, they cooked a little rice that the woman was carrying, poured it into a banana leaf, then put the lentils in to boil, making a watery *daal*. "Food!" Rafique said, relieved, a smile breaking through sweat, dirt and soot on his hungry face. In the river, they washed their faces, cleaned themselves.

Squatting under the shade of a tree, they ate together with the old man. In a far off corner, under the cover of her sari, the woman first gave the child her breast, then ate the single meal of the day from a banana leaf. Like a stone she sat in the shade, holding the baby in her arms.

"Tastes better than any *Eid* festival of *pilau* and lamb curry," Rafique said, as he licked his fingers dry.

"Never have I had a better tasting *daal*," Nazmul said, slurping it, relishing every last little morsel.

The old man came up, gently touched Nazmul then Rafique on the arm, thanked them, said his goodbyes.

"*Khoda* bless you," the old man said, a gleam of hope returning to his eyes. "*Amar natire tomra bachaiso*. You have saved my grandson," he said, tears rolling down his creased cheeks as he thought about his murdered son.

The woman looked at Rafique then Nazmul, clasped the child. Gratitude and thankfulness glinted in her eyes. Rafique and Nazmul parted, leaving the family with other refugees.

"Rafique, we need to find a place for the night. We can't go any farther today, and my feet are blistered," said Nazmul cursing, pulling the scab off another blister, as he saw only more rising hills and deeper forests ahead.

"Shsssh. Quiet Nazmul, I hear something," Rafique said apprehensively as they came to a clearing. A covey of Shaliks, bright yellow-beaked with shiny black and brown feathers, chittered and flurried, flitted in a high arching Sal tree branch, twitching their white undertails rhythmically. Rafique stopped, looked up at the darkening sky, and then seeing no one, continued to walk down to the edge of the river.

"*Haramir baccha* collaborators, Shanti Bahini, fucking Peace Committees, are everywhere! Everywhere," Nazmul said with bitterness.

"We are almost there," said Rafique.

"Yeah?" said Nazmul, his two feet festering sores.

"Yeah, a day's more walk to India, then the fun starts," Rafique said as he looked down the river for shelter for the night.

"More curves to this river than a woman!" Nazmul said as he tried to keep up with Rafique.

The banks were dense with life, lined with towering Garjan, Kanak, Chamal and Sal trees, and a *Lalmukh Bandar*, Red-faced monkey, swung from the green canopy, screeching, almost mocking them as it hung from the branches above. A jungle Mayna rustled from its nest, glided down and across the river.

Nazmul and Rafique stood for a moment in the thick of brush, surrounded completely by the green tropical forest, the bamboo, the banana, the earthy smell of rain on brown sweet clay, the mist blanketing the hills and the Salda babbling in front of them. The place was beautiful beyond imagination—dense, towering, tangled, impenetrable, impermeable, impassable jungle. The tops of the tall trees met high above, forming a thick green-vaulted ceiling.

"I sure hope those guys gave us the right information," Nazmul said, worry crossing his brow. "Hill-station just south of Agartala, hmm? I hope they are right."

As Rafique looked down the winding bank, around the next bend he saw an abandoned house, a speck, a stationary spot on the lens of his pupil. With the setting sun, they walked to the crumbling house, damp and overgrown with green algae and trees that covered the top of the exposed terra cotta facade. Stone steps went down to the river and the place was overrun with vines.

Inside, the air was stale. Exhausted, they collapsed in a far corner.

"Shit, sure is a spooky place!" Nazmul said. He swallowed hard and his pupils grew large as he looked at Rafique.

"Where else are we going to spend the night?" Rafique said as he made himself comfortable, laying down, pillowing his satchel.

The day had faded almost imperceptibly, the gloom deepening slowly into a clammy thick darkness. A cold white mist crept in from the surrounding hills like a great wet shroud. As night fell the house came alive, the strange sounds of an owl, the squeak of a rat, the shrill cry of a nesting bird.

In the dark starless night the river rustled like bare feet on grass. A bull frog burped, babbled, croaked. On the far side another answered and nearby another agreed, now in chorus.

"I don't want to spend the night here," said Nazmul.

"Relax Nazmul, we will be fine. I have a *biri*," Rafique said lighting it after a few tries. "You want a puff?"

"Yeah, sure." Nazmul said. Rafique passed it to Nazmul. Nazmul puffed, drew deep on the *biri*, the sharp smell filling their little corner.

"Now that we are, away from civilization, this war is becoming very clear, Nazmul. How green, how rich this land is; no wonder they won't let us have our freedom!"

In the mist-shrouded night, Rafique walked outside and squatted to take a piss. Just behind him he heard a sharp prolonged hiss. He turned his head slowly, focusing into the darkness, then into the cobra's tiny venomous eyes gleaming in a held anger, the flaring nostrils, the thin tongue flickering in between the curved dripping fangs. It arched, drew its neck back like a drawn bow, pointed, aimed. Then a flash.

Rafique jumped. The snake missed, reared back angrily like a snapping whip, struck again as he ran for the other end of the stone steps.

Shaken, Rafique stood shuddering on the steps of the abandoned house, lit another *biri*, breathed hard, puffed, blew the smoke into the air. He contemplated his life, Nahar. His own life had turned deadly, into this sinuous serpentine Salda river, full of surprises, constantly changing. What was Nahar doing in Sheetalpur? How were his parents? A bad premonition overcame him. And what were Bodor Morol and Neezam up to?

"I hope they are OK," Rafique said.

Nazmul looked at Rafique, took in a deep breath, exhaled. "I hope so too. Our worst enemies are these fucking collaborators."

Rafique sat by the river smoking the *biri* down to a stub, lost in thoughts about Nahar, his parents. He flicked the butt into the water, and listened to it slowly die out in an elongated fizz.

BEFORE THE FIRST LIGHT OF day, Rafique and Nazmul started on the last leg of their hike across the border into India. Bleary, Nazmul's eyes turned to the horizon in an infinite yearning. An invisible line had to be crossed to find shelter, a promised rest, regrouping, retribution, revenge, the fight for freedom.

They waded across a shallow section of the river bed. Dawn's cold blue gave way to the sun's warm crimson streaks. On the one road punctuating the fields and forests, on the journey into guerrilla country, in the quagmires of mud, the thousands who walked with them became family. Most of the refugees clung together, scared like sheep. They followed each other close, afraid to leave the dirt trail; there were persistent rumors of attacks, ubiquitous collaborators, thieves and dacoits picking off stragglers.

Nearing the border, Rafique and Nazmul felt a new burst of courage, a burst of energy. Tired and starving, Rafique turned around, walked backwards, arms spread out wide, and began to recite a poem he had just composed, a note of excitement in his rising voice,

> *"Oh ye lost stranger, burning in the sun, crumpled in the shade,*
> *The landscape beckons you with outstretched arms,*
> *On the horizon is the border*
> *Crawl, walk, claw to the other side,*
> *Death unfolds by the roadside,*
> *Darkness finds you weak, cold, hungry, homeless,*
> *The land beckons you with open arms*
> *On the horizon is the border,*
> *Oh ye lost stranger,*
> *Crawl, walk, claw to the other side,*
> *Freedom awaits just over the horizon.*

He was stopped by the sounds of a lanky man's hand-claps.

"Bah! Bah! Baash!" called out the emaciated man in a hoarse voice, his eyes blood-shot in his sunken, gaunt face. Both Rafique and Nazmul said their hellos, but the man, in his late twenties, said little, trudging along with them.

"Bhai, your name?" Nazmul asked.

After a quarter mile of a lumbering silence, he replied, "What's in a name? If no one is left to call you, names are worthless. Worthless."

Something smoldered dangerously in his eyes. In a trudging silence like walking in a graveyard, in a few phrases from two others who traveled with him, Rafique and Nazmul found out that this was Jewel, a man who had lost his wife, baby daughter, father, mother at the hands of the West Pakistani military.

Everyone.

"Bhai, are you joining the *Mukti Fauj?*" asked a sun baked, stocky

151

young man, Khalid, no more than nineteen, wearing a *lungi*, carrying a jute satchel, bare feet slippered in callused cracked soles, a farmer's son. In his heart-felt open laughter, in his wide innocent brown eyes echoed the simple soul of the Koel's song, the Doel's chitter.

Together walking with them were young men, some barely fifteen, students, teachers, farmers and peasants driven by hatred, passion and pain, seeking the hidden guerrilla camps just setting up on the border.

Once into India, past the patrols of Indian Army, safe, the dust hung like a ribbon on the road over thousands of refugees seeking safety. The Tripura sun beat down on the men. This was new ground, safe Indian territory, their visions for a free Bangladesh now brighter.

—❧—

BLISTERED FEET, HUNGRY, EXHAUSTED, RAFIQUE and Nazmul hobbled into the guerrilla camp a few miles south of Agartala.

They first registered at the refugee camp for a ration card. The guerrilla camp, a hilly, forested station. There they found Captain Jahangir, formerly of the East Pakistan Rifles. The young man in his early thirties, tall and sinewy, wearing a khaki uniform and brandishing a handlebar moustache, eyed Nazmul and Rafique in contained amusement. He looked them up and down, sizing them up along with the other young men who were now trickling into camp. "Did you take the journey, or did the journey take you?" asked Captain Jahangir to Rafique in a voice filled with mirth.

"I think the journey has taken me!" replied Rafique, and they both laughed looking down at the torn shoes Nazmul was holding, his feet raw, blistered.

Captain Jahangir looked at the men around him as they fell into line. They in turn watched him with unblinking eyes in determined faces. Repeating after Captain Jahangir's loud, commanding voice, Rafique, Nazmul, Jewel, Khalid took the oath along with two dozen other eager *Mukti Bahini* recruits, their loud voices resonating in excitement.

In the name of Almighty God,

I pledge allegiance to the lawfully created democratic
Government of Bangladesh.
I pledge to defend the integrity and freedom of my
motherland with the last drop of my blood!

Captain Jahangir held his Sten gun high in the air, screamed, "Joy Bangla!"

And the men repeated, "Joy Bangla," in a resounding chorus resonating through the tall Sal trees into the dense, echoing back in the frenzied calls of the wild, the birds, the monkeys seemingly woken up from silent shadows of the jungle.

"At any cost we will fight till we annihilate the enemy, rid our mother land of murderers!" Captain Jahangir yelled out to the men.

"Annihilate!" Jewel cursed with a fierce animal-like hatred.

The men stood shoulder to shoulder wearing *lungis* and shirts, pants and cotton singlets, *gamchas* and Panjabis. But they all breasted a common emotion.

Freedom and revenge.

They saluted the green, red and yellow flag of Bangladesh fluttering on the bamboo pole. In their eyes, young and old, burned the desire for freedom.

"Power comes from becoming the change," Captain Jahangir said to Rafique. "To do something you must give your heart, soul and life. Everything. Nothing less will do. You Rafique, you Nazmul, you Jewel, you yourself must become the change."

Like the slogan of *Joy Bangla*, like the fiery line of Bangabandhu, '*Ebarer songram muktir songram, ebarer songram shadhinotar songram,*' the passion in Captain Jahangir's voice was contagious.

Rafique, Nazmul now joined with Jewel, Khalid, Monzu, Nantu, Tajul, Altaf, Murad, Khosru, Hellal, Alam, Atta, Firoz, Hasan, Tanvir, Sonil, Raja, Hanif and Karim.

In this remote hill-station, they slept the first night under the open skies as insects and worms crawled over them.

Days later tents were pitched, but they had no pots or pans or utensils. Medical supplies were sparse and dysentery rampant. Used empty grenade shells became utensils. When Brigadier Pandey of

India visited their camp, he offered them plates and utensils.

"Give us guns and bullets instead," was the unanimous request by the *Mukti Bahini*. With every breath, the guerrillas clung onto their tenuous dreams. Hungry for freedom, these young men craved guns and grenades. Filling their bellies with cupped handfuls of pond water, smoking to kill their appetite, these men survived on one meal a day, nourished by that common dream, that common want, that common desire: freedom.

And in their shortened *lungis* and barefoot, they ran, shot and shouted in tongues of fire and fists of fury. Disheveled, disheartened young men became determined, driven *Mukti Bahini* guerrillas.

Here in this remote camp they felt safe. Away from the reach of the butchers from West Pakistan, they could regroup. All day and into each night, the talk, the laughter, the camaraderie, the jokes filled the air, lightened thoughts about home.

"Bamboo staves for training," Nazmul said.

"Wait, soon we will soon get arms," Rafique answered.

"We are still on March 7th, Ramna Race course standing," Jewel complained bitterly. "Barely any arms beyond these .303 rifles."

Next day Captain Jahangir taught them the basics of using a .303 WWII vintage rifle, the wood polished by a hundred hands, the trigger pulled a thousand times.

"Older than my grandfather," Nazmul quipped, gripping the trigger tightly, pointing and practicing.

During one of their exercises, they were on the ground crawling on their elbows under barbed wire, when Nazmul broke out laughing, "Your ass is showing Rafique! Your pants are ripped."

"Shit!" Rafique cursed. Khaild, overhearing this, came to the rescue.

"Don't worry Rafique Bhai," Khalid said as he ran back to his tent and brought Rafique one of his *lungis*.

"Khalid, what will you wear?" Rafique asked.

"Don't worry. I have one more," Khalid replied.

Rafique was used to pajamas, not *lungis*. Khalid took his *lungi*, untwisted it, shook it holding it like a hoop, pulling it tight around his waist then with a snap of his wrist, tightened the *lungi* into a knot. Twisting the unfurled end of his ankle length *lungi*, Khalid pulled it up between his legs, tucked it behind, transforming it into a short loincloth.

Nazmul cracked up as Rafique tried to properly tie the *lungi*. "Rafique, seems to me you lost to a *lungi*. What will you do against the military? Scare them off by showing your bare ass!"

Even Jewel, always quiet and somber, cracked up at this joke, a smile appearing on his lips.

A Sergeant Major trained the boys in small arms, while a Professor of Victoria's college ran the operations of the camp. The training period was very short—only four days.

After the basic training, Rafique was given a Sten gun: short brown metal, cheap, ugly and very deadly at short range. Light and small, Rafique liked that it was easy to hide under a chador. The hot moist metal warmed against him. The touch of metal against his skin gave him hope. It was automatic WWII arms and a grade up from the .303 Lee Enfield Rifles that the rest of the *Mukti Bahini* had. He felt power in the long magazine of 9mm bullets. He rubbed the barrel, felt it warm in his hands, and visions of revenge grew in his eyes.

Early next morning, springing to his feet, Rafique crawled to the front of the tent, where the bamboo pole held up the canvas. The guard stood holding a cup of tea, a .303 rifle in his other hand. Beyond him, the rest of the guerillas were gathered around the campfire, eating a little breakfast, smoking cigarettes and eagerly listening to the small battery-powered radio perched on a metal ammo case, crackling, hissing and coughing out news.

Rafique chewed on a Neem branch, then used the bristles to brush his teeth. He spat out the bitter taste.

Nazmul gave him a tin mug full of hot piping tea, and Rafique nodded a thanks.

They sat on their haunches, facing each other, blowing on the hot tea and dipping a dry hard old toast biscuit into the brew.

"Cigarette?" Nazmul asked. Rafique took out his last Charminar cigarette, a strong flavored smoke with a four pillared Minar on the box, handed it to Nazmul. Nazmul lit it and handed it to Rafique.

Puffing on the cigarette, Rafique spat out into the dirt and said,

"I know the fight is going to be hard, but look at the situation. No fucking asshole wants to support us. We barely have any arms. Not enough food. Little medicine. You know a poor Bangladeshis life is worth nothing. Dogs and cats, animals, have more value that our lives, Nazmul. Fucking bastards."

A rice gruel, thick and salty, was breakfast. Sometimes they were lucky to eat a concoction of vegetables and fish. At times, for breakfast, they would eat leaven bread and grams used as horse-feed. Lunch was usually watery lentil soup and rice, and more often than not there were leeches floating in the liquid. They casually picked them out, continued to eat.

"Better see if there's anything to eat. Two days since we had any *bhat*. What I would not give for a little rice and *daal,* some of my mother's *tangra macher dopeaza*. Even smoking does not kill this hunger anymore," Nazmul said.

Rafique and Nazmul finished drinking the morning tea, washed the two tin cups in pond water, the only ones they had. They handed them to two other guerrillas so that they could drink the brewing tea that had to serve for breakfast, maybe even lunch.

Later in the week they learned how to operate the submachine guns, how to charge grenades and prepare a bomb, how to swim across rivers without getting the weapons wet, holding them up high above their heads. They learnt how to clean the weapons and keep them clean of mud and dirt and water and how to plug the gun barrels against mud.

After the morning exercises, exhausted Rafique, Nazmul, Khalid, Jewel and a few others lay under the expanse of a large Sal tree, the smell of crushed grass under them, the air filled with a rich medley of inexhaustibly varied notes full of chirping, churring of Shaliks, sparrows. Khalid had a gamcha over his face, shading himself from the sharp Tripura sun cutting in through the leaves.

"Cigarette?" Jewel asked.

"*Biri,*" Khalid said, handing him a stubby leaf-wrapped *biri*.

Jewel lay on his back drawing in deep on the *biri*, blowing out the earthy acrid smoke.

"Jewel Bhai, your shooting was perfect. I think you will become our leader," Khalid said.

"Just give me a chance," Jewel swore under his breath. "Just one chance."

Dead leaves lay about rustling in the wind.

"My back!" Nazmul complained.

"My knees are scraped," Rafique added.

"Forget that, my belly is killing me," Khalid said.

Rafique turned on to his stomach and pillowed his arms. He dreamt of holding Nahar.

They men talked about homes, their villages and towns, their enemies and worries about their families they left behind.

"Ma's food tastes so good. There's magic in her hands," Kahlid said, remembering her cooking. He closed his eyes, took a deep breath, smelling the good food, the sweet earth, fish, rice, curries his mother made on festival days. "Ahhh," he sighed.

The men talked, reminisced about family, wives, remembered the ones they yearned to return to.

Finally, Jewel rubbed his index finger on his thumb, said, "I remember the silky spiral ringlets on my little daughter's forehead."

The wind rustled a bit.

"Jewel Bhai, is anyone left?" Khalid finally asked.

"All dead," Jewel said, his face wrenched in pain. "Collaborators, they pointed out our home. Killed my father, mother, only sister. My wife, my little daughter."

Jewel thought about the last time he touched his daughter's soft ringlets; her giggle echoed in his ears. His eyes filled with a sad unutterable expression of despair and hate. Revenge etched hard lines on his face.

The men were quiet, smoking the *biris*. Jewel sat up, the lines of his face now drawn in anger. He flicked away the butt of his biri, said, "In the historic battle of the Polashi war on June 23 1757, we lost because of Mir Jafar, one traitor who sided with Lord Clive and the British. Now we have hundreds of thousands of Mir Jafars. We need to annihilate all of these bastards."

"Now in Bengal there are thousands of Mir Jafars with the Shanti Bahini. They are your neighbors. Bangladeshi Brutus, you are the

Mir Jafars of today," Nazmul said.

Jewel muttered in a broken voice, his words slow, deliberate, "I held her, my body red with her blood, her forehead blown off by a fucking Pakistani butcher's bullet."

In a hoarse whisper he said,

"From my baby's eyes,
My tears red blood today,
My tears red blood today..."

—⁊⅀—

EVENING GLOW SHOWED THROUGH THE tied back flaps of the tattered canvas tent, propped up on each end by a short bamboo pole. Outside crackled the crimson of a campfire, eager faces cursed at a hand of cards or howled in happiness at what luck shone on them in a guerrilla camp of uncertainties. Now and then an excited voice cut through the soft overtone of the multitude. In the background someone played a harmonica, sounding a phrase over and over, trying for effect, reaching for that elusive feeling that floated away in the Tripura night.

Rafique and Nazmul, perspiring after a long walk from town, came into the darkening tent together. Rafique dropped the spotty yellow jack fruit in one corner of the tent with a thud.

"Whew, easily fifty pounds," Rafique said panting, wiping the sweat off his brow. The thick gnarled stem dripped rubbery white sap.

Nazmul, who had helped carry it part of the way, wiped his brow, sat down and inspected the large fruit; "Not quite ripe. Early, real early in the season, Rafique."

"Still, it's breakfast in a few days," Rafique said, his voice excited, his mouth salivating at memories of past feasts on jack fruit in Sheetalpur. "We only need a piece of bamboo shoved by the stem end to ripen it. Get Khalid, he'll know what to do." Rafique sat down, leaned and then stretched back flat on his back.

Nazmul came back shortly with Khalid who brandished a *daow* and curiously held a piece of bamboo in his hand.

"Rafique Bhai, you called?" Khalid asked. But before Rafique could answer, Khalid's nose perked up catching the slight fruity scent. His eyes widened as he saw the large jack fruit in the far corner. "*Kathol*, Jack fruit!" he muttered and like a fly to a feast he made for the fruit.

"Yes, let's ..." Rafique said, but before he could finish, Khalid went to work. He took the machete and whittled the bamboo stake expertly into a sharp point and shoved the stake into the stem end. He twisted it in, his hand now sticky from the white sap.

"Twenty-five paisas for breakfast for the whole crew, what do you think Khalid?" Rafique asked, a sense of victory in his voice.

"Great Rafique Bhai. No problem. Now this will ripen up quickly. We can have it for breakfast in maybe two, three days," said Khalid as he wiped the sap from his fingers and the machete on the grass just outside the tent flap. "Oh, before I forget, Jewel Bhai swapped his book for one he thought you might want to read. He went to Agartala and left the book with me. Just give me a second," Khalid said. He ran out of the tent and came back in a flash, holding a well-thumbed, slightly torn paperback in his hand.

"Jewel Bhai gave me this," Khalid said as he handed Rafique the book. "*Bideshi boi*, Foreign book."

Rafique's eyes widened. He looked at the book as if discovering treasure. "*The Wall* by Sartre. Wow what luck. I was just talking to Jewel about philosophy last night. This I have to read," Rafique said, his voice rising, running his fingers over the cover in admiration.

"Thanks Khalid. Scored big today," Rafique said looking at Nazmul. "Food for the belly, food for the mind. What more can a man want?"

Khalid lingered, sat next to the two men.

"Rafique Bhai, you know a lot, you can read, write English, Bangla?" said Khalid, a wanting coming into his eyes.

"Sure," Rafique answered.

"Rafique Bhai, everyone here writes home. Can you write a letter for me to my mother? I can't read or write. Never had a chance to learn," Khalid said looking down in shame.

Rafique patted him on the back, "Khalid, you are so smart, good with your hands. You know more about farming, about this earth, by doing than many men I know who spent all their days with their heads stuck between the pages of books. What do you want to tell your mother?"

"Just that I am OK and not to worry," Khalid said. "I will see her soon."

"Sure. Nazmul give me that piece of paper," Rafique said. "Go ahead, say what you want and I will write it for you, Khalid."

"Ma, *amaar salaam neeo*, my salaams. I am fine and have many good friends. Don't worry, I will return home soon," Khalid said, then he scratched his head for a second, searching for words, emotions flooding his mind. "Rafique Bhai, you keep the letter, when I think of something good, I will tell you and you please put it in, OK?"

"Sure Khalid," Rafique said as he folded the piece of paper with the few lines and stuck it in his shirt pocket.

Khalid, his face beaming with pride at having written part of a letter declaring his successes to his mother, jumped up and scurried out to see what was about by the small fire outside.

"I'm starving," Nazmul said, as he lay down on a piece of blue plastic tarp, stretched over wet, cold ground and looked up at the night sky through the tattered holes in the tent. Like the tent, his dreams of a free Bangladesh were still in pieces. From his pocket Rafique took a moist box, a red and blue butterfly labeled matchstick box, built like a tiny drawer. After three broken moist match sticks, he finally lit one. Cupping the precious flame, Rafique lit the cloth wick of the kerosene lamp. Nazmul raised the wick a tad and shook the last of the kerosene in the bottom of the lamp, trying to squeeze out a little light. A bubble of yellow formed around the two men, the rest of the tent drowned in shadows.

Rafique, his belly grumbling in hunger, wrapped his *gamcha* around a brick, and putting his head on it, squinted in the flicker of the yellow light at French existentialism.

"Something about reading French philosophy with your head on a brick makes it that much clearer," Rafique chuckled, as he brushed away the insects and moths that came to settle on the damp pages.

Rafique read in the splashed yellow light and flickering shadows, about the town in Spain and of Pablo Ibbieta, the guerrilla—the town next door and a continent away. He swatted at mosquitoes, breathed in the fruity smell of the jack fruit now filling the tent, salivated and continued reading about fighting a war that was a continent away, yet seemed very much the war Rafique was part of. What would it be like to be Pablo's comrade?

The singing, the card game died out and in its place the sounds of the night slowly crawled into the tent. Owls, frogs, monkey calls pierced the thick Tripura darkness. In the clear night a white half-withered moon brought little light, little hope. The wailing wind was moist, heavy and singing over the pond into the clefts of the hills.

— ꝛ —

"NAZMUL I FINISHED READING *The Wall*."

"Why do you need philosophy, French at that, in Agartala, Rafique?"

"Philosophy, Nazmul, philosophy is the core of our fight. The difference between these West Pakistani animals and us." Rafique squirmed on his back, then continued, "It's set in the Spanish civil war, and 'The Wall' is the wall where the revolutionaries are stood up and shot. Now get this: Pablo Ibbieta, the hero, along with two others in his cell, is sentenced to be shot. He is offered a chance at freedom if he collaborates and gives the location of his comrade, Ramón Gris. Well, he gives the authorities a false address. What the heck, he will go free and his friend is not there, right? But guess what? His friend has moved to the false address he gave! Ramón Gris is shot and Pablo is spared." Nazmul was quiet, Rafique then said, "What do you think Nazmul?"

"How ironic. Sounds like one of our squealing rats right here, Rafique. You know the worst enemy is the enemy within."

"But he thought it was a wrong address."

"So what the fuck, his comrade is dead, isn't he? False address or not. Collaborator, defector, fucking bastard. Just like a *makaal faal*, a fake melon, looks great outside, but tastes horrible inside."

"Yes, but that's Sartre for you! Lies spoken today can become the truth in the future! "

"How about truth today becoming lies tomorrow?"

"Can happen. Actually happens all the time."

"Reading Sartre to the smell of ripening jack fruit, a brick for a pillow, what a life, Nazmul!"

"You be Sartre, I'll be asleep."

"Nazmul let me borrow a piece of paper."

"What happened to your diary?"

"Filled up. Wrote all last night."

"What the hell you write? Love letter to Nahar?" Nazmul said, a mischievous twinkle in his eye. He looked in his satchel, found his notebook, tore out a piece of paper and handed it to Rafique. "Here."

"Thanks!"

"The story sounds great, but right now it's our blood that is flowing and Tikka's bastards are feasting in the Cantonments. But our time will come. Soon. Very soon," Nazmul said as he rolled over, exhausted, hungry, and soon asleep.

—⁂—

DEEP INTO THE CLEAR TRIPURA NIGHT, Rafique lay awake, and in the hilly air a cut glass star twinkled in through a hole in the canvas. Rafique and Nazmul's was the only tent lit against an impenetrable shroud of clammy darkness wreathed in tendrils of fog and mist.

Nahar's smile flashed up in his mind, her eyes two sparks reflecting the evening star. Rafique could hear Nahar's soft, shy lyric voice in his heart, the tones rising and falling in sweetness, the curious music of her chosen words tripping out in fluted notes. "Nahar Sultana," a shy voice whispered into his ear. He thought about the first time she said it. Lying on his stomach, making a clipboard of *The Wall*, he laid a piece of paper on top of the book and started to write. The golden butterfly of the lantern flame flickered on the lined paper.

Tuesday April 27, 1971

Dearest Nahar,
With Allah's help you will get this letter. And with all my heart I hope you, Abba and Amma are safe.

We are fighting a just war. And we will win this war. Pray for us all.

I hope to be with you in a free Bangladesh. There is so much to write about, but I cannot. In this war, every story, every horrible act, every atrocity is true.

We have heart, we have hope and we are determined. Like Hitler and Moussilini, Tikka and Yahya have attacked us with a ferocity unparalleled in savagery in the history of mankind. And we will attack them with the same ferocity. As soon as the monsoons come, we shall intensify our operation. When the Monsoon rains flood the land, the dry land soldiers will not be able to move swiftly like the Mukti Bahini.

Everyone here has heart and determination. But we need help. Arms. We don't even have a pillow. Only a brick with a gamcha wrapped on top to lay down our head under the Banyan tree.

Careful of Bodor Morol and Neezam. Keep your eyes open at all times.

I don't know when I will write again, but don't worry about me. Take care of yourself and take care of Abba and Amma and make sure you stay by their side.

Let's pray for a free Bangladesh. After you read this letter, destroy it. Don't give this to Amma. It will put them in danger. Tell them I am fine.

Pray but don't worry. Know that I am always with you, and through you, your eyes, your breath I will always be with you.

Nahar, as you look at the moon, know that I am looking at the same moon as you. Know that we share the same vision, even though we cannot share this night.

This night and always I am with you.
Forever Yours,
Rafique

Mukti Bahini

Gazipur, East Pakistan, late May, 1971

THERE WAS THE RISING WIND. The new moon and a few stars twinkled. An oasis of quiet, a bubble of protection, surrounded the ten. In these dry months, the months before the monsoon rains, the water almost disappeared, and the shallow wooden country sailboat scraped through a jungle of glossy long-stalked water hyacinth. The slight woody smell of water sloshing the bottom of the boat filled the air as the *kaash phool* caressed the foreheads and shoulders of the guerrillas in a gentle kiss.

The May atmosphere crackled with tension. Under Jewel's supervision, Rafique, Khalid, Sonil, Hasan, Raja, Habib, Tajul, Monju and Karim crouched low under the boom of the sail, as the river lapped gently at the boat's hull. On a mission to blow up a remote bridge, to ambush a convoy of Pakistani soldiers, this rag tag band of cavaliers was carrying a range of weapons: khaki satchels of grenades on their chests, Sten guns, a few .303 rifles, small antipersonnel mines, sub machine guns, SMG's, and a light machine gun, LMG.

At the front of the open boat, Rafique was perched by his tripod mounted LMG, his heart pounding against a pack of Charminars, craving a smoke. But he knew better. On his side lay a satchel full of more heavy 7.62 mm caliber cartridges for the LMG. In his nose was the faint smell of the grease inside the bore of the gun. He slowly moved his finger over the trigger. In his fingers was a certain power, a divinity of death he had never felt before.

Khalid touched his small copper *tabiz*—the talisman he wore around his neck on a black string—to his lips in a prayer. Tajul crouched low and guided the *majhee*. This was his territory: he had grown up here, swam these waters, tilled this land.

The *majhee*, wearing a faded blue *lungi* and a cotton singlet, held the rudder, gently guiding the boat with his long stringy limbs, his face weathered, imprinted by wind and sun.

"This the right way?" Jewel asked, concerned. His determination, his courage during training camp in Agartala had won him the leadership of these men. And he was focused on keeping them safe, in accomplishing the mission Captain Jahangir had placed on his shoulders.

Tajul nodded, assured him, "Yes, see that old banyan tree. Just after it at the next bend we have to go ashore. We will be safe at my home." A smile formed on his lips at the thought of seeing his parents.

Khalid, sitting on the bow, looked down into the dark water. In the silvery surface, two red-orbs of *rakhashi* daemon eyes peered back at him. The slow, rhythmic sway of the boat aroused in Khalid's mind thoughts of the *rakhashi*, the daemon queen his grandmother used to tell of in bedtime stories, whose vital spark lay in the shape of a black hornet inside a box, down, down below the waters of a huge lake. And this dusk there were many daemons and devils in this land. Daemonic *rakhashi* Razakars were gorging on this land of poets. And devilbroweddrunkfatjawed Yahya's military was merciless.

Suddenly, in the distance they heard the muffled engine of a launch.

"Military," the *majhee* whispered in a voice cracking with fear.

The approaching steady thumping, the steady sound of a bow slicing through water shattered the island of silence, the bubble of protection shrouding the men. The boatman headed them into shore, jumped into the water, put his shoulder to the boat, pushed it into the riparian bank. Muscling through sharp reeds, Sonil handed the guns and their bags to Hasan who handed them up the bank to Khalid.

Nervously, they followed a thin dirt trail. Tajul, in the lead, stepped on a twig. The sharp snapping sound made everyone jump back. Up the trail they heard voices. Zigzagging, quickly following Tajul, they cut through the trees away from the trail. They stumbled across fields, their only cover the darkness of the night. Weighed down with ammunition, Rafique squinted, peering ahead, careful not to trip.

THE STARS SHONE ABOVE, PINPRICKS of light, the wispy moon throwing a silver gleam. Guided by the keen eyes of Tajul on back dirt paths, they reached the edge of a clearing. Three straw-thatched huts, shuttered with plaited bamboo, stood a hundred feet away.

"Tajul, careful," Jewel whispered.

From behind the cover of a lychee tree, they watched as Tajul went alone to the houses. To the side stood a haystack and a huge clay watering bowl for the cattle. A fine acrid smell of burning jute twigs hung in the moist air, mixed with the earthy smell coming from the watering bowl.

Rafique held his finger to his lips, gesturing to the other men to be quiet. A tenseness gripped him. In the distance a dog barked, and above them an animal rustled the branches. Rafique heard a voice, then another, in the mud hut, and then a few minutes later the moving, swinging dim glow of a kerosene lantern shone through the mesh of the outer bamboo plaid fence. The lantern circled in the courtyard from the main hut to the adjacent hut. Minutes later Tajul came out of the house alone.

"It's OK. I told Ma, Baba not to make a sound," Tajul said softly to Jewel and Rafique.

"You sure, Tajul?" Jewel asked, looking questioningly into Tajul's eyes.

"It's OK Jewel Bhai, only Baba and Ma and my sister are here. We will be safe for the night," Tajul reassured them.

Weary, the band of guerrillas followed Tajul, stepping cautiously past the fence and into a grain silo room next to the cattle pen. The only sound was of the men breathing. Tajul brought the kerosene lamp and put it in the middle of the hand smoothed clay floor, empty except for some bales of jute in a corner and a large bamboo mesh crate used to store the harvested paddy.

"Khalid, you stand guard," Jewel ordered. Khalid went outside to the thatched veranda and then out to the edge of the lychee tree. Exhausted, the guerrillas collapsed on the dirt floor, leaning their guns against the mud wall, their satchels on the ground next to them. The sound of crickets filled the night air.

"Who lives around here?" Jewel questioned Tajul.

"The next door neighbors are farmers also. We are safe tonight. The army has not come this far, but the *Shanti* Committee chairman has come by and asked about me," Tajul said.

"And?" Rafique, unnerved, asked, gazing into Tajul's face in the flickering kerosene light.

"Baba told them I went Dacca to visit my Uncle. I don't think they believed him. Fucking rats are everywhere."

The men collapsed on the moist floor, pillowing their arms on their satchels. From the next hut across the small courtyard came the sound of cooking, the sweet smell of food in the air penetrating the heavy earthy odor of jute and paddy.

An hour after they arrived, Tajul brought a few tin and china plates, a jug of water and glasses.

"If they find out, it's all over for Tajul's parents and his sister," Rafique whispered to Jewel.

"We just have to leave early in the morning before anyone finds out," Jewel said, his brows furrowed in worry.

Rafique thought about Nahar and his parents. And what were Neezam and Bodor Morol up to?

Tajul's mother, a small woman, her soft brown eyes set in a round face lit with the excitement of seeing her son again, brought plates of rice and *daal*, some chilis and salt. She mashed potatoes and mixed them with mustard oil, onions and green chilies into a potato *bharta*. For the first time in over a week, the men had something decent to eat.

"*Khallama*, Auntie, you have given us new life," Raja said, "How can we ever repay you?"

"My sons, you are sacrificing everything for our country. The little we can do is nothing," she said, wiping her face with the *áchol* of her sari, smiling deeply.

"*Khallama* you are doing everything you can. Thank you," Rafique said. He knew his men ran on their bellies. Without food, they could not go even one mile.

Tajul fluttered about the room trying to be the perfect host, pouring water into the glasses, ladling out the rice, *daal, bharta*.

"*Daal* and *bharta* is all we have," Tajul said apologizing for the food, mopping his sweaty face on his shirt sleeve.

"Sorry? Are you crazy Tajul? This is heaven sent," Hasan said as he sat in a corner, licking his fingers, salivating at the tingling taste of mustard oil.

After dinner, the men sat around on the ground with their bent backs against the mud wall and smoked the last of their Charminars. Rafique, his neck sore from the heavy satchel full of cartridges, stretched his legs on the clay floor, arched the small of his back against the cool mud wall, and relaxed, his LMG leaning at an angle beside him, against the bamboo grain silo.

"We need more plastic, PK," Rafique said to Jewel.

Jewel, deep in his thoughts, his face lit by the light and shadow of the lantern, nodded.

"How much explosives would blow up the bridge clean?" Rafique asked.

"Twenty pounds of plastic would do it, but we only have ten," Jewel said in his quiet way. He crouched close to Rafique. "We need to scout out the bridge, make sure we place the PK so that at least part of the bridge is blown up."

"Let's blow it just as the Pakistani jeep goes over it," Rafique said. "That way we will kill two birds with one stone."

"We sure could use one more light machine gun against a convoy," Monju said, listening to the two men, drawing deep on the butt of a cigarette and blowing out a spiraling gray ring of smoke.

"We need more rounds!" Sonil broke in. "What good guns without ammo?"

"How long can we hold them up with these few rounds?" Karim wondered.

Wrapped in a common fighting fabric for freedom, for a free Bangladesh, huddled together in this small mud hut, tired, exhausted, the men became a guerrilla family—the *Mukti Bahini*. Their goal to accomplish the seemingly impossible, their weapons few, their camaraderie and courage focused, ferocious.

"You remember Captain Jahangir's words? We need to rebuild these bridges. Only damage the bridge. What we have in arms right now is heaven sent. No one has any PK, so be glad," Jewel said as his voice rose in a steely determination, as the lines on his face tightened. "Rafique, how many grenades, mines do we have?"

"Twenty grenades, ten balms, my LMG, three Stens, two SMG's and four .303 rifles," Rafique rattled off the list.

"Oriental balms, yes those small balm container-size mines will kill the pain permanently for the Pakistani soldiers," Karim laughed sarcastically. "Waking up to pineapple grenades for breakfast! How sweet!"

"For this mission it's nothing against the firepower of the Pakistanis," Sonil added, leaning against a bail of jute in the far dark corner of the hut.

"Hey, you guys forget two months ago they were killing us like dogs and cats. Now we have machine guns. If you can't fight, let me know, and I will send you home right now. Right now! We will manage. We must and we will," Jewel said, his rising voice filling the hut. "Listen, we will lob every grenade into the jeeps and trucks, that's our only chance. It will detonate some of their grenades and ammo and that will damage the bridge some more. We will use the enemy's arms against them."

The men shuffled, said nothing as Jewels words sank in. Someone coughed.

"The sun always rises in the east, and sinks in the west. Bangladesh will be free, and the Yahya's killers will surely fall," said Rafique as he looked out through the bamboo slatted window. Outside the deep dark of the night was pierced by a few flashing fireflies signaling in a secret code.

"The grenades are very good; if we can lob them right, they will stop almost anything," Jewel said.

"Almost," said Rafique. "We will certainly need a miracle for everything to come off as planned."

"Then we pray for a miracle," Jewel said as he clenched his fist.

Hasan and Raja were on the veranda, sleeping on the ground. Rafique rolled a *gamcha* into a tight roll, put it under his head, laying down on a dirt floor. Sleepy, Rafique touched his forehead against the butt of the LMG. He looked at the silhouette of the machine gun against the bamboo mesh of the grain silo. He looked into the metallic glint for freedom, and he saw the dead bodies of the students at Dacca University, at Jagannath, at Iqbal Hall; he touched the trigger, wanting to touch the dream of a free Bangladesh, and it sparked the loneliness in his heart for Nahar; he wanted to see victory in the long barrel, and in the sight of the gun, he saw a razed to the ground Shaheed Minar; he wanted to see, smell the turquoise green undulating fields of young paddy. And in his hands, in the 7.62mm cartridges of cold pointed metal, all he saw was more bloody battlefields, more dead bodies.

AND EVERY NIGHT THESE MEN moved. Never staying at the same place for more than a day. Over the course of a week, at night and during the early morning hours, Jewel and Rafique scouted out the bridge. From afar, they watched the Pakistani army convoys move on the road, carefully noting the time and the hours they came and went. They noted the pattern of troop movements. A jeep or two, maybe a convoy would move early in the morning towards Comilla from Dacca.

"We don't have enough explosives to blow this bridge, only damage it," Rafique said as he lay looking at their target from the safety of the nearby woods.

"We can put a dent in the mid section so that it's impassable. That will stop them for a few days at least," Jewel said.

"How are we going to set it up?" Rafique asked, as they walked by the side of the road. "Damn, wish we had a wireless set. How are we going to communicate?"

"Put Habib over there behind that tree a mile away from the bridge. Then we post Karim behind that tree a half mile away." Jewel pointed to a tree on the horizon and another half the distance. "When Habib sees the truck, he will wave to signal Karim and Karim will relay the message by waving to us. They travel at fifty miles per hour, maybe less; that gives us a minute window. Maybe a minute and a half, fine for what we need to set up."

Jewel peered at the bridge. Then with a determined conviction he said, "I will be under the bridge with the PK and Khalid can put the four antipersonnel mines on the bridge. When the first truck hits our mines, BOOM, an important column blows up."

"Will it work?" Rafique said, his eyes furrowed with a question.

"Sure."

"Let's hope so. But let's put in six or eight mines just in case they miss some."

"OK, Rafique. Courage and brains can defeat any enemy. The Pakistani army has all the weapons, but we can use our brains and make this work."

"Allah help us all."

"Allah help us, yes. But let's help ourselves with what we got first."

Slowly they walked back in the dark, the plan now cemented in Jewel's mind, and in Rafique's, questions grew larger. He said nothing.

IT WAS 3:00 IN THE morning when Jewel's group left their hiding position some five miles south of the road. The men crept through the darkness, through the cover of trees towards the edge of the open fields. Each man, loaded down with arms, walked slowly, deliberately, in silence.

Rafique felt the LMG, the sack of grenades, the clips for the gun dragging on his neck. In his mouth was a dry taste, an anxious lump lodged in his parched throat. On his right hand he carried the LMG, and with his left he pulled up on the straps of his satchel full of cartridges.

"Rafique," Jewel said.

"Yes," Rafique said, swallowing hard, as he saw Jewel look apprehensively towards the bridge.

"Anything happens, you're in charge. Make sure those Pakistani murderers are dead. When the operation is over, head for Agartala," Jewel said.

The odor of fear, the smell of a tense sweat, filled Rafique's nose. In the dark, Jewel moved first, Rafique next, then Kahlid and the men moved carefully into the open fields.

Rafique placed his feet cautiously, feeling the slippery mud under his shoes.

"After the PK blows, when the soldiers try to escape, aim carefully and fire," Jewel said to his men, his face stony, expressionless. "Remember what Captain Jahangir said. Think target. Let the man get up before you take a shot, not when he is crouched or laying down. Aim for the center of the back, for his chest, aim at a big target. Think target. Don't look at faces. Be a hunter, let's hunt them down."

Jewel deployed his force into two ambush positions near the small bridge, which intersected with the main highway. Trees and vegetation covered approaches to the bridge and offered cover for the men.

As planned, Habib took up a spotting position a mile away behind a tree, Karim a half mile away.

Jewel tied the ten pounds of PK to a center column of the bridge with rough jute twine, a wire running to a thirty-second detonator. Khalid waited with Jewel, six antipersonnel mines in his satchel ready to blow up the Pakistani jeep.

Rafique lay on his stomach behind the trunk of a mango tree on the eastern side of the bridge and watched it become daylight. He wanted to have the sun on his back and in the eyes of the army soldiers. He mounted the LMG on the tripod, curled his finger around the trigger, clenched his teeth and gathered his thoughts. Inside him stirred a closeness to revenge he had never felt. Rafique watched the road, watched the men take up positions on both sides of the bridge. He looked down the sight of his gun and aimed to the left of the white concrete sides of the bridge.

In the still of dawn, the dark became light, and the near dark bright.

To his left Rafique could make out Jewel and Khalid closest to the bridge. Backing them up were Sonil, Hasan, Raja and Tajul. And on the other side were Monju and Karim. Rafique prayed silently, and he wished they had just one more machine gun on the other side. He felt his chest tighten in tension as he looked at the bridge, and as he thought about his murdered friends at Dacca University, his finger on the trigger tightened.

The dew had wet him, and the dirt was soft. He felt the give of a small patch of green grass under his elbows. Below the bridge, a light mist floated on the water, clung to the paddy fields, hid the horizon.

Rafique pulled out the clip from the LMG. He turned the gun, cleaned off the barrel, blew through it, tasting a bit of earth on the tip of his tongue. A sweet taste. Turning the gun around, he slid the clip back in, felt it click. It felt good.

Rafique lay on his belly and waited.

Now the sun was glinting off the sight of Rafique's LMG. The rice husks undulated in a slight breeze, the green fields glistened golden in the warm May sun.

As he lay there, Rafique noticed a column of red ants marching across his line of sight, a few feet away. They carried pieces of rice husks, industriously laboring to their colony. He watched as the ants touched their little antlers in a kissed code transmitted down the line. As a child, he always called the red ants India, the enemy back in the 1965 India-Pakistan war. The red ants bite hard, and then they were India. Bad. Today, he looked at the red ants, and Rafique called the red ants Pakistan. Strange how one's own country became your enemy. Now the Indians were the black ants, the friendly ants. Red and black. Strange how roles reversed.

Under his breath Rafique uttered, "Khoda, Allah, help us today!"

And then he waited. And waited. Waited patiently for the Pakistani army jeep to come by as it always did every morning.

Like clockwork, around 9:00 Habib waved and then Karim signaled from behind the tree as a Pakistani jeep came into view.

And they watched the jeep from afar, as it approached. The signaling worked. Khalid ran up from underneath the bridge, placing the six mines in pre-planned spots. Khalid ran back and took up his position as Jewel triggered the thirty-second timer on the PK.

As the jeep drifted into view, Rafique held his breath, taking aim through the sight of the LMG. *Come on, come on.*

The tires skirted the first mine, then the second. Everyone held his breath. It passed the third mine. Nothing. Cold sweat beaded and dripped down Rafique's eyebrows.

Seconds ticked. And then simultaneously, a mine exploded and the plastic explosives detonated with a huge ear-shattering boom. The jeep flew in the air and landed on its side.

Rafique squeezed the trigger; Jewel and Khalid lobbed two grenades.

BAAA-ROWWWWWWM.

The grenades exploded shaking the ground, and the Pakistanis returned fire. As planned, everyone lobbed grenades into the jeep and a mangle of bloody limbs and bits of flesh lay scattered around the bridge. At the same moment, on the other side of the bridge, Monju and Karim opened up and their guns went rat-tat-tatting into the KABOOM of the jeep's exploding gas tank.

Of the four men in the jeep, two of the Pakistani soldiers had survived and scurried down, running for cover away from where Rafique lay with the sub machine gun.

Rafique breathed in short gasps through his mouth, the bitter hatred that filled him tasting acid in the back of his throat. Steadying his elbows, feeling the smoothness of trigger against his right index finger, he lined the front and back sights onto the center of the soldier's back and gently squeezed the trigger.

Against his shoulder, Rafique felt the sharp lurching of the LMG, a rhythm of revenge. He went with the flying bullets into the Pakistani soldier's chest, seeking sweet vengeance. On the road, the soldier buckled, staggered, fell to his knees, touched the blood on his chest, his face suddenly tranquil as he hit the road. From the other side of the bridge Rafique heard Sten gun fire rip into the other soldier who crumbled, then slid down the side of the embankment.

A black spot appeared on the horizon, grew larger. Rafique watched in horror as another large Pakistani truck pulled up behind the blown up jeep, and Yahya's finest poured out, taking positions behind the truck. Certain death.

From behind the truck, the Pakistani commander cried out, "*Mukti*, surrender or you will all be killed!"

"Joy Bangla!" he heard Khalid scream out before he lobbed a grenade.

Rafique, his elbows digging into the soft dirt, squeezed the trigger of his LMG, making a mosquito net out of the brown canvas top of the heavy military truck.

The Pakistani soldiers, a dozen, returned fire, and the machine gun they used pinned the men down. A volley of lead hit above Rafique and all around them. Branches, large mud clots came raining down. In disbelief, Rafique watched as Jewel crawled up the side of the embankment, into the line of fire, and lobbed a grenade into the truck.

"To hell you go, you fucking murderers," Jewel demonically screamed.

Backing Jewel up, Khalid ran up behind him firing his Sten gun into the truck.

Jewel, grazed in his left hand by a bullet, ran suicidally into the fire of the Pakistanis. As he lobbed two more grenades into the truck he screamed, "*Jallads,* you bastards you are coming with me."

At that instant a grenade exploded at Jewel's feet sending dirt, debris and his body flying through the air. He landed with his torso ripped open, his eyes open, empty of life.

Khalid, just behind him, took shrapnel through the right side of his chest, cutting into his lungs.

Screaming in pain, holding onto his side, Khalid fell. Inside him a thousand tiny Tikka Khans were digging into his flesh with bayonets, each taking revenge, savoring in taking away his very breath. "Rafique Bhai...," he screamed.

Leaving his post, Rafique ran to the two men and dragged Khalid down the embankment. Each time Rafique moved him, Khalid screamed. Sonil followed Rafique and pulled Jewel's body down. Rafique threw Khalid's bloody body on his shoulder, handing his LMG to Raja, and he hobbled for the cover of the trees. Here, Rafique laid Khalid down on the dirt. He felt the hole in Khalid's chest. Khalid screamed again when Rafique's fingers slid along the slick wet inside of his shirt. He took a *gamcha*, the only thing that he had, and plugged the hole as best as he could.

Khalid gurgled, blood oozing from his mouth, "Tell my mother I died a *Bir*, a hero. My letter..."

Khalid had given over to weak groans, too exhausted to scream any longer. "Ohh Allah, La Ilaha Illa-Allah..."

Rafique was bathed in Khalid's blood.

"Letter..." Khalid said drawing his last breath, pointing to his blood-soaked shirt pocket.

Inside Rafique something snapped.

ON A SMALL RISE, CAPPED by a dense canopy the afternoon sun strained to reach through, the men shouldered and then placed Jewel's and Khalid's blood-covered bodies on the ground. Worried about a counterattack, the eight men hastily burrowed into the moist red earth with bayonets, clawing with their bare hands, trenching out two shallow graves. Without water to cleanse the bodies, without white cotton clothes to cover them, they hurriedly wrapped them in two chadors.

In a brown chador besmeared in blood, Rafique and Sonil lifted Jewel's body. Rafique held Jewel's head and Sonil his legs. Slowly they lowered the body into the earthen grave, watched earth worms move away as the dark moist earth embraced one more soul. Gently Rafique touched Jewel's eyelids, shutting them forever. Bowing down, they placed him onto the floor of the grave. As Rafique turned Jewel's turgid face west towards Kaba, facing Mecca, a solitary tear fell from Rafique's eyes onto Jewel's forehead.

Hasan and Raja placed Khalid's bloody corpse, covered in a chador now crimson and wet, in the grave. Rafique turned Khalid's swollen blood-streaked face slightly towards Mecca. He knelt on the mound of dirt and looked at the two men who gave everything for freedom, for a free Bangladesh.

Rafique stared at Jewel's face. A strange happiness shone there as if he was playing with the soft curly ringlets of his daughter's hair.

And Khalid, once vivacious, effervescent, now lay quiet. A farmer's son, the soil that was under his fingernails all his young life was now embracing him forever.

Standing up, Rafique crumbled a fistful of dirt onto the body of Khalid, then another onto the body of Jewel. The other men followed. Specks, handfuls, covered the men—the good earth, motherland. Using the butts of the .303 rifles as spades, they pushed the dirt over the bodies, and the small mounds they padded with their hands, the two small mounds, side by side, where Khalid and Jewel could keep each other company forever. Forever they would be companions walking into that near eternity, laughing, joking, looking up at lush green, the moistness of the earth they fought, died for, keeping them warm.

The men standing around the graves raised their hands in a *Janaza* funeral prayer.

His head bent, Rafique stood with the seven others. "In death, with their last drop of blood, they found that little ground, this earth, they fought so hard for. Bangladesh. Jewel didn't die today, and not here. He died months ago in that village where his daughter stopped giggling. He died that day with his family."

The onus of leadership now fell on Rafique's shoulders. In the distance, he could see Jewel determined as he was to the very end, and he repeated to himself his words, "Courage and brains can defeat any enemy." Yes Jewel, you showed what courage and brains can do today, but you knew, knew from the start that you would never return from this mission.

Rafique herded his men, heavy with the burden of death, now veterans of war, towards Agartala to regroup, to come to terms with the death of two of their own. Eight men: Rafique, Sonil, Hasan, Raja, Habib, Tajul, Monju and Karim. Silent in their mourning, lost in their thoughts, they trudged with heavy feet and heart on a narrow dirt trail towards Agartala. Less two. They tried to speak, to comfort each other, but sorrow locked their lips.

Rafique touched the folded letter in his shirt pocket. Khalid had never given him an address for the unfinished letter, a letter to his Ma.

Where would he post it?

To an unknown address, to a Ma who waited for news.

Pounding against his heart was Khalid's bright beaming face, his earthy heartfelt laughter, all in a single line etched in crimson,

"Ma, died a *Bir*."

Rhythm of the Rumble

❧ ❧ ❧

June 1971, East Pakistan

JUNE INTO AUGUST, LOWERING SKIES shroud Sheetalpur in dense, wet Southwest clouds that push and stack deep and dark into the horizon. Animated by lightning and thrummed by the tabla of continuous rain, the earth grows a voluptuous green that bursts forth along vast undulations of water.

Sky, earth, rain were in a drenched embrace. In Nahar's brown eyes danced the braided ripples of water in great sheets of silver, and in Nahar's heart the Chowdhury house was veiled in an air of emptiness, like the empty rooms inside her heart.

Outside in the courtyard chickens cooped up in the thatched *dhenki* hut were pecking at the worms in their wiggled journeys on the wet clay courtyard. Boochu scurried after the chickens in a melee of raucous clucking and barking.

Out in the kitchen Amina boiled a kettle of water for the morning tea, and Jahanara and Nahar gathered around Chowdhury's prized radio, the textile grill and polished wood cabinet sitting prominently on the teak wooden dining table. Nahar stood behind her mother-in-law, her green sari *áchol* demurely draped over her head, eagerly awaiting the news.

Chowdhury touched the radio, a present from Rafique, touching Rafique's war, his dreams of a free Bangladesh. *Swadhin Bangla Betar Kendro,* Radio Free Bangladesh, was on the border, somewhere near Rafique. Turning the dials, Chowdhury felt close to his son, and through the airwaves he felt one in the fight for freedom, one with Rafique and Nazmul and thousands of the *Mukti Bahini.*

Stirred out of his thoughts by the clinking of Amina putting a cup of tea on the table in front of him, he cleared his throat, and said to Nahar, "*Bou Maa*, any news from Rafique? Any letter?"

"No, Abba, nothing new. Only that one letter, a month old," Nahar replied.

"Yes, I remember Rafique wrote about how when the monsoon rains came, the military would get stuck in the mud of Bangladesh and the *Mukti Bahini* would launch their attacks," Jahanara said.

"In this rain their equipment will get stuck, but it is the collaborators who are going to make us lose the war," Chowdhury said, his voice seething with frustration and anger, as he carefully turned the small metal tuning knob, trying to get the early morning hour of news, music and programs on Radio Free Bangladesh that usually came on for a short hour around 7 or 7:30. He looked up at Nahar, asked, "How are Naila and Shihab doing? Any news from Chittagong?"

"No, Abba," Nahar replied.

"It's been four months, and no news from Chittagong. Rahman doesn't have any news either?" Mustafa said, concern in his voice.

"No," Nahar said, wondering about her sister. She pulled at her looped *áchol*, prayed for her sister, Naila, her husband Shihab, for their safety. These days there was little news. And most of it bad.

Jahanara sighed deeply, her face darkened, thoughts about her son now gone for two months clouded her mind. Two months and just one letter.

Food was on her table.

And what was on her son's plate this monsoon morning?

Treasured memories gathered in her mind. Memories of Rafique as a baby, his first day at school, running home to her arms, so happy. She chewed on some *paan*, betel nut, mixed with sweet minty *masala*, and her mind drifted far away to the guerrilla camp where

Rafique was. She remembered a certain gesture Rafique would make with his chubby curled fingers when he was just a boy, calling her to him. Today Rafique was gesturing for her from a hundred miles away, from Agartala. Her husband's voice brought her back to the conversation, back to the dining table in Sheetalpur.

Jahanara looked up across the table at Mustafa and asked, "What is Neezam doing?"

"Neezam and Bodor are leading the *Shanti* Committee in the village," said Chowdhury. "These days they are inseparable."

Jahanara, silent for a moment, chewed the *paan*. In a voice shrouded in shame she said, "How could I have told Rafique, my own son, I didn't believe him. I said Neezam cannot be a traitor. I can't even start to think that Neezam could do this. We brought him up. I was the first one to hold him when he was born!" Biting her lip, cursing herself, she looked out into the courtyard as the sun battled the dark gray clouds and lost. The skies had opened up and the rain and the wind cut swaths into the silvery landscape. She exhaled a long discontent, "Allah..."

Chowdhury, not wanting to talk about Neezam, changed the subject. "Jahanara do you know just yesterday, Yahya Khan announced that the 500 and 100 Rupee notes are going to be worthless, demonetized."

"Which bills?" Jahanara, distracted, asked Chowdhury.

"Five hundred and one hundred rupee notes," Chowdhury repeated. "Everyone will have to run to the bank. And if they are in India, they will be in big trouble. That's Yahya's great idea, to financially cripple people against him."

In Nahar's heart thoughts about Rafique flowed like the rain, in great sheets. Last night, in a fitful sleep, she had dreamt about Rafique, dreamt about the Fair. On the way back from the *Mela*, Rafique asked by the water-lily adorned pond, "Nahar, you want some *podmo phool*, water lilies?" As she reached out to take the lily, his body, then his hand disappeared in the murky water. She had screamed awake, the image of his fingers disappearing into the water kept her up all night.

Talk about the 500 Rupee notes brought Nahar back to the conversation. She thought about the notes that she had sewn in into the belt folds of Rafique's pants, one hundred and five hundred rupee notes. Tightly she gripped the back of Jahanara's chair, worrying what Rafique would do now.

"How about the fifty rupee notes?" Jahanara asked.

"Those will be fine." Chowdhury replied.

"Some people will not have enough money to even buy food," said Jahanara.

"If the only money they have becomes worthless paper, yes, they will surely starve," said Chowdhury.

Things were going from bad to worse, and there was no end in sight to this war, Nahar thought, watching as Boochu ran around in the courtyard getting wet. Was Rafique sheltered this morning in this endless rain? Why had he not written again? A jumble of thoughts and emotions kept surfacing, her mind becoming unclear, unfocused.

Chowdhury played with the dial of the radio, and tuned in *Swadhin Bangla Betar Kendro*. After the static, the light hiss of silence, the welcome uplifting sound of Radio Free Bangladesh washed over Chowdhury, Jahanara and Nahar. With the morning program marched in "*Chal Chal Chal*, Let's go, go, go," one of Kazi Nazrul Islam's rebellious uplifting songs. Nahar felt Rafique in the surging sounds, amplified a thousand times. With passion in his deep resonating voice, she loved how Rafique would recite Nazrul's patriotic poems. She yearned to hear his voice once more, to hear him call her name just once.

"*Chal, Chal, Chal.*"

"*Chal, Chal, Chal,*" Nahar formed the words on her lips.

Intangible ephemeral songs floating in through moist air, riding on the wings of clouds, wings of hope, became indestructible edicts of strength. The hope-starved Bangladeshi hearts thrummed in rising rhythms to the beat of *Swadhin Bangla Betar Kendro*.

"Rafique's favorite, isn't it *Bou Maa*?" asked Chowdhury.

"Yes, Abba. One of Rafique's favorites," Nahar replied with conviction.

Amina came in with three more fresh piping-hot cups of tea, placed them in front of Chowdhury and Jahanara and one in front of Nahar.

"Amina, bring the *mooa* and the *naru*," Jahanara said.

"*Jee*, Amma," she said, as she twisted open the wooden top latch on the netted *misriv* cupboard in the corner and took out the puffed rice balls and the coconut candy sealed in a glass container. Even in the sealed glass, the moisture had softened the molasses coated puffed rice balls. Monsoon and moisture had permeated into the very soul of Bengal.

"On the eastern horizon, the sun has risen, *Purbo Digonte Shurjo Uthechhe,*" Subol Das' song flowed out loud and clear.

"A new sun of freedom, and I hope Rafique can help raise it," Jahanara said. She imagined Rafique coming home in a free Bangladesh, coming back home to them. "Soon."

"The sun is going to rise. And victory will be ours," said Chowdhury.

"Amina," called Jahanara.

"*Jee*," Amina said pulling her wet *dupatta* around her waist, tying it into a knot.

"Call Halim and that Boochu; it's wet out there. Make sure you dry him. Stupid dog. Dry that puppy and give him something to eat."

"*Jee*, Amma," Amina said, as she ran out to the veranda calling to Boochu.

Nahar watched the worry lines grow in the faces of her in-laws as they listened to the news about Nixon's support for Yahya Khan.

"Abba, how come we are getting no support from the international community?" Nahar asked. "No one is willing to even recognize us as a nation, even though the Mujibnagar Government is trying so hard. The only support we have is India and Russia, really."

"We will get support," Chowdhury said, his voice rising. "In the beginning of any revolution it's tough getting the support that you need."

"But right now," Nahar asked. "We need support right now. Rafique and Nazmul need help now, not tomorrow."

"Poor people count for very little. And Yahya has clamped down on the press. Even the UN thinks that East Pakistan is an internal affair. Well no more. Not with the refugee crisis spilling over into India," Chowdhury said as he took one more sip of his tea, looked at Jahanara and Nahar's *āchol* covered face behind her. Fear had gripped Sheetalpur. No one came to the Chowdhury *Bari* anymore. No more evening gatherings in the front courtyard. Now, Nahar was the only one left to discuss the news with. The only one safe to share his thoughts with, the only one who understood.

"Abba, we need international support," Nahar repeated, her eyebrows narrowed.

"Nahar, we will get international support. But a Bangladeshi's life is not worth much. Nixon and Kissinger are too busy with Vietnam. And with Chou En Lai's Chinese support for Yahya, well Yahya is Nixon's pal in connecting USA with China. So we are nobody. Nobody," Chowdhury said bitterly. He turned off the radio, now that the hour of morning programs was over. Outside the rain was coming down sideways in silver ropes, a constant beat on the roof.

"The refugees are dying right now without food," Nahar said.

"If the UN mission does not support Yahya, then he will not get the money he wants," said Chowdhury. "People like Kennedy are going to support us. Everything is not lost," Chowdhury said. "Everything is not lost."

Chowdhury got up and walked to the doorway. He would have to make a trip to the bank, and fast. Or else the money would be worthless.

His mind drifted to the safe and the five hundred and one hundred Rupee bills he had there. He stood looking at the sheet of water stretching into the horizon. The paddy fields, the few that were planted were already under water, not even the tops showing.

"Jahanara, open the *almira* and give me the Habib Bank book," said Chowdhury. "I have to go to the bank."

Jahanara sat still, a distant look in her eyes.

"Jahanara, I have to go to the bank," Chowdhury repeated.

"In this weather?" startled Jahanara said, her voice fearful. "The town is crawling with army and Razakars."

"If I don't go?" he said slowly, contemplating his decision, uncertain of the outcome. "I have to turn in the notes."

Jahanara reached for the keys knotted on the tail end of her pale blue cotton sari. Knotted in her heart strings were thoughts of her son.

—⁂—

Comilla, East Pakistan-India Border

IN THE BORDER VILLAGE, CUTTING a swath across Rafique's line of vision were more men, women and children pounded into mud by the monsoon, the slanting sheets cutting into refugees walking towards the border. A lanky tall man walked with a shorter stocky companion behind him. Just like Jewel and Kahlid. Rafique squinted, tried to refocus.

In his shirt pocket Khalid's unfinished and unaddressed letter rose and fell with every breath.

Rafique's small band of *Mukti Bahini* guerrillas, eight in all, squatted next to him as he tried to tune in *Swadhin Bangla Betar Kendro* on the radio. In the veranda in front of the corrugated tin and mud-walled hut, for that day their camp and shelter, they were huddled around kneeling in a prayer, seeking guidance from the in-exile Bangladesh Mujibnagar Government, maybe some uplifting news, humor from the commentators and actors on *The Ultimatum*, *Charampatra*, and *Butcher's Court, Jollader Dorbar*. And of course Mujibur's historic lines from his rebel-rousing March 7th speech, and patriotic songs to uplift the soul.

The small weathered transistor radio sat on a wooden stool, its volume turned up all the way.

On the Comilla border, the *Mukti Bahini* K-sector had launched a counteroffensive.

Into the hearts of this motley crew, *Charampatra, The Ultimatum*, came in an energetic monologue dripping with humor about the plight of an increasingly beleaguered West Pakistani army. It started in chaste Bengali and drifted into a rich and humorous old town Dacca dialect. *"Chhokku Mia, bashonti rong, ek gada peek phaliya, Dha-in! Ki oilo ki oilo, Larkanar nawabjada pyare Julfikar Ali Bhutto, Yahyar ek gelasher dosto,* Chokku Mia,... the nawab of Larkanar, Bhutto and Yahya are one whiskey glass friends." The sarcasm, the jokes made the guerrillas burst out laughing.

"Joy Bangla!" went up the cheer.

The program was primarily in Bengali with Urdu and English sections, the Urdu directed at demoralizing the Pakistani soldiers.

As the announcer's voice excitedly described each round of

successes by the *Mukti Bahini,* he drew cheers or moans from the guerrillas. The *Mukti Bahini* with the EPR was now pummeling the Pakistanis. The international news was not that positive, as Nixon and Kissinger were siding with Yahya, given the support Yahya had from China. Russia was supporting Indira Gandhi and India.

"Joy Bangla," screamed two of the guerrillas, raising clenched fists and boxing the empty air.

A group of village kids had also gathered with the *Mukti Bahini,* listening to the radio, finding communal strength. First there was the jovial song, and then a comedy skit mocking the Pakistani Army. Everyone listened intently, breaking out in laughter at the caricature of Tikka Khan and Yahya Khan. In their hearts what they wished they could do to these murderers, the announcer and actors at *Swadhin Bangla Betar Kendro* were doing. This was a time to laugh, a venting relief from fear.

Through the airwaves, *Swadhin Bangla Betar Kendro* kept the fiction of Bangladesh alive. Out of the radio tumbled the music and slogans to drive the guerrillas into action, to keep hope alive in their souls and hearts, even against insurmountable odds.

"*Aji Bangladesher hridoy hote,*" by Tagore, "Today from the heart of Bangladesh," melodiously lifted the spirits of men, women and kids, alike; here, in the deep of the village, in a secret place, was truly on this monsoon day the soul of Tagore's Bengal.

"*Lathi maar, bhangra tala,* Kick, shatter the locks!" screamed the enthusiastic crowd.

"*Ebarer songram muktir songram,* This struggle is for freedom!" yelled another guerrilla, lifting his Sten gun in the air in a salute.

They gathered close, closer even to strain their ears to hear any news, hopefully good. The voice crackled over the constant buzz, as Rafique ever so slightly turned the dial and then twisted the antenna.

Then came the bad news about the demonetized notes.

"Did you hear the news that the 500 and 100 Rupee money notes need to be taken into the Banks?" said Rafique.

"Yes," said one of the guerrillas. "So what do we do?"

"Send someone to Dacca?" one of the guerrillas said after a moment.

"And get them killed?" said Rafique. "A countrywide trap by Yahya."

Rafique felt the folds of his pant's belt loop, remembered how Nahar had sewn a few 500 Rupee notes into it.

He thought about Nahar. His Nahar. She always had thought about everything. His parents. How were they doing in Sheetalpur? Through the guerrilla grapevine he had heard of the Razakar activity led by Bodor Morol and Neezam, and in every breath, he was praying for the safety of his parents, Nahar, Amina and Halim.

In the far dark horizon, fighting the rain, refugees struggled towards the border, and in that vanishing line he could see Khalid's wide smile, in his ears echoed Khalid's calls of "Rafique Bhai." And he now saw what he had not wanted to recognize—the suicidal determination of Jewel.

From *Swadhin Bangla Betar Kendro* a song blew in with the wind and rain,

Tir hara eai dheuer shagor pari debore

Through angry waves, we shall cross this boundless ocean,
We a few young sailors grip hard and fast onto the wheel,
Eagerly our lives we sacrifice in this war,
Taste we not the sweet nectar of life,
Lost our address, our homes,
As day and night mesh into one,
Into the unknown we fly,
Relentless is our charge, on and on,
Sail this ship we must,
I, the Captain in this pounding tumultuous ocean.

Rafique touched Khalid's unaddressed letter, felt Jewel's madness for vengeance.

—❧—

IN A FLOODED FIRST LANE, Kalabagan, Dacca, a sparse handful of rickshaw-wallahs pulled passengers covered in blue plastic tarps through knee-deep water. Behind the closed pharmacy, prominently displaying Yahya's picture and festooned with triangular green and white crescent moon Pakistani flags, in Samad Uncle's abandoned 'safe-house' Nazmul, along with Firoz and Rintu, was hiding in a corner storeroom. With the morning came a pale light into the small room through the green metal bars of the one little window. Except for a quilt on a mat, a bed, and a wooden *alna* for hanging clothes in the corner, the store room was empty.

On the middle of the floor, a tea cup ashtray was full of butts, in the corner of the bed and on the *alna* were drying shirts, cotton singlets, underwear, *lungis* and *gamchas* of the three *Mukti Bahini* guerrillas who called this home.

Nazmul sat in a *lungi* and a cotton singlet. Suddenly there was a knock on the door. Nazmul, Rintu, and Firoz sprang up. Nazmul went for his Sten, only to realize that the visitor was the *durwan*, bringing them a pack of cigarettes and the newspaper.

"Saar, money no more good," crackled the *durwan*.

"What the... what are you talking about?" Nazmul said. "*Oi*, did you smoke some Ganja?"

"*Naah*, Saar, paper," he said, taken aback, as he put down the rain-sprinkled newspaper on the bed next to them. The front lines announced in bold letters that all five-hundred and one-hundred rupee notes were demonetized.

"They demonetized the Pakistani 100 Rupee and 500 Rupee," Nazmul read out loud.

"Yeah, a trap. I don't have any money. You have any 100 or 500 Rupee notes?" Firoz asked.

"I have just a few 100 Rupee notes," said Nazmul. "We need someone we can trust at the bank and get them changed, or we have no money. Nothing."

"This is a great way to trap the *Mukti Bahini* movement. What a fucking ploy." Firoz said.

"*Oi*, who do you know in the bank, Firoz?" Nazmul asked, a puzzled frown on his face.

"How much money we have?" Firoz asked.

190

"Next to nothing!" Nazmul said sarcastically, wondering about when Rafique would join him. He needed ammunition, money and most importantly Rafique's brains in masterminding their operation.

"My brother-in-law can take it in," Firoz reassured Nazmul.

"Rafique, that's who we need to get this operation into high gear," Nazmul said quietly, in an even emotionless voice.

A guerrilla June in Dacca.
Planning.
Hiding.
Surviving.

Their lively talk and laughter helped pass the time. Conversations changed. Instead of planning the next month, they talked about plans for the rest of their lives. Planning one's life was easier than seeing past the day in this a seat-of-the-pants kind of operation.

"Anything in the newspaper?" Rintu asked.

"America is sending another Apollo mission to the moon," replied Nazmul.

"At least they gave fifteen million dollars to our refugees in India," said Firoz. "The UN sent the money right?"

"We sent a message to the UN, alright," chuckled Nazmul. "Those three pineapples on the porch of the Intercontinental woke up UN Refugee High Commissioner Prince Sadruddin Aga Khan. Yahya's cover-up is not going to last forever. Those pineapples did the talking for us!" laughed Rintu.

"Talking about grenades, what happened to the plastic explosives we were supposed to get?" Nazmul asked.

"We only got twenty pounds," Rintu said. He stubbed out his cigarette butt inside a cup, then added dryly, "We need about eighty or ninety pounds."

"When?" Nazmul questioned, unsure, without any answers.

In the early afternoon, Firoz and Rintu came back, dripping wet, tired from an afternoon of scouting out a power station.

"'Bell-bottom Guerrillas' that's what Major Zia called us at Agartala when he came to visit. That's so funny." Rintu chuckled and added. "I think our commander Major Musharraf is proud of us."

"Yes, we are it, brother. Bell-bottom guerrillas. The scorpions. Right here and now," said Nazmul, as he put on his dry *lungi*, and spread out his wet bell-bottoms on the *alna* in the corner. "Wet bell-bottom guerrillas," Nazmul said. "Firoz you have any cigarettes?"

"Yeah, sure, here," Firoz said as he handed Nazmul a brown and gold hard pack of 555s.

"Thanks." Nazmul said as he picked out one of the last cigarettes, ritualistically thumped it's end hard against his palm, packing in the tobacco.

The three of them have been there since early afternoon; their wet clothes in the corner by the window will never dry in this moistness. On the bed lay two books: Jibananondo Das's *Rupsahi Bangla, Beauteous Bengal* and a dog-eared copy of *The Diary of Anne Frank.*

Nazmul brought out the deck of cards and laid it out.

A WET DAY DISAPPEARED INTO the soft sounds of evening. Nazmul sat on the thin quilt, resting his head on an arm pillowed against the cement wall. Like the cradled head of a newborn, on the pillow lay the small battery-powered radio. It was eight o'clock and Nazmul was busy tuning in *Swadhin Bangla Betar Kendro*. On the floor, leaning against the bed sat Firoz and Rintu, ears perked to the sounds on the radio.

The tabla of rain falling on the tin veranda roof, the swish of the wet leaves, the bell-like tinkle of water running through the gutter into the drains fluted a soft riff as Nazmul rotated the metal dial, his mind on the missions ahead. The narrow alleyways and wide streets of Dacca were now infested with swarming Pakistani soldiers and the rat Razakars. He stretched the antenna trying hard to tune in the spirit-lifting news of Radio Free Bangladesh.

Like water to a parched throat, music to the ears, *"Joy Bangla Banglar Joy,* Victory to Bangladesh" blared from the radio. A sparkle of hope, a glimmer of the promise of freedom came into the eyes of the men.

"I heard Baitul Mukarram is now crawling with Pakistani soldiers?" asked Nazmul, as he pulled out a cigarette. He struck a sulphur match stick, it burned blue until the little wood stick caught, lighting Nazmul's thought-engrossed face. He lit the 555. Took a long drag. Nazmul, face shrunken with hunger, chin mottled with stubble, eyes blood-shot and red-rimmed, exhaled a ring of smoke that dissipated into the mosquito net hanging from four posts of the bed.

"Yes," answered Firoz, "not only crawling, but shopping. Those bastards are busy buying everything for their families in Pakistan while murdering ours."

"Rafique Bhai is supposed to come here, no?" Asked Rintu.

"Yes. But first he's got to find someone to take care of his unit. Rafique was successful in blowing up that bridge, but Jewel and Khalid gave their lives in that operation." Nazmul took another long drag on the cigarette killing the gnawing hunger in his belly. Today was a one meal day, and that one meal did not amount to much. Nazmul thought about Agartala. About the last time he saw Rafique and Jewel and Khalid and the other men. He exhaled a long breath. Every time he closed his eyes, images of Jewel and Khalid filled his mind.

Nazmul, Firoz, and Rintu smoked cigarettes and put them out on the teacups, and laughed at the jokes on the radio program. When the program was over, they turned off the radio and concentrated on planning their guerrilla activities deep in the heart of enemy headquarters—Dacca.

"We need to get some information about the movement of military there," Nazmul said to Rintu and Firoz.

"You guys take a rickshaw in the morning. Shave first, and no guns. Go to Baitul Mukarram and look like you are shopping. Don't attract any attention. Wear *lungis*, shirt. Take my shirt, it's dry, Rintu." After a moment, Nazmul, furrowed his brows, looked at the rain outside, and said, "And I am going to Dhanmondi. We need to scope out a car we can hijack."

"Sure," Firoz said, as Rintu laid out the worn cards.

In this ramshackle store room, bleak and barren, on the cold floor on a thread bare hand-stitched quilt, these men share an intimacy of discomfort. Hundreds of miles apart, Rafique and Nazmul were looking forward to going "back home" to pick up where they left off, carrying emblazoned flags of freedom. A common thread wove them together into the fighting fabric of the *Mukti Bahini*. Firoz and Rintu were still caught up in the excitement of the gypsy lifestyle they enjoyed—dreams of Ché wrapped in Jibonanondo Das's *Ruposhi Bangla, Beauteous Bengal*.

They talked.

They laughed.

They dealt cards.

They dealt their tenuous guerrilla lives on the ramshackle card table of Dacca, planning, plotting, bombing.

Refugee

East Pakistan-India Border, 1971

Refugee.

NINETEENSEVENTYONE.

Assam, Bihar, Meghalaya, Tripura, West Bengal, Agartala, Salt Lake, Calcutta, Sabrum, Khasi-Jaintia Hills, Cherrapunji.

And every border city.

A strange world.

Little boy eyes watered and dried over and over again. Dried, tears no more.

He is young, very young, his bulging eyes as old as death. Soon, very soon, he will be as old as the earth. Bloated belly, he clings to the side of his skeletal mother. He is one and he is a million, his mother dying, his father dead. He is one, he is many.

And hope, hope drains eternally from eyes of sorrow, eyes never to see breath-taking wonders. The green, the good, the divine. Eyes so big. Only to have seen evil, black and hell. Oh, little hearts so weak trying to cherish a little breath, a little life.

Eyes so big. Unsmiling. Bleary.

Eyes of

NINETEENSEVENTYONE.

Crows fat and sleek. Where vultures feast fat, strong in monsoon wet. Gaunt by the serpentine roadside, the refugees, barren and hopeless in rain, under a blinding sun, wander the roads. Refugees followed eagerly by scavenging birds, dogs, jackals.

Aimless and hopeless.

NINETEENSEVENTYONE.

On the Akhaura road, on Jessore road, the panting muddy refugees slosh in the tempestuous monsoon. They drag broken bodies into India. Broken souls.

Crouched like an animal, on all fours she crawls across the border. Only the sari on her back, the crooked walking stick by her side, pain in her eyes, back broken under the weight of youth lost forever. Her neck twisted, her hair a gray scattered cluster, her flesh sunburnt, her fingers digging into the mud, she peers and stares with a serene surreal expression; her cheeks hallow and gaunt, like a corpse. In her pained eyes visions of atrocities unfathomable.

She is

NINETEENSEVENTYONE.

Deep from the heart of the Bay of Bengal, the heavy ominous dark clouds march up the skies over the bloated body-ridden Padma, Meghna, Jamuna and tear at the backs of the dying refugees, tearing with wind and pounding with rain.

Over the Ganges delta and over the variegated canopies march in monsoon's heavy clouds. The wind blows howling and whistling, high in the air, then silent and low, and it roars in the canopies of the banyan and swishes in the branches of the mango and jack fruit. The monsoon clouds, thick grays, pile and push against a dark horizon. The rain breaks into its own incessant, steady beat, rain that is torrential, cold, cutting. By the muddy roadside, in the rain, under the trees, wind-whipped tent cities sprout up. And millions of children, swollen bellies and big round eyes, look hauntingly at the dying light. Strong men break down and cry.

Hopelessness for their dying children.

NINETEENSEVENTYONE.

And because they are terrorized, and because they are jointly running away from death, they huddle together, they share their lives, their hunger and they share the hope for a free Bangladesh. They carry each other's loads when they cannot even carry themselves. Huddled listlessly by the roadside, wandering aimlessly. Stories bring them together, stories of atrocities, of slaughter, of looting, and burning, of rape, of harassment and abuse by Pakistani soldiers and the Razakars.

Under the gentle canopy of father banyans' outstretched limbs and gargantuan roots floating from the sky, many sleep in a safe embrace, afloat like tendrils trying to reach for freedom.

Tender tendrils reaching toward freedom.

NINETEENSEVENTYONE.

And the endless rain falls. Paddy fields become muddy rivers. And in the cold cutting rain the refugees press together in their tents. In leaking tarpaulin tents stillborn babies are born to malnourished mothers. Old people curl up in corners and die. Monsoon pounds. The water rises. And the people sit bare, naked and wet in the *lungis* and saris and *gamchas*. The tents, islands of anguish, stand in muddy brown water, and the refugees stand in knee deep water. And the children cry, and the women look away, for there is nowhere to go anymore.

All night thousands stand out in the open in the rain, shriveled like their hope. Women with babies in their arms. Water, water everywhere, rising, rising, rising to their knees.

Pneumonia in the morning and death in the afternoon.

NINETEENSEVENTYONE.

Over the rivers, and down the highways and countless muddy jungle paths, East Pakistan streams into India: an endless flood of refugees, ragged clothes on their heads, carrying sick children and the old.

Endless human columns pushing day into night, thousands, hundreds of thousands seen wandering in the countryside without food, without shelter, sleeping in schools, in the wet fields and in the shade. Wrinkled starved faces, tales of terror etched in lines of pain. Dead by the roadside. No one to bury them.

Carrion for the claws, in the mud, on the side of the dirt road, hundreds of thousands died never to be buried.

Unburied bodies.

NINETEENSEVENTYONE.

Pencil-limbed peasants along rain swept roads, the gaunt faces, vacant stares, and caved-in stomachs of malnutrition. Millions starve eating roots.

The processions of families plodding by with children with silent eyes, bony heads, with bare ribs curving upward under the thin veil of skin. Starving black angels in human guise.

On their lips a prayer, on their heads sacks of grain, in front millions, behind, millions, big tin suitcases underarm, last legs under their frame.

In their eyes fear. Escape.

The stricken skeletal ox-carts plough through mud and in despair, weighted down with all the earthly possessions, the father pointing, the oxen following the endless human chain of refugees.

The chain of pain.

Anemic, drained,

Refugee.

NINETEENSEVENTYONE.

Fleeing the bloody talons of Tikka Khan, hundreds of thousands of refugees living in concrete pipes on the outskirts of Calcutta. Packed together in camps, the luckier ones with tarpaulins to keep out the rain, others with makeshift thatched roofing and a sea of mud for a floor.

Overworked relief officials struggling: no food, no shelter left. The smell of misery in the pouring rain, in the overpowering stench of death, in the sight of malnourished children. Dysentery drains the bowels of big-eyed infants. Drained at once, drained to death's open embrace.

In the corner. There. Yes. No more than twelve. Little girl no more. Ranting in whimpers and whispers. No one left. Just her emptiness and pain, and in pain she dances her wrists, twirling palm to palm, the dance of the strange. The strange of loss, the strange of nothing left. No more sadness. No more pain. No more hope. No more laughter. Her lips move, but no sound comes out. In her dead eyes, there is the song of loss, of once and no more.

And yes, she is

NINETEENSEVENTYONE.

The endless line for the ration card. Penniless families squat near the river, offering their utensils for food.

Miles along the old Jessore road north of Calcutta towards the border of East Pakistan millions of people sit huddled together. Waiting for food. Que up in endless lines for refugee registration cards. Camp on the roadside under hastily constructed lean-tos.

Relief. The relief card. The relief sack of rice and sack of lentils. And after three days the ration is gone, and day four and day five and day six and day seven the hunger attacks through the belly and eats out the brain. The children cry with hunger. No food. And the men gather together and the women huddle in a corner. And their faces grow gray with terror. The whisperings rise like puffs of smoke and in this miasma of fear, the fear turns into anger, and the anger into revenge against the Pakistani army.

The line.

NINETEENSEVENTYONE.

A child paralyzed from the waist down, never to walk again; a child quivering on a mat in a small tent still in shock from seeing his parents, brothers, sisters executed before his eyes; a 10-year-old girl out foraging for something to cover the body of her baby brother who died of cholera minutes before.

A crematorium. A crematorium, the greatest need.

Joy Bangla. Sickness comes. Pneumonia-measles-cholera. Death cures all. Death the one drug. Ten million refugees. Nowhere to go. Six million farmers. Three million laborers. Two million city folk. Half a million artisans. Nowhere to go.

East Pakistan.

NINETEENSEVENTYONE.

Yet hope. Hope rides on radio waves into the camps. The most

199

powerful of hope, dreams, aspirations float in on the ethereal waves of the transistor radio. Hope from *Shawdhin Bangal Betar Kendro*, the *Kendro* playing the *Charampatra*. The welcome news is read by Deb Dulal Bandyapadhay, and the tears and pain vanish and the faces light up. Hope grows eternal and ethereal on the sounds of the transistor radio.

Hope. Fear. Horror. Tears. Terror. Death.
NINETEENSEVENTYONE.

Refugee
you are
NINTEENSEVENTYONE.

࿐

While My Guitar Gently Weeps

Concert for Bangla Desh, August 1, 1971,
Madison Square Garden, New York, New York

ON A CORNER OF 8th Avenue, gazing at the marquee spelling out Madison Square Garden in white letters on black, Rachael blew out a long breath of sharp, earthy smoke into the August humidity of New York City.

Filling her was the haunting image she had seen of the young baby, bloated belly, hollow eyes full of hunger, holding a few grains of rice in a large aluminum bowl, a last piece on his chin.

Rachael leaned back against the hot skyscraper wall to get out of the way of the throng of concert goers charging by. "Something in the baby's eyes," Rachael said, her long wavy blonde hair flowing loose in a slight breeze. "Like he's holding onto the last hope for life."

David leaned over, took the joint from Rachael's hand and took a long drag. "Wow, this place is mobbed. Beatle's power's buzzing today." Standing a block away from Madison Square Garden, where young concert goers swarmed like bees, he wiped the sweat off his forehead with the sleeve of his blue T-shirt. David pushed in the tickets behind the pack of Marlboro's in his bell-bottom jean pocket, took another hit and passed the joint to Ryan. "Shit, can you feel the electricity in the air guys? This concert's going to be fantastic!"

201

"Ten million refugees. That's a lot of starving people!" said Ryan, holding the joint in his left hand, his only hand, looking at the towering neon Coca Cola sign high up on a building as it spread the virtues of soft drinks to the thirsty concert-going crowd. His empty shirt sleeve hung limp over the place where his right hand should be. His shoulder length auburn hair was tied back with a beaded peace sign headband. "We're just freakin' lucky to have these tickets."

"Yeah luck was camping out for days!" David laughed sarcastically.

The hazy afternoon sun reflected off the glass of circular Madison Square Garden into the faces of clustered, frenzied concertgoers. The sun glinted off of the silver bracelet on Rachael's left wrist. She touched the band, a six-year-old Christmas gift from Frank, his last Christmas. She turned it and read the engraving, *'To Rachael with love always—Frank.'*

"Frank would've loved to see Dylan," Rachael said. "Was his favorite."

"I'm so sorry, Rachael," David said, gently squeezing her hand.

The front of Madison Square Garden was lined with white Police barricades, and behind the barricades a crowd had gathered: the mostly young hippie crowd wearing cotton T-shirts, torn jeans, sporting long side-burns, ruffled long hair, Afros.

"It's great George Harrison is helping the refugees. We gotta help the ones who are alive," Ryan said, his blood-shot eyes reflecting the red neon signs in front of the Garden. "Coke and a burger, those two and you hold the American dream in your hands. Oh, I meant my left hand. I contributed the other one to the dream!"

Ryan laughed, snickered at some cosmic joke he blew smoke at. David and Rachael looked at the passing crowd in silence.

"This is a great chance to see George and Ringo together," Rachael said.

"Shit, Harrison should be good," said Ryan, doing a little dance step in a slight break in the flow of concert goers, swinging around on the metal post of the street light in front of them, running his fingers over the intricate metal filigrees. He bowed in front of Rachael. *"Lucy in the sky with diamonds!* And madam, the next dance?"

Rachael took up his request, swung around and around with

him on the hot sidewalk, her right hand in his left. David clapped to the cadence of their feet as they danced an Irish jig, stomping and jumping, Ryan twirling Rachael.

"Yeeeeeeehaaaaaah!" Ryan screamed.

Exhausted and sweating, they finally collapsed against the side of the building.

"You guys should be on stage," David laughed. Ryan brought out another joint from the corner of his Marlboro packet, lit it, took a long puff.

"The matinee was great," Rachael said. "Everyone's talking about it."

"Too bad John and McCartney didn't make it. Could've been a Beatles reunion!" Ryan said.

"Yeah, I guess no Ono, no John. He was supposed to be here. McCartney never wanted to do it anyhow," David said as he handed the joint back to Ryan. "Good shit, dude."

"Colombian Gold, Sinsemilla buds," Ryan said. "Just scored from this vet at the VA."

"Had some great Thai sticks in Vietnam, man," said David playing air guitar.

"No end to drugs in 'Nam: heroin, ludes, weed, you name your poison," added Ryan, the first whispers of paranoia knifing through his drug-fuzzed mind. He looked up at a clear New York skyline over the towering columns of mirrored glass where he stood. "Can't forget those whirlybirds buzzing in the air all the time. But they

---

The master, Ravi, came to the pupil, George, and asked for help for the dying, starving people of his land. For his guru, guru of the sitar, George Harrison went all out in single-handedly organizing the Concert for Bangladesh.

My friend came to me with sadness in his eyes,
Told me that he wanted to help
Before his country dies,
Although I couldn't feel the pain
I knew I had to try -
Now I'm asking all of you
To help save some lives
George Harrison.

The Concert for Bangladesh, the first benefit mega concert, the Woodstock of

are busy running dope in Thailand, not dropping no aid to these refugees!"

Ryan struck a pose as a flamenco dancer, hands on hips, head in the air as he tap danced in his sneakers on the concrete. David and Rachael clapped to the beat. "Eeeeeehaaaaa!" Rachael said laughing at Ryan's antics.

"Yeah, what kept us going was the dope. Knew a guy on tranquilizers, and when he got shot, shot dead, he looked so damn peaceful. Dead," said David. "What a way to go huh? I don't think he even knew what hit him."

"You really into the peace movement?" asked Ryan, looking at Rachael.

"Yeah, my brother Frank died in Vietnam. For what? What good is this war doing?" Rachael said.

"I'm really sorry," Ryan said. "Didn't mean to pry."

"Naah, that's alright. Hard to get over it when it's your brother," Rachael said.

"I guess he would've loved to see this concert," asked Ryan.

"My brother got to see Bob Hope and this Indian goddess in the middle of the war," said Rachael.

"Really?" said David. "USO show?"

"Indian goddess?" Ryan's eyes lit up.

"Yes," Rachael said. "The last show he saw featured an Indian Miss World, Reita Faria, with Bob Hope. It was the first year that he was there. Christmas 1966. Frank was all excited about it. His first

---

benefit concerts, tied to the spirit of peace, love and music, was an unprecedented event, initiated by Ravi Shankar and organized primarily by George Harrison in a very narrow time frame.

Without Ravi Shankar and George Harrison's efforts, much of the suffering endured by the Bangladeshi people at the time would have gone unnoticed. Few noticed that millions of East Pakistanis were being killed, raped, forced to flee to refugee camps. After the Concert, everybody knew the name of Bangla Desh as overnight the word spread far and wide and world attention focused into this tiny war-ravaged country.

It was the '70s, the Vietnam years, the psychotic years, the psychedelic years and the year of the Holocaust in East Pakistan.

George Harrison started to call on friends with an obsession, drawing on his

Christmas in Vietnam and his last Christmas anywhere," Rachael said.

Across the street limousines were pulling up, taking the musicians and celebrities into the Garden. The crowd mobbed each car, trying to get a glimpse of the celebrities inside.

"Did you kill anyone while you were there?" Rachael asked looking at David then turning to Ryan.

David fidgeted, put his hands inside his jean pockets, looked across to the police barricades around the Garden. Ryan blew out a wisp of smoke. It hovered like a tiny cloud in the humid Manhattan summer.

"What the fuck do you expect when you give a soldier a machine gun and the license to kill? Huh?" asked Ryan. Like a kaleidoscope, images swirled inside his mind, of the faces of dead bodies, mud covered, writhing in pain.

"Guys went crazy. Even shot cows dead, blew out their brains. Most the kids who went there hadn't see anything outside of their home town. And then there you are, in the middle of this fucking muddy gook country," David said.

David gingerly held the dwindling joint, the rolling paper now a tarred light brown, in between his thumb and index finger. He took another hit, shook his head and spoke from the back of his throat without exhaling, "How much shit can a nineteen-year-old take? This crap from the Generals. Just how great things are and how soon we will be out of there. Never happens. And you are holding pieces

---

extensive web of show-business connections. The concert came together quietly, as Harrison spent June into July putting together the pieces that would lead to a first of a kind benefit concert.

August 1, a Sunday, was the only day the Garden was available and so that day was booked.

Because tickets to the evening show sold out so quickly, a matinee show at noon was added. Two concerts took place and 40,000 people attended.

The Concert for Bangladesh lives today in its lasting legacy of being the first benefit concert of its magnitude in the history of the world—that it spawned so many benefit concerts—a precursor to Live aid, Farm aid, Live Earth and the like. It serves today, as it has served yesterday, as the model of love, concern and peace embodied in hundreds of philanthropic musical efforts since.

of your buddy. You take it out on the first moving thing you see."

Images of malnourished East Pakistani refugee children starving to death, Vietnamese civilians in the rain running from gunfire fused into each other in David's mind. "A great cause," David said, running his fingers through his hair, shaking his head, trying to get his mind off of flashbacks of Vietnam.

"Fuck man, my buddy Joel kept saying, 'I don't want to die, God.' Then he said, 'Mom, I don't want to go. Mom, I don't want to go.' He had just gotten a letter from his mother. Just nineteen. And when he died in my arms, man I freaked. I fucking went berserk." Ryan stopped, slapped a brick hard.

"Frank, he killed a little kid by accident," Rachael said.

"Shit, that's fucked," said Ryan. After a minute he asked, "Where was he?"

"Mekong Delta," Rachael said.

David passed the joint to Ryan. Holding the roach in his yellowed index finger and thumb, Ryan took the last lung filling hit off the joint, held his breath.

"My brother killed a family. Accidentally killed this little kid. It was part of an operation they were in. All there in his diary," Rachael said looking up at the last streaks of sunlight brushing gold shadows on top of the long concrete canyon of buildings stretching down Manhattan as far as her eyes could see.

"Sadly, it happens all the time," said Ryan. He lit a Marlboro. "Cig?"

"Yeah, sure," David said. Ryan passed the hard pack of Marlboros.

Other firsts included the first live appearance for George Harrison after the breaking up of the Beatles. Bob Dylan made his first stage appearance since the Isle of Wight Festival in August 1969; it was the first live performance of "While My Guitar Gently Weeps."

It featured an all-star group of performers that included Bob Dylan, Eric Clapton, George Harrison, Billy Preston, Leon Russell, Badfinger and Ringo Star.

"It was the most moving and intense musical experience of the century," said Ravi Shankar.

George Harrison performed classic renditions of "Here Comes the Sun," "Awaiting On You All," and "What Is Life?" Ringo Starr's highlight is an excellent version of "It Don't Come Easy."

The Concert for Bangla Desh was filmed and recorded. Ticket sales and royalties

David lit a cigarette, rubbed his bloodshot eyes, blew smoke circles above his head, said nothing.

"A part of him died with the little boy. I think that was what caused him to lose it," Rachael said, stared blankly down at the pavement. "And then he was shot trying to save a buddy. The whole thing was like a bad omen."

"Vietnam's so fucked up," David said.

"A two-year-old boy slowly bleeding to death in his arms and nothing he could do. He was all torn up," said Rachael.

"Seems like war really has become about killing innocents," Ryan said. "But no one wants to admit it."

"How are your parents doing, Rachael?" asked David.

"Dad's quiet, lost in his thoughts. Mom, she cries, mostly by herself, reading Frank's letters and his diary. Searching for some answer. They wanted me to be here away from home, away from all of Frank's things. Get away from it all," Rachael said, her voice dropping to a painful whisper.

"U.S. foreign policy comes in two flavors, fucked and royally fucked!" Ryan said baying like a wolf at the sky, his empty sleeve thrashing in the air.

"I remember the day that they came to the door. The one time you don't want to answer the door. My mother answered and she just didn't want to believe it. She was in shock for a week. Frank was her everything," Rachael said.

"The dreaded death knock," said Ryan. "A parent's worst nightmare."

---

generated by the movie and three-record set raised approximately fifteen million dollars for the relief effort for Bangla Desh. Tax related problems and non-profit status issues, however, crippled the final efforts to get the money promptly to the refugees. But even though the money was slow to reach the needy, aid and attention were quickly brought to help the refugees all due to this concert.

A unique relationship between Ravi Shankar and George Harrison bloomed into a one-of-a-kind concert and overnight Bangla Desh was on the tongue of the world, bringing much needed attention to the cause of the war ravaged country, and the desperately needed international aid efforts for the refugees. August 1 was four months into the genocide in Bangla Desh and as it turned out smack in the middle of the nine months that it ultimately took to liberate the country. The timing was perfect.

For a long minute Rachael looked at the Madison Square Garden sign across the street, now glowing in the little light of dusk. "The hardest part for us was she kept thinking she could have stopped Frank from going to Vietnam somehow."

"The human ego is a strange thing. Absolute power can even destroy a nation," David said. "Here in Bangla Desh one General is killing millions, dumping them into rivers, and in 'Nam another General is filling body bags. Counting twice."

"Frank would have loved seeing Dylan. Loved him," Rachael said. "He was into that kind of music, loved poetry, wrote all the time."

In front of Rachael were images of malnourished Bangla Deshi children hanging limply in their mothers' arms; in her mind's eye, Frank was holding onto the bloody body of a dying Vietnamese child.

"TIME TO GO," DAVID SAID to Rachael and Ryan, as the concert hour neared.

"Rock and roll," Ryan said, twirling around as he played air guitar, jumping up and down. They slowly headed towards the Garden, crossed 8th Avenue.

Rachael, David and Ryan joined a long line of people winding around Madison Square Garden, waiting to get the once over by NYC's finest. The crowd grew louder. Once past the entrance, the three were swept away by a thick crowd cramming into a tight corridor that led to the sports auditorium, the home of the New

---

The birth of Bangladesh, aided by the Concert for Bangla Desh, has been a seminal seed that has flourished in man's humanity towards his fellow man.

In the matinee show and in the evening show, the following artists played:

Eric Clapton - guitars
Bob Dylan - vocals, guitar, harmonica
George Harrison - vocals, guitars
Billy Preston - vocals, keyboards
Leon Russell - bass, keyboards, vocals
Ringo Starr - drums, vocals, tambourine
Ravi Shankar - sitar
Ustad Ali Akbar Khan - sarod
Ustad Allah Rakha - tabla

York Knicks, and now George Harrison's philanthropic ensemble. From the rafters to the basketball court, Madison Square Garden was jam packed, fans screaming, jumping, dancing at the chance to see George and Ringo, Clapton and Dylan and all the other superstars. Most of the concert goers were in their late teens to early 20s, a Beatles crowd with a sprinkling of Deshis.

"This is great!" David yelled out over the sound of the crowd to Rachael and Ryan. They meshed into the delirium of activity as bright lights washed over the excited fans on the floor.

The stage was huge, set up to hold Harrison and his friends, the mass ensemble of almost thirty musicians and singers. Rachael, Ryan and David were surrounded by the throng of excited fans, packed in so tight they could barely move.

"George, yeah!" David shouted.

"Ringo!" Ryan screamed over the crowd.

As the concert began, a bearded, long-haired, elated tall and lanky George Harrison came up on stage, dressed in a tangerine full-sleeve shirt and a white suit, a small Krishna in Hindi embroidered in red on the lapels.

"I just want to say before we start the concert, that to thank you all for coming here, and as you all know it's a special benefit concert. We've got a good show lined up. I hope so, anyway," said George.

The roar from the crowd was deafening.

George Harrison introduced Ravi Shankar, asking the crowd to settle down.

Then Ravi Shankar and his troupe walked onto the stage, each

Kamala Chakvaraty - tamboura
The Band
Jesse Ed Davis - rhythm guitar
Tom Evans - acoustic guitar
Pete Ham - acoustic guitar
Mike Gibbins - percussion
Jim Keltner - drums
Joey Molland - acoustic guitar
Don Preston - guitars, backing vocals
Carl Radle - bass guitar
Klaus Voorman - bass guitar

carrying their instrument, and sat down in a shallow arc, Ravi on the far left, Ustad Ali Akbar Khan on the far right with the sarod. Alla Rakha on tabla, Kamala Chakravarty on the tamboura in the middle.

"Ravi!" Rachael screamed out. The crowd applauded, clapped, the sounds echoing against the high Garden wall and ceiling.

"Quiet! Silence please. For this we need silence," Ravi asked the screaming crowd, their hands up in the air.

"Friends, as George told you just now they will be participating in the second part. The first part is going to be us playing for you on the Indian Instruments. The Indian Music... We are trying to set the music to this special event, this historical program which is not a program as usual but which has a message. And to make you aware of a very serious situation that is happening...through our music we would like you to feel the agony and also the pain and lot of sad happenings in Bangla Desh, and also the refugees who have come to India... Thank you so very much."

The instruments went out of tune due to heat from the bright lights, and for a couple of minutes Ravi and group tuned, tightened the strings, plucked. When they were done tuning, the crowd, mostly unfamiliar with Indian music, clapped, thinking that was a set.

"Thank you! If you appreciate the tuning so much, I hope you will appreciate the playing more. Thank you," Ravi said, a beaming smile on his face.

The first piece, *Bangla Dhun,* set the tone for the rest of the concert.

The Hollywood Horns
Jim Horn, Allan Beutler, Chuck Findley, Jackie Kelso, Lou McCreary, Ollie Mitchell
The Backing vocalists
Don Nix, Jo Green, Jeanie Greene, Marlin Greene, Dolores Hall, Claudia Linnear

Afternoon show
"Bangla Dhun"—Ravi Shankar, Ali Akbar Khan, Allah Rakha, Kamala Chakravarty
"Wah Wah"—George Harrison and Band
"Something"—George Harrison and Band

"I love the sitar," said Rachael.

Ravi starts to pluck melodiously on the sitar in a duet with the master of sarod, Ustad Ali Akbar Khan, while rhythm is provided by Alla Rakha and Kamala Chakravarty.

In a momentary break, the applause. The duet rises into an intense piece. Ryan, his eyes closed, nods his head in sync with the beat of the tabla.

At the end of the performance, there is huge applause, the crowd loving every minute. Ravi and the Band get up and bow to the crowd, carrying their instruments away.

The whole stage now shifts to George Harrison and his mass ensemble of musicians, singers, instrumentalists—altogether almost thirty.

"Wah Wah" is the first tune played by George Harrison and the band. The whole stage comes alive bathed in an electric purple light as Harrison rocks the crowd.

Next up is "My Sweet Lord." The rhythm slows down, Harrison twangs an acoustic guitar, gently rocking the crowd.

Third up Billy Preston with his rocking rhythm and blues brings the house down. Preston takes the crowd to a church revival meeting with "That's the Way God Planned It." The spirit is so strong, the groove so deep, that Preston jumps up from his keyboard in the middle of his set. The music is free-flowing and melodious, and the band is just jamming, and Preston in the spirit of the moment does his jabberwocky shuffle across the floor, hopping, skipping and dancing and Harrison and the rest of the band are jamming away,

"Awaiting On You All"—George Harrison and Band
"That's The Way God Planned It"—Billy Preston and Band
"It Don't Come Easy"—Ringo Starr and Band
"Beware Of Darkness"—Leon Russell and Band
"While My Guitar Gently Weeps"—Eric Clapton and Band
"Jumpin' Jack Flash"—Leon Russell and Band
"Young Blood"—Leon Russell and Band
"Here Comes The Sun"—Pete Ham and Band
"A Hard Rain's A-Gonna Fall"—Bob Dylan and Band
"Blowin' In The Wind"—Bob Dylan and Band
"It Takes a Lot to Laugh, It Takes a Train to Cry"—Bob Dylan and Band
"Love Minus Zero/No Limit"—Bob Dylan and Band

tripping away at the beauty of the show.

The energetic crowd sways like tall grass blowing in a breeze, as resounding melodies saturate every corner of Madison Square Garden. The energy from the gospel music explodes like a gust of wind, the frenzy climbs to a peak, in a perfect unison as Preston captures the revival spirit.

"Lord help us," screams Rachael. "That's the Way God Planned It."

"Feel like I'm back in church," David says.

"That's the way, that's the way God!" Ryan yells out at the top of his lungs.

Accompanying guitars join the melody, then an intense burst as the entire band erupts. Drums pounding, tremors of bass and guitars screaming wildly, a raging storm of musical energy in perfect harmony.

George Harrison says,

"I'd like to introduce you to a few people here. Everybody here came at very short notice and some people even cancelled a few gigs to try to make it, and nobody was paid for anything."

"We got on drums, Ringo Starr." The crowd went wild, applause filling the air.

"Also on drums, Jim Keltner. On bass ...Klaus Voorman."

"We've got a whole lot of guitarists. Mr. Jesse Ed Davis. An old friend of mine, Mr. Eric Clapton."

The applause, the screaming is deafening.

"Just Like a Woman"—Bob Dylan and Band
"Hear Me Lord"—George Harrison and Band
"My Sweet Lord"—Bob Dylan and Band
"Bangla Desh"—George Harrison and Band

Evening show
"Bangla Dhun"—Ravi Shankar, Ali Akbar Khan, Allah Rakha, Kamala Chakravarty
"Wah-Wah"—George Harrison and Band
"My Sweet Lord"—Bob Dylan and Band
"That's The Way God Planned It"—Billy Preston and Band
"It Don't Come Easy"—Ringo Starr and Band
"Beware Of Darkness"—Leon Russell and Band

"Somebody I'm sure you all know now on piano, Leon."

"I don't know if they're coming through on acoustic guitars, but it's an Apple band, Badfinger."

"And we've got a whole lot of singers out there. The singers are all from all different parts of the world, give them a big hand."

"And the Hollywood Horn players, led by Jim Horn. And we've forgotten Billy Preston."

By now the applause has reached a fever pitch, the screaming kicked up a few decibels.

After the introductions Ringo sings *While My Guitar Gently Weeps* with Eric Clapton.

"Go Clapton," Ryan screams.

"Yeah Ringo!" David yells out.

Rachael sways to the beat, in hypnotic gyrations. Her hips shimmy, she moves to the rhythm, holding her hands above her, rocking side to side, swinging, surging to the undulating rhythms.

Finally after six songs and "Here Comes the Sun," performed by Pete Horn, the reclusive Bob Dylan walks onto the stage from out of the dark shadows. Wearing a faded blue jean jacket, looking like an Oakie, carrying his acoustic guitar and a harmonica clipped onto a metal holder, his tangled curls wreathing his stubble-mottled face, Dylan warbles in his twangy, nasal style, "A Hard Rain's Gonna Fall," "Blowin' in the Wind," and "It Takes a Lot to Laugh," amongst a half dozen songs he performs accompanied by an elated George Harrison, ecstatic that his reclusive friend makes it onto the NYC stage.

"While My Guitar Gently Weeps"—Eric Clapton and Band

"Jumpin' Jack Flash"—Leon Russell and Band

"Youngblood"—Leon Russell and Band

"Here Comes The Sun"—Pete Ham and Band

"Hard Rain's A-Gonna Fall"—Bob Dylan and Band

"It Takes A Lot To Laugh, It Takes a Train to Cry"—Bob Dylan and Band

"Blowin' In The Wind"—Bob Dylan and Band

"Mr. Tambourine Man"—Bob Dylan and Band

"Just Like A Woman"—Bob Dylan and Band

"Something"—George Harrison and Band

"Bangla Desh"—George Harrison and Band

A long concert draws to a close with the final song, 'Bangla Desh,' composed and sung by George Harrison. George Harrison sings the final song with a penetrating conviction, twanging the electric guitar with his long fingers, sax riffs rising, drums thrumming, jamming into a musical crescendo.

My friend came to me, with sadness in his eyes.
He told me that he wanted help before his country dies.
Bangla Desh, Bangla Desh
...

Bangla Desh, Bangla Desh

—⸕—

LATE IN THE EVENING AFTER the concert, on the north bound Broadway subway train from Penn Station, Rachael, Ryan and David swayed to the rhythmic rumble of the rails as it bent and twisted through dark steel and concrete tunnels. As Rachael hung on to an overhead strap, her wrist swung, hitting a metal pole, Frank's silver band making a rhythmic clicking sound in sync with the sway.

"How many refugees are dying crossing the border? Who knows?" David said, as they rounded a curve.

"With ten million refugees counted, even if a few are killed, die from starvation, that's a few hundred thousand, maybe much, much more," said Rachael.

"Man, we're the cherries, the FNG's, then in a body bag. Just a tally, a number to count who won the war," Ryan said.

"They kept on counting bodies. Gooks. Us. One day we won. Next we lost. Like a General's body count score board," David said.

"Strange how we were winning the war one week and the next we were losing, and we were on the same shitty piece of ground. Same fucking ground, and the big wigs they called it a victory 'cause the count was in our favor. Well hell, next week we lost because our body bag count was larger than the gook count," said Ryan. "Fucking slimy plastic body bags."

"Strange how the only thing that mattered in Vietnam was the body count," Rachael said.

"Yeah, and it's the exact opposite in East Pakistan," Ryan said. The subway train rocked. And Ryan leaned against a metal pole for balance. Lights in the car flashed on and off. The sharp sounds of wheels scraping against the rails.

"The West Pakistani General's victory is the lack of a body count," Rachael added. Watching the subterranean world flash by like a filmstrip in the graffittied darkness, then in flashes of light, she saw Frank's beaming face from the Christmas of '66, radiant and happy. She saw the faces of pale, gaunt refugee children. Images of children starving, hollow eyes of hunger, filled her head as the subway rolled through the black damp tunnels, her brain still on a musical high.

"It don't come easy. No easy independence for East Pakistan."

"That's for sure," said Ryan.

"We just supported the refugees. Ravi, George, Leon, everyone did. People for people. And Nixon is busy giving arms to the West Pakistani killers," said David.

"War is hell." Ryan said. "Anywhere. Everywhere."

"And sure as shit is easier to support a fucking dictator than a legit government. Look who they have up the flag pole in Vietnam. Another gook who is a spook and got his fingers in the grease and the honey. Same shit another fucking country, Pakistan. Support another genocide. Another fucking dictator," said David.

"Strange man. Some fucked up shit, I don't get," Ryan sang out in sarcasm, twirling around the subway pole. "I'm the refugee on Main Street, America, refugee of Vietnam, looking for my mind. Who's gonna take care of me? No one? Vietnam Vets don't matter anymore?"

The signs of the stations flashed by: Port Authority, Columbus Circle, Lincoln Center, 72nd St, 79th St, 86th St.

"Thanks for the ticket to the concert," Ryan said. He looked at Rachael and David, an emptiness in his eyes.

"Anytime, Ryan," David said, hugging him goodbye.

"See ya," Rachael said kissing Ryan on the cheek, squeezing his left hand.

On 96th St, Ryan got off before the Columbia University stop at 116th.

215

"Gotta go see about a prosthetic arm at the VA tomorrow, David. See if my donation there brings me anything," Ryan said as he stepped off.

The train rolled on. With the sharp clanging cadence of the subway, Rachael's mind echoed with music and the cries of starving refugees.

—❦—

DOWNSTAIRS, IN THE COLUMBIA DORMITORY hallway, the coin-operated telephone was a black metal box bolted to the wall above the hall table. Rachael lifted the heavy receiver to her ear and dialed. After a few moments, as prompted, she dropped a handful of quarters into the slot, waited.

"Dad!" she said, the familiar voice on the other end bringing warmth into the long empty hallway.

"Rachael how are you?"

"Fine Dad. Great. How are you guys doing?"

"Good. And how was your concert last night?" asked Jack.

"Fantastic! You should have been there," Rachael said.

"Let me get your Mom. Hang on."

After a few seconds of transcontinental silence Laura said, "Rachael, how are you? How are things at Columbia?"

"Fine Mom, you should have seen the Concert for Bangla Desh. It was just great."

"What a great thing George Harrison and Ravi Shankar did! Priti told me about it. Everyone is talking about the concert."

"Priti?"

"Oh, that's right. You haven't met her. Priti Kumar, a student of mine doing her Ph.D. at UCLA. She's from Calcutta. Wonderful girl. You definitely should meet her when you are back home."

"'Holocaust in East Pakistan,' that's how Geraldo Rivera described it on channel 7," added Jack.

"It's wonderful all these musicians have come together for such a great cause," said Laura.

"Can we help somehow?" Rachael asked.

"I'll ask Priti. She has relatives in East Pakistan who are now refugees. She should know," Laura said.

"Thank God for the Concert for Bangla Desh; it's brought so much attention to the genocide in East Pakistan," said Jack. "Just senseless killing. Senseless as Vietnam."

"I feel terrible for those sad eyed refugee children, frozen on the laps of their parents, bombed into some strange numbness," Rachael said.

"It's so horrible," Laura said. "In war children suffer the most."

"They are organizing into guerrillas, determined to fight for their freedom." Jack said, his voice now expansive. "Freedom is never free."

"Mom, Dad, got to go. Tell Uncle Joe and Scott I said hi. I love you," Rachael said.

"Call us next Sunday Rachael. I'll talk to Priti, see what we can do to support the refugees," Laura said.

"Bye Mom! Bye Dad!" Rachael said as she hung up. Slowly she walked down the long hallway. With deliberate steps, Rachael walked to the stairs and climbed up to her room, humming,

... My Guitar Gently Weeps for you
Bangla Desh, Bangla Desh.

❧

Bell-bottom Guerillas

❧ ❧ ❧

July-August 1971, Dacca, East Pakistan

GRENADES, A STEN GUN AND plastic explosives clanged to the
rhythm of Rafique's leaps of faith across puddles on First Lane,
Kalabagan. With green *moola* tops poking conspicuously from
the jute grocery bag, Rafique, his heart racing, turned the corner
into the alley, jumped across another puddle, and threw his brown
chador over his cotton Panjabi. He hiked up his worn bell-bottom
pants and adjusted the straps of his slippery sandals as he tried to
navigate the flooded alley. In a tense morning's journey from the
outskirts of Dacca, Rafique had bypassed two army checkpoints,
thanks to the knowing tendrils of the *Mukti Bahini*. Desperately
he sought shelter for the night at Dr. Samad's.

Under the leadership of Khaled Musharraf, Sector Two
Commander, Dacca was buzzing, a hive of guerrilla activity. A
shroud of terror weighed on the city. At every turn a machine gun
brandishing soldier looked you over. On the corner was a military
truck ready to haul anyone off to an MP Hostel, a death camp.
Hopelessness was etched in lines of fear on the common man's face,
fear darkened his downcast, averted eyes.

Rafique hurried down the alley and as he turned the corner, his eyes focused on the Red Cross sign, a beacon of sanctuary, painted on the yellow wall of the closed pharmacy in front of a house. As the rain started to plow up the muddy side streets, thoughts of the recent battle rattled inside Rafique's head, and Jewel and Khalid's deaths gnawed at his insides.

Coming out of his trance, Rafique knocked on the metal front gate, looked up at a brick and cement two-story yellow house. Signs of abandonment showed in the rusting metal grill of a second floor veranda, the moss covered wall above now like a droopy eyelid.

This section of Dacca, centrally located around First Lane, Kalabagan, was as Rafique had remembered it; a long narrow road, with alleys shooting off, lined with houses and shoehorned shops cramped into every little corner. Off to the south lay blocks of Government Staff Quarters, yellow mildew stained five and six story apartment complexes. The buildings eyed with metal bar windows adorned in drying laundry.

He knew the yellow house well, had been here in the pre-March 25 days with Nazmul. The house belonged to Dr. Samad, now helping treat refugees in India.

Rafique tried to avoid the scrutinizing gaze of the next-door *durwan* as he knocked once more on the gate. Every eye seemed to be riveted on him.

This late morning only a solitary shivering rickshaw-wallah sat under the drawn top of his rickshaw. Wrapped in a blue plastic tarp usually reserved for passengers, parked in front of the closed pharmacy, he smoked a *biri*, trying to warm his insides, cold after pulling passengers through knee-deep water. The street was deserted, as the monsoon rains had driven everyone in Dacca inside. Inside the houses in fear, inside themselves, inside their souls for answers to the whys of their upturned lives.

Rafique, drenching wet, cast furtive glances as he knocked again on the metal gate.

The rickshaw-wallah said, "Bhai, Pharmacy closed. Anyone inside?"

Rafique knocked once more.

Finally the *durwan*, old, haggard, wearing a stained cotton

undershirt and green and grey checkered threadbare *lungi*, opened
the side metal door and looked at Rafique.

"Chan Mian, how are you?" Rafique said.

Recognizing Rafique, the *durwan's* tired eyes instantly widened,
and he flashed a red *paan* stained grin through his missing teeth.

"Rafique Bhai, *keemon acheen*, how are you?" said the *durwan*
in a splintered voice, like a note on a cracked bamboo flute. He was
a small man, with fear in his flat, hard eyes. Chan Mian pulled
Rafique in and quickly closed the metal side door behind him with
a bang, locking it.

Inside the compound was a padlocked first floor office, a small
enclosed courtyard with a few unkempt coconut palms, a scraggly
papaya plant and neglected rose bushes.

"My motorcycle!" Rafique exclaimed in joy seeing his bike parked
under the stairs.

"Samad *Shaaheb* left it," Chan Mian said, his face reflecting
Rafique's joy.

The *durwan* led Rafique to the back where there was an empty
storeroom. On one side of the small room was a quilt on a bamboo
mesh mat, a bed with a bare bed roll, and in the far corner a wooden
alna.

"Nazmul?" Rafique inquired of the *durwan*, who stood staring
at him with a questioning look in his eyes.

"Nazmul Bhai in the afternoon," said the *durwan* in a humble
voice and then added, "Bhai, *keechu lagbe*, need something?"

"*Naa*, nothing," Rafique said, his voice weary and drawn, his
arms rags, his blood-shot eyes closing in on him. "The quilt will
do."

Rafique lay down on a hand-stitched field of birds and flowers.
All day he had felt someone was twisting a metal wire around his
chest with a pair of pliers, increasing the tension constantly, almost
reaching a breaking point. Laying down, looking at the ceiling,
exhaling a long, deep breath, he said, "Allah *amaree bachaichee*,
Allah saved me."

A little light seeped in through the green bars of the small corner
window along with the sweet earthy fragrance of the moist July air.
Rafique took out, tapped, and lit the last of his cigarettes. He blew

smoke rings towards the ceiling. The rings lingered and then floated down in the airless room.

He thought about Nahar. His father and mother. And Sheetalpur.

The room was dark and empty around him and the rain filled the afternoon, a steady beat on the tin back porch, sleepy and soothing, the cars rushing by on Mirpur road a half mile away.

Rafique toyed with the trigger of his Sten gun now warm beside him. He cocked and depressed the trigger, then slowly released it, his mission clear. In his jute sack were the five pounds of yellow putty-like plastic explosive, three grenades and two thin pencil timers. He felt his mind, usually focused, alert, fade to thoughts of Nahar, his parents, Sheetalpur.

Thoughts of a girl who had peeked at him, blushing under a pink *dupatta*. The girl he had married, and for four months had not held. Nahar.

"Nahar," he whispered.

Rafique fell into a deep sleep on the mat in the corner of the store room, in a bell-bottom guerrilla hideout in Dacca.

NAZMUL CAME IN THE LATE afternoon, stood in the doorway. Startled, Rafique sat up and reached for his Sten hidden under his chador.

"Rafique, don't shoot!" Nazmul cried out.

Rafique focused, looked at Nazmul's face. Suddenly realizing where he was, he put down the Sten gun, Nazmul silhouetted in the doorway like an apparition.

"You're OK!" said Nazmul as he embraced Rafique in a deep rib-crushing hug. A smile as wide as the Meghna filled Nazmul's face. Like a trophy, Rafique held Nazmul in his hands, stepping back to look him up and down. Nazmul looked aged in his scraggly beard—disheveled, hollow-eyed and tense.

"How are you Nazmul? I thought you guys must have blown up all of Dacca by now!" Rafique said, his weary eyes coming to life.

"Blow up all of Dacca? We're too busy hiding most of the time!"

Nazmul, warmed by Rafique's hug, asked, "How is the rest of the group?"

Rafique looked away, walked to the small corner window and grimaced. "Jewel and Khalid became martyrs." Rafique looked out at the steady rain. A long moment passed.

Nazmul approached him, patted Rafique softly on his back, "I know Rafique..."

"How is Nahar? Abba and Amma?" Rafique asked.

"Last news that I got is two weeks old. They were fine," Nazmul said.

"And Neezam, Bodor?"

"Neezam's men came by our house. My parent's said nothing. The military has not entered Sheetalpur yet," Nazmul said, and a darkness surfaced in Rafique's expression.

Rafique strode out to the veranda, scratched the rough of a two-day-old beard.

"Cigarette?"

Nazmul handed Rafique a cigarette, lighting it for him.

"Samad Uncle is in Agartala?" Rafique asked.

"No, he was. From there he left for the Salt Lake refugee camp outside Calcutta to treat sick refugees."

"What's going on in Dacca?" Rafique asked, looking at the glow of his cigarette, watching the curling smoke hang heavy in the moist air.

"A lot. June was really busy; the grenades we lobbed at the Intercontinental Hotel were a great success."

"How's the power station operation going?" Rafique asked.

"We'll need 80 to 90 pounds of PK to blow it up. The boys have been moving about 8 to 10 pounds a day into the power station, hidden inside the inner cover of a car door. That is why it's taking so much time," Nazmul said drawing on his cigarette. "We don't have enough PK in Dacca. We need more from across the border. After we have moved enough PK inside the power station, we can blow it up. Meanwhile we keep the Pakistani troops distracted by other guerrilla actions."

"How many hideouts?" Rafique asked.

"More than twenty. In Hatkhola, Dhanmondi, Maghbazar, other

areas."

"Safe?"

"Safe for now, but we can't stay at the same place for too long," Nazmul said solemnly. "Safe till some bastard rat squeals. We have to move every few days."

Rafique put out his cigarette and went inside. He pulled up his jute sack, opened it.

"August is going to be a very busy month," Rafique said as he pointed to the thin pencil timer and the PK.

A faint smile crept into Nazmul's weary, worry-creased face.

—⁂—

LATE INTO THE AFTERNOON, NAZMUL went all out to have the *durwan* cook some rice-and-*daal khichri* and even get some green chilies and a lime.

"Saar, not enough," Chan Mian had told Nazmul.

"Put in more water," Nazmul had said, as the last of the onions, the rooted potatoes were all gone.

Chan Mian brought a plate of *khichri*, a green chile, a slice of lime with a little salt on one end of the plate. Sitting on the edge of the bed, Rafique looked up. The *durwan* put the food on the bed, to the side of Rafique. He set a glass of water next to it.

Starving, Rafique devoured the *khichri*, breaking off the end of a green chile as he licked the taste of lime off of his fingers. "Rough week on the road from Agartala, Nazmul. *Dosht*, thanks! The *khichri* is great."

As he licked his fingers and slurped the last of the *daal* on his tin plate, Nazmul, eager to feed his best friend, called the *durwan* over and told him to bring another plate of *khichri*.

"Saar, no more."

"What about mine? Bring my plate," Nazmul whispered to Chan Mian.

"Nazmul you aren't eating?" Rafique asked.

"Oh, I had a great lunch just before I came," Nazmul said. While Rafique ate, Nazmul sat chatting, smiling. Nazmul drank a glass of water and lit a cigarette; seeing Rafique lift up the plate and slurp the last of the soupy *khichri* made him forget his gnawing hunger pangs.

Rafique walked out to the veranda, poured the water out of a glass and washed his hands. He looked up at Nazmul and asked, "Got anything to read? Bhuddhu Dev, Mailer, Dostoyevsky, Uris?"

"I've a Bhuddhu Dev and Uris's *The Exodus*," said Nazmul.

"Bhuddhu Dev! Like old times again, Nazmul," Rafique said as he relaxed.

"Like old times."

IN THE EVENING, FIROZ AND Rintu joined them, dripping wet from the relentless rain.

"Rafique Bhai," they both exclaimed hugging Rafique, smiling, their faces radiating a newfound confidence. Endless questions filled the small room—about the bridge operation, about operations in Dacca, about the goings on at the guerrilla training camp at Melaghar—and the men told stories of lucky escapes, bombings, guerrilla operations into the early evening. In their hearts was the fear of capture, death at any moment, and on their lips this evening in this small smoky storeroom was laughter and humor.

Firoz and Rintu, both from the city, dared not stay at home for fear of capture. Having the luxury of sneaking home once in a while to shave, shower and eat a home-cooked meal, they looked in much better shape than Rafique or Nazmul.

"Ran out of cigarettes. Firoz you have any?" asked Nazmul.

"Yeah, sure, here," Firoz said, his anxious eyes lit up as he handed Rafique a freshly opened brown and gold hard pack of 555s.

"Thanks." Rafique said.

The four guerrillas sat in a semi-circle on the quilt, leaned up against the bed, the sweating cement wall.

Nazmul brought out the deck of cards and laid it out.

As the overcast day turned into a wet night, the card game took prisoner the minds and hands of the four guerrillas. Except for Rafique's fits of swearing, they played without much talk. The card game in this wait-and-see time allowed them a dependable silence, masking and comforting them in the solitude of their fears.

Nazmul shuffled and Rafique, Rintu and Firoz held their cards close and they held their thoughts closer. Nazmul cut the cards and put out a lay, slowly and deliberately. Nazmul stared at his hand, pretended a lack of interest. He flounced the card together and turned around to Rafique, studying his face intently, wondering about Rafique's thoughts.

"Shit, wish I had an ace," said Rintu as he threw down his cards, his small round face filled with disappointment.

"Don't throw out your luck on little stuff. You ain't going to have it when you need it for real!" said Rafique. "Keep your wishes for your life, and forget the luck on the cards."

"Rafique," Nazmul said, "it's your play."

Rafique draws an ace from the deck, avoids looking either at his hand or at the card. He slaps it into the discard pile. Nazmul, holding two aces, decides he will wait until his next turn to pick it up.

Thursday 22nd July 1971

In large and small ways, Rafique, Nazmul, Firoz and Rintu's lives were defined by the sounds, whispers, looks and stares they faced on the streets of Dacca. A sudden noise, a peering gaze, made them wince, step faster, breathe harder. The ubiquitous Razakars were everywhere.

In July and August the bell-bottom guerrillas carried out frequent sorties into Dacca, operating at Baitul Mukarram, Malibagh rail crossing, the Election Commission, the television tower on top of the DIT building.

"Rafique, the city is submerged in water. I have never seen such a heavy downpour in recent years," Nazmul said under a mid-morning sun blotted out by heavy clouds.

"There's water in our compound. The road is under knee deep water. It was almost dry only a couple of hours ago. It's coming down in buckets!" said Rafique.

"The bloody Pakistani army is up a river without a paddle," said Firoz, usually quiet, laughing.

"Can the Pakistanis swim? We will drown them now," Rintu said. "They're not used to our big rivers and lakes."

Rafique looked at the newspaper in the corner of the room and cursed under his breath. "Martial Law Regulation no. 159 allows the Razakars to arrest anyone without a warrant, and they have been given the weapons and license to kill."

"Yahya is in a tight corner. Tikka has to strengthen the Razakars and raise more new killers," Nazmul said.

"The government is bringing in militias from West Pakistan— the ones wearing gray baggy pants and knee-length *kurta* shirts," Rafique said. "You see them manning the check posts around Purbani Hotel."

"Yes, I spotted a few on Mirpur road," said Nazmul.

As the light dimmed in the western horizon, and the room fell silent and dark, Rintu said, "No water or electricity today!"

"The power sub-station near the P.G. Hospital Shahbag power station has been blown," said Nazmul.

"And don't forget Ulan and Gulbagh power stations," added Firoz.

"Avoid the P.G. Hospital area," Rafique said. "Rampura, Khilgaon and Shahbagh areas are being searched house to house."

When the cacophony of the day's events was heard, Rafique said, "We need to make a car bomb. Any ideas?"

"We found a car we can hijack," Nazmul said.

"What are we going to bomb?" asked Rintu, excitement and suppressed fear in his voice.

"Soldiers at Baitul Mukarram," said Rafique.

"Ganny's department store on Jinnah Avenue was hit. That was a big hangout for the soldiers shopping," said Firoz. "They just walked in and started brush firing with a Sten. Killed a few Pakistani soldiers. What a great operation!"

"Baitul Mukarram is just crawling with military. And we are going to blow up this car in broad daylight?" asked Rintu, his eyebrows raised.

"No, during the late afternoon." Rafique answered.

"And how much plastic explosives do we have?" Nazmul asked.

"We have five pounds." Rafique said. "And there's another five I can get."

Rafique opened his sack and showed them the yellow plastic explosive that looked like wood putty.

"How are we going to time it?"

"With a pencil timer."

"You have one?" asked Firoz.

"Yes," Rafique said as he pulled out the small chemical timers.

"How long?" Rintu wanted to know.

"Fifteen minutes. Had a choice of thirty or fifteen. Fifteen is better. If we sit around they will get suspicious."

"How does it work?" Firoz asked.

"You pull out this small safety strip paper, and then crush the end of the thin copper tube containing the cupric chloride with pliers, crush the tube to break the glass vial. There's a detonator inside the pencil and that will explode the PK. Fifteen minutes, then boom!"

Rafique passed the pencil timer to his men and they inspected it as if it was something magical.

—⚜—

August 7, 1971 Dacca

BY DHANMONDI LAKE RAFIQUE LEANED on his motorcycle and looked down the road skirting the row of white brick houses. Nazmul leaned up against an arching tree and smoked a cigarette, staring up at an afternoon graying sky through dark limbs and dense leaf clusters. Rafique's eyes moved over Dhanmondi lake, at the now empty bamboo and wood fishing platforms dotting the near edge of the water. Bloated bodies floated in the lake now. Gone were the anglers; missing, the once ever vigilant fishing ticket collector. For a week, Firoz and Rintu had been scoping out the green Fiat that belonged to one of these houses.

This afternoon the car came out of the gate with the solitary driver. He had dropped off a passenger and was on his way to pick up someone. This routine played out every afternoon. Like a green turtle, small round eager headlight eyes protruding with circular chrome rings, whitewall tires and shiny smooth hubcaps, the Fiat 600 puttered down the street in front of Rafique and Nazmul towards the next block where Firoz and Rintu were anxiously waiting. It was a four-seater with two flimsy doors, a rear 600cc engine and a front trunk.

The motorcycle was idling. When the fiat passed, Rafique and Nazmul hopped on the bike and raced after it. As precisely planned, Firoz and Rintu jumped out in front of the fiat at the intersection, Firoz brandishing his Sten gun as Rafique and Nazmul skidded to a stop behind, blocking the rear. The four had the car surrounded.

"*Mukti Bahini!*" shouted Rafique as he shoved his Sten from under his chador into the scared, colorless face of the driver. He gestured with a flick of the drilled barrel for him to get out.

"Joy Bangla! Saar, no shoot!" said the driver, his trembling hands pressed together in a plea. "Joy Bangla."

Firoz yanked the passenger door open as the driver scampered out, repeating his Joy Banglas. Rafique hopped in the driver's seat, as Firoz got in the passenger seat and Rintu slid into the back with the briefcase loaded with PK.

Nazmul torqued the bike out towards Mirpur road, as Rafique tried to catch up.

"Shit, brakes are not worth a damn," Rafique cursed over the sharp squeal, biting his upper lip as he tried to get used to the puttering idiosyncrasies of the little Fiat. "Worse than that old VW bug my Masud Uncle and I used to push through mud."

Rafique accelerated, using his left hand to downshift, to slow down without screeching the brakes, without drawing any unwanted attention. They crossed over the Mirpur road, into Kalabagan, up winding alleys, avoiding main streets.

A long hour later, after bypassing all the Pakistani army checkpoints, Rafique, Firoz and Rintu made it to Baitul Mukarram. They circled their target building and after three attempts parked in front of a military truck, next to some sari and fabric stores. The shopping center was full of military personnel.

Rafique smiled. Baitul Mukarram, the mosque and the adjoining area had become the bastion of the occupying forces.

Even before he had parked the car, a young street kid, a boy hardly seven or eight, came running up to them, "*Saar*, guard car?" he asked poking his sweat-stained grimy face against the driver's side glass window, bare feet, his shorts torn, a stained shirt with a missing sleeve. His hot breath made steamy nose rings on the glass.

"*Naa*," Rafique said turning off the Fiat.

"*Attem*. Orphan, Saar, no food all day," two begging eyes pleaded at Rafique. "Saar," he pleaded holding out an empty cupped hand.

Rafique quickly said, "*Oi*, go with them," he pointed to Firoz and Rintu who had already stood on the sidewalk.

Rafique took a deep breath, looked around. A light drizzle started to fall.

The streets emptied. Soldiers and Razakars shopped at the fabric and sari stores, their pockets heavy with the spoils of war.

Rafique slid over the gear shift to the passenger seat. He reached over with his right hand, pulled the grey plastic briefcase off the rear seat, lifting it ever so gently. He placed it on his lap, and then he snapped open the latches. Inside, padded by rolled up newspaper, on the side of the yellow PK tightly wrapped in clear plastic, the pencil timer stuck out. Taking a set of pliers from his pocket, Rafique squeezed the pencil timer hard, heard the sharp snap of the glass vial break. The fifteen minute fuse was triggered.

He adjusted the elastic metal band of his Citizen wrist watch. 4:30 exactly. Breathing through his mouth, Rafique closed the briefcase and then carefully hid it under the frayed passenger seat. His heart racing, he wiped the sweat off of his forehead on his sleeve.

In the corner of his eye, in horror he saw a Pakistani soldier coming towards him. Rafique froze. He counted his breaths. One. Two. Three. Slowly he turned his face away from the soldier. The green turtle had swallowed him in a cocoon of steam and sweat.

Twenty-five. Twenty-six...Thirty.

He dared not turn around. Now the light drizzle had changed into a strong steady rain, beating out a drum roll on the Fiat's top. Thararump. Thararump. Thararump. Drops of water dripped through a leak in the roof. Rafique glanced through the corner of his eye.

No one. The soldier was gone.

This was his chance. He pulled at the door handle, heard it click open. He slid out into welcome rain drops pelting his face and neck. It felt good. Looking straight towards the next side alley where Rintu and Firoz were waiting, waiting with the street kid. Rafique exhaled, steam escaping his mouth.

He noted the time on his watch. 4:35.

He walked with measured steps and joined them.

"Here," Rafique said giving the little kid fifty paisas. "Now go over there and find someone to bug," Rafique said pointing away from him.

"Saab, may you live long," the boy said as he hid the coin somewhere in the folds of his tattered shorts and ran, splashing through puddles in the other direction.

Rafique, Rintu and Firoz walked down to the next street, to the rickety corner chai stall supported by a rusting round metal electric pole, overhead wires like branches spreading out in every direction.

Nazmul rode up with the motorcycle and parked it angled in front of a rickshaw. Trying not to attract attention, Rintu and Firoz walked farther down the road, staying within the direct line of view of Rafique and Nazmul, to a mostly deserted bus stand. They huddled with a few stranded passengers.

"New Market, New Market," an eager conductor kid yelled out hanging from an approaching bus, banging on the side, a tinny evocation spreading out.

"Two cups of chai," Nazmul said sitting down on the wooden time worn bench under the corrugated tin awning that also served as the front wall of the stall.

"Waiting for someone?" asked the storekeeper. Flat-faced with a hooked nose, the man wore a long beard, a white skull cap, and a curious gaze.

"Yes," Rafique replied.

"By bus?" the storekeeper asked.

"Yes," Nazmul said, looking towards the bus stand.

Rafique looked at the tiny stall. A picture of General Yahya

Khan was prominently displayed, adorned with a flapping line of triangular green and white crescent moon and star Pakistani flags glued to a jute twine. A few yellowing bananas on a jute string hung in front, and tightly screwed glass jars held hard biscuits for dipping into the chai.

"A pack of Wills," Rafique said, shying away from the inquisitive looks of the storekeeper.

Rafique opened the pack, and reached for the lighter hanging on a string. The store keeper flicked the lighter and lit Rafique's cigarette. Leaning close, a tiny smile in his eyes, he said, "Are you guys *Mukti*?"

"*Mukti*, yeah, sure. I am the leader of the *Mukti Bahini*," Nazmul said laughing, and agreeing, exaggerating the humor, swallowing hard. He bit his lip and looked away.

Rafique looked at his wrist watch. 4:45. Fifteen minutes.

He took a drag on the cigarette, tapped his fingers ever so lightly on the bench. Catching himself tapping, he looked at the mostly empty shelves of the chai stand, spat out a tiny piece of tobacco on the tip of his tongue and said, "Not much merchandise?"

"Saar, these days, *maal nai*, no merchandise," the storekeeper said.

Rafique turned his wrist, nonchalantly looked at the time again.

4:50.

Rafique looked at Nazmul. He checked his wrist watch again. Drenched in nervous sweat, his shirt now stuck to his back like glue.

He stood up, and Nazmul, drawing close, said softly, "I will go."

"No," Rafique said in a strained voice. "Naah!"

"You sure the timer was not thirty minutes?" Nazmul whispered.

Thirty minutes? Could it be? Rafique wondered. There were no markings on it. He looked at his watch. It was 4:50. Thirty minutes. That would put it at 5 o'clock. Rafique felt a lump growing in the back of his throat. He swallowed hard but it remained.

Firoz and Rintu walked past them, looked with shifty glances, nervous twitches. Then they walked back to the bus stand, waiting for a signal, a sign. Rafique looked towards Rintu and Firoz and scratched the top of his head. For a moment they stood looking back.

"New Market, New Market," the barely teenage conductor called out, slapped the side of the green and white bus, making a tinny banging sound. Past the outstretched hands of the conductor hanging on to the doorway handle of the bus, Rintu and then Firoz stepped inside. The bus spewed out blue smoke, slowly creaked out of the stand.

5:10. *Over thirty minutes.* Glancing furtively from side to side, his shirt soaking wet, water dripping off his long hair, Rafique walked towards the Fiat. With its windows fogged up now it looked more like a green dragon, an explosive-rigged trap. Glancing both ways, he opened the passenger door, closed it. For a moment Rafique sat in the fogged up car. Slowly he reached down, and pulled out the briefcase, and put it in his lap.

He took a deep breath. No, not a thirty minute timer Allah. It was 5:15 exactly. He could hear his heart beating with the sound of the rain on the roof.

Thararump. Thararump. Thararump.

He sat with the briefcase on his lap, his open palms on the plastic top wet from rain leaking in. His knees shook. His fingers trembled. And for an eerie moment, Rafique saw the bomb blowing up in his face.

Slow, he said to himself. Slower. Go slow.

"Shit," he cursed through clenched teeth, as his fingers trembled. "Shit!"

The hard shell briefcase had two latches. He flipped open one.

OK, OK, so far so good. The other latch was stuck. Rafique's fingers were wet and the latch would not budge. With the keys of the Fiat he pried.

"Shit."

Rafique took out the pliers and hammered the key into the latch. It broke open.

The muscles at the base of his spine squeezed all the way up to the base of his neck, every nerve, every muscle tightening.

Sweat beaded on his forehead, dripped into his eyes. He wiped his eyes with his sleeve.

Heart racing, Rafique took a deep breath, exhaled and then looked down into the open briefcase. Yes, he had crushed the tube containing the chemical. He had done everything exactly as planned, correctly. The detonator was triggered but had not fired. He checked the safety in the pencil timer. Yes, he had pulled it. Now the PK was getting wet from the water leaking into the car.

An ugly afternoon was turning into an uglier dusk.

He disconnected the wet timer, reached into his shirt pocket for the second detonator. His fingers trembling, Rafique dropped the detonator between his legs.

"Shit," he said, this time louder.

He picked up the detonator and connected it to the plastic explosives. He took out the pliers in his pocket. Saying a prayer he squeezed the timer as hard as he could. He heard the crack sound of the breaking vial, triggering the timer, slid the detonator into position. Rafique double checked. Yes. The safety was pulled.

Yes.

He used the sleeve of his shirt to wipe off the sweat. He licked the salty perspiration on his lips, his throat parched. He lay the briefcase down at his feet, the floor now wet with rain water.

Slowly he opened the passenger door, looked both ways and he started the walk back towards the chai stall.

"Ten pounds, fifteen minutes," he murmured as he looked at his watch.

5:20. Five minutes had passed. He was too scared to notice the time he had set off the detonator. Fifteen minutes. 5:33, 5:34 maybe. Rain, salty with sweat, poured over his face, dripped from his moustache down his neck. It felt good.

Nazmul stood at the chai stand, under a blue tarp strung on ropes tied to bamboo posts. The rain dripped off the ends of the tarp, forming larger and larger puddles. The *naala* behind the chai stall churned with rain water.

"Give me your cigarette," was the first thing Rafique said to Nazmul. He took a deep drag, blew it in the air, grabbed the chai Nazmul was drinking and poured it down his parched throat.

Nazmul looked into Rafique's colorless, drained face.

Rafique took another desperate drag at Nazmul's cigarette. Both Rafique and Nazmul stood, smoked, breathed hard. Rafique looked around to see a group of soldiers headed for the army truck parked behind the fiat.

He flicked the cigarette into the *naala*.

'KABOOOM!' The car exploded into a raging inferno, disintegrated in a huge, fiery, and ear shattering explosion that blew debris and glass hundreds of feet into the air. The plate glass windows in a nearby store exploded into shard daggers. The two doors twisted outward like giant slapping hands, knifing through the soldiers and vehicles. And one of the tires, ripped out of its bolts, flew through the air, the rim a spinning cutting disc, ricocheting against the building. A wall of sound knocked Rafique and Nazmul backwards.

Getting up, Rafique jumped onto the motorcycle, kicked the starter. The bike sputtered. People were running in every direction.

"Fuck," Rafique screamed. "The petrol valve!" He turned it on, kicked the starter and the bike came alive, spewing out blue smoke. Nazmul jumped on. Rafique revved his motorcycle, winding out the two-stroke engine. The bike lunged into the roadway and leaned into a deep left turn. As everyone ran in every direction for their lives on the other side of Baitul Mukarram, Rafique gunned the bike, twisting and turning through rickshaws, buses, private cars and skirting street hawkers, and pedestrians.

"Time for you fuckers to go home," Rafique screamed at the top of his voice. "A one-way ticket on me!"

His head down and pointed into the traffic, Rafique was on a high on the streets of Baitul Mukarram, racing through back streets, bypassing the army checkpoints. His head buzzed, his vision blurred.

"Careful, don't kill us!" Nazmul screamed into Rafique's ear. The back of Nazmul's khaki shirt was flapping in the wind like a banner as Rafique's hair spiked up in the air.

Veering into a long sloping turn, flying past the traffic circle in front of Balaka Cinema, blurring by the newly painted Islamic street signs, Rafique's Honda leaned deep towards the muddy pavement, cutting into the turn, drifting over the center divider line, the frame scraping pavement and finally rolling into the front of the Red Cross sign on the pharmacy.

With a sharp flick of Rafique's wrist, the engine decompressed, and he downshifted, leaving a short skid. Through the side gate, they pushed the bike, parked it under the stairs.

They ran to the storeroom and turned on the radio. From Calcutta floated in a famous Khudiram song,

Ekbar biddai de Ma ghure ashi

Don't hold me back, Mother, I would smilingly go to the gallows for the cause of the nation.

Rafique sang with the radio. Nazmul lit a cigarette.

"Let me have a drag," Rafique said. Blowing out the smoke, he ran his fingers through his wet hair, his heart hammering against his rib cage.

"Free ticket home to hell you butchers!" Rafique said.

He strutted on the back porch of the building, smoking, swearing.

—⚜—

August 30, 1971 12:30 A.M.
First Lane, Kalabagan

RAFIQUE LAY IN BED, LISTENING to the night sounds in the street outside—the rustled dance of leaves, the mournful howl of a lonely dog. He looked past Nazmul sleeping on the quilt on the floor, to the empty bedrolls. This night Firoz and Rintu were hiding at a friend's. A truck rumbled by on Mirpur road. At this time of night, it could only be a Pakistani military truck. Through the bars of the open window the distant street light threw long shadows and narrow swaths of light on the floor. Restlessly Rafique turned in bed, felt comfort in the trigger of his Sten.

Sleep would not come. His breaths were shallow, the muscles along the side of his neck twisted into a knot. For the last week the tension in Dacca had been rising. Ticking up a notch every day.

Everywhere Rafique looked, eyes were riveted on him. Today when he had turned into First Lane, he saw an unknown face staring at him from the far bend, marking him.

"Nazmul."

From outside the gate came a scraping, clawing noise. Nazmul lay on the quilt. Quietly listening.

"Nazmul."

"Huhh," Nazmul muttered half-asleep, sitting up.

"Trouble," Rafique said softly, rolling off the bed, the Sten in his hand. "Get your gun." Rafique cocked the gun and Nazmul gripped his revolver in his right hand, pointed the muzzle at the door. Rafique covered Nazmul as Nazmul slid open the large wooden latch and clicked down the metal hasp.

Chan Mian was fast asleep, snoring on a bamboo plaid mat in the front room.

From the direction of the front gate, a dark silhouetted shadow moved towards them. Gasping for breath, two terror filled eyes shone in the suffused light.

"Don't shoot Nazmul Bhai, *amii* Firoz, I am Firoz" cried out the figure, his hands held high in the air.

"Firoz!" Rafique said, fear knotted his stomach, still covering him with the Sten. Firoz wore only pants, his right forearm was cut, bleeding, his hair disheveled.

"They got Rintu!" Firoz said doubled over, panting for breath, his pale face drenched with perspiration. "I escaped. They got Rintu." Firoz ran into the room, went straight for the *alna*, grabbed a shirt and said, "Shit! Run right now! I jumped over the back and barely escaped." Pulling on the shirt he added, "They have picked up Rahim, Jamal, Hanif, Murad, and Shaheen. We need to get out of Dacca right now! Right Now!"

Rafique's eyes were wide open. He tried to gather his thoughts. His brain refused to register a single word.

"We have to move, over the back wall, right now," Firoz said, frantically bandaging a *gamcha* around his bleeding forearm.

Dreamland. They had been in a dreamland to think that the Pakistani intelligence would not catch on to their safe-house hideouts

237

in Dacca, Rafique thought to himself.

Nazmul ran for the front room to wake up Chan Mian.

"Get up, get up Chan Mian," he said. Chan Mian woke up startled. He flinched at the sudden light in his face, full of questions.

"Clean up everything, the beds, the *alna*, roll everything up. If anyone comes tell them no one is here. Do you understand?" Nazmul said.

"Saar, military?" Chan Mian said, waking up to a nightmare unfolding around him.

"Clean everything. Hurry and leave, Chan Mian," Nazmul said as he ran back to the storeroom.

"Someone squealed! How else could they get the address of all our safe houses?" Rafique said, as he grabbed his jute bag that now held just the Sten gun, and headed out.

"Inside job," said Firoz as he followed Rafique.

"Someone told. Remember Sartre's Spanish rat? We have a *Makal faal*, a squealing rat amongst us!" Rafique cursed out aloud.

"A rat. A stinking rat," Nazmul said following Firoz and Rafique.

With adrenaline pumping, fingernails scraping brick, toes trying to get a hold onto the mortar of the wall, Firoz, Nazmul, then Rafique clawed over the back wall, scampering for their lives. As they landed on the hard ground by the *naala* with a thud, the front of the house lit up with search lights.

"*Darwaza kholo*, open the gate," came a barking sound.

Just my fingers around that bastard's neck, just one minute, Rafique thought as he smashed his clenched fist into the wall, bloodying his knuckles. He picked up the jute bag and ran for his life behind Firoz and Nazmul, scrambling as another jeep screamed into the alley from the opposite side of First Lane, their escape route through the alley blocked by blinding tunneling headlights.

They were cornered. Cutting across the alley, pushing and pulling each other, they scampered over another wall into the dark compound of the opposite house.

"Fucking rats," Nazmul cursed, pushing Firoz up the side of another steep wall, into the next compound. Dogs were barking, and lights started to come on, one by one. They could hear voices as Firoz landed hard on his ankle. He hobbled, one arm draped over Rafique and Nazmul's shoulders as they ran down another twisting alley.

Nazmul felt the ragged rasp of Firoz's breath on his face, heard the hoarse panting of Rafique, and the sounds of voices and a distant muffled cry.

He murmured, "Chan Mian!"

No Tomorrow Like Today

ঝ ঝ ঝ

September 1971, Sheetalpur, East Pakistan

BITS OF BAD INTERNATIONAL NEWS competed with the enthusiastic tone of the announcer: "*Prime Minister of Bangladesh Tajuddin Ahmed has announced ... we will be victorious ... Commander-in-Chief Osmany...Joy Bangla...*" The battery-powered transistor radio sputtered to life with the hour of evening programs from *Shawdhin Bangla Betar Kendro* as Nahar sat on the edge of the bed, Rafique's copy of *Sanchita*, Kazi Nazrul Islam's collection of poems, in her hand, the flickering lantern throwing a yellow filigree of light and shadow over her face. The radio squealed, clicked, coughed several times and then fell silent.

Nahar turned it off, then on. It crackled back to life, and out sputtered '*Ultimatum, Charompatra*,' a satirical program narrated in a thick delicious Old Town Daccaia accent, poking fun at Yahya Khan, Tikka Khan and their henchmen.

'*Larkanar nawabjada pyare Julfikar Ali Bhutto, Yahyar ek gelasher dosto,* Larkana's Nawab Zulfikar Ali Bhutto, Yahya's one peg favorite buddy,' the program ridiculed.

Nahar looked out over the desolate landscape. A little evening breeze rippled across the surface of the pond. Boochu barked into the horizon, sniffing the air.

241

She turned the small volume knob all the way up. The singer jumped into an ocean of emotions, sweeping Nahar away in the uplifting patriotic song by Apel Mahmud.

Mora ekti phool ke bachabo bole juddho kori,
...
Mora akti mukher hashir joono asro dhori,

To save one flower, we wage war,
For the laughter in one face, we bear arms.

The words carried her away. Nahar tied her *dupatta* around her waist, swayed from side to side, moving her head and tapping her feet. Her Rafique was fighting to save one flower, to see the sweet smile on one face.

One flower.

One face.

She opened the wooden *almira* and ran her hand across Rafique's shirts, his Panjabis. All neat. All organized. Like the taste of a lingering kiss, the lover gone, Nahar felt Rafique through his things. She touched his shawls, his pants, his books on the desk, his pen, notebooks. As she crushed his shirts in her arms, buried her face in Rafique's faint fragrance, Nahar was crushed by the weight of loneliness, lost in a chasm of emptiness. Here was his room. Here was everything. Everything but Rafique.

Shattering the calm, bursting with angry emotion, Poet Kazi Nazrul Islam's signature song plucked at her heartstrings, shaking the very core of her soul.

'Karar oi louho kopat
Karar oi louho kopat
...
Lathi mar bhangra tala
Lathi mar bhangra tala

Shatter those iron gates of prison
Shatter those iron gates of prison
...

Kick, shatter the locks!
Kick, shatter the locks!'

"*Karar oi louho kopat!'* she sang out loud, filled with fight. Then louder. In sync with Nazrul's rebel rousing rhythm, Rafique's favorite, Nahar's head went side to side; she kicked and then kicked higher. 'Kick, shatter the locks!' she said, her lungs bursting with, *'Lathi mar bhangra tala, Lathi mar bhangra tala,'* churning out like a ferocious cyclone. She jumped and kicked. Kicked again. Then she kicked once more to 'Kick, shatter the locks!'

Exhausted—her mind a mosaic of memories: Rafique, March 25th, Neezam, Bodor Morol, Naila—Nahar sank onto the bed wrapped in her *salwar kameez.*

—❧—

A THIN MIST DESCENDED ON the paddy fields. Dusk had given way to evening. A cool September breeze came up from the courtyard bringing with it the humid earthy smell of drying jute and freshly chopped firewood. Across the courtyard, Nahar could hear the chatter of Amina and Halim as they stacked firewood against the mud wall of the thatched *dhenki* hut.

Earlier in the day, Nahar had helped Amina crush rice into a fine powder under the pestle of the foot driven, heavy wooden *dhenki*, to make some *pithas*, sweet rice cakes. The pivoting of the *dhenki* and the pounding rhythm, the subtle creaking and rhythmic smashing, the swinging foot motion, the swaying of women's hips, the woman's hands clearing the rice husks while the pestle was up in the air, still beat in her ears. The gentle rhythms of *gram* Bangla played in Nahar's heart.

A crescent moon was arching up in the sky and a little light filtered in through the wooden slats of her window. Energized by the songs on *Shawdhin Bangla Betar Kendro*, Nahar felt warm on a chilly night.

The sound of voices. The slap of bare feet on the clay of the courtyard. Suddenly the loud creaking of Amina running up the wooden stairs awakened Nahar out of her trance.

"Nahar Appa! Nahar Appa!" Amina burst out in excitement as she entered Nahar's room.

"What is it?"

"Rafique Bhai, it's Rafique Bhai. He's outside," Amina said trying to catch her breath. "In the *dhenki* hut."

"Rafique! Rafique?" Nahar said. The words sounded strange, distant, echoing against the walls of the room after four long war-weary months.

"Rafique! Rafique!" Nahar repeated louder this time, as if they were incantations to break a spell. A spell of loneliness. A spell of hopelessness.

"Yes, Rafique Bhai!"

"What are you saying? Why is he not here?"

"He says too dangerous. Only to tell you, only you. They are watching the house."

"Who?" Nahar said as she raised her eyebrows, narrowed her eyes. "Who's watching the house?"

"Don't know." Amina said, her chest heaving in excitement. "Rafique Bhai tired, very tired."

In a flash, Nahar put on her sandals, threw a shawl about her shoulders, and flew down the wooden stairs behind Amina. Jahanara was on the prayer mat with her hands clasped together in an unceasing prayer. Tired and worried, Chowdhury had gone to sleep.

Nahar and Amina went out the side door into the darkness. Quietly they made it across the courtyard to the *dhenki*.

Lost in the deep shadows of the lantern light, Rafique sat smoking silently on the heavy wooden *dhenki*, his legs crossed, rolling the cigarette slowly between his thumb and index finger. The tip of the cigarette, a red glow, lit the creased worry-filled lines of Rafique's face. The smell of earthy threshed, husked paddy mixed with the acrid cigarette smoke.

Eyes wide in disbelief, her knees giving way, Nahar braced herself against the corner post of the hut.

"I go bring water, food. Rafique Bhai starving," Amina said. She ran back around to the main house

Rafique turned around and looked at Nahar. In his crumpled

blue Panjabi and muddy bell-bottom pants, Rafique, disheveled and exhausted, sported a scraggly beard, his hair an uncombed mess.

"Rafique!" Nahar said as she rushed to him, threw her arms around him. She held him tight and close, his touch electric, every nerve in her body came alive as she murmured in his ear, "Rafique Rafique Rafique!"

"Nahar," Rafique drew her in tightly in his arms as she wept against his shoulder. Her hair—fragrant, intoxicating, sweet—filled Rafique. He kissed her again and again, crushing her in his sinewy arms. Each kiss and touch bordered on pain, the longing so intense. Their bodies entwined, Nahar drew him out of death and war, out of guerrilla camps, Dacca hideouts, near starvation, near death, into her soft arms, into an intoxication, into a swollen passion, into a longing that swept both away.

A long minute passed. Then another. Nahar felt the skeletal leanness of his body. She felt Rafique's Panjabi, damp from sweat and humidity and she could feel through her palm a palpable fear, a mounting frustration.

Boochu, Nahar's puppy, barked a little pleasure yelp, wagged his tail and sniffed at Rafique's sandals. Rafique patted his head.

Nahar laid her face on his shoulder and said, "Why are you sitting here? Did someone follow you?"

"They got almost everyone in Dacca. We're in trouble. Big trouble," Rafique said as he stood up, his eyes locked with hers.

Nahar bit her lower lip, gathered her emotions, sat quietly on the *dhenki's* large wooden beam.

Rafique lit another cigarette, paced up and down. As paddy husks crunched under his sandals, Rafique took another drag on the cigarette, and blew the smoke into the musky air.

Questions tumbled out of Nahar. "What happened? Where is Nazmul?" Patiently she waited for Rafique's response.

"A raid. Nazmul and I barely escaped. Barely. They got everyone." Rafique stopped pacing, blew out a tense breath of smoke, flicked the cigarette butt into the bamboo bushes. Its red burning embers exploded in the dark. "Nazmul left for Agartala, the same time I came here. Dacca is a disaster. They captured most of the guerrillas, raided over twenty houses. Someone inside gave the addresses of our safe houses in Dacca. I don't think the captured *Mukti Bahini,* our friends, are alive anymore. I don't know." Rafique buried his face in his hands.

Amina came hurrying back, balancing a water jug, a glass and a plate of sweet rice flour *pitha* cakes. She stood behind the side wall, clearing her throat.

Nahar looked up and said, "Come."

Amina placed the food and water beside Nahar on the flat of the *dhenki.* She poured a glass of water.

"Nahar Appa, Amma went to bed. Abba and Amma are sleeping. I didn't wake them. I already put soap, towel and water bucket and mug by tube well. Everything is there. Food almost ready. Please come. The back door is open."

Amina turned to go.

"Good. Amma will be scared to see Rafique in this shape," Nahar said. *How would her in-laws feel if she kept Rafique's presence from them?* "Wait Amina. Go quietly and tell Abba and Amma that Rafique is here."

"Tell them not to come here. I'll go inside," Rafique added.

"He is coming to the dining table. Get the food ready, quick. Tell Halim to draw some water for a bath for your Bhaia," Nahar said.

"*Jee,* Appa," Amina said, and dashed back to the house.

Nahar poured water into Rafique's cupped hands from the jug as he splashed it on his face, then rinsed out his mouth. Water dripping from his face, he ate the *pitha* cake and gulped down a glass of water.

"Nahar, I can't believe you are in front of me here..."

"Eat," Nahar said as she poured another glass. Rafique drank deeply, thirstily, chewing on another *pitha.*

Rafique turned to Nahar. He wanted to forget everything but her, to kiss her again and again. Nahar's enticing sweet attar, her soft lips made him forget. Forget the war. The world smelled of love and excitement, and Nahar was sweet, inviting, and tonight in his arms after four long hard months of guerrilla war.

"Quick, Rafique, let's go," Nahar said getting up and pulling Rafique towards the tube well behind the house.

In a bubble of lantern light, surrounded by pitch darkness, Halim threw his weight on the handle of the rusty tube well. Pumped up and down. With a sucking, swirling sound, water gushed out into the metal pail.

Halim's face lit up, bright, radiant, his voice bubbling forth, "Rafique Bhai! *Bhaijaan ami ebar apnar loge jamu*, fight *kormu*. This time I will go with you. I will fight! I will free the country."

Stepping on the jack fruit planks around the tubewell, Rafique walked up to Halim, ruffled his hair and said, "Halim you are so young. Soon you will go, InsAllah."

"Halim has only one thought. He will go to war, to fight. If he joins the fight freedom will come sooner, much sooner," Nahar said smiling at Halim.

"Halim is right, if everyone thought like him, freedom would come much sooner," Rafique said, pouring the pail of water over his head. Halim pumped another pail of water, panted excitedly, "We will free the country soon Rafique Bhai!"

Nahar smiled at Halim. "Go help Amina," she said.

Excited, Halim danced and hopped his way to find Amina.

Nahar bent over Rafique, pouring water from a mug over him, lathering his hair and back with the bar of soap, washing off four months of dirt, dust and life on the run. Rafique grabbed her wrist, pulled her down into his wet bare chest, kissing her face, running his fingers over her soft cheeks, tasting the sweetness in her lips. In this embrace, entwined around each other, parts of a whole, once broken, now restored, Rafique held Nahar.

Finally, Nahar, wet and blushing said, "I'm going. You come. I have to change."

Rafique laughed and squeezed Nahar's nose in between his fingers and said, "I want a little one just like you."

Nahar laughed, twisted out of Rafique's grip and ran into the house, her feet barely touching the floor.

Dripping wet, running behind her, Rafique came up the stairs chasing Nahar. Like a doll, he picked her up in his arms, and gently lay her down on the bed. "My little pearl," he said, biting her ear lobe, crushing her in his wet embrace, kissing her soaking wet body passionately, tasting the sweetness of their reunion. She closed her eyes. Dreamt the dream of longing, not believing Rafique's touch all over her body. Tonight Nahar's dream droplets glistened again in the moonlight on half submerged green leaves.

From downstairs, through the closed doors, the sounds of Chowdhury and Jahanara's voices came into the room.

"Not now, Rafique. Let's go downstairs, let's eat first," Nahar whispered. Slowly, Nahar uncurled from under Rafique, unlocking his grip around her. The sounds of Chowdhury clearing his throat got louder, breaking the lovers' trance.

Nahar took out a clean Panjabi and pajamas for Rafique. "Let's go Rafique," she said nervously.

Both Jahanara and Chowdhury were waiting by the base of the stairs. Their eyes met Rafique's as he flew down the stairs and touched their feet. Jahanara embraced her son, holding him close, her face wet with tears.

"Baba Rafique, Baba how are you?" Jahanara said as she kissed his forehead, his brow. Chowdhury hugged Rafique, held him tight against his chest for a long moment in a somber silence.

"Come, Baba. Come eat," his mother said, looking at a skeleton that was once her son.

Rafique sat down at the table across from his father. His mother stood next to him, while Nahar stood beside Jahanara, her *dupatta* draped over her head. Amina ran back and forth to the kitchen, heating and bringing the food to the table.

"Baba, you have become skin and bones," Jahanara said as she piled rice and curry on Rafique's plate, ran her hands over his back.

The table was laden with *daal*, rice, chicken curry, *shootki* dried fish curry. The pungent smell of *shootki* called out enticingly, as Rafique mixed the *daal*, the *shootki*, his favorite, and squeezed some lime into the mix. He rolled a ball of rice between his first two fingers and thumb, tore at a piece of chicken and rolling it again, put it into his mouth. Nahar put a piece of mango pickle and a slice of lemon on Rafique's plate. Amina ran in again with a plate of freshly sliced red onions.

"Nazmul?" Chowdhury, asked, his words filled with anxiety and worry.

"He's OK, Abba. He's fine. He left for Agartala. There was a huge raid in Dacca. Unbelievable disaster. You must leave immediately for *Khallama's*, Auntie's place. Immediately. It's not safe here right now."

Chowdhury peered at Rafique. "What exactly happened in Dacca? We got news of your operations on the bridge. Then you went to Dacca. We have been hearing of the bombings."

"Abba, the *Mukti Bahini* blew up power stations. We killed a lot of soldiers and Razakars. But someone inside squealed. A rat," Rafique said looking up from his plate.

"Hmmm," Chowdhury said and nodded his head as a shadow cast over his face. "Did you guys think the West Pakistani army was going to let you do whatever you wanted inside Dacca? Problem is within us...our people, the collaborators," Chowdhury said with a certain frustration in his voice.

"Baba, eat, you must be starving," his mother said as she piled more rice and chicken onto his plate. Nahar played with the end of her *dupatta* and turned her head to hide her smile.

"How many boys were captured? Do we know anyone?" asked Chowdhury.

"They caught most of our group. I was lucky. Extremely lucky. Firoz saved our lives. You must leave right now," Rafique said, the pitch of his voice rising steadily. "They know about me. They are looking for me. You need to leave right away,"

Chowdhury was silent.

"Abba, you are not listening to me, Neezam and Bodor are up to no good. I know it. I can feel it. You need to go to *Khallama's* at least for a few months."

Rafique took the white-embroidered-cotton cover off his glass and drank the water dry. Nahar refilled the glass to the brim from a white china pitcher adorned with a red rose, and Rafique drained the glass again. Amina came, stood beside Rafique and fanned him with a palm-leaf hand-fan.

"Abba, are you listening?" Rafique repeated.

"Yes, Rafique, we will go immediately. We were waiting for you. I also have a gut feeling that Neezam is up to no good," said Mustafa Chowdhury.

"Abba, you should leave in the morning, first thing for *Khallama's*,"

Rafique repeated.

Nahar looked at Amina, "Amina *chaltar achar.*"

In one corner of the dining room, stood the netted *mirsiv* cupboard. Amina went to it and got out the bottle of *chalta* pickles in mustard oil she had made. Proudly she put a plate of it in front of Rafique.

"Amina, ahhh, *chaltar achaar.* Life is heaven," said Rafique as he chewed on the fiber of a *chalta*, put another handful of rice and *daal* with *shootki* into his mouth. "Amma, the *shootki* is great!" Rafique said as he licked his fingers clean. "How I missed your cooking! Sure beats grams we ate in Agartala."

"Grams?" asked Jahanara with her eyebrows raised.

"Yes, grams for feeding animals. We boiled them and drank the water, Amma," Rafique laughed, then noticing a tear start in the corner of his mother's eye, he became quiet, moving the food about on his plate, biting on a green chile.

"Ahh!" Rafique writhed in heavenly chili flavor, full. Then narrowing his eyes, he asked. "How is Rahman Bhai?"

"He returned to his job at the University," Nahar said. "He had no choice. They will stay in Old Town with some friends."

"How is Selina Appa?" Rafique, remembering how sick she was in April, asked. "How is the baby? Boy or girl?"

Everyone suddenly went mute. Finally Jahanara broke the uneasy silence.

"It was a girl. So sad. Selina is OK now, but March 25th was too much. She just could not take it. And then the journey here."

Rafique became quiet. Jahanara sat down. Nahar bit the end of her *dupatta*, held the edge of Rafique's chair. She thought back to March 25th, about Selina Appa. The journey, the escape. No, nothing would be the same again. The world had changed. Forever.

"Go Rafique, go get some rest," Chowdhury finally said.

Jahanara looked at Nahar and saw how she was smiling.

"Nahar go take some rest," Jahanara said. "Amina?"

"Yes Amma," Amina replied.

"Bring us two cups of tea," Jahanara said, as a long lost glow crept into her face. And just as quickly, she thought about how in a few more hours Rafique was going to leave. She bit her lip, and

250

her face darkened.

Rafique hugged his parents once more and went out towards the veranda.

Slowly Chowdhury got up and unfolding the *Jai Namaaz*, sat down to pray. In the corner hung the painting of his father, Mohammed Asgar Chowdhury, seated, in his fez cap, long black *sherwani*. Mustafa looked up at his father's picture and drew a long breath. He gazed up into the eyes of his father, searching for some meaning, answers to the unfolding mayhem around him.

On the other side of the room, on the bed, Jahanara sat on her immaculate prayer mat, opened her Koran and thanked Allah for keeping her son safe, bringing him back to her.

RAFIQUE PACED ON THE VERANDA outside.

"Bhaia, cigarettes," Halim said handing him a packet of Chowdhury's cigarettes and a cup of tea.

Rafique thumped the pack of Wills against his palm. He paced up and down on the veranda and lit a cigarette. The red glowing tip moved back and forth, back and forth. Rafique crushed it into the tea saucer. From behind, Nahar snuck up on Rafique and hugged him. Rafique turned, pulled her close and kissed her, kissed the nape of her neck.

"Rafique let's go down to the pond" Nahar suggested.

"Everything has changed," Rafique said to Nahar as they walked. "Everything."

They walked across the clay courtyard, past the dark pasture to the cemented steps of the ghat. In the moonlight, the world was a negative of its daytime self.

They sat close to each other. The rustle of betel-nut palms carried on a slight breeze, and with it floated the sweet fragrance of its flowers. A croaking bull-frog glided by on the shimmering silver surface of the pond, which broke into ripples as Rafique threw a dirt clod, skipping it three times and into the center. In the cascading rings, Rafique lost his fragmented thoughts. He lit another cigarette, blew out the smoke, flicked the ashes.

Nahar sat listening to the whispering ripples. She tried to think of a future, of freedom, of a new life, but only darkness, images of Dacca University flashed in front of her eyes. She wanted to scream. The more she tried to imagine a wonderful life, the more haunting the images became. Tonight the only thing she wanted was to hold Rafique. Her Rafique. Her Rafique for a few precious hours.

Tears rolled from Nahar's eyes, down her cheeks.

Rafique, put his arm around her and said, "Nahar, everything is fine. Look, Nahar, look at me. I am here."

"Rafique just hold me tight right now."

Nahar felt Rafique in the darkness squeezing her hard, as her feelings of hope mixed with fear.

"Nahar, love's the only truth. In war, death lays bare everything. In war love is the only thing that remains," Rafique said holding her as the wind whipped off the surface off the water.

"How long can we survive, Rafique?"

"Nahar, can you see how the cement of the steps are worn where the women put their earthen water jugs?"

She followed his gaze, nodded.

"Like earthen pots wear out stone, we will wear down the enemy. We will see a bright sun of freedom. I can feel it Nahar. I know it."

"Yes, Rafique."

"Nahar, life will become wonderful again. We'll ride on my bike, we'll go to the *Mela*, I'll pick lots of *padma phools* for you, I'll buy you glass bangles."

Nahar's mind wandered back to when Rafique came back from Dacca for a few weeks in February. February 15th. Their first marriage anniversary. Like butterflies, they floated over the village riding his motorcycle to the *Falgun Mela*. She wore the red sari Rafique had brought for her from Dacca. Her sari *āchol* floated, she floated, her mind a butterfly.

On the way back home, Rafique stopped on the side of the pond. Rolling up his pants, he waded into the water and picked a water lily for her, told her, "Happy anniversary."

That day was the first time Rafique told her, "Nahar, when I first saw you on *Eid* day, in your pink dress, I thought of you as my little pink lily. I used to sit here alone and think of you looking at the lilies waving gently in the breeze. I used to dream you were waving, calling me."

Nahar remembered those days like dreamy *rupkotha*, days like fairly tales.

"Now in the garden of lilies, my dream lily, lily of my heart floats. I must capture this wondrous moment," Rafique had said as he took her photo that memorable day.

Today, Nahar looked into Rafique's eyes. "Rafique when will life be like that again? When?"

"Very soon Nahar," he said, kissing her cheek, tasting the salt of her tears. "Very soon."

The wind picked up, the breeze coming off the rippled surface of the pond. Rafique held Nahar closer, as the wind tugged at their chador, the lilies danced on the waves, glistened in the soft suffused light. A glimmer caught Nahar's face, and Rafique saw the moon glinting off her nose stud.

Time lost its meaning in a night with no tomorrow.

"Nahar, next year I will pick two *padma phools*, one for you and one for ..?" Rafique said as a mischievous smile appeared on his face. "I want lot of babies like you."

Nahar hid her face in Rafique's chest.

"Can you give me that photo I took of you in front of the lilies?" Rafique asked.

"Oh I left those at Rahman Bhai's. Nazmul has the copies and negatives."

In the mysterious moonlight, holding Rafique, Nahar thought. *No more tomorrow. No more tomorrow like today.*

—⋇—

RAFIQUE TURNED DOWN THE wick till the room was lit only by a wedge of moonlight creeping in through the open window.

Curling his fingers through Nahar's hair, Rafique drew her close, his arms tightened around her body, the sensation of her breath on his face, the taste of his salty perspiration on her tongue.

Nahar dug into Rafique's chest with her forehead. She felt his want, his eagerness, his longings after four long war torn months, his thirst. And they lay with their pain, they lay with the happiness of holding each other.

"Rafique," Nahar murmured. "Rafique, hold me tight."

He opened the palms of his hands and ran them over her long silky hair, down along the concave of her back. His fingers snapped off the buttons of her *salwar kameez*, then slowly peeled back the fabric from her shoulders.

He touched her body with his cheeks, his nose, his tongue.

Nahar felt a new battle-hardened Rafique—a man full of hope, still the dreamer—tough like the glistening bamboo staves they had raised together in the March sun of the Ramna Race Course Maidan.

The sweat between their bodies joined them together. Their bodies lost in a sinuous rhythm, her body swollen. He lost himself in her, in the soft silken song of her flesh. A fever possessed them.

Like a lily, she opened to him. Rafique bit Nahar's earlobes and bit her shoulder, fierce and ferocious. As he crushed her body into his, she could feel his heart beating against hers. Deep within her, Nahar felt complete.

In this moment between now and forever, nothing mattered more than this—this oneness, this melting, this completeness, this world of make believe that stole the meaning of time.

Nahar looked at Rafique's watch lying on the small night desk. 3:00 a.m. Soon, this dream, this happiness would be over. She lay with her head on Rafique's arm. "Rafique, what are we going to do?" she said, feeling his body tense up again with the passing minutes. Tears flowed down her cheeks, wet his forearm.

"Without you, how am I going to live?" Nahar asked again, as Rafique lay still, silent.

"One day when we are back here, in a free Bangladesh, I'll hold you again and never have to leave," Rafique said, his voice filled with the conviction gained over months of fighting, after the sacrifices of Jewel, Khalid, Rintu. A conviction instilled with the blood of friends, now martyrs. A conviction that victory was close.

"If I could only hold you forever like this, Rafique, so that you would be etched in me forever. Every part of you, Rafique," Nahar said as she ran her palm over the stubble under his chin. In the dark he smelled of a place far away.

Nahar reached for the lantern on the wooden floor, its flame low. She twisted the small metal knob and the orange-yellow fire came to life through the sooty glass cover.

She held the flame in front of Rafique's face. With a penetrating gaze she peered into his eyes, and asked, "It won't be long, will it?"

"No, not long."

Rafique looked up at her, and mustering all the conviction that he could said, "Yes, yes, we will be back together. Here. Before long. Yes. Everything will be the same." He smiled. "And we'll have children and be free."

Nahar looked into Rafique's eyes. She set the lantern down. As a wave of sadness filled her heart, she opened her arms wide and drew him into her, as she whispered,

"No tomorrow like today."

—❦—

IN THAT INDISTINCT IRON GRAY before dawn, Rafique had to leave. Nahar straightened out her *dupatta*, flitted about the room like a bird, getting the things that Rafique would need.

Rafique walked out the door wearing a new *khadi* Panjabi, a clean pair of bell-bottom pants, a cotton satchel Nahar had packed hanging on his shoulder.

Her knees weak, Nahar steadied herself holding onto the side of the railing, stepping on the time-worn stairs. Downstairs Jahanara sat on the *Jai Namaaz* spread out on the bed, her Koran open on a wooden book holder in front of her.

"Amma," Rafique said softly as Jahanara touched his cheeks and brushed back the hair from his forehead. As Rafique bent down to touch her feet, Jahanara recited a *Surah* and blew a blessing on his forehead. Gently she embraced him, kissed him on his brow.

Rafique got up and walked across to his father sitting on his prayer mat, looking out through the doorway. Chowdhury finished praying and held his son to his heart. His son, the tiny infant, the child he held in his arms, the toddler he taught to walk, to swing a cricket bat—leaving once more into a most uncertain darkness of a merciless war. Chowdhury stared out into the darkness of the paddy fields, and further into the darkness of the horizon.

"Baba, be careful," Chowdhury said.

"I will ..."

Chowdhury assured his son, even before Rafique had the chance to mention it, "We will leave by evening for your Aunt's place."

Rafique got up and walked out the door onto the veranda where Amina and Halim stood, tears in their eyes. "*Tora shabdhane thakis,*" he said. "You guys be very careful."

Jahanara and Chowdhury joined them on the veranda, and Halim, trying to hide his tears, stood behind Chowdhury. Rafique went behind his father, rubbed Halim on the back and said, "Next time I will take you with me."

"Rafique, Baba, here is a *tabiz*. Put it around your neck," Jahanara said, her hands trembling. "Put it on, Baba."

"Don't worry, Amma, I will."

In her mind's eye floated a vision, a bad omen. She had been praying and reciting *Surahs* from the Koran all morning. Something had fractured deep within her, and the cracks were running through her like dark waves. Her mind was unsettled, a premonition of disaster, some foreboding preying heavily on her mind.

Rafique put the *tabiz* behind the cigarette pack in his shirt pocket, pushing it in deep next to his heart. He bent down and touched her mother's feet again.

Rafique's father took his chador and in an arching motion put it over Rafique like a protective wing. He then embraced his only son, and kissed him on his forehead, something Mustafa Chowdhury had not done since he used to carry Rafique proudly in his arms when he was only a toddler.

Rafique held onto his father, and then suddenly breaking away walked across the courtyard towards the *dhenki* hut. Nahar followed him.

Boochu came and sniffed Rafique and gave a yelp of pleasure, the yellow spots over his eyes batting in excitement, and on a kind word from Nahar, sat down and wagged his little tail on the dirt.

Tightly wrapped in her shawl, Nahar went to the *dhenki* and sat on the middle, looked into the silver and black of the darkness touched by pale moon beams. She covered her face at the ghosts in the shadows.

Rafique searched behind the stacked firewood, moved a few pieces, and grabbed his hidden Sten gun. He reached for Nahar. And as he held her tight, he whispered, "I want you to remember this night Nahar. 'Til I get back, 'til we are free, remember that I love you more than anything in this world, and in this war, whatever happens I will always be with you. For a thousand lifetimes, I am yours, Nahar."

"Rafique take me with you. I can't live without you." Nahar started to weep. "Don't leave me."

Rafique was silent. He struggled to find words to console her. With the eastern skies lighting up in a pale swath of crimson and blue, Rafique drew Nahar close, the thrumming of his pounding heart pressed against hers. He kissed her—her neck, her chin, her lips, her eyes.

Holding his Sten gun in one hand and clutching Nahar to his chest, he said,

"You are the *padma phool* of my life,
the water lily of my heart,
bejeweling my dreams,
lighting my dark nights.
In the depths of darkness,
I will always swim to you,
search for you,
afloat on the braided ripples of the deep green water,
ever my pink water lily,
filaments of saffron and gold.
In your eyes glisten little pearls,
droplets on green leaves of the water lily,
shimmering, shattering the sunlight
into a thousand rainbows in my heart.
Nahar I love you,
My *padma phool.*"

He kissed her again, a gentle lingering goodbye kiss, the touch of parting pain.

Rafique faded into the darkness. Turning, Nahar thrust her face, steaming and wet, into the bend of her arm, and went on crying, not caring any longer to dry her face.

Rafique walked on the slender *lail* between the paddies, between the stubble of unplanted coffee-colored fields. In his mind's eye, he held the image of Nahar looking at him: her sweet musk, the taste of her soft lips, her touch, so soft, her whispers, kind and deep and forever. His water lily.

He glanced back as he threw the end of the chador over his shoulder. His chador covered his Sten gun, and his *tabiz*, and the lingering smell of Nahar. He swooshed Boochu to go home, to take care of Nahar, but the little pup wagged his tail and with the tinniest of yelps, followed Rafique.

"Joy Bangla," Rafique said to Boochu, as he walked away.

Boochu barked.

Nahar held onto a post. Across her tear-blurred vision, Rafique's cigarette cut arching red trails along the thin dirt path in between rice paddies and flooded fields, and finally disappeared into a distant wall of impenetrable jungle.

❧

Enemy Within

Sheetalpur, East Pakistan, early September 1971

"*B-ismi-llāhi r-rahmāni r-rahīm*" Nahar recited as she stood facing Mecca putting her hands together in her afternoon prayers. After Rafique left, Nahar had slept fitfully for only an hour.

As the afternoon skies started to get dark and ugly, as a storm brewed on the western horizon, fear and uncertainty tore at Nahar. Thoughts of Rafique's quick visit the night before, his warnings, and the fear of Razakars turned Nahar's weary mind into a quagmire like the red Bhawal earth outside.

An uneasy haste filled the house. Downstairs, she could hear the sounds of packing as Jahanara readied to leave with everyone for her sister's in the next village.

A bad premonition throbbed inside Nahar. She could hear Boochu yelping. She furrowed her brows and listened, wondering what it was Boochu had been fretting about, nervously sniffing the air all afternoon. A red rooster on top of the *dhenki* on the outer courtyard squawked raucously, flapping his wings in a warning to the hens and chicks pecking industriously at the scattered rice husks.

Behind the house, Amina was washing a flask at the tube well. Standing on a plank, Amina had her sari scrunched between her knees, and was perched like a stork over the tube well, its angled spout spewing out water in spurts into the metal pail. Hurrying to do some last minute cleaning, she cursed the pump.

Suddenly, Amina stopped, had the eerie feeling someone was watching her. She turned around, saw no one and resigned herself to the jitters after Rafique's surprise visit last night. But then she heard it again. A distant sound. A distant rumbling. She looked up at the horizon. The slow rumbling of engines came closer. Amina dropped the clothes, ran out towards the *dhenki* hut, and looked into the distance at the dirt road that wound around the hillocks towards Sheetalpur. She tried to scream, but could only rasp out a faint, "Military!"

"Military!" Amina screamed as she ran towards the main house. "Military jeeps are coming. Military!"

Chowdhury was pacing by a stack of papers and land titles. He looked up, his whole body tensed, his hands became rigid, the blood ran out of his face.

"Nahar.…Jahanara," Chowdhury yelled. He froze. *Escape. But how?* This time louder, he yelled, "Nahar, Jahanara!"

"Amma!" Nahar screamed out as she ran out of her room. The rumbling of approaching engines made her insides cringe. A thousand thoughts went through her.

No, this cannot be happening. She flew down the stairs to find Jahanara, Chowdhury and Amina by the front door, speechless, their eyes wide in horror.

"Military, Military!" she heard Halim cry out from the outer courtyard. *Had they captured Rafique?*

NO!

Chowdhury grabbed Nahar's hand, and gesturing to Amina said, "Now! Under the hay stack, right now!"

Pushing Nahar and Amina out the door, Jahanara said, "They must not find you two here! Run! Run! Go, hide under the haystack!"

"Nahar Appa! Now!" Amina said to Nahar, pulling at her.

Nahar looked back at the ashen faces of her in-laws, as Amina pulled her across the courtyard to the haystacks.

Just on the outskirts of the courtyard, on the side of the *dhenki* hut, were two haystacks pointing up like stubby yellow umbrellas.

Perspiring, shaking, Amina's face frantic with terror, she whispered, "Quick, Nahar Appa! Hide!"

Amina crouched by the haystack. Nahar stood for a moment looking back towards the house, the veranda where Mustafa and Jahanara were now standing. She heard soldiers screaming orders in Urdu.

"Appa, this is our only chance," Amina said as she scampered on all fours. Frozen in fear, Nahar, now on her hands and knees, watched Amina disappear under a haystack. Breathing hard, she knelt in the mud, bent forward, looked under the second haystack. Inch by inch Nahar crawled on her hands and knees, worked her way under. As she pushed, coughing through hay into the small cavity around the bamboo in the center, the hay cut her face, her neck and forearms.

The ground beneath her hands was wet and littered with cow dung and chicken shit. The smell of the rancid cow urine suffocated Nahar. Gripping the bamboo pole, she gasped for breath in this small noxious cavity. Her head was spinning. Arching her back into the hay, with one hand she held her stomach and with the other she covered her now muddy face. She vomited in dry heaves. Vomited again and again.

Crumpled flat on her stomach, Nahar began to mutter prayers, "Hey *Khoda, La ilaha illa anta, subhanaka, inni kuntu minaz-zalimin,* there is no god but You, You are far exalted and above all weaknesses, and I was indeed the wrongdoer."

The wind blew towards the haystacks and carried with it the soldiers' voices. Nahar heard their loud Urdu commands. Then Neezam. Neezam's voice.

Boochu ran out barking and yelping towards the soldiers. One of the soldiers cursed, "*Chootia koota,* fucking dog," whirled and viciously kicked him like a football. Boochu landed several feet away. Whimpering he got back up, and barked again. Taking the butt of his sub-machine gun, the soldier smashed Boochu's head. Boochu yelped in agony, as thick red blood came out of his mouth, nostrils and smashed brain. A final twitch.

At the first sounds, Halim had found a space behind the stacked firewood in the corner of the denki hut to crawl into and hide. Now

261

with the sounds of approaching soldiers, Halim ran from the *dhenki* hut out towards the pond. Away from the military. Slipped and fell. Got up and ran again. As he zigzagged, one of the soldiers fired. The bullet ricocheted off the hard bark of one betel nut tree and whistled by, hitting another. Through the trees the sound of splintering bark echoed for a moment. The soldier, now on his knees, took careful aim with the rifle.

He fired again. A loud crack.

A thud.

The wind picked up, blew towards the hay stacks, and the sounds of the soldiers became louder. The military and the Razakars had the compound surrounded. More yelling. Shouted orders.

Neezam and Captain Daud lead the group into the courtyard. With them, eight West Pakistani soldiers, four Razakars, and Bodor Morol. Captain Daud, a tall moustached sharp-featured man, high cheek bones, his black straight hair cropped, stood in the middle of the courtyard, ordered his men, "Surround them!"

Three soldiers ran up to the veranda, surrounded Chowdhury and Jahanara, their bayonets drawn. Pushed by the soldiers, Jahanara and Chowdhury stumbled into the middle of the courtyard.

Guns drawn, Neezam and Captain Daud confronted Chowdhury and Jahanara. Neezam looked at them, his eyes narrowed behind dark aviator glasses, his black leather shoes shining, his pants creased.

The gun shot still ringing in her ears, Jahanara said, "Neezam! *Tui,* you!" her voice shaking in anger. "How dare you bring the military here? To my home?"

"Where is Rafique?" Neezam asked. "We know he was here last night."

"He is not here," Chowdhury replied holding his ground.

"Neezam," shouted Jahanara as she raised her hand and went to hit him. One of the soldiers shoved a bayonet at her chest, stopping her.

"Where is Rafique hiding?" screamed Neezam. "He was here yesterday, I have news."

"Rafique is not here. He left for Dacca to the University," said Chowdhury, his voice seething in anger, his glaring eyes wide open and fixed on Neezam's face. His fear was overwhelmed by a fierce sense of betrayal. "Leave now Neezam!"

"And Nahar?" Neezam laughed sarcastically. "Where is Nahar?" Bodor Morol, half-hidden behind Neezam and Captain Daud, smirked.

"She left with Rafique," Chowdhury said, his voice tremulous, as one of the soldiers poked him in the back with a bayonet. "Now you leave!"

Exhausted, heart racing, the taste of vomit in her mouth, Nahar lay suffocating on her back in the mud, eyes blinded in tears as she looked at the little light fringing the edge of the haystack.

Captain Daud shouted, "Enough. That bastard *Mukti* is hiding somewhere around here."

Neezam pointed to the house.

"Search the house!" Captain Daud ordered his men. "Make sure no one escapes. Shoot first!"

Three of the Razakars and two Pakistani soldiers entered the house.

"Neezam, you traitor! I should have killed you when you were born. I raised you with my own two hands," Jahanara cried out, her voice now spent.

"You bastard traitor, you brought this upon us." Chowdhury could not believe Neezam's feral metamorphosis. "We raised you as our son, Neezam! Leave from here now!"

Nahar heard the sound of doors being kicked in, the sounds of breaking glass and china, piercing guttural orders, crashing chairs, and shelves. Then thuds, rifle butts against wood and a shot, as they broke the door off the armoire. The sounds disappeared into silence. Finally after a few minutes she heard in Urdu, "No one here."

"Where are they?" Neezam screamed. "Tell me or else!"

"No," Jahanara screamed out. "Don't take him! No!"

"Look over there. We won't leave without them," Neezam said.

"Abhi goli mardo, Shoot them right now," Nahar heard an angry commanding voice say in Urdu. Crouched, Nahar shuddered, her insides wrenched, she prayed. *Allah! Allah!*

"No! No! No!" she heard Jahanara cry out in anguish. Nahar

263

heard three shots in rapid succession and an echoing thud.

"Mustafaaaaaaaaaaaaaaaa," she heard Jahanara scream.

Another revolver shot rang out.

"Aaaaaaaa!" Nahar heard Jahanara groan.

Then silence.

Sounds crashed inside Nahar's spinning head. She held her hands over her ears.

Everything went dark.

—❦—

WHEN NAHAR WOKE UP, SHE found she was laying on her belly. She moved away from her vomit, gasped for a little air low to the ground. She wanted to cough badly, wanted to sneeze, breathed ever so slowly in long painful wheezes.

Urdu barks and yells. Boots slapping in mud.

Her pulse accelerated. Her lips trembled. She could hear her heartbeat loud in her ears. Stop Nahar. Death awaits. Just a sneeze and you are dead.

Through the hay and mud strewn about, Nahar could see the bottom of the haystack where Amina was hiding. A prayer stuck to her lips. She kept repeating *"Lailaha illallah hu…"*

Voices approached. Closer.

"Look over there!" Nahar heard Bodor cry out. She tried to swallow, but her throat was parched, her heart hammering against her rib cage, her head spinning. She tried to focus. Did they see the tracks she left?

Amina? What was Amina doing?

"She must be here," Neezam said with conviction as he paced by the haystack. "I know it! I know she is hiding around here. No way she has escaped."

"Maybe a *magi* whore is hiding under there!" cried out a Razakar, as he shoved his bayonet into the hay, missing Nahar's feet by a few inches. Nahar cringed away, slowly crawling in the other direction.

In the dim light by the edge of the haystack, Nahar could see the muddied Pakistani army boots. Big and black, steel-toed, they dug into the soft earth, darkening her vision around the edges of the haystack. Cornered, Nahar thought to herself. *Don't sneeze! Don't sneeze!*

More boots. More shouting now towards the other haystack as they shoved bayonets into the sides of it.

"Bastards, where did the whore go?"

Suffocating, her arms and legs numb, Nahar lay praying. With every breath, she fought her urge to sneeze.

The soldiers set the haystack on fire. Smoke and soot filled her nose, her lungs. Somehow she clawed towards the dim light a few inches at a time, making headway through the mud to the edge of the haystack, to the light. The hay stack was now engulfed in flames, the heat intense, the billowing smoke eating up the last of the air, the sound roaring in her ears, the taste of hot soot and smoke now choking her.

She needed strength.
Think about Rafique.
Yes.
Think about water.
No.
Think about air.
No.

❧

Eye of the Storm

September 1971, Sheetalpur, East Pakistan

AS FIRE RAVENOUSLY TONGUED its branches, the bamboo bush near the haystack curled, crackled, exploded like agonized fingers twisting away from the whistling wind, away from the flames, away from the burning haystacks.

Amina, covered in soot and manure, singed, wheezing for breath and coughing, crawled out from under the inferno. Stumbling, she tried to run. Captain Daud caught up to her, rifle butted her in the back and as she lay in the mud, kicked her in the ribs.

Right behind Captain Daud, Bodor Morol kicked her once more and Neezam grabbed Amina's hair with his fist, holding her head like a hunting trophy, pulled her face close up to his and spat in it.

"*Magi, khanki,* whore, bitch. Nahar, where is Nahar?" Neezam yelled into her face as he savagely shook her head from side to side. Amina watched in horror as fire engulfed both haystacks.

"Nahar?" Neezam asked again. Slapped her hard. Blood flowed down Amina's cut lips.

Amina had to save Nahar. She had to tell.

Amina nodded her head. Pointed towards the haystack next to the one she was hiding under. Quickly, Captain Daud motioned to two *jawan* soldiers, who, kneeling, could see a flash of white, a white *salwar* under the hay. As they pulled Nahar away from the flames by her traitorous *salwar*, it came off.

Humiliated in her futile efforts to hide her nakedness, only wearing a *kameez*, smeared in manure, chicken shit, urine and mud, Nahar was now dragged towards the main house by two soldiers, past the butchered bodies of Jahanara and Mustafa that lay in a growing pool of blood, spreading into the brown clay of the courtyard like a dark, black omen, lay in the middle of a courtyard built by Mustafa Chowdhury's father, Mohammed Asgar Chowdhury, Neezam and Rafique's grandfather, built as a place for his grand children to play. And here, on this courtyard, one grandchild had murdered his Uncle and Aunt.

Chowdhury's eye still glared open, turned upward, the sightless stare of a corpse. Jahanara lay at the feet of Mustafa, her green sari now a dark crusted red, her left hand outstretched, limp over Chowdhury's legs, in a rejected plea for mercy. Rejected by Neezam. Jahanara's arms had nourished Neezam, the child. And Neezam's hands had taken her life, silenced her forever. Lips that once kissed Neezam, now mute flesh.

Two souls silenced by hatred; spawned by a hideous greed.

Dragged past the bodies, Nahar's mind revolved over and over beneath her closed eyelids. Mercifully, she reeled into unconsciousness.

Like a slaughtered animal, the soldiers dragged Nahar up onto the front veranda. When Nahar came to, she found her hands were tied to the corner wooden post with jute twine, her legs tied together at the ankle. Like a crumpled rag doll, semi-conscious, she lay naked except for her *kameez*.

Nahar started to shiver. She heard a moaning, "Allah, Khoda." In the corner of her eye she saw Amina, in a torn blouse and ripped petticoat, tied to a beam on the other side of the veranda. Amina writhed, twisted in mid-air, like a goat ready for the butcher to knife into pieces, her feet stretched below her barely touching the ground.

Nahar's head reeled with pain and dizziness. Her teeth started to chatter, her shoulders shuddered in involuntary convulsions. She wanted to screech out her grief. But her voice was hoarse, her speech strangled.

She heard the sounds of soldiers going through the huts, the house, searching, the distant sounds of loot being loaded into trucks. Their home now a death trap. Shouts and yelled orders filled the air. Nahar watched, her vision fading in and out of focus, as the soldiers dragged the bodies of Mustafa and Jahanara away from the courtyard towards the pond, leaving a trail of blood.

Nahar looked at Chowdhury's chair on the veranda, and below it a saucer from last night where Rafique had put out a cigarette. Gray ash lay in the saucer. The wind picked up, blew it into disappearing bits. Where was Rafique? What would she tell him? What?

"Amma, Abba," Nahar cried. Her head hung limp. Light melted into the gloom of early evening, closing in on her, deepening slowly, gripping her in its clammy fingers.

Bodor Morol turned to walk towards the house. As he passed her, Nahar called out to him in a last plea, "*Chacha*, you know me from my childhood. I played and grew up with your daughter Nazneen, went to school with her. Please help me! Please *Chacha*!"

Bodor pulled up his *lungi*, went up to the doorway on the veranda. Behind him, Neezam stopped to laugh at Nahar's pleading. His eyes blazing and merciless.

Nahar tugged at her tied wrists, and the twine cut into her, drawing blood. She tried to scream out of this nightmare. Only half-formed rasped syllables passed her cut lips.

Neezam stooped down to Nahar. Like a mongrel ripping at an injured rabbit, Neezam pulled her hair, his face close to her's and barked, "Where is Rafique?" A vicious confidence grew in his voice. "Tell us right now, or else death, death right now!"

"*Shourer Baccha*," Nahar murmured under her breath. She could smell whiskey on his breath. "Son of a swine."

"*Ki bolli?* What did you say? *Haramzadi*, bastard," Neezam cursed. "So, you thought you would get away, *Magi*?"

Nahar gathered the spit in her mouth into a ball on the tip of her bloody tongue and spat into Neezam's eye.

"Fucking bitch, *chootmarani khanki*, whore, I will kill you right now," Neezam said slapping Nahar hard as he shook her head violently, ripping out a handful of her hair. He struck her again across the face, this time drawing blood from her mouth.

"Allah, *bachoow amare*, save me," Amina screamed. Cold, cutting laughter shadowed Amina's every cry for mercy. Two Pakistani soldiers were upon Amina. Beating her with a cane. Kicking her with their steel toed boots. Soft-thudding blows against unresisting flesh.

Neezam stepped back, took out a handkerchief to wipe the spit off of his face.

Horrified by what they were doing to Amina, Nahar found a deep pool of untapped courage and screamed, "Stop, she is innocent! Leave her, please leave her. She is innocent."

Captain Daud heard Nahar screaming, paused. Leaving his men, he walked over to Neezam. Wearing an ironed khaki uniform, carrying a staff cane, with hard eyes he scrutinized Nahar's bloody face, her body.

"Leave her, please leave her. She is innocent," Nahar screamed again.

As Nahar looked up, Neezam peered down at her, murder in his eyes. He spat into Nahar's face and screamed, "*Khanki,* whore, I will kill you right now." He pulled out a pistol from his pant pocket, chocked Nahar by the throat and held the gun to her ear.

"Stop it!" Captain Daud called out from behind. He glanced fiercely at Neezam, moved him aside with a flick of his cane, and examined Nahar like an animal, shining a bright flashlight into her face. He narrowed his eyes, raised his thick eyebrows. Captain Daud, a grin on his moustached lips, pulled Nahar's chin up to his face with his staff cane. He now saw Nahar in a new light. Daud stepped back. To the two *jawans*, he said, "Put these two on the truck." Looking into Nahar's glazed eyes, he said, "How many Pakistanis has your husband killed so far? How many operations?"

Nahar looked down.

"Where is your husband?" Captain Daud asked, his voice rising.

Nahar heard the questions. She was silent.

"Your husband was here, we know. We have information. Tell us or you will die right now!" She heard in Urdu.

Die? Death would be an easy escape, Nahar thought. They had

stopped beating Amina. Nahar struggled to regain some composure. She wanted to die with some dignity.

"You can cooperate or die," Captain Daud said.

Nahar's silence only made Captain Daud angrier as he brought his staff cane down hard on the wooden post in front of Nahar. Reflexively, she shuddered.

"Next time, it's going to be your face!" he said, stroking the cane. Captain Daud turned away from Nahar, called out to one of his soldiers in the middle of the courtyard, "We have to leave right now, or we will be stuck in this fucking muddy *Mukti* hole tonight."

In a loud sharp voice he ordered the soldiers to load the women into the jeep.

He turned to Neezam and Bodor standing beside him. Daud tapped his cane on Neezam's ironed silk shirt pocket. "Make sure you take care of this village, make sure there is no *Mukti* here."

"Yes sir! We will set up camp here, sir," said Neezam saluting him, a curling smile crossing his lips, his tone calculated, emotionless. Neezam sauntered towards the main house with Bodor closely following behind. Bodor eyed the Chowdhury estate in an entirely new light.

Holding an end of his *lungi* up with one hand so that it would not get pulled through the mud and blood, Bodor turned and said, "Neezam, all this is yours now."

Neezam's voice slowed and deepened, and he said with a smile, "Yes." After a minute, pulling out a cigarette and tapping it on his gold case, he added, "Mine."

Two soldiers dragged Nahar and Amina towards the olive jeep. They hoisted Nahar up and threw her on the back seat. Tied her hands to the metal tubing of the front seat. They threw Amina next to her, like a sack of rice.

It started to drizzle, a light rain. With the rain all of Nahar's dreams dissolved, like droplets dripping off green water lily leaves.

Tied to the back of the jeep, Nahar and Amina were trophied pieces of bloody hunted animals.

❦

Beyond All Borders
❧ ❧ ❧

Salda River, East Pakistan-India Border, September 1971

IN THE WANING AFTERNOON, THE sun climbed up towards the top of the Tripura foothills, its slanted light kissing the hilltops. By the river, along the spreading bamboo and waving bananas, a shade crept in.

Silent as a stalking tiger, Rafique stepped quietly to the water from out of the brush. At the river's edge, he looked at Salda as it snaked like a mighty python gorged on the feast of monsoon rain gushing down from the northern ranges of the Longtharai, the Atharamura.

A yellow breasted blue *machranga* skimmed smoothly only a few inches over the water surface and harpooned a *puthi* in its beak. It twisted its head from side to side, swallowing its meal, before beating its wings hard, rising up, finding a perch in the shade of an arching bamboo.

Rafique knelt down, ran his fingers over the still surface of the water, clearing it, and washed his face. After walking all day, his throat felt like sandpaper. Cupping the cool water in his hands, the September sun reflecting in the clear liquid, drank deeply. He drank again, filling his empty stomach, and again, dulling the pangs of hunger stabbing at his belly.

A blackbird suddenly skittered over him. Rafique jumped back, his neck strained, his eyes bloodshot. Still crouched, he raised his head, looked across the river; here the Salda was too wide, the currents too swift to cross. He took some *chira,* popped a handful into his mouth and chewed. Where he and Nazmul had crossed just a few months before, the meandering rivulet Salda of April was now a wide gorged river of September. Hoping he could find a shallower spot, he hiked through the brush further downstream.

Pushing through thick ferns, grasses, and mosquitoes, on a winding trail at the edge of the river, Rafique journeyed downstream. He took the last of the hard round block of palm sugar Nahar had packed for him three days earlier, bit off a piece and chewed on its sweetness.

Through a forested shore lined by tall Chamal, Garjan, Kanak trees, Rafique looked across to the other side. So close to the border, he could almost smell the sharp Charminars of Agartala, hear the excited conversations of guerrillas at Melaghar, feel the welcome touch of deadly pineapple grenades—the reedy harmonica playing by the campfire, searching, trying for that illusive effect.

Rafique had heard on the *Swadhin Bangla Betar* news that Tajuddin Ahmad, the Bangladesh Government's Prime Minister in exile, had asked for additional arms and training from the Indian Government. Hopefully, when he got to Agartala tomorrow, there would be enough arms to go back and launch another assault in Sheetalpur or Dacca.

Nazmul and Firoz were, he hoped, in Agartala. Chewing on the *chira,* Rafique recounted the events of the last few hectic deadly days and the last few hard months of guerrilla warfare. Sheetalpur, Nahar, his parents. Had they safely reached his Aunt's?

Dacca, Rintu, Khalid, Jewel. All the captured guerrillas. He wished Nazmul was with him. And Rintu?

Out of the death camps in the M.P. Hostels, Cantonment and Barracks of devilbroweddrunkfatjawed Yahya's soldiers the only thing that escaped were tales of Nazi style torture: fingernails torn out, electrocutions, degrading humiliation before death, death by kicking and stomping.

En route to Agartala, Rafique had spent the night with a few Sector Two guerrillas going back to Dacca for a bombing operation. This time they would stay outside of Dacca. Ambush and run. He remembered the conversation.

"Two options in the death camps of Dacca. One. If you admit you are guilty, you will die. Two. If you don't admit you're guilty, you will be tortured endlessly. You may live. But death is more likely."

"Burned by acid, yes that's common."

"Finger nails ripped out, very common."

"Electric shock, very very common."

"Upside down hangings, a dose for every *Mukti*, a must."

Thoughts of Rintu, laughing, joking, of Rintu being tortured, his finger nails being pulled out, his body convulsing in electrocutions bayoneted into Rafique's thoughts. He shuddered, swallowed, looked down the path, then across the Salda, felt the Sten in his satchel banging against his back, wanted to take it out, empty the magazine into the mouth of the snitching rat who gave them away in Dacca. "*Mir Jafars*," he cursed under his breath, remembering Jewel's words about the enemy within.

On the same route, going to Agartala in April, he and Nazmul had met Khalid and Jewel. Khalid, a smile as pure as the good earth. Jewel, determined and ferocious, vengeance in his eye. Khalid's unfinished letter, address unknown, weighed down his satchel, the message still undelivered. Jewel, Khalid, Rintu, all the guerrillas. Brave beyond his wildest expectations. Rafique wanted to be alone today, alone with the many thoughts that filled him. The water gushed on, the swollen river pushing through with its monsoon might.

He lit his last cigarette and dragged at it ceremoniously. As he flicked the white ash, he looked up at the azure sky entombed in green. Today the sunshine seemed more golden, the sky more bright. It was getting late. He wanted to cross the Salda.

He crushed the empty cigarette pack, threw it away, and then he noticed the *tabiz* that his mother had given him was gone from his shirt pocket. He scrounged in his pant pockets. He looked in his Panjabi pockets where he had last seen it. He dug through his cotton satchel.

Nothing.

He had lost his talisman, lost his good luck.

A bad omen.

Rafique bit his lip. He ground his teeth. He thought about what Nahar had said about being careful, and that she would be fine, and to take care of himself and not worry about her.

"Take me with you, Rafique," she had said. He now wished, wished even through these Razakar maggot-infested routes, he had brought her and his parents with him.

Rafique fought with a growing fear inside, a fear larger than when he was in the Fiat with the unexploded bomb, greater than when he blew up the bridge. This battlefield, this battle was inside Rafique.

He exhaled a long breath. Reflexively his hands kept searching his pockets, patting down his pants.

What was going on in Agartala?

"Focus Rafique," he said to himself, trying to reel in his thoughts as he kept on walking.

The wind rushed in the tops of the bamboo and sounded in the dead *Sal* leaves as they scudded on the ground in front of Rafique. Row on row of waves lapped the banks of the river. As quick as it had come, the wind died down. The *machranga* left its bamboo haven and flitted and skimmed over the river southward. The Salda had narrowed now.

Taking off his father's chador, he put it in his cotton satchel. He shucked off his pants, peeled off his shirt, put them inside the satchel. He tied the strap of his bag like a headband, perching it high on the arch of his back. He held the Sten above his head as he waded into the water. The river bed came alive, tugging and pulling at his legs, pushing him deeper. He felt the strong current as he sank knee deep into riverbed mud, almost losing his balance. He stopped. Holding the Sten high above in both hands like a balancing stick, Rafique stepped from one muddy hole into the next. Gingerly he felt his way, avoiding being stabbed by a sharp buried branch. Up to his nose in water, his satchel wet, Rafique swam a dog paddle, holding the Sten barrel up and dry with one hand. He switched the Sten from hand to hand, paddling with one, until he made it to the other side. With endurance, finesse and sheer will, Rafique climbed the bank, holding a dry Sten. He put his satchel by the base of a tree, sat down exhausted, wished he had one more smoke.

At the river's edge, Rafique lay on the grass, pillowing his satchel on a toe-like gnarled root of a giant *Sal* tree.

As he looked up into the afternoon autumn sky, slow like locust came the vultures in the horizon, cutting an arc in his vision, filling the sky and the day with the wind of death. In a spiral they rode the warm air, slowly turning, dropping lower in a great tightening circle, ugly harbingers of death, dropping down towards the edge of the river uttering low guttural croaks.

Rafique sat up. Squinted. His body tensed. His spine arched. Death was near. As he looked across, towards the middle of the muddy river, two bloated corpses slowly floated by. A water snake, twisting its periscoped head, swam side to side towards the corpses, then skirted them.

Voices. Cupping his ears, Rafique listened. Squinting hard, he could make out a group of soldiers maybe a quarter of a mile across the river. With them, tied hostages, captured refugees, being kicked, shoved and booted to the far edge of the river. He could barely make out Urdu orders, unable to catch all the words.

Rafique edged down to the water, getting a closer view of the soldiers and their captives.

The sound of a baby's cry pierced the air. Then a piercing shriek of a woman. The sound of slaps and beatings. A *Lalmukh Bandar*, red-faced monkey, screeched from high atop the branches. It screeched again, louder, harsher, shattering the peace of the jungle.

Wanting blood, his gritted teeth bared, his stomach knotted in disgust, a total and utter hatred, a seething killing anger rose in Rafique's throat as he watched the hostages being beaten mercilessly.

He felt like he was a spectator in a ruthless Roman gladiator gallery watching the sport of killing. *This was not to be, not in front of me, not now, not ever. I will never be able to look at myself in the*

mirror, never.
Never.
And I could never look Nahar, Abba, Amma in the eye, never forgive myself, if I do not help them.

In a split second, throwing his bag under a dense thicket, Rafique camouflaged his Sten by wrapping it in a green *gamcha.*
"Wish Nazmul was here," Rafique murmured to himself, his hand clenched in anger, gripping onto the barrel of his gun.
By a single flick of his wrist, his *lungi* became a loincloth. Making a satchel out of the fold of the *lungi*, he hid his last grenade. He eyed some driftwood by the edge of the river. Wading in, he tied the Sten with the *gamcha* to the top branch. He hung underneath, floating down the river with the current, using his legs to paddle towards the other side. The water swirled around his neck, and Raifque felt bare, wished he still had his mother's *tabiz.*
Mid-stream he could make out an officer and two *jawans*, and with them three *lungi* and khaki shirt wearing, rifle toting Razakars. The soldiers were wearing half-sleeve khaki shirts and pants and netted helmets.
The gorged Salda was swift, and Rafique drifted with the current like a hidden tiger, only his nose and gun above water. In his mind flashed his father's childhood stories of the Royal Bengal Tiger floating between islands deep in the Sunderbans.
Echoes of yelled orders, the pleading voices of the hostages bounced off the surface of the water as Rafique's eyes sparked in anger. They were beating one of the men into a pulp, his face a bloody mess. Babies screeched in horror and the women tried to smother their mouths.
Hidden behind the driftwood, nearing the other bank, Rafique could see a young man, possibly a *Mukti Bahini* guerrilla, wearing pants, kneeling, his hands tied behind his back. Lined up to be shot by the river's edge were three *lungi* clad men, trembling stick figures, two women in saris, one clutching an infant to her chest, the other shaking in fear, holding onto the two naked children—whimpering, wrapped around the legs of their mother like tendrils. Nine souls.
Kneeling, being beaten, the pant wearing man pleaded for their

278

lives, "Saar, we are innocent, *amaderke mairen naa*, don't kill us." One of the Razakars kicked him in the groin. The man fell over. As the man lay unconscious on the ground, the Razakar continued kicking him in the side.

Unable to stand, the woman holding a baby in her arms crumpled to the ground.

A bit upstream from the soldiers, Rafique found a spit of mud. Hiding in the riparian reeds, he marked his prey.

"*Gooli maroo*, fire," barked the commander in a beret.

Triggered by the order, fighting through the reeds, Rafique stood up, aimed his Sten.

"Captain! *Mukti! Ooper pass*, over there!" cried out one of the Pakistani soldiers, pointing toward Rafique.

The soldiers forgot their captives, fell forward, started shooting at Rafique. In the fray, the refugees escaped into the jungle, away from the river.

Rafique gripped the magazine of the Sten in his left hand, as he squeezed the trigger with his right, shouldering the metal handle. In rapid bursts, the recoil hit his shoulder, jarring him, as he sprayed 9mm bullets at an upward sweep, emptying the magazine into the soldiers and Razakars. Hit, a Pakistani soldier and two of the Razakars fell instantly.

With his free left hand, pulling out his one grenade from the folds of his *lungi*, Rafique bit off the safety with his teeth. He held the grenade in his right hand for a moment, shortening the time to explosion, gauging the distance, and like the cricket balls he had lobbed a thousand times, he lobbed it hard in a high arc. A few feet in front of the now cowering soldiers, the grenade bounced. It lay still for a second. The exploding shrapnel tore into the soldiers, killing them all, wounding the officer behind.

The Pakistani commander squeezed the trigger on his machine gun. A hail of bullets scattered around Rafique, cutting into the water.

The ack-ack-ack sounded like a death rattle, a demented last laughter, as one bullet tore through Rafique's stomach and another went clear through his left shoulder. He felt like someone had taken a bat to his shoulder. A dark cloud of red spread around him, his stomach bleeding badly.

The wounded officer threw a grenade, and it erupted in the water just behind Rafique. Rafique felt himself slammed forward from the blast, his Sten gun left his hand and sunk into the mud.

Rafique lay hurt gasping for breath, bleeding on the edge of the river, his left hand pushing hard into the gash that was once his stomach. The pain grew as his body stiffened, the shock now hardening into an agonizing pain. The Captain came towards Rafique pointing his rifle. "*Mukti chootia*, I will show you," he said approaching Rafique.

Rafique feigned death as he lay head down in a pool of blood. Like a cobra arching it's head back, Rafique coiled all the strength left in his body—every muscle, every nerve was taut, tight and coiled like a spring.

Up close the officer pointed the rifle at Rafique's head. Rafique pounced. Grabbing, ripping at the barrel, he yanked the Captain down into the river. The officer's fist crashed into Rafique's face with the force of a club, but Rafique hung on. The rifle came loose, sank to the muddy bottom.

Choking the officer in a vise like grip, Rafique clawed into his throat just above the Adam's apple. They locked eyes. Cold killing eyes looked into Rafique's face, the head turned from side to side trying to break free of Rafique's deadly grip.

Rafique felt stones under his feet. Screaming in agony, he used his battered left hand to pull up a heavy stone, smash it into the officer's ear.

The first blow made a soft crunching sound, as blood oozed out and the officer released his grip on Rafique's neck, screaming in pain.

"I'm taking you with me you murdering bastard," Rafique spat his own blood into the face of the Pakistani.

From deep within, Rafique's death anger came welling up in an atavistic primal explosiveness he had never felt before—March 25, the bridge, Jewel, Khalid, Rintu, their deaths, his life, the unkept promises of returning to Nahar, his parents. Everything, all Rafique's anger exploded into the smashing of the stone into the face of the Captain.

"Maur khooni, Maur! Maur! Die murderer, die! Die!" Rafique screamed.

Rafique hit again and found the Captain's forehead with a dull crunch, his face now a bloody pulp. He brought down the stone harder and harder each time with the thud of crunched skull, spattered brain. He struck again and again, smashing the officer's pulped head.

Exhausted, Rafique released the stone, but not the soldier's bloody neck. He gasped for air, his throat now dry, his body drained. Slowly, he loosened his grip and watched the body of his enemy sink to the muddy bottom.

Rafique recited, *"La ilah illa Allah; Muhammad Rasul Allah,* None is god except Allah; Muhammad is the Messenger of Allah."

The Salda lapped at his sides, cold water caressed him, gently soothing, drawing him in deep, the burning dissolving into the river. Like a mother's bedtime song, the river slowly lulled him into a dream. Rafique took in a long breath, filled his lungs with the sweet moistness of Bangladesh.

He could see the softness in his mother's eyes. On the courtyard, his mother running after him trying to catch him as he played hide-and-seek with her. She was bathing him, caressing his forehead ever so gently before bedtime. He was holding on to the strong, sure hands of his father, walking beside him down the village trails. His father was calling him from across the lush green paddy fields, "Rafique, Rafique," putting his warm chador over him.

Rafique whispered, "Forgive me Abba, Amma. I could not keep my promise to return. Nahar, forgive me."

Lifting off the gossamer red veil of Nahar, face glistening golden, Rafique held a bright glow, a blush, a rose, velvety, blooming in his hands, smelled her hair and skin, heard her sweet laughter.

With the gentle caress of water, like the velvet of rose petals on his cheeks, the colors dissolved, like glistening pearls on green leaves, rolling off, becoming one with the white, the silver surface of the Salda.

281

In the depths of darkness,
I will always swim to you,
search for you,
afloat on the braided ripples of the deep green water,
filaments of saffron and gold.
In your eyes glisten little pearls,
shimmering, shattering the sunlight
into a thousand rainbows in my heart.

Silent Screams

❧ ❧ ❧

September 1971, Dacca Cantonment, East Pakistan

TETHERED TOGETHER, AMINA AND NAHAR were jerked out of the jeep, dragged violently by two *Hawaldars* towards one of the holding cells at Dacca Cantonment. Whimpering, Amina tried, tried desperately with tied hands to cling to Nahar.

"*Kutti choop ho ja*. Bitch, shut up," the *Hawaldar* screamed at Amina, and his sadistic eyes bored into Nahar's face as he threw the women into the bowels of a rancid, dark bunker. The dozen women inside scurried to the farthest corners, covering their bruised faces with their hands, cowering from the light. Beaten, shivering, with hopeless faces and empty eyes.

The *Hawaldars* untied Amina and Nahar, pulled hard on the jute rope, drawing blood, cutting into their wrists. Amina collapsed onto the floor, shaking violently, bloody, soaked in sweat, stinking of manure. Next to her, Nahar, on her knees, gasped for air.

Captain Daud stood in the doorway, inspecting Nahar like a prize catch in a pen. "*Wo aurat ko Major Shikander ke pas baich do*. Send that woman to Major Shikander's. She is the wife of a *Mukti* leader. They need to interrogate her," he said, pointing his cane at Nahar. Then with a loud thud, the *Hawaldar* closed the door, plunging the women into a fetid darkness.

Sobbing, Amina reached, held on to Nahar's shoulder, her eyes sunk in terror, kneeling, fearfully looking at the other women in the bunker. "Appa," Amina sobbed. Nahar held her tight, felt Amina's

285

heart thumping hard against her.

"Appa," Amina whimpered again. Nahar felt like a chicken in a coup awaiting slaughter. She remembered how gently the feathers were plucked from around the neck, bare, clean, little bright veins, before the butcher's knife bore down drawing blood, cutting through the skin, severing the head.

They awaited the butchers.

—⊰⊱—

"Naah," Amina hardened, screaming into the glinting hungry eyes that shone at her in the dark room. "Naah, Appa, Nahar Appa, *bachow*, save me!"

"*Rundi*. whore!" The *Hawaldar* growled at Amina as he dragged her away, her hair clenched in his hands.

"Appa, Appa," Amina cried out as Nahar held onto her arm. The women huddled into a corner, weeping as Amina was yanked towards the open door.

"*Rundi, kutti*. Whore, bitch," the *Hawaldar* yelled as he slapped then punched Nahar away from Amina.

"*Naah*, Stop". Nahar shrieked at the top of her voice as she tried to free Amina from the *Hawaldar's* grip. The other women cringed, crossed their clenched fists over their chests, trembled.

The *Hawaldar* threw Nahar against the concrete wall.

"Amina," Nahar called out as she hit her head on the wall and collapsed.

Then the *Hawaldars* gripped another begging woman—several scrapes and bruises on her face, a welt over her eye—by her hands and dragged her out of the bunker. Her pleas fell on merciless ears.

"Appa, appa..." Amina's empty cries filled the bunker, echoed inside Nahar's head.

The door slammed shut.

The women cringed. They were next.

Clawing her way, Nahar got to the heavy door and bashed her bloodied forehead against it, banged again and again with her clenched fists.

"Amina," Nahar choked.

"Mad, have you gone mad?" hissed a woman in her early twenties, wearing a petticoat and torn blouse. She stood next to Nahar, looked into her face. "If you try to stop them, you will be killed. You have to survive. Survive!"

Amina's shrieks for help rang in Nahar's ears, dying out into the far end of the compound.

"Play their game or you will be dead before morning," the woman said to Nahar.

"Amina," crumpled by the door, Nahar wept.

"Amina*re*."

AMINA STEPPED ON LEGS, stumbled and fell on a still warm body. In the darkness of this empty bunker she scampered away, thrashing at the floor like a bird with broken wings. Naked, she crawled to a corner and held her stomach with her hands as she coughed in dry heaves. She vomited. In her mouth was the bitter taste of blood and vomit, on her skin she still felt cold clammy fingers, clawing hands, talons of torture. Blood ran down her leg, as she gasped in air heavy with the stench of death, of feces and urine.

Outside was the sound of soldiers talking and laughing, an occasional loud grunt. Amina ran her fingers through the tangle that was once her beautiful long hair, her knee-length long hair, her pride. All her life she had taken such good care of her hair, washing it, putting mustard oil and combing it—now disheveled, bloody, rancid.

She lay motionless on the cement, her right knee swollen, red. Through the hair that lay covering her eyes, she fixed her gaze on the ceiling—a 'u' hook for a fan. As she focused on the hook, she heard the sound of a jeep engine as it slowly faded away.

Her mind, her legs felt numb. Amina hobbled to the middle of the room, gathered all her strength and stood up. She stood on her tiptoes and reached for the hook but it was beyond her reach.

In the corner of the room was a metal pail full of urine and feces. A flood of uncontrolled tears rolled down her cheeks. She clenched her teeth, wiped her tears away with the back of her hand, slowly edged to the pail, turned it over, spewing the waste on the floor. Amina put the pail under the hook, stepped on it and stretched. Her finger tips trembled in empty air as she arched her feet, tip toed, stretched her back, the hook just beyond her reach. The glinting metal eye, the hook to escape, escape from the hell of torture she had descended into was inches away.

Her knee gave way. Amina fell down hard on the concrete floor. She pushed up, looked around. The room was empty except for the body of the woman. She took a deep breath and crawled to it. Amina's hands trembled as she touched the woman's hands, still warm. She pulled. Nothing. Grabbing the woman's legs, she pulled. Painful inch by inch, Amina dragged the body to the center of the room under the hook.

"Allah, *amaree khoma koiro*, Allah forgive me," Amina panted as she balanced the bucket on top of the woman's back. She tried to stand on the bucket, but lost her balance. Fell again. Breathing hard, Amina pushed the body aside and put the bucket upside down on the cement. Reaching into the very last of her strength she raised the body and laid it over the pail.

"*Khoda amaree maap koiroo*, God forgive me," Amina murmured as she stood on the body. Her toes pressed into the back of the still warm corpse. Through the nerves of her feet to her legs, to the base of her spine and up her neck, an icy chill crept up Amina's body. Her head spun. She shuddered. On tiptoe her fingertips brushed the bottom of the 'u' hook. On her fingertips was the touch of cold rusty metal, under her feet a body still warm.

Freedom.

Exhausted Amina got down and sat against the wall. For a minute she held her hand against her neck, feeling the softness. She felt her throat rise and fall, rise and fall with her every breath.

Panting, Amina rasped a prayer, asking forgiveness to Allah.

"Our Lord! We have wronged our own souls: If thou forgive us not and bestow not upon us Thy Mercy, we shall certainly be lost."

She looked up at the ceiling. There shone the 'u' hook. It was alive now, calling her, squinting in a daemonic one-eyed gaze.

Amina ran her hand through the kelp of her disheveled hair. With trembling hands she braided one side of her hair and noosed it around her neck. The braid was too short. Amina started to tear away the hair on the other side of her head. Her hands turned red with blood as she pulled out more and more hair. Amina braided the torn hair into the end of the braid already noosed around her neck, extending it.

She tightened the rope of hair around her neck. She held the tail end of the braid, pulled at it, feeling the pressure on her neck.

She whispered words from the Koran.

"He has created the heavens and the earth with the truth; He makes the night cover the day and makes the day overtake the night, and He has made the sun and the moon subservient; each one runs on to an assigned term; now surely He is the Mighty, the great Forgiver."

Amina hobbled to the body, prayed, "He is the Mighty, the great Forgiver."

She stepped up and stood on her toes on the back of the woman's body, inserted the braid through the 'u' hook. In the near distance Amina heard sounds approaching. Soldier's voices. Laughter.

Quickly she pulled at the tail end of the braid now threaded through the hook, felt the noose tightening around her neck. She took the tail knotted it once and then again around the hook. Amina pulled at the braid and the knots tightened, held.

"Allah, forgive me," Amina uttered closing her eyes. Gritting her teeth, she stepped off the body.

Her head felt congested, her body swung wildly. The braided rope cut into her neck, drawing blood, mixing with the blood that flowed from her scalp. Amina swung naked, a pendulum of time cutting the bonds of misery noosed in braids of pride.

Light flooded the room, her eyes jeweled in a certain shining, a revelation of eternity. Amina floated like the white cranes of winter over the wetlands, a million visions scintillated in her iris irradiated in green, red and yellow, in palpable textures of music, of the lone *Baul's aktara*, that now filled the earth and sky in a soulful serenade of freedom, the golden yellow pollen of a million mustard flowers swirling trails in the air. She floated over water, her hands outstretched as she had run under the mango trees when she was a child. The little *puthi* fish was poking its tiny mouth and Amina could see all the way to the bottom of a crystalline pond. The fishes swam in elongated circles of dance. Flocks of birds floated overhead, flying in arrowed paths cutting across the blue towards home.

Her mind wandered to the caressing *kaash phool* by the bend in the river where she ran, frolicking with her playmates, Halim and Boochu. Halim, with his big wide eyes, was reaching out. His hands stretched out like a plane, he ran in a foot race down the dirt trail, with Boochu yelping behind him, through the glittering green and gold of the dancing paddy into the distant horizon. She was chasing Boochu and Halim into an eternity of emerald lushness—into the blue hue, into the wondrous and the free.

Amina, a swinging pendulum.

The rhythm slowed.

The swinging stopped.

Amina was free.

One World

Wednesday, November 24, 1971, Brentwood, California

"LAST OF THE SEASON," JACK said proudly, holding a wicker basket overflowing with butternut squashes and baby carrots from the small backyard patch. He set it on the kitchen counter next to Laura.

"Looks great, Jack," Laura said, looking up from paring and slicing Granny Smith apples, turning the slices into a large glass pie plate. As the cold November day curtained to a close, Laura, busy making preparations for Thanksgiving dinner, found herself lost in thoughts of Frank. She looked at Jack as he took off his jacket and washed his hands in the sink.

"Even with the mulch, it's getting too cold. I think this weekend I'll till up the patch. Mix in some compost."

"I'll put the carrots into the salad for tomorrow, and put in a few peppers, tomatoes, a little sprig of cilantro. Priti and Alok will like that."

"Do you have everything for your great stuffing?"

"Yes," Laura sighed, as she put down the paring knife. "Remember how Frank loved my stuffing?"

"Sure. He could eat a whole plateful and then some. How Frank loved Thanksgiving. Cranberry, a drumstick and stuffing and he was in heaven."

"Another Thanksgiving without him," Laura said. Tears flooded her eyes, poured down her cheeks.

Jack came and hugged her, wiped her tears away, gently kissed her on the cheek.

291

"We have to go on, Laura. If not for our sake, for Rachael's. By the way, where is Rachael?" asked Jack.

"Next door at Sarah's. She is going to have dinner there."

"Sarah could have been our daughter-in-law."

Laura washed the carrots and put them in a bowl, and Jack put away the rest of the winter squashes.

"Frank would have been twenty-four now," Laura said. "He never talked much about it, but I know he loved Sarah so much; she's mentioned so many times in his diary."

"Twenty-four," Jack repeated the words slowly, his chest rising and falling in a held pain.

"Remember how we dressed him up on his second Halloween as a tomato with those silly green leaf ears? Do you remember that Jack?"

"Yes. Frank thought he really was a tomato!" Jack chuckled, then went quiet.

"What fun that was," Laura said, pain choking her voice.

Jack looked out through a parting in the kitchen window curtains at the small vegetable patch, out in the far corner of the lawn, by the base of the pines. He could see Frank as a toddler, like a beaming bright tomato himself, sitting in the dirt between the tomato trellises and eagerly picking and putting tomatoes into the basket.

"He loved playing in the dirt, pulling up ripe tomatoes. Just loved digging with his little spade in the soft earth. Remember that picture of him with that big smile, squatting with his farmer hat in the middle of all those ripe tomato vines?"

"Yes, I have it put away. He was always so proud of helping you fill those baskets. His face would gleam as he showed them off to me," Laura said as she wiped her eyes with her sleeve, still holding on to a tomato in the other hand. "What good, what single good did Frank's life do?" Laura asked Jack. "To die for a war with no end, so far from home?"

She put away the bowl of carrots, the pie plate, washed her hands. Handing Jack a cup of coffee, then pouring one for herself, she walked over to the couch in the living room and sat down.

She took a sip of coffee, then smiled. "I forgot to tell you the great news, Jack. Priti called. She is expecting."

"How wonderful," Jack replied as he paced around the room, holding the cup of coffee. "When is the baby due?"

"Not for a while. It's going to be tough with her studies, but she is done this semester and in the spring she will be off."

"How's her dissertation going?"

"The committee has signed off on it. She has a chance to get an offer next year teaching a course in South Asian studies."

"Great!" Taking another sip, Jack put down his cup on the coffee table next to a small, weathered, brown leather diary.

"I see you've been reading Frank's diary again," Jack said.

"Frank would have been such a great writer."

"Yes, writing was his passion."

Laura sat motionless, her eyes searching the far corners of the room for something lost.

—⚜—

JACK LOOKED AT THE BRASS mantle piece clock. 5:00. He went to the TV, and turned it on, switched the channel to the national news. He turned the knob on the roof antenna rotator.

"There," he said, finally happy with the picture.

Harry Reasoner, ABC news anchor, came on wearing a wide tie and read the headline in a deep resonating voice for Wednesday, November 24, 1971.

"India gives its troops power to cross into Pakistan for self defense; reported Indian tanks in East Pakistan Sunday due to threatened Pakistan attack. Pakistan says it repelled a number of drives along the border and killed 200 Indians fighting with East Pakistani rebels... Reports of badly hit town issued."

Overpowering images of bloody bodies filled the screen. In the first few minutes, they showed an Indian village, Harihar, Gola, right on the far Eastern side of the border with East Pakistan, heavily shelled by the Pakistani army.

"Oh, God! Look at that child the mother is holding; his foot is half blown off!" Laura said.

Moaning cries filled the air as the camera panned over relatives grieving at the bodies of men, women, children dead on the ground.

Mother's cried, clutching the dead bodies of their children to their chests.

"Look at that village! Leveled! And no medical help," Jack said.

"Priti was telling me only last year that the worst typhoon wiped out hundreds of thousands of East Pakistanis in the southern low lying islands and low lands in the Bay of Bengal. Strange how devastated a country can be. Torn apart by nature. Now torn apart by man."

"I guess third world lives don't matter much."

'Via Satellite' was overlaid on the screen as Peter Jennings, surrounded by *Mukti Bahini* guerrillas, reported from a border village not far from the major East Pakistani town of Jessore. Around him the guerrillas were crouching, shooting and firing into West Pakistani army positions across the paddy fields.

"...as the afternoon fades, the day-long silence is rent with an exchange of fire," Peter Jennings reported, on his haunches, wearing a short sleeve khaki shirt in a dense tropical surrounding. *Mukti Bahini* guerrillas crouched around him.

"Doesn't it look a lot like Vietnam and Cambodia?" asked Jack.

"Yes. All those paddy fields."

After the Jennings piece from the border, the image cut to Howard Tuckner in Dacca, standing in the middle of a sparsely travelled main road in the capital. A few rickshaws, an ox cart, a bus and a truck were on the street, the few people's faces grim, cheerless.

"Dacca is a city expecting to die before it can live again," Howard Tuckner reported, his expression sombre. The divided Dacca road in the center of town behind him was almost empty, a few rickshaws, baby taxis and a truck passed by, a traffic policeman wearing a pith helmet and white uniform brandished a stave directing what little traffic there was.

"Looks like it's over for this government," said Jack.

"I sure hope so," Laura said.

The picture on the screen changed to a view of an almost deserted downtown Dacca. Only a few customers looked at clothes in an open bazaar. A roadside shopkeeper, wearing a skull cap, squatted in front of empty wooden shelves in his tiny stall, with hardly any wares to offer. "There is little support for the Pakistani army," Howard Tuckner stated. "Guerrillas were confident that they would topple the West Pakistani military junta entrenched 80,000 plus in Dacca," he continued.

The report on East Pakistan was most of the newscast. Following Howard Tuckner, Ted Koppel, ABC diplomatic correspondent, reported on the United States looking for an end to the crisis before the imminent fall of Yahya's war machine to the hands of the Bangladeshi guerrillas and to Indira Gandhi's troops.

An attractive woman appeared, cleaning the top of a piano with Johnson's Lemon Pledge, the sponsors of the ABC national news program for the evening. The mirror-like shine on the piano reflected her image.

"I remember talking to Priti about Yahya Khan's ping-pong diplomacy with his buddy Chou En-Lai on behalf of Nixon. Yahya is the go-between the US and China, and for that reason I guess Nixon wants at all costs to save Yahya's genocidal regime now, even in the face of imminent defeat," said Jack.

"Like Priti said, Nixon needs Yahya. Saving Yahya is higher up on the agenda than saving starving kids."

Later in the news reporter Jim Giggans came on with an overlay on the screen, "Tay Ninh, South Vietnam." He stood by highway Route 22. Behind, large army trucks lumbered, loaded down with South Vietnamese soldiers and heavy artillery.

"South Vietnam hopes to relieve enemy pressure on Phnom Penh and destroy enemy base camps," reported Jim Giggans.

"South Vietnam and the U.S. are in this symbiotic relationship. —similar to the Indian army and the *Mukti Bahini* guerrillas," Jack commented.

"Yes, and sadly so many innocent civilians are getting killed in both wars. Only East Pakistan has more palm trees and the cows in Cambodia looked larger."

"One world unified by death. Doesn't matter Vietnam, Cambodia or East Pakistan. The Archangel of death is color-blind," said Jack. "And the grim reaper has made South East Asia his home base."

"One world unified by the death of innocent men, women

and children," Laura sighed. "I wish we could help some of those children."

After the commercial, the news changed to the My Lai court martial where Colonel Oran K. Henderson underwent cross-examination about the massacre in Vietnam by American soldiers.

On the screen the reporter said, "Henderson says twenty and the chopper pilot says he saw 100 dead on the ground."

"Don't you think Henderson is a scapegoat?" Laura asked.

"You give drugs and arms to young soldiers and then when things go wrong like My Lai, there has to be a scapegoat," Jack replied.

At the end of the news there was a commentary by co-anchor Howard Smith reporting from Washington on Nixon and the chances of the United States regaining its influence in the world.

"...Russia supports India and is on very bad terms with Pakistan. China has declared for Pakistan and is on very bad terms with India. ...The larger danger... is that given their commitment the two neighbors, Russia and China, could come into conflict... Suppose China as some people expect moves her troops to India's borders to make India back down. Russia would almost surely bring counter power to bear against China somewhere."

The commentary ended with how the U.S. could influence both Russia and China to join it in seeking a political settlement in East Pakistan. How America could use the situation in the Indian sub-continent and find its way back to prominence in world diplomacy.

"America losing its way in the world. That's new! Wonder what brainiac figured this out." Jack said.

"A Sino-Soviet conflict in that area would be a disaster and Nixon knows it," said Laura.

"East Pakistan is a chess pawn in the hands of the superpowers," said Jack. "World War Three over East Pakistan? Russia and China getting involved in the Indian sub-continent?"

Jaw clenched, he turned off the TV.

"My Lai is just one massacre. How about the hundred more no one ever finds out about?" Jack said.

Laura repeated the question again to Jack,

"What good, what single good did Frank's death do?"

QUIET FILLED THE ROOM. JACK got up, and with a slow, thoughtful cadence walked towards the kitchen. For a moment, Laura looked outside, listened to the whisper, the rustle of autumn leaves in the wind. She remembered again the photo of Frank, a toddler, sitting on the ground by the tomato patch. His cheeks gleamed in the sun like two ripe red tomatoes. Getting up, slowly she followed Jack.

"Thought I'd make us some fresh coffee," Jack said as he poured water into the coffee maker.

"Great," said Laura, distracted. She took some homemade oatmeal raisin cookies from a jar on the counter and set them on a plate.

Laura walked back into the living room, placed the plate of cookies on the coffee table, and sat down. She picked up Frank's diary, and opened it to the first of many dog-eared pages. "Frank Patrick McKensie," was written in a neat cursive script on the front page. Jack set the two cups of steaming coffee on the table and sat down beside her.

Laura turned to the last page, a picture of Frank. A warm smile on his lips, Frank was dressed in a new marine-blue uniform, a crisp white hat on his crew-cut sandy brown hair. His eyes shone in pride, in hopes of a bright future. She gently touched his face, her fingertips caressing his smile.

"Frank was such a great writer, such feeling he had, such thirst for life," Laura said. Her mouth quivered, trying to say something, but nothing but a long slow exhalation of a tortured breath came out.

"Can I have a look?"

Laura closed the diary, handed it to him. To a much-thumbed page, Jack opened the dairy, cleared his throat, and started to read.

Homeward bound on the Mekong Delta Line
April 5, 1967, Vietnam

Buddy of mine, so fine.
Young wife, young man,
Our laughter, our camaraderie so fine,

My buddies and me, on the Mekong Delta line,
In banshee-like tracer light,
He stepped, stepped on a VC mine,
Then he bled, bled in his red banshee flight,
In my arms, a river of blood, buddy of mine so fine.
Dead on the Mekong Delta line.
Home-ward bound to young wife
A last salute, a last cold caress,
Plastic body bag to cold aluminum transfer tube,
Buddy of mine so fine,
Homeward bound on the Mekong Delta Line.

❧

JACK CLOSED THE DIARY, AND held it in his hands, running his fingers along the tattered, feathered edges. In the roughness, he felt the grip of Frank's tender hands as he used to hold him waiting with his little notebook for the school bus. How eager Frank had been holding his first notebooks, young eyes shining in the amazement of life, life so new and fresh. In these rough frayed edges, Jack felt the twenty years of his son all come flooding through him.

Jack handed the diary back to Laura. He took a sip of the coffee and rubbed his forehead—he wanted to howl, to cry out.

Laura swallowed and a sadness sank down into her chest, dissolving into her heart, filling her lungs. It filled her like a heavy burden, a rock, a coalesced mass of all things she did not want to remember, but could never forget.

In the far corner of their living room, the piano was suffused with the reflected light from the chandelier. Jack looked outside, as a waxing harvest moon threw long shadows on a silvery backyard. Finally he said, almost in a whisper, "The thanks missing in our Thanksgiving is Frank."

EXCERPTS FROM THE DIARY OF FRANK P. MCKENSIE

March 12, 1967, Vietnam

Late last night, I was kissing Reita Faria in my dreams. I was the lucky soldier on that USO stage.

She held herself so well. The silk dress tucked in the left hand. Her hair in a bun, that petite wristwatch and dark fabric with the white patterns, the long earring and graceful stance. She stood in front of the mike, so sure, so confidant, taking away every GI's breath.

If Gandhi was in Vietnam would he smoke a peace pipe with me over my dead buddy?

If Gandhi had lived in South Vietnam, instead of his early life in South Africa, would Vietnam be different?

And what the hell would he tell the VC?

Lay down your arms?

World problems solved?

Gandhi and me, smoking a peace pipe in 'Nam.

Did I do something really wrong in my last life to be here suffering and paying penance for unatoned sin?

As I look out of my bunker there is about a hundred yards of brush and tall grass. We are camped on this hill and it gently slopes down into a small river. And after that rice paddies for about a mile. Into the horizon you can see the Central Highlands.

In this land of make believe, here I sit looking over rice paddies, thinking I am looking over the blue Pacific. Just now, I wish I could dive into the cleansing pure waters of the Pacific and wash myself of this mud and muck, wash away a war with no end.

April 17, 1967, Mekong Delta, Vietnam

Some politician and some General put me here, so they can sit in their padded leather chairs while I wipe the shit off my butt in this stinking fox hole with mud.

Everyday, less and less of us believe in this war.

And policy? And why is it that one strike of a pen kills so many?

With 5,000 villages, this place has lived on a rice economy for 2,000 years. And out of the blue, by Johnson's orders, overnight, we have to build a democratic nation around the most corrupt local officials? A land wrapped in a hundred years of ugly corrupt colonialism, nepotism, in the middle of a twenty-year war.

God help us! I can think of easier things to accomplish!

April 19, 1967, Mekong Delta, Vietnam

If I could have given my life, I would have, to save his. Helpless, I held him as he died in my arms. Blood smeared his face, blood spurted out of him soaking me. And I just held him.

We had burnt the village to the ground, looking for the VC. I didn't even notice 'till Bill and Doc yelled out. I heard this muffled cry and under the collapsed bamboo hut, in a corner, was a little boy, maybe two years old, his arms twitching, tore up by a grenade I had lobbed.

I picked him up. Held him in my arms, his heart throbbing, fading away against my ribs, bleeding, dying. Coughing, spraying blood from a punctured lung. Then he gasped.

I died with him, died as he lay in my arms, bloody, muddy and dead. I would have given my life there if it would have saved his.

I died with him.

God forgive me.

Dreamin' of Home
May 1967, Vietnam

Dreamin'
To taste the promises of forever,
Lingering on Sarah's parted lips.
California brilliant sunshine,
Aflame in the bougainvillea's branches,
Bursting sweet in the melons of summer.
Chasing Ruff into the cold crashing surf,
Of the blue Pacific, bejeweled in a million diamonds.
Halloweens. Thanksgivings. Christmases.
Mom. Dad. Rachael.
Dreamin' of Home.

❧

Intelligentsia Genocide

❧ ❧ ❧

December 14, 1971, Dacca University

I N THE COLD GRAY OF a cheerless December morning, Professor Rahman sat in the living room sipping a lukewarm cup of black tea. No sugar. No milk. None to be had. All night, while Indian Mig-21s strafed military targets in and around Dacca, sleepless, bleary eyed, he intently listened to All India Radio reporting the impending fall of Dacca to the hands of the approaching *Mukti Bahini* forces and the Indian Army.

Victory was at hand.

A cold December breeze filtered in through the cracks of the plastic sheeting now covering the window panes, the glass shattered, still unrepaired after March 25th. And on the radio was percolating the news from BBC, Voice of America and Calcutta Radio about the relentless march of the combined forces towards Dacca.

"Freedom, soon," Rahman said taking a sip of tea and slumping back wearily into the sofa. "Soon."

Under the bamboo-print cotton curtains, on the glass and wooden bookcase, a candle entombed on a china plate lay burnt into a stub; wax had dripped off the edges of the plate onto the bookcase. The faint fragrance of melted wax on wood mixed with the smell of the freshly cooked *chitoi pithas* from the kitchen. Eerily quiet, no sounds of traffic or voices drifted in from the street.

"*Pitha*," Selina said walking in from the kitchen and placing a

303

plate in front of Rahman. She wiped the beads of perspiration from her forehead with the *áchol* of her blue cotton print sari and exhaled, "We only have *daal* for one more day."

Rahman took a bite of a *pitha*, chewed, tasted bits of rice kernels, sipped a little tea, gave her a hope-filled smile, and said, "Selina, freedom is just around the corner." He drew the gray shawl tight around his shoulders, and pulled his plaid *lungi* around his ankles. "Don't worry."

"Don't worry?" Selina said, adjusting the edge of her sari, tucking it in her waistband. "What will the children eat?"

She peeked into the adjoining bedroom. After a restless night of sporadic shootings, excitement and the anticipation of a free Bangladesh, Tia, Babul and Moina were fast asleep—Moina with her arms wrapped around Tia's neck and Babul curled up on the side of the bed. Covered by a cotton blanket, they looked peaceful and very tired, as if they had fought many battles and won. Selina went and pulled the blanket up a bit over the children.

The crackle of distant gunfire fingered into the Dacca University campus, ricocheted off the walls of the long stairwell leading up to the door of the Rahmans' fourth-floor apartment, and rang in his ears. With the echoes of guns, visions reverberated in his mind—Nilkhet slum burning, screaming women shot with children in their arms and students' bodies piled in front of the Halls—of March 25th. Rahman looked at the large calendar on the wall.

December 14, 1971.

March 25.
April.
May.
June.
July.
August.
September.
October.
November.
And now, December 14.

Nine long, arduous, months of carnage and killings, blood and struggle, sacrifice and sufferings.

Rahman took another sip of tea, gripped the cup for a little warmth. His eyes grew cold and his face darkened as he thought about the murders of Mustafa, Jahanara and Halim. For over three months, Nahar and Amina were missing, presumed dead.

"*Khoda*," he said in sheer pain, gritting his teeth, thinking back to the April day he said goodbye in Sheetalpur to Rafique and Nazmul. He took off his black thick-rimmed glasses, set them next to the cup, and rubbed his bloodshot eyes. *Where was Rafique? Nazmul?*

Under his Panjabi and undershirt a chill went through him, the hair on the back of his neck stood up, anger and anguish tore at his insides. It had been a long, sleepless night, the large clock ticking out the relentless seconds against the wall. Since March 25th, he had aged a lifetime. Rahman scratched his hand over his face mottled with day-old salt-and-pepper stubble, surprised it had not all gone gray in the last few months.

It was not without fear, misgivings and debate that he had returned from Sheetalpur in August. With three young mouths to feed, life in Sheetalpur for an extended period was impossible; it was a dire struggle to find powdered milk for his children, to even gather the daily bare necessities for his family. He put his head down on his folded hands, rested. After a few long minutes, he raised his head, put his glasses back on, wrapped the chador tighter around his shoulders, thought about shaving.

"Tia'r Ma, were you making some breakfast?" Rahman called out to Selina, his stomach grumbling.

"Coming, let me finish warming the milk for Moina," Selina said, juggling the cooking without any help once again. She had lost the baby in May, barely had time to recover. She had picked a name. *Shapna*. Dream. A baby girl—her dream—who would have been six months old now, if Shapna had lived.

In August they had come back first to live with relatives in Old Dacca, and then in September moved back to their apartment. Hunched over the kerosene stove, out of the corner of her eye she looked at the jute sack of rice, the lentil, the pail of water. All the stores were closed. The powdered milk for little Moina was running out.

"*Khoda, ai dojok theke amake uddar koro.* God, save me from this Hell," she coughed through the smoke from the stove.

Rahman ran his fingers through his thinning hair, thinking back to yesterday. When he had come home in the late afternoon, bare handed, frustrated from trying to gather some groceries, Selina said in a strained voice, "A student came looking for you. Tia opened the door. I was taking a bath. 'Bangla Department's Professor Rahman?' he asked Tia."

Rahman swallowed, his eyebrows narrowed. "Student? What did he look like?"

"I don't know. Tia just told me someone, maybe a student was looking for you. I am scared to death."

After a long moment, he said, "Tia'r Ma, don't worry. Victory is around the corner. Nothing will happen now."

"Any news from Chittagong?" Selina asked, lost in the fate of Nahar and Amina, the murders of the Chowdhury family. She wondered if Nahar and Amina were even alive, wondered about Rafique and Nazmul.

"Nothing. No news from Naila and Shihab. I pray they are OK," Rahman said.

"How will we face Rafique when he comes back?"

"Victory is just around the corner," Rahman repeated, collecting his thoughts. "Soon, a free Bangladesh."

An appetizing aroma filled his nose as Rahman picked up the *pitha* again. He took another bite, chewed on the sweetness, the first *pitha* of winter. From the kitchen came the faint sound of the metal scratching of a spatula in Selina's hands rubbing against the blackened surface of the frying pan, turning over a *roti*. The apartment complex was deserted except for the Salaams downstairs.

The quiet of an empty Nilkhet road was broken by the sound of a vehicle.

Sounds of footsteps in the corridor.

Then a knock.

Who could it be at this hour?

Rahman looked up at the clock.

8:30

"Who is it? Salaam Saheeb?" he asked. Slowly, Rahman got up, turned to the door, the blood draining from his face, his eyes glazed with fear.

"*Ke*, who?" he said, approaching the door.

"Professor Rahman *ache*, home?" an unknown man's loud voice asked in Bengali.

Rahman could feel his heart thump against his rib cage. He coughed on a last bit of *pitha* in his mouth, his throat now dry, his hand hanging at his side, helplessly numb.

Selina ran out from the kitchen, her face ghostly white. She stood beside Rahman, her stare fixed at what lay beyond the door. Her eyes widened and she whispered, "Don't..."

"Professor Rahman *ache*, home?" now louder, the voice called out.

More pounding knocks.

As Rahman opened the door, two young men burst past him.

Another two men stood in the doorway, blocking any exit. The four men were in their twenties, wearing cotton pants and khaki shirts. One of them brandished a pistol. A fifth man, a short, stocky, older man, stood outside wrapped in a brown chador, sporting a thick beard, his eyes hidden behind dark glasses.

The older man took out a piece of paper from under his chador and stepped forward to scrutinize Professor Rahman's face. "Professor Rahman?" he asked, his voice authoritative. "Our commander needs to talk to you for half an hour," he said in broken Urdu. A grin of capture appeared on his lips. "Hands up!"

The jab of a cold revolver barrel against his spine, Rahman reluctantly raised his hands. *Students?* He looked at the four young men in khaki shirts and cotton pants. *By their heavy accent, clearly not native Urdu speakers. They are not West Pakistani army. Bangladeshi. Maybe I have a chance.*

Shaking, Selina stood firm next to Rahman.

"Who are you? What do you want with him?" She asked in a tremulous voice, her breathing in short, anxious spurts. The men ignored her. Babul, Tia and Moina ran to their mother. Little Moina, blinked, rubbed the sleep from her eyes, clutched her mother's sari with both hands, shivered against her. Tia and Babul, barely awake, huddled next to Moina and Selina.

"Baba, Baba," Tia cried out, looking first at the men, then at her father with his hands raised.

"He hasn't done anything. Where are you taking him? There is a mistake. He..." Selina's pleading was cut short by the commands of the chador clad man.

"*Choop raho!* Quiet!"

"No!" Selina said, as she pulled at Rahman. "NO, you cannot take him. NO!"

Babul tugged at his father. The two young men shoved Selina and Babul away.

For an instant Selina and Rahman's eyes met. He nodded, a finality, a parting in the gesture.

"My pants," Professor Rahman pleaded.

"No need! Let's go! Now!" barked the chador-clad man.

One of the young men took Rahman's gray chador and blindfolded him with it. They pulled his arms back sharply and tied his wrists with a jute rope.

"Let's go," commanded the man wearing dark sunglasses, as they shoved Rahman out the door. Rahman trudged along, blinded, the rope cutting into his wrists.

"Where are you taking him?" Selina pleaded as she followed them into the corridor.

"Baba! Baba!" Babul screamed as he and Tia followed Selina. Moina had wrapped herself around Selina's leg, crying in fright.

They dragged and pushed Rahman down the long flight of stairs.

Pleading, Selina and the children followed the men down the stairs. She cried out, "Where are you taking my husband?" And as they lead him down, she began screaming out, "Help, *bachaow*, Allah, *Khoda bachaow*, help, please." The corridors, the stairs, the whole building echoed with her empty pleas.

Once outside on the front playground, standing on the chalk-marked cement where the children played *aka-dooka*, one of the young men pulled out a pistol and shot into the air and shouted, "Don't follow us or you will be shot," in broken Urdu.

Shoved from behind, Rahman stumbled towards a mud-splashed

THE SILENT AND THE LOST

white microbus, the tires encrusted in brown clay. He tried to stall, but two of the men dragged him at gunpoint to the truck and shoved him into the back seat.

The microbus sped away.

Selina looked up from the outside landing to see a nervous Professor Salaam with his wife standing beside him on the third-floor balcony. "Professor Salaam," Selina screamed. She stumbled and fell as she started for the stairs. Helped by Babul and Tia, she got up and ran up the stairs. Breathless, Selina gasped, "Salaam Shaheb, please...Please they are taking my husband. Can you help? Oh *Khoda* please!"

In tears, Tia, Babul and Moina were holding onto a hysterical Selina on the third floor landing. Professor Salaam with his wife standing behind him, looked at Selina, the children, concern mixed with fear in his eyes. Would he be next?

"Baba," Tia cried out clinging onto Selina. Selina stood in shock, disbelief. Two of the Salaam's children poked their heads out from behind their parents. Selina looked down at the empty street where the microbus had been a few minutes ago. As her head spun, she stumbled back towards their apartment. She got to the second step when she collapsed.

Professor and Mrs. Salaam ran to Selina. Mrs. Salaam put Selina's arm around her, rested Selina's head on her shoulder, and she pulled and pushed Selina up the steep stairs to the fourth floor. Exhausted, Mrs. Salaam, laid Selina down on the couch and collapsed beside her.

Mrs. Salaam wetted a towel and put it on Selina's forehead. Selina came to, writhing in pain, turned her head from side to side, screamed out,

"Rahman!"

—❧—

SELINA WAS IN SHOCK.

She lay on the bed, drained, surrounded by the children. Mrs. Salaam sat next to her, wetting a towel in cold water and pressing it to her forehead. After an hour that seemed like a whole day, Selina slowly got to her feet. Moina wanted some milk. Babul and Tia were hungry. She dragged herself to the kitchen, and with Mrs. Salaam's help warmed up some *pithas* for Tia, Babul and Moina.

Selina sat down at the dining table, looked out the window, as the children quietly nibbled at the *pithas*, pushing the food around on their plates. Tia looked up at her Ma from time to time.

"Ma, Baba will come back," Tia said, wrapping herself around her mother, her voice quivering like that of a lost child wondering if she would ever be found.

"Baba, Baba," little Moina cried out at every sound, running to the door.

Selina looked at the pictures of her wedding on the wall, of her and the children with Rahman. The books, the *alna* with Rahman's pants. Everywhere Selina saw Rahman.

That morning into the afternoon time passed with a dreadful slowness.

Selina sat at the kitchen table with her forehead clutched in her hands. Her temples throbbed. Her mind was blank.

Who could help?

Who could she call?

All her life, Professor Rahman had taken care of all these things. She clutched the edge of the table, tried to think. How was she going to get hold of anyone? How? Her disbelief now yielded to helplessness.

Summoning the last bit of strength Selina had, she pushed up against the table, slowly got up, walked towards Rahman's small desk in the corner of the bedroom, leaning against the wall for support as she went. As her knees gave way, Selina sat down on the bed. The earth was spinning around her. She reached for the diary, opened it, the pages all a blur.

Exhausted, she clutched the diary to her chest and lay down.

A knock on the door.

"Baba, Baba," Babul, Tia and Moina screamed. Babul flung open the door. Professor Salaam. Babul shrank back.

Professor Salaam stood silent, looking at Babul and Tia.

Selina walked into the living room, pulled her *áchol* over her head. Her eyes, tear filled, searched for Rahman in the doorway. "Any news Professor Salaam?"

"I just got the news. They took a few others from the area," Professor Salaam said staring at his feet. "Don't worry, I'm sure they will release them soon. The war is over." He tried to feign a smile, but looking at the long faces of the children, his smile disappeared.

"Professor Salaam, do you know anyone..." Selina asked, her voice cracked. "Someone you can call?"

Professor Salaam stood with a vacant expression in his face, and after a long moment, he reassured her, "Let me see what I can find out."

Embracing Tia, Selina went back to the bedroom, rolled out the *Jai Namaz* and sat down to pray, her hands clasped towards Mecca. She looked down at the interlaced motif in the green *Jai Namaaz* woven in intricate arch patterns.

"Allah, *Khoda*, bring back to my children their father," she prayed through tears, drops falling on the *Jai Namaaz*. Drop by drop the circles of despair spread, grew darker.

Quiet, the children sat in the living room. Through her parted palms held in prayer, Selina saw her children, Tia, Moina and Babul, little faces now holding on to a last hope, their eyes fixed at the door, their thoughts about their Baba returning.

Selina rubbed her palms on her face, finished her prayer and went into the living room.

"When will Baba come back?" Moina ran to her and got on her lap.

"He will come back soon," Selina told her children, trying hard to believe her own words. "Yes, yes, your Baba will be back this afternoon."

Tia was sitting, holding little Moina. Tia looked strikingly like her father: big forehead, wide brown eyes, pointed chin. Just like Rahman. Babul was only four, but so much like his father in his manners, his curiosity, his considerate ways, always looking out for his sisters, running to their aid every time.

In a torturous slowness, every sound marking time, the day went by without news. And every hour added to the crushing accumulated weight of hopelessness.

Yet another knock on the door. All three children—Babul, Tia and Moina—ran towards the door, hoping, praying to open the door and see their Baba's face. Selina sat with hands clenched in prayer. It was Mrs. Salaam. The light went out of the children's faces, and Selina stood, her eyes wide once again filled with disappointment.

"The phone is dead. Professor Salaam tried but no one knows anything," Mrs. Salaam said, coming over to Selina and hugging her. Before Mrs. Salaam left, she told Selina, "If you need anything, send Tia." For a long moment Mrs. Salaam stood by the door, looking at the desperation on Selina's face, unable to step out. She thanked Allah that they had not taken her husband, that her family was safe.

The afternoon ticked into a cold dusk. Then the light went out of the sky and out of Selina's heart.

She fed Moina, warmed the last of the food for Tia and Babul, sat at the dining table, looked across to Rahman's empty chair.

"Tia'r Ma, were you making some breakfast?" Startled, she looked up. No one. She looked away, got up and stood in a corner as her eyes filled with tears. He had gone out the door hungry. "Allah," she murmured. She wished she had just made him the *roti* a few minutes earlier. At least he would not be starved. Selina could no longer touch any food.

She went to the living room. The plate of *pithas*, cold, lay on the living room table, a bite of one taken out by Rahman. She brought the plate back, covered it with another plate and set it on the dining table. Yes he would come back. The *pithas* would be fine for a while longer. Yes. Just a little longer, he would be back, hungry, she could heat up the *pithas*, he could finish them.

When the children had finally gone to sleep, in a delirium Selina saw over and over again the look in Rahman's eyes—that last anguished look before they blind-folded him. Sleepless, she lay with Moina curled up against her side. She stared up at the ceiling. As the long hours passed she saw Rahman as he was when she first set eyes on him—young, thin, tall, shy, distracted, studious with those thick rimmed glasses.

"Rahman," she murmured as she touched Moina's silky hair. Three children, just young children. Thoughts rose like dark bubbles to the surface of her mind—denial and doubt faded into sorrow.

—❧—

December 15

WITH RAISED HANDS AT THE *Fajar* prayer, Selina promised Allah many things, promised Allah everything.

In the cold darkness before dawn, in the stinging desperation of a December morning, Selina sat on the *Jai Namaz*. "To Allah belongs what is in the heavens and on earth, and Allah encompasses everything!" she prayed that this would be the start of a new dawn. She looked at the little light filtering into the room, thought of the impending day and its promise. Yes, Rahman would be back today.

She remembered that night of March 25th. That horrible night. How they had survived that night. Now this night was the longest, and she was alone, all alone with the children who lay sleeping after a restless night.

On March 25th, Rahman was by her side. Rafique and Nazmul were presumed dead. But Rafique and Nazmul had come back alive. Surely, Rahman would be released, he was going to come back, just like Rafique and Nazmul had appeared. *Yes.*

All day every sound, every knock, every car horn brought the children from the depths of despair to the dazzling pinnacles of hope, only to be dashed down into the ground, crushed on opening the door to see an empty corridor.

Morning had turned into a waiting afternoon. In the afternoon Mrs. Salaam had come up, brought rice and *daal*. And afternoon turned into an evening of heartbreak.

Late in the evening, Moina, Tia, Babul lay asleep on the bed beside Selina, legs, arms entangled.

Selina got up, went to the outside window overlooking Nilkhet road. The wind crackled against the plastic sheeting as she held on to the cold bars, looked out at diffused shadows. The burnt slum had been cleared away. The charred Dev Daru trees were dead.

Under the thin membrane of her skin, someone had taken a bayonet and sliced her insides, shredded every organ. She closed her eyes. A sense of loss staggered her. The whole world was hostile, frigid like a corpse. She shuddered.

Selina wrapped her hands around herself trying to remember Rahman's warm embrace.

The silent sadness of the night, pierced by tears shed by lonely stars, the chill of the winter wind rustling the dead barks of the Dev Darus gripped Selina's soul.

Red Sun of Freedom

December 16, 1971, Dacca Cantonment Barracks

"Joy Bangla, Joy Bangla, Joy Bangla!" Penetrated the fetid darkness of this 20 by 10 feet bunker, an infernal pit holding eleven tortured, raped, starving women—bloody, bruised, near death. Ushering in victory amongst the ruins of surrender by the West Pakistani Army, the Bangladeshi flag fluttered—a yellow map of the country inlaid in a red sun of freedom rising in a lush green field—victorious and proud on the jeeps and trucks of the rescuing *Mukti Bahini* guerrillas.

December 16.

Victory Day.

Victory. Hope. Freedom. A new life.

"Joy Bangla!" muttered Hadija and Nahar in fading voices, trying to scream out those two words of freedom—their voices trailing off.

"Joy Bangla!" rasped Fatima in a feeble whisper. Breathing in spurts, fourteen-year-old Fatima lay with her head on Nahar's lap. Fatima's nose was thin, her cheekbones high, sweeping down to a pointed chin so that her face was heart-shaped, now wrenched in pain. Abducted as she walked to school, Fatima had been imprisoned the last six months in Military Hostels and Mirpur rape camps, raped innumerable times.

"Joy Bangla!" Nahar said through her cut lips, her breathing labored, her hair cut short, in a torn petticoat and blouse. The soldiers had cropped the women's hair, taken away *dupattas* or shawls or saris—anything to hang themselves with.

In Nahar's eyes was a glazed, weary look of resignation as she held Fatima's head in her lap. Sitting on the cold concrete, in her own vomit and urine, Nahar's head was spinning, her vision blurred.

"Joy Bangla!" the women tried to scream out at the top of their lungs, but only broken shrill calls of help from cracked voices escaped to the outside world, to the ears of the *Mukti Bahini* guerrillas and the Indian Army now scouring the grounds of Dacca Cantonment. From outside the sounds of Bengali orders, the sounds of freedom, came into this hell. Sounds they had prayed about for weeks, months.

Abandoned to die, for the last two days these eleven women had heard the sounds of running boots, barked orders, shouts of an army in retreat, ready to surrender.

Screams and shouts for help for the last day had brought no one to this infernal dungeon, where they had been kept for months, pulled out, raped, then thrown back. Over and over again.

Anticipating freedom, the eleven women had huddled and prayed. For two days, Nahar heard the the dull dead panting of the women. The scurrying claws of rats over her leg woke her up, made her skin crawl. The humans were done. Now it was the animals' turn.

Fatima lay motionless, barely alive, her pulse almost imperceptible. A day ago she had uttered a sharp cry, "No, Naaah!" Her shoulders shuddered, she fainted. And for two days Nahar whispered kind words into Fatima's ears, gently touched her colorless cheeks as she lay unconscious.

"We are going to be free, soon," she whispered trying to keep Fatima's spirits up. "Free." Nahar, herself fading, felt helpless, forlorn in a dark abyss.

"Joy Bangla" shook the eleven entombed women in a thunderous shout from a *Mukti Bahini* guerrilla, followed by loud, repeated boot kicks to the padlocked, heavy door that held them.

316

As the door splintered into pieces, sunlight lit the urine, feces and blood covered floor. The shaft of light entered through the portal of hell and transformed it into the passageway to freedom. The women cringed in shame, dishonor into the very corners of this vile bowel of captivity.

Blinded by the light, Nahar shielded her eyes with her hands, squinted as blue spheres floated before her. She called out, "Rafique."

Over the last day, with freedom on the horizon, the women had whispered,

"In our society, who will accept us?"

"No honor, no one!"

"No one," was the answer that hung heavy in their souls, filling broken bodies with broken dreams.

"No one!"

Nahar looked at the bits of the door. Her head spun, she gasped for air.

"Rafique," Nahar murmured. "Rafique."

Nahar reached out her hand, her right index finger trembling in the beam of light thrown by the flashlight of the *Mukti Bahini* guerrilla. "Rafique," Nahar said with all the strength she could muster.

If only Rafique was here, he could glue the pieces together, and life would be golden again, whole and wonderful. Yes. Rafique.

From outside, Nahar heard a kind voice, "Ma, you are free."

Ma?

Ma?

For four months, she had been called many things bitch, *harami, haramzadi, khanki, magi,* names you wouldn't call an animal. Now Ma?

"Ma," Fatima whispered, the first sound she had uttered in a day. "Ma."

"Ma," Nahar repeated, caressing Fatima's sweat covered forehead. "Fatima, *amra shadhin,* we are free!"

There was a strange ring to this syllable.

Ma.

All around the Cantonment, outside and in the buildings,

military equipment, trucks, guns, ammunition lay abandoned, the last vestiges of surrender strewn about by the West Pakistani Army. Scouring the barracks, the *Mukti Bahini* handed the women what they could find—*dupattas, gamchas,* shirts, *lungis,* chadors, curtains, blankets, bed covers and saris—to cover their bare bodies.

Laying Fatima's head on the floor, Nahar dug her fingers into the squalid concrete floor to crawl towards the light, searching for Rafique. As she crawled on her hands and knees, inch by inch, she searched for something lost, a last scintilla of hope.

"Rafique, Rafique..." she murmured.

Hadija, barely able to stand, her short hair tangled and sweaty down the sides of her face, came up to Nahar, now halfway to the doorway and called out, "Appa, Appa, Nahar Appa, get up, please, Appa. We must go now."

Hadija said, "Nahar Appa, for you," as she handed her a blanket and a torn cotton curtain.

Hadija helped Nahar wrap the curtain, tucking it into her tattered blood stained petticoat. Then Hadija and Nahar wrapped Fatima in a white blanket, covering her body as best as they could.

Nahar dragged herself to the doorway and asked, "What day is today?"

"Victory day. Today is December 16, Victory Day," the bearded guerrilla, outside the door brandishing a Sten gun, said to Nahar.

"Rafique?" Nahar asked staring at his face. "Rafique?"

The young *Mukti* smiled tentatively and said, "Appa, you are now free. We are all free."

"Free! Free? Where is Rafique?" Nahar asked. "My husband?"

The guerrilla fidgeted. Then in a reassuring voice said, "He will come. Now everything will be OK."

Nahar's head rested on the crudely carved doorway. She held on to the portal to their prison, between the dark past and the light of freedom. The trees gently danced in a December breeze. Nahar looked out into the verdant grass glistening in the sun, and shivered as she still felt the touch of many cold Satans creeping on her skin.

"Nahar Appa! Nahar Appa!" She turned to find Hadija calling

her. "We must leave."

"Leave?" Nahar asked. "Where?"

Who was alive? Rafique? Naila? Selina? Rahman? Who?

"*Khoda!*" Nahar exhaled. "Allah!" The sudden realization of her freedom, the uncertainty of what lay ahead hit Nahar. As she collapsed, her forehead crashed into the jutting piece of wood forming this dim doorway to this unknown.

Now outside, Nahar and Fatima lay sprawled on the ground by the side of the bunker.

"Rafique, Rafique, my husband, he is a *Mukti Bahini* commander. Please. Please, tell him I am alive," Nahar pleaded to the guerrillas handing her some water to drink. Fatima lay unconscious, pale and barely breathing.

"They need immediate medical attention," said the student guerrilla to the *Mukti Bahini* commander, a lanky bearded man in his early thirties.

"Take them to Dacca Medical College Hospital immediately," the commander ordered.

The *Mukti Bahini* took the other women in better shape to another room, giving them first aid, water, food.

From other holding cells, more women now gathered in this office room. Like trained imprisoned animals, they followed the orders today as they had been doing in these barracks for weeks and months. Some started to cry hysterically, some laughed out loud like crazed psychopaths. And some were in complete silence. Their eyes dead. Their faces colorless.

"If you have an address you want to go to, please tell me," asked the *Mukti Bahini* commander. He took down both Dacca and village addresses for those who had two addresses, asking them where they wanted to go.

"Your name? Your address?" he asked each of the now freed women.

"*Amar too koono thikana nai*, I don't have anywhere go to," whimpered one of the women.

"Don't worry, we will take care of you," the commander said in a kind, reassuring voice. A look of disbelief clouded his eyes at the pain etched in the faces of these broken women.

A student guerrilla, stunned at the inhuman depravity that these raped women had faced, first carried Fatima into the waiting jeep. Then he helped Nahar. Fatima lay unconscious, her head resting on Nahar's lap. The sounds of slogans, laughter, and an occasional "Joy Bangla" hung in the December dust as Nahar held Fatima's cold hand and rubbed it, looking into her fading face.

"Hold on, just a little more, just a little more," Nahar whispered into Fatima's ear.

"Go, go!" the commander ordered the two guerrillas. As the jeep jerked, then rumbled away from the Cantonment barracks headed for the Dacca Medical College Hospital, Nahar held her stomach with one hand, felt deep within the tiniest flutter.

In the open jeep, a chill gripped Nahar. She squeezed Fatima's hand. Nahar remembered the night Amina was next to her in a jeep like this.

"Amina," she cried. "Amina*re*."

They sped towards Dacca, down deserted roads, war torn, ripped up by heavy tank treads. The sound of the engine, the jeep flying along the empty road brought back memories of a time past, of a place Nahar once knew.

As they got closer to Dacca, people gathered on the streets, screamed out, "Joy Bangla," and shook their clenched fists in the air in a sign of victory.

"Joy Bangla," the two guerrillas screamed back, raising their hands, their fingers held high in a V for victory sign.

On the jeep, tied to a bamboo stave, a large Bangladeshi flag fluttered in the wind, a snapping song of freedom, rippling and swirling to the rhythm of the rumble of the jeep, the chorus of "Joy Banglas" by the jubilant crowds.

The red sun of freedom had risen by the roadside, had risen in the villages, in the town, in the cities, in the hearts of free Bangladeshis, and in the undulating dancing fields of green.

March 7th, Ramna; March 25th, Dacca University; and now December 16th, Victory day.

"Joy Bangla," she said energized, buoyed up with the chanting, dancing crowds by the road. Reaching, touching hands, hands kind and free. Her trailing voice fluted over the crowds in the song of freedom, in the song of *Shadhinata*. "Joy Bangla."

The jeep surged and rode over a bump as the breeze blew through Nahar's hair, and it tugged at her. She felt she was flying, free. She breathed in deep. Held her breath. The last light of the day streaked in through the trees by the side of the road, painting flashes of light and shadow on Nahar's face. Faster the jeep rumbled on to the Hospital.

Slowly, with the diffusing day, the gleam of freedom left Nahar's eyes.

"Rafique, Rafique slow down I will fall," Nahar screams.

"Hold on to me tighter," Rafique says. "Tighter Nahar, hold on tighter."

Her red sari *āchol* is snapping in a breeze to the rhythm and roar of the engine, flying, free, flowing in the late afternoon air through lush orchards, mango, lychee, the sun slanting into her face, her flying red sari, Rafique, the world, an intense heightened romance. Free.

Nahar, desperate, grips hard.

Then she is falling, disappearing into an abysmal darkness.

Nahar rests her forehead on Fatima's and whispers, "Rafique, won't you pick me one more lily, one more..."

Light liquid like water flooding the ground envelops Nahar. Rafique's voice floats with her, a distant voice, embracing and soft, suspended like particles of gold shimmering in the last crimson glow.

On Wings of Freedom

December 16th, 1971, Dacca, Bangladesh

LIGHT FOOTSTEPS SOUNDED IN THE cemented stairwell. A soft mid-morning rap on the door. The room filled with sudden anticipation, an unfolding hope. Tia ran to open the door, only to find Mrs. Salaam standing on the small landing, her soft face masked in worry.

Mrs. Salaam hesitated as she turned into the dark living room. Selina sat with her head down, clad in a crumpled olive green sari. Moina clung to her neck and Babul stood beside her gazing demurely at the floor. Street noises cut through the silence, diluting the eerie quiet of grief. Mrs. Salaam walked purposefully and laid her hand on Selina's shoulder, comforting her. Selina's eyes were sunken, swollen, a void from where despair wrenched into the lines of her face.

With a deliberate effort Mrs. Salaam sat down on the couch, clasped the hem of her sari in her hands as if trying to squeeze out some good news. "The army is going to surrender. They are going to surrender today." Mrs. Salaam offered this news wrapped in an air of hope, forming the words slowly.

For Selina these words found a hand hold of hope in a splintered corner of her heart. *Certainly, if they surrender, would they not release the hostages?*

"Everyone is saying... I mean with the surrender... they will surely let the hostages go," Mrs. Salaam said.

Let the hostages go, echoed in Selina's mind. *Yes, they will surely let the hostages go, yes.*

"Today Baba will come home Ma," Tia said as she jumped up and down. Moina, now sitting on Selina's lap, gathered her mother's face in her arms and kissed her and exclaimed, "Baba, Baba!" Tia and Moina joined Babul, jumping up and down, excited at Mrs. Salaam's news.

"Yes, yes, they must let him go," Selina repeated to the children, clinging onto this last shred of hope. *Yes,* she thought, *they no longer could keep Tia'r Baba captive.*

SOUNDS OF LIFE. STIRRINGS OF people on the street outside. A few slogans.

The morning passes slowly as the sun climbs into its zenith.

More vehicle sounds.

Selina kneels on the kitchen floor and digs into the jute sack.

At the bottom of the sack, deep within it, under grains of rice, under her hidden gold jewelry, lay Professor Rahman's neatly folded flag. There is the metallic jingle of the jewelry. Grains of rice spill out from the edges of the jute sack forming a white wreath on the

---

On the Crippling of a New Nation:
Rayerbazar Razakar Buddhijibi Massacre

I read the names. Twenty-two in all. Names followed by one line addresses. Eight with tick marks against them. The names are written in a sharp, jaggy, stabbed handwriting on a small lined 1971 diary on display at the Liberation War Museum in Dhaka. The two pages dated April 9th Friday to April 12th Monday.

In a cold calculating hand, here is etched the murder of the bejeweling brilliance, of a yet unborn Bangladesh, the precious seeds of creative genius of a new nation.

    √Wakil Ahmed Bengali

    36E UQ

The UQ, an acronym for University Quarters, and the Bengali referring to the department at Dhaka University. IER refers to the Institute of Education and Research, Dhaka University.

    √Dr. Faizul Mohi IER

    35 G UQ

    √Saduddin Sociology

cement floor. Folded, hidden since the 26th of March, the flag covered in a fine dust of rice.

Professor Rahman's flag. The same flag that on the eve of March 25th, he had risked his life to take down from the roof as terror descended all around them.

Selina holds the flag, the red, the yellow, the green close to her chest.

She walks back to the dining room and lays the flag on the table next to the uneaten plate of stale *pithas*. She exhales a long breath and unfolds the flag, and grains of rice scatter on the table.

"Babul, Moina, Tia, let's go and raise the flag on the lightning rod, the same place your Baba put it," she says, biting her lip.

"Baba will come back and be happy to see the flag," Tia pipes.

The children jumped up and down, ran up the stairs to the roof. Selina followed slowly, clinging to the bannister, focusing on the light flooding through the open door at the top of the stairs. On the rooftop she breathed in the fresh air. They tied the flag to the metal grounding pole, just like in March.

Surrender was certain. Surely Rahman's return also.

Professor Rahman's flag fluttered and snapped in a breath of wind. With the flag, hope fluttered in Selina's heart. Tia, Moina and Babul clapped their hands with joy and sang out, "'Baba's flag! Baba's flag!'"

---

16 D UQ
√ Dr. Murtaza
14 A UQ
√Dr. Akhtar Ahmed IER
11-D UQ
√Dr. Abul Khair History
35 B
√Munier Chowdhury Bengali
14 F
Further on down the lined page,
√ Anawar Pasha Bengali
30-E

These two pages were dug up from 350 Nakhal Para in Dhaka after the liberation of Bangladesh and are from the personal diary of the assassinator, the leader of the Razakars, who dragged these men from their homes on December 14, 1971 just two days before victory, tortured them mercilessly, and then killed and dumped their

"Helicopters," Tia screamed pointing to a line of the mechanical birds that rose up and above the green dots of trees marking the horizon.

Freedom was coming in waves, carried on the wings of helicopters. A group of helicopters with Indian markings roared above them headed towards Ramna Race course.

As the afternoon wore on, jubilant crowds, men, women, children, ran alongside the trucks of the *Mukti Bahini* and the Indian forces, cheering and greeting them loudly, shaking hands, patting backs.

The crowds danced in the streets. Rippling out in graceful folds to the chants of "Joy Bangla" under a spotless sky, Professor Rahman's flag fluttered in the wind. And Selina wept in a corner.

People cannot believe they have survived the nightmare of nine months. The women, hiding for so long, came out of the houses, out of the apartments, breathing deeply of dignity in a free Bangladesh.

Over Professor Rahman's cherished radio, in the evening came the news:

"You are listening to the Bengali Service of BBC."

"Today the Commander of Pakistan's Eastern Zone, General A.K. Niazi, has removed the badge from his shoulder, placed it on the table in front of Indian Acting Commander of the Eastern Zone, General Jagjit Singh Aurora, and signed the surrender agreement in Race Course of Dacca. A new nation, Bangladesh, came into being

---

bodies, some at Rayerbazar brickyard.

Systematic Genocide. Targeted murder of intelligentsia. Tick after tick of death. Detailed. Planned. Executed.

At the inception of the killings on the grounds of Dhaka University, on March 25, 1971, with the killing of Dr. Dev, a targeted hand-written list of intellectuals, professors and faculty were the first lined up and shot. From similar execution lists, starting in early December and extending past Victory Day, Razakars systematically executed an estimated 991 teachers, 13 journalists, 49 physicians, 42 lawyers and 16 writers, artists and engineers.

December 18, 1971

The sky was torn, the earth cracked, the cold December wind scathing, the stench unbearable. Hundreds of tortured, mutilated bodies of professors, teachers, journalists, intellectuals—the future of a free Bangladesh, blindfolded, faces slashed, eyes gouged out—lay strewn about on top of discarded bricks, rotting in a few inches of seeping water. The harsh guttural cawing of vultures fighting over the bodies was punctuated by the agonized screams of relatives grieving over their loved ones.

in the world map from today."

Selina stared at the plate of stale *pithas*. The edges had started to dry out.

The radio sang out, *"Joy Bangla, Banglar Joy!"*

"Joy Bangla, Banglar Joy!

Millions of masses have woken up in the dark night, this is the time for sunrise."

The last sunset of the war. Selina had clung to Professor Rahman on the first. She pressed her hands upward now, clinging to a prayer.

—❦—

Morning, December 18th

A SHARP KNOCK ON THE wooden door. Selina looks up with sleepless bloodshot eyes from the *Jai Namaaz*. She rises, her mind weary, and opens the door.

Professor Salaam and his wife stand on the dark landing. Behind them shuffle five *Mukti Bahini* guerrillas, scraggly beards, carrying Sten guns and SMGs.

Selina's face contorts in disbelief. Through tears of forsaken hope, she looks at Professor Salaam and then behind him the gaunt, disheveled guerrillas, their pants and boots encased in a dried reddish black clay.

Mrs. Salaam walks in, followed by Professor Salaam. The five

An apocalyptic vision of surreal, demented horror.

Less than ten miles from Dhaka University, at a bend of a wide estuary of the Buriganga river surrounded by the Razakar slaughterhouses of Mohemmudpur, Rayerbazar brickyard had become a shallow open grave to the gems of an embryonic nation.

Holding a handkerchief, a *gamcha* or a sari *āchol* to their noses to ward off the horrible stench, relatives, friends, neighbors, looked for any trace of their loved ones, roamed the brick yard, mourned in agony at the sight of so many tortured, mangled bodies. Tossed like discarded bricks, some with their faces in the water, their hands tied, some on their sides, the brightest of Bangladesh lay about in mangled heaps, the sacrilegious burial ground of the best.

Here lay a grotesquely wounded civilization, a crippled new nation.

The henchmen of the Pakistani army, the Al-Badar and Al-Shams Razakars, carried out these heinous killings and silenced a large voice for truth and justice that ultimately would have spoken out against the collaborators.

Twisted on her back, in the agony of a tortured death, Selina Parveen, editor of

Mukti Bahini guerrillas stand outside.

Selina sits down quietly, and Mrs. Salaam comes and sits beside her, anchoring an arm around her.

A suffocating silence presses the air out of the room.

Professor Salam sits mute for a few minutes, distracted.

"You have any news Uncle?" Babul asks helplessly. Getting up, Professor Salaam pats Babul on the shoulder.

"Why don't you go take Moina and Babul into the bedroom," Selina says looking at Tia. Selina looks again at the five *Mukti Bahini* guerrillas outside, her mind a dizzying empty vacuum. One of the guerrillas outside clears his throat.

Scared, the children huddle together in the doorway, Moina and Babul with their arms around Tia.

"Rayerbazar," Professor Salaam says, biting his lip.

Selina's mouth works into a scream. Her lips move. But no sound. Finally a tearing, raspy "*Naaah*," fills the room as Selina collapses into Mrs. Salaams arms.

"*Naaaaah!*"

✳

Shilalipi, lay blindfolded with the *gamcha* she was using in her kitchen when she was abducted.

Some of the corpses were but bones, carrion for the fighting vultures tearing and ripping at the flesh.

In another pit eight bodies lay of healthy, strapping men. Dr. Rabbi, a cardiologist, with his chest open, his heart torn out of his body by the most vile of creatures.

Nearby was the body of Muneir Chowdhury, now ticked off on the killer's diary.

Dr. Yakub Ali, Chairman of Ramana Union and Sirajuddin Hossain of the *Ittefaq* lay tortured, mutilated.

On these killing fields, mound after mound, marsh after marsh, grotesquely murdered bodies of the intelligentsia of Bangladesh lay in a twisted allegorical tale—the forever lost gems of a nation not yet born.

War Within

❧   ❧   ❧

December 17, 1971, Dacca Medical College Hospital, Bangladesh

THE CLEAR SALINE DRIPPED, DRIPPED down from the plastic bottle hanging from a high metal bar of the window, through the long clear plastic tubing, through the intravenous needle into Nahar's veins, and in her glazed, unfocused eyes flowed out as salty tears. Dream-like, time dripped away in synchronicity with each tiny drop.

Nahar looked up at Fatima's cot. They had unhooked her i.v. Taken her away. Another patient now lay in her place.

"Fatima," Nahar whimpered through cracked lips. As she lay on a dirty patchwork quilt on the cold Dacca Medical College Hospital floor, light streamed in from the tall, arched window and cast a pale shadow across the ghostly grimace on her face.

"Amina," she moaned. She had failed, failed twice in saving Amina, sixteen, and now Fatima, fourteen. Amina's death resonated in Fatima's death. Amina whom she knew from the age of four. Fatima whom she knew only in shared suffering.

"*Pani, pani,*" an old woman's feeble cries for water came to Nahar's ears. In the corner of the ward, on a cot, was the body of a young *Mukti Bahini* guerrilla covered up by a dirty sheet, his hand hanging out, fingers clenched.

Nahar began a desperate prayer, "Allah forgive me...Fatima... Amina..."

Vaguely she heard the doctor call for the nurse and order her to inject a sedative into the i.v. tube.

"Allah*goo*, Allah, *Khoda!*" echoed in Nahar's ears. Nauseated by the pungent smell of phenolic disinfectants, the smell of Savlon antiseptic, sweat, the stench of festering open wounds, bodies, she wanted to scream out, "Fatima, Fatima." Only whispers came and sobs rocked her body.

Faces peered through the haze. Faded away. Voices distant. Then near. Faces. They wore nurses uniforms and white caps. They talked rapidly. She heard voices.

"Do you hurt?"

"Do you know who you are?"

"I know who I once was. And yes, I hurt everywhere," she said drifting off.

Fatima, floats light as air, twirling around on her toes like a classic dancer. She looks as gorgeous as a pink water lily in full bloom, then fades away into a rainbow, into a thousand Krishnachura's aflame in her hair. Her red *dupatta* shimmers ever so lightly against her bare back and arms, and Fatima twirls in her *Anarkali churidar*. Lightly she touches her peacock feather fan to her lips and blows Nahar a parting kiss. A strangled cry. Fatima turns in a questioning gesture, her eyes wide and apprehensive. Then she fades, a receding moon disappearing behind dark clouds.

ON THE WAY TO DACCA Medical College Hospital, Nazmul and Mrs. Sahana Alam drove past a desecrated and razed Shaheed Minar, the pillars pounded into dust by the West Pakistani army. Here jubilant crowds celebrated, waving the Bangladeshi flag. Young and old jumped up and down in the streets, waving, screaming "Joy Bangla!"

"Rafique Chowdhury?" Mrs. Sahana Alam asked as they drove.

"No news. Nothing." Nazmul said as he downshifted the commandeered Toyota. Wearing the shirt and pants he'd worn for the last week, he scratched his scraggly beard, bowed his head and thought about how he was going to face Nahar, what was he going to tell her about Rafique.

"Any chance?"

"I don't know. Nothing since late August," Nazmul said, his voice choked with the pain of denial. "I waited in Agartala in September. He did not show up. With our victory march into Dacca, I was hoping for some news. But nothing. No one has seen him. Nothing."

Nazmul looked away trying to hide his anguished face. They entered the road leading into the DMCH.

"When did you last see Nahar?" Mrs. Alam asked.

"I saw her last the day Rafique and I left for Agartala at the end of April. I just can't believe what has happened."

"Don't say a thing about Rafique."

"No."

"And nothing about Rahman."

"Nothing."

"Nahar is barely alive. Make up anything to lift her spirits, Nazmul."

"How can I face Nahar?" Nazmul said as he gripped the steering wheel hard, barely controlling the tears filling his eyes. Mrs. Alam patted Nazmul gently on his shoulder.

He down-shifted the Toyota to turn into the long driveway. Today the three-story building was a sanctuary for the wounded, the suffering, the dying.

Nazmul stopped. In front of him was a cart blocking the turn.

Corpses were being stacked on top of a flat bamboo slatted push cart. Mrs. Alam turned her face, gripped the door handle. Nazmul watched as two men, one holding the shoulders, the other the legs, swung the rigid bodies one on top of another, stacking four bodies like pieces of lumber. Grotesquely twisted, arms and legs bandaged, some of the bodies were almost naked, wearing *lungis*, cotton singlets. Minutes passed. The line of cars and baby taxis behind Nazmul grew longer. Someone honked. Then finally, after what seemed an hour, the three men pushed the cart out past Nazmul and Mrs. Alam.

Nazmul made his turn and parked.

"Mrs. Alam?" Nazmul asked as Mrs. Alam steadied herself getting out of the car. "Are you OK?"

"Yes," she said, voice muffled by the end of the sari that covered her mouth.

They climbed the wide steps that led into the long corridors of the Hospital. As they entered, Mrs. Alam's sharp features dulled, her eyes glazed, her gentle lips trembled. Looking at the wounded men, women and children strewn about, crying out for help, drawing a long breath, she said, "Allah, help us all."

A wall of putrid chemical smell mixed with the stench of open wounds hit Mrs. Alam as she held the *āchol* of her sari to her nose, trying to filter the suffocating odor coming from the overcrowded maze of sick patients. She paused, trying not to vomit. Coming from an affluent family, raised as the only daughter, early on she had been sheltered from much of the harsh realities of life. But she had seen much in her forty years, worked for women's social support groups. This was nothing she had seen before. Here on the floor was the urine of sick patients, red *paan*-stained walls, discarded syringes and gloves. Long fluorescent bulbs and ceiling fans hung from the high ceiling metal I-beam, shed light and air on a squalid mess of men and women. The edges of the long dank corridors were lined with sick patients, some even lay under the concrete stairs with their relatives by their sides, squeezed into every corner.

They reached the steep concrete stairs leading up to the upper floors. They paused. Mrs. Alam looked at the inverted heart pattern in blue on the wrought iron railings of the stairs. She gazed up at the stairs leading to more broken souls. Her eyes searched for someone familiar, an orderly, a doctor, anyone to ask for help. Suddenly, her eyes lit up at the sight of Dr. Ismail rushing down the corridor.

"Dr Ismail!" Mrs. Alam called out, as they ran towards him.

"Sahana Appa, you?" Dr. Ismail asked, unshaven, wearing a soiled white jacket, a stethoscope strung around his neck.

"Dr. Ismail! Thank God!" Mrs. Alam said.

"What brings you here?" Dr. Ismail asked.

"We are looking for someone. Nahar Sultana. She is Rafique Chowdhury's wife. This is Nazmul Islam, Rafique's friend."

Nazmul reached out and shook Dr. Ismail's hand.

Dr. Ismail's face darkened at the name. He hesitated, then said, "Yes, she's here on the second floor. And Rafique?"

"Missing," Nazmul replied. "No news for four months now."

Dr. Ismail pursed his lips and uttered a solitary "Oh!" Then he added, "They brought her here barely alive. Please, follow me."

Nazmul, Mrs. Alam and Dr. Ismail stepped around men and women sitting on the stairs, patients waiting for a bed, exhausted relatives, their heads buried in their hands.

They followed Dr. Ismail to Ward 8, a large open room with tens of cots, filled with patients. Many sprawled by the wall, on the ground on dirty quilts and torn old bed rolls.

"Take them to Nahar Sultana," Dr. Ismail said to the orderly at the door. Turning to Mrs. Alam, he said, "I have to run to surgery. I will check in later."

"Thank you," Nazmul said. "Thank you Dr. Ismail."

"Please come back when you get a chance," Mrs. Alam pleaded as Dr. Ismail rushed off.

Pushed up against the wall, Nahar lay crumpled, an i.v. stuck into her arm.

"Nahar?" Nazmul said. "Nahar!"

A vague, skeletal resemblance of what was Nahar lay before him, face pale, a welt above her right eyebrow, lips cut. Nazmul looked away.

Mrs. Alam sat down on the edge of the quilt. She drew close to Nahar's face, listened to her short, struggling breath, looked at the saline dripping into her arm.

"Nahar," Mrs. Alam said softly. She touched Nahar's emaciated cheeks. "Nahar. Wake up, Nahar."

His heart pounding against his rib cage, breathing hard, Nazmul hunched down, sat down by Nahar's feet.

Nahar groaned, her voice dimmed into a distant, "Rafique." She opened her bleary, dull eyes and looked at Mrs. Alam, and then tried to focus on Nazmul. "Rafique! Rafique!"

"Everything is fine, Nahar," Mrs. Alam said through her tears as she embraced her. Nahar wept bitterly on Mrs. Alam's shoulder.

After a few minutes, Nahar's eyes lit up as she looked past Nazmul. "Rafique? Rafique? Nazmul... Rafique? Amina. Amina!"

Nazmul bit his lip.

"Everything is fine Nahar, you need your rest. You need to get well," Mrs. Alam said holding Nahar's hand.

Nahar's questions came in sobs.

"Naila Appa? Naila Appa? Rahman Bhai? Selina Bhabi?"

"Rafique will come soon," Nazmul said breaking his tortured silence, his voice trembling. "Rahman Bhai, Selina Bhabi are in the village. Naila Appa will be here soon," Nazmul said.

Letting go of Mrs. Alam, Nahar slowly crumpled onto the quilt, a rag doll, closed her eyes in tears, held out her empty palms, slightly twirled her hands. For a long painful moment Nazmul and Mrs. Alam looked at each other.

"Nahar, Nazmul will be by you, let me find the doctor," Mrs. Alam whispered into Nahar's ear. "Everything will be fine. Nazmul you stay here, let me find the doctor."

Suddenly there was a commotion on the other side of the ward, as two nurses and a doctor tried to sedate a young *Mukti Bahini* guerrilla struggling with them.

"No, not my hands!" cried out the young man from across the room at the top of his voice. "You can't amputate my hands! No!" The orderly came running and held down the young man as the doctor pushed a needle into his arm.

"Gangrene," the doctor said. "No choice."

The guerrilla writhed in anguish.

"Don't take my arms Doctor," the man yelled out. The medicine took effect, he slowly lost consciousness.

Jarred by the screams, the pain of looking at Nahar's bruised face, Mrs. Alam got up and hurried off to find the Ward doctor, to see if Nahar could be put in a cot, to see about finding some clean clothes.

Nazmul sat at Nahar's feet, he stared at his empty hands, and then moved by Nahar's head to sit, pressing the small of his back against the cold wall.

Nahar opened her eyes, looked up. "Rafique? They killed Amina. They killed Fatima."

Nazmul put his hand on Nahar's greasy hair. The ridges of his palm scraped against the welt on her forehead and she cringed.

"Rafique?" Nahar repeated. She twisted, turned her head from side to side.

Out of Nazmul's eyes the glow of victory went out like the gleam of Nahar's once radiant face, went out like the gloss of her once silky hair, went out like the softness of her lips, went out like the sweet rhythmic tones of her fluting voice. He touched Nahar's crumpled curled hand once then shrank back, his victory spirit now crushed like the crumpled frame of Nahar.

Nazmul sat looking at the Nahar he had known from a young age, the wonderful spirit, the radiant warm face. Nahar drifted off. "Nahar," he murmured.

A slow thick fog encircles Nahar. Suffocating, she tries to breathe. Water fills her lungs. "Rafique," she tries to cry out through a heavy crashing weight. Nahar touches her chest as she lies at the bottom of the Chowdhury's pond. A lily has rooted in her heart, its long stem runs out of her chest, all the way through the murky water to the shimmering surface, the sun catching in the ripples high above. The sinuous long stem of the water lily vibrates with the throbbing of Nahar's heart.

"Rafique!" she screams again.

Rafique tries to pull at the stem, to get her a lily. Long stems of the water lily are wrapped around his legs, his knees. He tries to pull again, and he pulls at Nahar's throbbing, encircled, empty heart.

"Rafique!" she tries to scream but only groggy, water-filled sounds escape.

Nahar is looking up at the light. She is sinking, deeper, deeper, enveloped inside a glowing murk. She claws at the sides, scratching, lunging, pummeling, but the walls are slippery. Her body begins to twitch convulsively. She tries to look, to find a little light, but she cannot see anything except an impenetrable maroon glow. Nahar flails about. She cannot breathe, her mouth and nose swamped with mud and water. Her heart thrums into the roots of the lily, harder, faster as a cry from deep in the water vibrates through the sinews of the stem up into Rafique's hands and strums his heart strings.

"Rafique!" she chokes.

Rafique's water eaten, colorless face, his dead white open eyes look down at her.

"RAFIQUE!"

— ❧ —

"*KEO ASHEE NAI?* NO ONE came?" asked the curious elderly woman visitor to the patient in the cot next to Nahar. The Hospital was now filled with hundreds of visiting relatives, some carrying food in tiffin carriers, eyes full of hope. Patients' faces lit up at the joy of seeing their loved ones.

And Nahar saw no one. Her sister, Naila Appa, brother-in-law, Shihab Bhai, no one. Where was Professor Rahman? Selina Bhabi? Are Tia, Moina, Babul OK?

Keo ashee nai? No one came? echoed inside Nahar's numb mind. Surely, Naila Appa would come. She was OK in September. Were they not alive? But Mrs. Alam and Nazmul said they were OK. Nahar tried to stay brave. Maybe Rafique was lying in a hospital wounded. Just like her. Waiting for her. Yes, that was the reason Rafique was not here. Yes.

And did Nazmul not say the Rahmans were in the village? The roads must be bad, the bridges blown up on the main highway to Chittagong. That's right. Naila Appa would be here soon.

Soon.

— ❧ —

December 21, DMCH

ON THE FIFTH DAY, THE day of her discharge, the nurse helped Nahar take a long shower, helped her put on her sari. Nahar waited for her older sister, Naila Appa and her husband Shihab Ahmed. They were coming with Nazmul and Mrs. Alam.

She waited anxiously. They had discharged her, needed her bed. She sat back against the wall, closed her eyes, remembered what it felt like when her mother gently caressed her forehead when she was sick with a temperature. Her father's voice, loud and reaching across the courtyard, was in her ears the way he used to call her in the early evenings to his side when she was just a little girl running around in her yellow frock. "Nahar, Amma Nahar, Nahar."

She opened her eyes and got up. A kind of forlornness filled her. Slowly, barely able to walk, she edged the wall to the far doorway, leaned her head on the frame of the door and gazed for a long time down the corridor crammed with relatives and patients.

Hundreds of relatives, visiting. And Nahar saw no one.

As she waited, she forced herself to think pleasant thoughts of times gone by, of moments precious. We are free, we have a free country. She felt Rafique's soft touch, his gentle gaze into her eyes, his smile, his strong voice calling out to her, "Nahar."

She and Rafique would go to the *Mela* this year. They would spend time in the honeymoon cottage at the Rahmans'.

AS IF THEY CARRIED THEIR burden across the Padma, Meghna, Jamuna, as if they had climbed up Tiger Hill in Chittagong lifting sorrow, grief and pain, Mrs. Alam and Nazmul with Dr. Ismail climbed wearily, slowly up the steep stairs, their faces grim, dark.

It was 11:30, getting late in the morning.

"Where are you going to take her?" asked Dr. Ismail.

"Dr. Samad's at First Lane, Kalabagan. You know my Uncle Samad." replied Nazmul. "She can recover in a quiet place there."

"Yes, I know Samad from college life. It's not going to be easy for Nahar. The trauma she has been through," Dr. Ismail said. "But Samad is there. I hope Nahar can hang on."

"I already had a discussion with Samad and his wife Mila. I told them I will come by and check on her," said Mrs. Alam.

"I have something to discuss with you," Dr. Ismail said to Mrs. Alam.

Nazmul went on ahead, alone.

"Rafique," Nahar cried out from the distant doorway seeing Nazmul's bearded face.

Ismail pulled Mrs. Alam aside, outside the door of Ward 8. He stood for a moment, looked down the long hallway, drew a long breath and said,

"She's pregnant."

❧

Bironganas
❧ ❧ ❧

January 1972, Dhanmondi Women's Shelter, Dacca

ARALYZED, NAHAR SAT ON THE rickshaw beside Mrs. Sahana Alam. Breathing in anxious short gasps, she clung to a ball of clothes wrapped in a sari, crushing it against her swollen belly, desperately clinging on as if the softness would nourish her on this gnawing day. A chill, a shiver of uncertainty went through Nahar, veiled under a dark burqa today, the same burqa she wore on March 27 escaping from Dacca University. Then it was to hide from the Pakistani invaders. And today it was to hide from a liberated free Bangladeshi society's prying, condemning eyes.

"Everything will be fine," Mrs. Alam said reassuringly, as she pressed Nahar's clasped hands. The wind in the rickshaw tugged at Nahar's veil, revealing her tear-streaked face. She held onto the rattling bamboo slats of the rickshaw top, in her ears the metallic click-clang-clicking of the angled brace holding the bamboo slats together.

With the bright spinning of the rickshaw's spokes, with the sounds of the horns, the bells on a winding First Lane, Nahar's mind spun. In Nahar's ears lingered Rafique's voice, "shimmering, shattering the sunlight into a thousand rainbows in my heart."

Into the impenetrable jungle, into the dim of that morning, Rafique had disappeared, the glow of his cigarette fading out into the darkness. Now, Nahar looked down the long tarred road, hard, hot in the sunlight. Dust draped the sidewalk in front of the shops as people filled the streets. Her eyes darted about the hundreds of faces, searching, seeking.

Where was Rafique?

Jolted out of her daydream by a bump, the sound of horns, bells, Nahar was brought back to what Mrs. Alam was saying.

"They will take good care of you at the Hostel," Mrs. Alam said, her voice full of kindness. "The other girls there can give you company. Nahar, you need lots of care in this bad health."

The rickshaw-wallah peddled harder, zigzagging through the oncoming trucks and diesel-spewing overcrowded buses on Mirpur road.

"Selina Rahman called yesterday. Asked how you are," Mrs. Alam said, as she held onto the rickshaw.

"Selina Bhabi came a few days ago with my belongings that I had left in March at her place." Nahar closed her eyes. *If only my life could be returned, if only Rafique would come back.*

Mrs. Alam inhaled a long breath, released it ever so slowly, trying to hide her sorrow, her pain at Nahar's last held hope for Rafique's return. For Nahar the whole world was blotted out. A cloudland of dreams all based on the return of Rafique.

Two days ago Dr. Samad and Nazmul had come to visit Mrs. Alam at her office, requesting that she admit Nahar to a *Birongana* Hostel.

"Why? What does Nahar do?" Mrs. Alam had asked.

"Nahar wanders around the house, especially the store room where Rafique stayed. Wanders around touching the walls, the floors, smelling, looking for Rafique, whispering, murmuring 'Rafique, Rafique' to herself. And she screams out almost every night. My wife is scared. When guests comes we have to hide her or lock her in the store room."

"It has become difficult for them," Nazmul added. "They wanted to help Mrs. Alam. But now, now it's out of our hands."

"Neighbors are gossiping, looking at her in strange ways," Dr. Samad said.

Nahar bounced on the hard block rickshaw seat, as the rickshaw-wallah, beads of sweat flying from his dark brow, rang his bell and peddled through the traffic headed towards Dhanmondi.

"*Birongana* house," Nahar murmured under her breath.

"They will take good care of you there," Mrs. Alam said, gently squeezing Nahar's hands.

Nahar knew Dr. Samad and his wife did not want anyone to see her. Not the neighbors. Not the visitors. They hid her in the storeroom, on the roof when visitors came. The attitude of the servants, whispers and words she heard, derogatory remarks, downcast looks made her crumble into pieces, made her feel like a piece of dirt.

As they passed a large metal gate, the vegetable-wallah balancing the large bamboo basket called out eagerly, "*Shaak, shobjii lakbee naki.* Need vegetables?"

Mrs. Alam wondered about Nahar's family, her older sister Naila. Over a month ago she had a conversation with Nazmul who had contacted Nahar's brother-in-law Shihab Ahmed in Chittagong. Nazmul had called many times, but Nahar's brother-in-law's response was the same.

"We cannot come," Shihab Ahmed had told Nazmul. "If anyone finds out about Nahar's capture we will not be able to show our faces."

He and Naila were leaving soon for London for his Ph.D.

Mrs. Alam struggled with the question of whether she should ask Nahar about her sister. Nahar sat next to her, but her thoughts were distant.

"Did your sister contact you?" Mrs. Alam finally asked.

As the rickshaw bounced and rolled on, the wind tugged at Nahar's veil covering her in a bubble of protection. She looked at the hard road, said nothing. A few minutes later she murmured, "No. She is not going to contact me." Her voice dropped to a thin whisper, and she added. "They had my *janaza* prayer. In shame they have buried me alive."

When she was young, Nahar used to play hide-and-seek with her sister Naila. Today it was a game of hide, but no one, no one was seeking Nahar.

343

Like a little girl, Nahar suddenly turned to Mrs. Alam and said impulsively, "Rafique will come back Appa. Everything will be back to normal, you will see. Everybody will accept me. Rafique will come back *naa*?"

Mrs Alam looked away, then wrapped her arm around Nahar. The pretense gone from her voice, she said "Yes, everything will be just fine when Rafique comes back." Fidgeting with her gold wedding band, Mrs. Alam thanked Allah that her son, her daughters and her husband were safe. She was lucky, very lucky.

Nahar looked through her veil at Mirpur road, the tarred, hard road. As a little wind came off Dhanmondi Lake, bringing up the burned tar smell of the road, she tightened her hold on the bundle of clothes.

Everything will be fine soon. Mrs. Alam had just said so. She just had to wait for Rafique's return. When Rafique comes back she won't have to hide behind this black veil. She can visit Selina, and see Tia, Moina, Babul again. Rafique will take her to the *Mela*, Bolaka Cinema Hall, New Market. Her sister, relatives will accept her. Yes. Society will accept her. Yes, everything will return to normal.

Yes.

"*Appa*, Dhanmondi, by the Lake? Which road?" the rickshaw-wallah asked looking back from his seat, perspiration drenching his cotton singlet and his *gamcha* tied *lungi*.

"Left there," Mrs. Alam pointed with her finger. "Then right at the alley, over by the tea stall."

The rickshaw creaked, bounced and rolled to a stop in front of the Dhanmondi Women's Shelter.

"*Aare, Birongana* house. You should have told me before," the rickshaw-wallah said.

THE SHELTER HAD A TALL metal gate and a high wall plastered with black and white handbills. By the small side gate a scruffy, threadbare *lungi*-clad *durwan* sat on a wooden stool and squinted at them in the morning sun. A few rickshaws—glinting in the sun with meticulously hand painted tigers, lions, and village sceneries on their backs—were parked at sharp angles with their front tires poking into each other.

This morning thoughts of the past, the present and the future tumbled inside Nahar. She stumbled getting off the rickshaw as her legs gave way and Mrs. Alam grabbed her wrist to keep her from falling.

"How much?" Mrs. Alam asked.

"*Naa, Memsaab*, nothing" he said, looking at Nahar, wondering about her fate, as thoughts about his own sister, his wife filled him.

Mrs. Alam took out a one Rupee bill and pressed it into his hand.

Nahar steadied herself as she walked towards the gate. As her sponge sandals slapped on the concrete driveway, she dragged herself into the two story, white-washed brick building, dark black and green mildew stains running down its sides.

Nahar walked hidden under the burqa. Men loitering by the gate near the street peanut vendor stared at her as she walked into the compound. Nahar felt peering eyes stabbing her, bayonets in her back, whispers pouring salt on open wounds.

"*Birongana,*" they whispered.

Birongana. Heroine. Yes, I am your spat-on heroine.

On the tiny tea stall radio, a song lamenting love lost floated in with Nahar as she raised her sandaled feet and stepped over the threshold into her last address, the secluded sanctuary of the Dhanmondi Women's Shelter.

Here, in the silent entrance to the world of *Bironganas*, Nahar stood.

Eyes shrouded in dark circles of sleepless nights and hopeless days followed Nahar as she walked through the shelter. The music drifted in, and like dust settled on the broken souls who stood by the doorway to the building, some leaning, some holding onto the wall.

"*Aye, Aye, tooi, tooi,* you, you, haah, haaah," all of a sudden a gaunt disheveled woman, her eyes possessed, started to laugh hysterically, pointing to Nahar. "You she-devil! Seed of the murderers in your belly!" she screamed at Nahar. *"Tooi, tooi."*

"Aaaah," Nahar gasped and fell back onto Mrs. Alam.

"Insane. She's mad," Mrs. Alam said, startled as she anchored Nahar with her arm and pulled her away down the hall.

Shaking, Nahar shrank into herself, desperate to cover her dishonor. Blouse, petticoat, sari, burqa, all her clothes did nothing to hide her shame.

She was the naked *Birongana*.

Dishonored. Forever.

Naked.

One of the social workers, a white sari-clad woman in her thirties, watching this scene unfold, pulled the crazed woman away into the adjacent room. A minute later she reappeared and asked, *"Madam kar shathe dekha korben?* Madam who do you want to see?"

"I am Mrs. Alam. Is Mrs. Pasha here?" Mrs. Alam said as she pulled her starched blue sari *áchol* tight around her shoulders.

They followed the woman past the concrete stairways, into a small room. "Mrs. Pasha's office is in there," she pointed to a corner room.

Nahar saw in the corner of this small room two pregnant women lying in cots. One rested her arm on her forehead. Rags, they no longer appeared to be women. Sorrow colored their expressions.

"Tooi, tooi, tooi, you, you, you," kept reverberating in Nahar's head, shaking her very core.

MRS. ALAM KNOCKED ON THE office door.

"Come in," a woman's voice said from inside.

"Salam Aleikum, Please sit," said Mrs. Pasha, a woman in her mid-forties who wore a stern official look older than her years. She adjusted her thick rimmed glasses, looked up at Nahar and then Mrs. Alam. "How are you?"

"Walekum Assalam. Good," said Mrs. Alam as she sat down, Nahar sitting beside her. The small clean office held a desk, and a large calendar draped with *kadom* flowers hung on the white-washed wall. A carved wooden country boat sat on Mrs. Pasha's desk. Behind

her a variegated pothos vine sat on the windowsill, curling and crawling up the metal bars of the window.

Lifting her veil, Nahar looked sheepishly at Mrs. Pasha.

"Your name?" Mrs. Pasha asked peering at Nahar's face over her glasses.

"Nahar Sultana," Nahar said blankly staring at her sandaled feet.

"Address?" asked Mrs. Pasha.

Nahar sat silently. Images of her life flashed then tore like a ripped movie reel, thrashing and shredding. She said almost inaudibly, "Sheetalpur Village."

"Sheetalpur Village, Kapasia," Mrs. Alam repeated louder.

In the large green register, Mrs. Pasha etched with her fountain pen the pertinent information, and looked up. "You don't have to worry. We will take good care of Nahar," Mrs. Pasha assured Mrs. Alam, a softness in her eyes. "All the facilities are here and our staff is most helpful."

Mrs. Pasha looked into Nahar's eyes. She reached over the small desk, brushed the tears off of Nahar's cheeks with her fingertips.

"Everything will be fine," Mrs. Pasha said.

Nahar clasped her hands in her lap and looked down, trying to hide her tears. "*Tooi, tooi, tooi*, you, you, you," echoed in her ears.

Mrs. Pasha got up from her chair and walked over to Nahar. She gently rested her palm on Nahar's head. "You know Nahar, life is not always as you plan it. Sometimes life seems very simple. It's like a straight line. Next day. The day after. All fall into one line. Then suddenly, in just a day, everything changes. One day, one moment, changes the rest of your life. Forever. Suddenly there is a bend. Like light going through a prism, the path of everything changes, changes forever. And then you must be strong. In the worst moments, remember Allah is with you, we are with you. But you must be strong Nahar."

Mrs. Pasha walked back to her chair, sat down, pressed down hard on her pen. She glanced at Mrs. Alam then Nahar and said, "I understand you want to keep the baby?"

Nahar nodded.

"You know," Mrs. Pasha started, looking at Nahar, "you know, that the babies cannot stay in this country. It's government policy."

"Yes, we know," Mrs. Alam replied. Nahar stared blankly at the edge of the desk.

"*Naah, Naah,*" suddenly the sharp shrieks of a *Birongana* echoed down the hall, reverberated in Nahar's ears.

"I'll be right back," Mrs. Pasha said as she jumped up and ran to an adjacent room. There Rabeea, eighteen, late in her pregnancy, was flailing about, thrashing her hands, her short hair drenched in sweat. Mrs. Pasha went to a cabinet in the corner of the room, opened it. She took a tablet and handed it to one of the social workers. "Give her this sleeping pill! If she won't take the pill, give her an injection."

Nahar's hand started to tremble. Mrs. Alam gripped her wrist to steady her. Mrs. Pasha, returning, saw the fear in Nahar's eyes. She laid her hand on her shoulder, and gently ran her hands over Nahar's back, trying to calm her.

"You better go to your room and lie down. Nahar, Mrs. Alam, please follow me." Mrs. Pasha walked them to the stairs and told one of her assistants to show Nahar to her bed upstairs.

"Nahar, you rest," Mrs Pasha said, gently touching her on the arm. "Everything will be fine."

Once Nahar was settled, Mrs. Alam followed Mrs. Pasha back to her office. There Mrs. Pasha sat down and exhaled a long breath. Regaining her composure, she looked at the concerned face of Mrs. Alam. The two women were alone.

"How many women are here?" asked Mrs. Alam.

"Fourteen."

"Mrs. Pasha, how many women were raped in this war? How many others are there like Nahar?"

"Obliterated by the arithmetic of war, how many women were raped, you ask? Two, maybe four hundred thousand. No one will ever know. What does it matter to Nahar how many? What does it really matter, when the number is one and it is you?" asked Mrs. Pasha, deep pain in her eyes.

"Yes, what are numbers if you are the victim," Mrs. Alam sighed.

"Nahar is in very bad health. We only have a few pregnant women. Most of the women here have had abortions and many have nowhere to go," Mrs. Pasha said. "Many have no family. After the army killed their families in front of them, they raped them. Many of their families have disowned them. They have nowhere to go. Nowhere."

Mrs. Pasha got up, walked over to the small wooden boat on her table, touched it lightly, and said in a distant voice, "I wish I could sail away from the grief that these walls hold, but I just can't. Sometimes at night I feel like I was the one who was raped. I keep reliving the nightmare of the *Bironganas* here."

Mrs. Alam stayed silent, her eyes focused on the edge of the table in front of her.

"A *Birongana's* life is on a knife's edge. Especially some of these girls. Abandoned. One step away from suicide," Mrs. Pasha said. "Nahar wants the baby. But she cannot keep it. Do you know what that will do to her? The baby is all these women have. Even if it is a symbol of everything evil, they have nothing else to hang onto. What thought have you given to what will happen when we have to take away Nahar's baby?"

The question hung heavy in the air between them, filled the room in an uneasiness. Mrs. Alam, sitting in the chair, looked down, adjusted the accordion pleats of the skirt of her cotton print sari, fidgeting with the hem of the fabric. They were never right: too loose or too low or too high. Never right. Finally, in a thin uncertain voice she said, "She is in a dream world, constantly saying Rafique will return, Rafique will return. Maybe after the birth she can adjust back to normal life. I just don't know."

"And her family?" Mrs. Pasha asked. "Does she have anyone..."

"The only one she has left is her sister in Chittagong. She is married to a wealthy, reputable family. They don't want anything to do with Nahar. Nothing," Mrs. Alam said as a darkness came over her face.

"Many of the girls, especially the younger ones, cry so much after their baby is born we have no choice but to sedate them with sleeping pills." Mrs. Pasha said. "Their baby is the last thing they have. When it is in the belly, they have a different feeling. Then,

349

maybe they don't care. But when they hold their babies, things are completely different."

"Do you have a good home for Nahar's baby?"

"Oh yes. We want as much as possible to find good homes for the children. All of us here, and the social workers, are devoted to helping the women. The Bangladesh Government has responded to the needs of the *Bironganas* in two ways: first abortion and then instituting adoption laws. Initially, there were a lot of protests. Some people protested the adoption of Muslim babies by Western Christian families. But who will take them? Not the people protesting!"

The muscles of her face and jaw tightened. Mrs. Pasha could feel herself clenching her fists, her molars grinding down on each other.

"There was a girl who came here. She was no more than sixteen. Late in her pregnancy, so we could not abort. We had to sedate her for a period of a week to calm her down when the baby was sent away." Mrs. Pasha looked up. "For Nahar's sake, it's best if she does not even see her baby."

Mrs. Pasha walked to the window, looked out and continued, "You know Mrs. Alam, it was as if the army had been given an order. No woman was killed before being raped first. I wonder what we women did to deserve so much hatred. We weren't responsible for this war. Yet we were treated like the West Pakistani army's worst enemies."

—❦—

NAHAR'S LAY ON HER BED, in a small room with two other women, pillowing her head on her sari-wrapped package. She put a hand on her belly and the other on her forehead. As the baby moved inside her, she felt a dizziness and shuddered.

"*Pani lagbo*, water?" Nahar heard a voice ask. She looked up into a young face. Maybe sixteen, a sari clad girl with a bulging belly.

"Amina?" Nahar asked. "Amina?"

"*Naah*, Bilkis," the young girl replied, taking a step back.

She thought about what Mrs. Pasha said about the bend in one's life, the day that changes all other days forever. "Fatima," she muttered.

"*Pani*," Nahar said in a hoarse voice placing her palm on her burning forehead.

"*Accha. Neea aschi*. OK. I'll get it."

Nahar looked up. A silhouette. The light entering through the open door was cut by Mrs. Alam as she stepped into the room. She sat down on the edge of the narrow bed.

When Nahar's young roommate returned with the glass of water, Mrs. Alam asked, "What's your name?"

"Bilkis," she said as she withdrew to the other corner of the room, and stared blankly at her bare feet.

"Where are you from?" Mrs. Alam asked.

"Khulna," Bilkis said, looping her sari over her head.

"Khulna," Mrs. Alam repeated. She looked at Bilkis's black eyes that cradled a deep, welled-up sadness. "I'm going to be back. This is Nahar your new roommate. Can you keep an eye on Nahar for me, Bilkis?"

Bilkis stood silently, fidgeting, pulling at the edge of her sari, and digging her toes into the bare cement floor.

"*Accaha*, Madam, OK," finally she said.

Mrs. Alam gently touched Nahar's cheeks, said her good bye and walked out into the veranda. Three other pregnant *Bionganas,* soft closed lips, dark deep eyes that spoke volumes, stood on the veranda, their backs to the cement white-washed wall, warming themselves in the February mid-day sun. As the sun fell on their pale, gaunt faces, a darkness rose from the depths of their torn souls, floated on the mirror-like surface of their eyes.

Mrs. Alam said her good bye to Mrs. Pasha and walked out of the gate, turned and gazed at the dark stains running down the sides of the building. After he helped her get a rickshaw, the *durwan* closed the gate. As the rickshaw pulled away, Mrs. Sahana Alam looked back.

It was a late afternoon on a cloudless, dusty, lonely day.

❧

Tarred Road

❧ ❧ ❧

'Birongana' House, Dhanmondi Women's Shelter,
March 1972, Dacca, Bangladesh.

A S DUSK GATHERED, so did the women outside Nahar's room
on the veranda, breathing, whispering in the little breeze.
From the tall minarets, from loudspeakers the high-pitched
soundscape of the *muezzin's* ululating the faithful to the *Magrib*
prayer reverberated in Nahar's ears as she sat on her bed. She looped
her sari over her head, as did the three *Bironganas* outside.

The cars honked on the road below, the rickshaws clanged their
bells.

On this hot, sultry evening, Nahar sat listening to her roommates
outside. As she looked past them, across the road, the Krishnachura
tree was aflame with the red blooms; in the dim light of evening it
looked like blood on the surface of a still, lifeless river.

"Marium's husband divorced her."

"What happened?"

"She went back and her mother-in-law beat her up."

"Her husband does not want to take her back."

"She's back here."

"And her family?"

"They want nothing to do with her. Nothing. This is her last address."

Nahar sat silently, listening to Marium's tale. Slowly, cradling her belly, Nahar got up and walked to the veranda, stood at the railing, gazed at the men, women, children and rickshaws milling about.

For the last two months Nahar had heard it all.

In hushed voices the women spoke of their tragedies. What they whispered was little, in broken phrases.

"Am I welcome at home? No!"

"Am I welcomed by the village where I grew up? No!"

"Am I welcomed by my husband? No!"

"Is my life left to only my flesh? Dishonored flesh that must now become the morsel of prostitution?"

"Burma? India? A life as a prostitute. What do I have to give, to sell?"

"Rangoon. Calcutta. Yes."

"Only my body, that's to sell."

"Prostitution in Burma? Anywhere is better than here."

Birongana. War heroine.

Heroine?

No.

Magi! Khanki! Dog! Bitch!

The heroines of Bangladesh, *Bironganas*, the givers of all, for what, to where, to now, to then, to death, to body, to torture, to being shunned by mothers, slapped, kicked and tortured by husbands, beaten by mother-in-laws.

Theirs was a life of dreams that would never be, dreams torn to bits by the talons of '71.

Only despair.

Defamed. Dishonored. Disowned.

Denigrated *Bironganas*.

—❀—

"Allah, Allah, Khooda!" The deep silence of the night was pierced by a shrill scream. Jolted by the cry, Nahar, half awake, unable to sleep, sat up in bed. Downstairs Parveen was screaming out in her nightmare. At first her family members had been sympathetic. "Ma, I will come back for you in a few days," her father had told her. But a few days had become weeks.

Each day, and into each hopeless night, awake and asleep they relived their tortures of '71. Over and over again the screams pierced the silence of a night shrouded with visions of torture that tore at these women.

Nahar lay in bed, the baby moving in her belly. She lay with her eyes closed, with her arms protectively across her belly and let the sensation fill her with many shades of emotion—pain, joy, hopelessness.

She slowly sat up and looked over to where Bilkis and Lubna were sleeping in the cots next to her. She opened her palm, and in it were the two white sleeping pills, two small unblinking white eyes peering at her. They were little pearls, the pearls Rafique said glistened in her eyes, hard coated with strange markings, hardened tears from sleepless nights—shimmering like pearls of sorrow.

Swinging her legs over the side of the bed, holding her stomach with one hand, Nahar sat on the floor. From under her bed she pulled out a small brown suitcase, the suitcase she had left at the Rahmans' on March 27th, the one Nazmul had brought to her. She opened it.

Under her clothes, at the bottom of the bag, was her photo album. Inside it, her one anniversary picture. A last photograph. In the side fabric pocket of the bag, in an envelope, dried *bokul* flowers, a gift from Rafique, brought back that sweet fragrance lingering in the cool night air—old songs, unfinished conversations, her incomplete life, empty pages of an unfilled album.

In the dim light Nahar could barely make out her picture in front of the pond of water lilies. Yet in her mind, like the sun suddenly flooding through dark clouds, the picture brought everything rushing back.

Everything.

The water lilies floating in a held moment of innocence, the blue sky reflecting off of the ripples in the water, life green, alive. In this picture, she is aflame in that red sari, the innocence of a life lost, so precious, is captured forever in that single click.

Nahar took the sleeping pills, crumpled them inside a piece of paper along with others she had saved. She held the small ball of paper in her hands, pearls of crumpled dreams, pearls of lost glistening tears. She put the pills in a corner of the bag, under the sari and the picture album.

— ❦ —

"ALLAH-U AKBAR, ASH-HADU AN LA ILAHA ILLALLAH..."

From the Dhanmondi Mosque, the sound of the azhan. From the stretched vocal-cords of the *muezzin* echoed the call to the faithful for the morning *Fajr* prayer.

Nahar, after one more sleepless night, walked out to the veranda, walked out into the light of dawn fighting with a vast darkness.

Searching, seeking an Allah unknown, Nahar looked at the thin line of light on the eastern sky. She looked skyward, and said, "I, Nahar Sultana, *Birongana*, am God-made in a man-made hell of memories. The rules of man are false and lies. And war is the biggest lie of them all."

She looked down at the street, heard the sounds of women sweepers hard at work, sweeping, cleaning the tarred road. Today was March 27. The day of escape. And even a year later, the blood of martyrs was caked in the tar of the road, the stains deep, embedded into the asphalt, seeping into the hard earth, staining the concrete.

Jakosh, jakosh, the scraping of the circular brooms rang out in Nahar's ears. Yes with their broom, and their sweat, they were trying to clean the stains of blood of martyrs from the tarred road. Her ears rang with the *jakosh, jakosh* sounds. Nahar thought, yes, they could bring the old Nahar back. Yes, yes, clean off the shame, clean off the *Birongana* stains on her. The sweepers knew the secret, the secret to cleaning the streets, yes, they could clean the blemish, the taint, the smear from her torn soul, too.

Fourteen souls, *Bironganas*, entombed alive, were screaming inside Nahar's head. For over a month, she had relived 1971 in '72.

The screams, the crying, the whimpering, the unspoken pain.

"Rafique!" she murmured, her eyes searching the faces by the little light on the street. Rafique, only, Rafique. Yes, he will be back and Nahar will be the Nahar in that red sari. Yes.

The baby moved. And Nahar whispered, "Babu, Rafique will buy toys for you. Don't move too much, Babu. You need rest. We will go to New Market. Yes. Rafique will be back soon. He will bring you toys, Babu."

NAHAR, HIDING HERSELF UNDER THE blackness of Amina's burqa, stepped out of the whitewashed brick building, stepped out onto the driveway, and kept walking towards the high iron gate. Inside this black shroud, in a silence that was louder than a million soul-wrenching cries in the dead of night, she raced for the gate. She pulled it open, the hinges creaking, brushed past the *durwan*, and kept going.

Escape. Yes, escape from '71 lay beyond the gate. Rafique was waiting. She heard a voice calling her. No point in looking back. Only concentrated misery and agony was held up in the *Birongana* house and hope, hope had vanished.

Running, she headed towards the solitary rickshaw in front of the restaurant.

Dacca was asleep. A dog was scavenging about in the open refuse dump. In the corner, the restaurant-wallah was busy readying his wares. A few early morning walkers were sauntering out and about.

"Rickshaw!" Nahar called out.

"Appa?" the rickshaw-wallah, a stick-like, grey-bearded man in a yellowed cotton singlet and frayed plaid *lungi* answered.

She hesitated for a moment. Where? Nilkhet? No.

"First Lane."

"Appa! Appa!" the *durwan* called out to her as the rickshaw pulled away.

"Keep going. Don't look back! Keep going!" Nahar, breathing in quick, hard gasps, told the startled rickshaw-wallah. "My husband Rafique is waiting for me at First Lane."

The rickshaw's front wheel pointed out of Dhanmondi. Nahar's mind was spinning as she looked at the tar of Mirpur road once again; in her ears was the creaking of the rickshaw, the squeaking of the slats of wood under her feet, the flapping of the sponge sandals of the rickshaw-wallah on the pedals. The old man, breathing hard, flicked his head back at Nahar, looked at her out of the corner of his eye, and uncertain of his passenger, asked, "Where?"

"First Lane," Nahar repeated.

With sweat dripping from his chin, the rickshaw-wallah peddled and weaved towards Kalabagan.

Yes, Rafique was waiting. He was waiting at Dr. Samad. He needed help. *I'm coming. Wait, Rafique, I'm coming.*

She felt the baby move inside her. Yes, she was going to get her life back again.

The world was going to be whole again.

First Lane flashed through the shiny spinning wheels of the rickshaw's spokes.

"That way," Nahar pointed.

The rickshaw-wallah turned the corner.

In the distance, her eyes focused on the Red Cross sign, a beacon of hope painted on the yellow wall of the pharmacy, in front of Dr. Samad's house.

"Wait," Nahar called out. "Rafique, I'm coming."

❦

Into a Thousand Rainbows

※ ※ ※

Dhanmondi Women's Shelter
April 1972, Dacca, Bangladesh

THE BABY OPENED HIS EYES. Looked as if he was going to cry. Just skin and bones, barely five pounds, his ribs stuck out under a wrinkled skin. Through tired eyes, Nahar looked up from the birthing bed as Komola, the midwife, wrapped him in a small hand-stitched green quilt and laid him beside Nahar.

Breathing rapidly, the baby with tiny brown eyes blinked in wonder and gazed at Nahar. Nahar held him close to her breast, cut off from the whole world, in a secret sphere all her own.

Nahar looked into the pale, tiny doll-sized face, smelled the sweet innocence of his skin, touched the wisps of hair that cupped the little head. She caressed the miniature purple cheeks. The baby, eyes now closed, yawned contentedly in his mother's bosom. Komola, soft-eyed and understanding, studied the combined figures of mother and baby, a transient image of the moment.

Nahar felt the sharp painful prick as the needle punctured her skin, pushed deep into her arm. Startled, woken out of a dream within a dream, still holding the baby tightly, she looked up in surprise at the face of the nurse as she pulled out the syringe. Her heart raced. The cold metal pierced through this inner sanctum of mother and child.

The baby cried out. Nahar's head spun and her tight grip around the baby relaxed. "Naah, naaah," she screamed, her voice fading into empty echoes in her spinning mind.

The baby's tiny fingers wrapped around Nahar's little finger, a tender tendril clinging precariously to a trellis.

The nurse gestured to Komola. Komola, hesitation in her eyes, lingered for a moment beside the bed. She drew a deep breath, looked at Nahar's thin, pale face. As she took the baby out of Nahar's arms, Nahar's eyes blurred into a blank expression, her mind receded into darkness. She collapsed onto the bed, her fingers still reaching for the baby. Incoherently she whimpered, looking at the empty wooden crib beside her.

Nahar pursed her lips.

Nothing came.

DAYS PASSED.

A darkening, withering evening sunlight diffused through cracks in the wooden shutter, illuminated an empty room with Nahar sitting on her small cot, her silver box of *kajol* in her palm, wearing the dark pink-magenta *Jamdani* sari with glittering golden and silver flower motifs—Rafique's gift from their last visit to Dacca.

In a miasma of hopelessness, one thought filled her mind— Rafique. Yes, Rafique was going to come. Tonight. Yes. Yes. Rafique

---

Dustbin Babies

"…do not throw them in the dustbin. Bring them to us if they are alive."

Mother Teresa

1972 Dacca, Bangladesh.

And to these babies Mother Teresa gave unconditional love. That was what Mother Teresa was about, and it was through her personal intervention that many war babies were saved in 1972. Through the efforts of Mother Teresa and her colleagues at Missionaries of Charity, and the Government of Bangladesh's Ministry of Labour and Social Welfare, two Canadian organizations got involved early on in the adoption process. They were the Montreal-based Families for Children, and the Toronto-based Kuan-Yin Foundation. There were, in addition, many other organizations, such as the US-based Holt Adoption Program and Terre des Hommes.

In 1972, amid the turmoil of a war-torn nation, the war-baby issue had to be addressed. Society as a whole failed to deal with this issue, and to tackle the problem

was coming.

With her index finger, Nahar smeared the *kajol* around her swollen, sleepless, red eyes. She found her comb in the suitcase spread out on the bed. Nahar tried to comb her once silky and soft hair, now unkempt, knotted, tangled.

"Rafique," she murmured. No! Rafique would not see her like this. In a deadening silence of a dark future, a silence that is virulent, clawing, Nahar walked toward the mirror.

She stared at herself in the cracked mirror, her face fragmented into pieces in the reflection. She dragged at her disheveled hair. As she ran the back of her hand across her eyes, the *kajol* smeared her cheeks.

She walked backwards, pointing her finger, laughing hysterically at the mirror. She sat down on the edge of the bed and stared with empty eyes at her photograph, the last photograph Rafique took on their anniversary day. A short life, an afternoon, all framed in the black and white of a three by five.

She ran her trembling hands over her cherished things—a silk *salwar kameez*, a blue cotton *kameez*, the white sari she wore on the 7th of March, the photo album. These things had remained as it always had been.

I want my life back, just like these things. I want my life back. Nahar Sultana's life back.

Her photo album, an anniversary gift from Nazmul in 1971, lay unfilled. She smoothed out the empty pages, one by one; pages she and Rafique could have filled up. But the pages would remain

---

abortion was made legal for a limited time. Distinct features such as sharp noses and high cheekbones distinguished these war babies as children fathered by the West Pakistani soldiers. They were born guilty. Not integrable into the soft-featured Bangladeshi communities. Under these difficult circumstances, Bangabandhu Sheikh Mujibur Rahman declared that all war babies be sent out of Bangladesh to adoptee families.

Through President Sheikh Mujibur Rahman's intervention and personal request, the U.S. Branch of the Geneva-based International Social Service (ISS/AB) was the first to come forward to assist the government. In the implementation of these adoptions, two local voluntary agencies, the Dacca-based Bangladesh-Central Organization for Women Rehabilitation and the Family Planning Association, worked closely with the International Social Service Organization.

blank. Empty.

The many-hued afternoon of two years ago dissolved into blurry streaks as Nahar's eyes filled with an expression of bitter betrayal.

"*Naaah! Naaah!*" she screamed shaking her head again and again, pulling at her tangled hair. A *Birongana*. Her red eyes flamed as she held the photo close to her and screamed, "Yes, yes, Nahar Sultana, I want my life back!"

Her head reeled from the sleeping pills. She walked to the latched door and pressed her forehead against it.

From horizon to horizon, the ear shattering clap of thunder vibrated the very earth. A dark spring storm, a *kalbaishaki*, was brewing in the sky outside. As the wind swung the single dusty light bulb, flickering phantom shadows, blurred silhouettes, ghostly apparitions danced on the walls.

Nahar unlatched the door. The wind rushed in, a roar in her ears, slamming her. She braced herself, held on to the open banging door. She pushed into the howling wind. Dust clouds ran along the road outside. Leaves tore past her, and with a hiss, particles of dirt clawed her face, her eyes. For a long moment she swayed in the wild wind, caught in a precarious balance of freedom.

The rain slashed down into the earth, raising a moist smell of a dry world drinking thirstily.

Memory.

Song.

Wind.

Tears.

Rain.

All became one.

Barefoot, lashed by the winds, an age passed as Nahar inched her way down the corridor, gripping at the wet roughness of the plastered walls.

Shutters banged fiercely against the windows.

Nahar's sari ripped by the cutting *kalbaishaki*, snapped like a flag.

"Rafique," she screamed. Like the swirling dust, Nahar's mind spun, as she reeled from the pills.

On the roof, Nahar looked at the sky. The afternoon had

faded into an immense impenetrable darkness. A *rakhoshi*, eyes of smeared *kajol*, burnt umber cheeks puffed like the billowing clouds, an ominous crinkled forehead wreathed in *kalbaishaki* clouds had swallowed up the whole earth.

Devoured by the *rakhoshi*, Nahar gasped as the cold rain bit through her skin, poured through her veins, flooded her mind. In the dark *kalbaishaki* Nahar saw a sky framed in innocence. With heightened senses, she held her breath, wanting to dissolve into the drops, forever cleansed into a time past.

In her sudden hallucinatory vision, a thousand images flashed before her eyes. And in a three by five, in black and white, an afternoon captured in the lens of time, the tranquility of a reflected blue sky in between the nodding pink *padma phools*, the red radiance, the peaceful green of a tree-lined horizon, the sweet song of the red-whiskered Bulbuli. Nahar believed again. She heard the music of her soul, she heard the unspoken promise: the promise of love, the promise of freedom. Nature had opened her arms and embraced her, hugged her close to her bosom, the long abandoned daughter welcomed back into her fold.

As abruptly as it started, the *kalbaishaki* storm died down, leaving the smell of a quenched earth.

In her unveiled heart, the last faint spark of a silent anguish fell like the stillness of the last rain drops.

In the trees outside, a green cloud, a swirl of parrots broke away from the top of the Krichnachura, rising from a rippled red river of flowers, red beaks crying out into dawn skies, swirling, rising, rising into the deep hue and breaking into a thousand rainbows.

※

Book Three

Journey into the Heart

Winging Over the Bay of Bengal

❧ ❧ ❧

September, 1997, Singapore-Dhaka

"*Naah! Amar kichu nai! Amar kichu nai! Ami amar Baper Mar kache jaita parum na!* No! I have nothing! Nothing! I cannot go back to face my parents and my family!" cries out the barefoot young man in handcuffs being escorted to the far corner of the Changi Airport waiting area. Alex turns around to watch the sunken, macerated face of a young Bangladeshi migrant worker in his twenties, empty eyes, just skin and bones. His disjointed words die in echoes between the walls. Turning to the passenger seated next to him, Alex asks in curiosity, "What is his crime?"

The man, short-cropped dark hair, broad shoulders, clean shaven, a faint hint of cologne on his skin, looks to be in his early thirties. He looks up from the book he is reading and asks Alex in fluent, English, "I'm guessing you are not from Bangladesh?"

"No...yes, I am. But I grew up in California," Alex answers looking away towards the handcuffed man.

"He said he has nothing. Maybe he was given false papers for a job. Probably he sold everything on a false hope for a better life."

Alex, surrounded by fellow travelers in the waiting area of the

"Orange County."

"I've a friend who lives in Irvine. Wonderful place."

"Do you visit Bangladesh often?"

"Not really, but after I got married this year I am visiting every other month," Zaman says laughing as Alex joins in chuckles and mirthful head-shakings. "I'm waiting for a visa for my wife, so she can join me in fulfilling my American dream. The white picket fence with 1.5 kids and two cars."

"Yes, the American dream."

More and more Bangladeshi passengers gather in the waiting lounge. Alex sits and watches how the crowd is so distinct and different, secure in groups. The migrant workers sit in separate crowds, laborers who sport huge grins, returning home after long indentured service of modern-day slavery in Singapore, Malaysia and other countries in the fringe of Asia. Gentlemen crowds, some Asian and white non-resident Bangladeshis, travelers with families and kids or business people now fill up the lounge.

"Wow, so many Bangladeshi laborers working in Singapore?" Alex comments noticing the long line of laborers, some in yellow jumpsuits.

"Yes. But they are not only from Singapore; some are coming from Malaysia and other Asian countries. Most laborers from Bangladesh today work in Saudi Arabia, Kuwait, Dubai, Abu Dhabi, Libya. Mostly in the oil states," Zaman continues. "Actually Bangladesh runs on the migrant money coming in. Billions of dollars every year."

"Really?" Alex asks.

"Yes, oil money. No one really talks about it. But right now the money fueling Bangladesh is migrant money sent home. Most of the men travel leaving family behind. Religiously they send money back every month. Labor is Bangladesh's biggest export. By far. But sadly there are guys like that laborer, guys going home penniless."

—❦—

As ALEX BOARDS THE SINGAPORE Airlines' Airbus A300, the sound of planes taking off and landing fills the air. There is the smell of jet fuel, the sound of babies crying over the constant hum of humanity. The plane is wide, seating three, four, then three.

The plane finally screams down the runway, the engines alive with a tremendous force, a muscular force that pushes back time. Its fuselage shudders as the jets blast. The speed gives the plane a sleekness, and the power rocks Alex in his seat into a sudden awakening, an awaking to what lies ahead.

The Airbus climbs through the cloud bank, then makes an arching left turn to the north-west—a four-hour flight to Dhaka. Alex takes out the complementary airline magazine in the front pocket below the pull down tray. He flips through the in-flight tax free shopping guide and unfolds the world route map with thin black arching lines connecting far-flung destinations.

Los Angeles. Tokyo. Singapore. Then Dhaka, Bangladesh.

His fingertips trace his journey across the world. In his ears echo Sangeeta, Laura and Jack's words to be careful. Laura's kiss goodbye. Jack's hug. Sangeeta's last kiss still sweet on his lips.

Like the arc-shaped routes etched on the map, Alex is shooting himself like the trajectory of an arrow, back twenty-five years, back into the circumstances of his birth.

Over the Bay of Bengal, the flight is bumpy. Alex feels his stomach tighten as they drop a thousand feet in an air pocket, and the pilot comes on and asks everyone to fasten their seat belts.

Alex looks out the window over a churning Bay of Bengal far below, where cargo ships are specks. Into the horizon, front and center is the delta of Bangladesh, to the left India, to the right Myanmar, and beyond Myanmar on the horizon are Cambodia and Laos and Vietnam.

In the cool cabin air, with the sound of Miles in his ears, Alex squeezes his forehead between his thumb and index finger. From the ashes of the phoenix rises the new sun, and from the death of his older brother Frank, Alex thinks of his adoption, the sinuous path that is his life.

The plane levels off above the clouds at 31,000 feet. Lunch is served. Alex sits eating rice and chicken curry with a side of green beans.

The shapely, slender Singapore Girl air hostess slides by in between the rattling beverage cart and the seats, smiling at Alex as he looks up, asks for a beer. She places a Singha beer on the pull-down tray where it rattles in the slight turbulence over the Bay. Alex takes a long swallow, observes the golden dragon logo on the label of the Singha. He leans his head back, finishes his beer in one swallow, closes his eyes, runs his hands through his hair.

Weary, his mind drifting, Alex looks down again, imagines December 1971 on the Bay below. The USS Enterprise floats into the Bay with a Russian nuclear-armed sub shadowing it before the Enterprise turns back to the South Seas of Vietnam.

Did Nixon want another war on his hands while Vietnam was going on?

Don't think so. If Vietnam had not tied Nixon's hands in 1971, I wonder what the outcome of the Bangladesh War of Independence might have been?

Alex looks to the skies above in an infinite yearning, then closes his eyes, drifting to the soft riffs of Coltrane in his ears. The plane banks, making a slight leftward turn over the southern edge of Bangladesh.

In a primal pull, like the rainbow trout swimming to spawn in the river of their birth, we always go back to the same river we were born in, a force beyond our logical mind, pulling us back to our birthplace to find, to search for answers our souls ache for.

Your soul is not the combination of your mother's egg and your father's semen.

Maybe souls are put on a tree and plucked and put into the baby when it is born. Complete. Distinct. Separate from the identity of the parents.

The plane hits another air pocket, and Alex feels his stomach free fall. The Captain's voice jars him. "To the right of you is Chittagong. We will be landing at Dhaka in thirty minutes."

Through the columns of Southwest monsoon clouds, below a wide, silvery *áchol* embroidered in cadmium, brown islands fan out into the depths of the Bay. In sync with the flow of the great Padma, Jamuna, Meghna, Alex's heart thrums, the pace faster, as

Bangladesh appears like a dream. The fuselage of the Airbus slices through the clouds, cutting through decades, pulling towards water, towards soil, dark, mysterious.

The Riaspora

Zia International Airport, Dhaka, September 1997

WHEN THE AIRBUS TOUCHES BANGLADESHI soil at Zia International Airport, its wheels skidding and smoking on the runway, a burst of anxious energy is released in a wave undulating through the Riaspora. The returning Diaspora, with a mass unclicking of seat belts while the plane is still moving, jump up to grab their bags from the overhead compartments. On cue, like a mother hen herding her brood of chicks, the flight attendants herd the overly anxious passengers back into their seats.

Finally the plane comes to a stop at the gate. Most of the passengers immediately jam the aisles, the doors still closed. Still seated, Alex feels the suffocating squeeze. Within a few minutes the doors are opened and the passengers stream their way out of the plane as the crew thanks them for flying Singapore Airlines.

There is a great commotion in the back of the plane when the hand-cuffed barefoot prisoner screams, *"Ami jamu na. Ami namum na, ami namum na, ami shob khichu beicha bidesh gachi, ami aai deshe kee kurrom. Jamuna. Jamuna!* No I won't go. I won't get down. I won't. I sold everything to go foreign. What will I do in this country? No I won't go. No I won't go."

As Alex walks up the ramp into the brightly lit airport, security personnel run past him into the plane.

373

"BACK HOME! WE ARE BACK HOME!" The Bangladeshi passengers echo these words in their excitement, in their resonating conversations.

Alex makes his way with everyone else following the signs that say, "ARRIVING PASSENGERS." He feels the warm humidity. The dry skin of his knuckles now surprisingly smooth, moist in the Dhaka air.

Looking down the long, brightly lit corridor he sees a yellow sign overhead. On it is the word. "Welcome."

In the bustling terminal building are passengers from an earlier Emirates flight. Among the passengers are hundreds of sunburnt Bangladeshi laborers returning home from the Persian Gulf, women in burqas and saris, some Asians.

Towards the left, another sign reads, "Foreign Passports Only," separating the shuffling passengers in the capacious Custom's area with tall vaulted ceilings and bright fluorescent lights. In front, in small wooden cubicles are the seated Customs officers, cursorily inspecting and stamping entry dates on the passports.

The questions are short. Curt.

"Visa?"

"Yes, yes."

"Please fill up card. Complete visa section."

"Yes, Sir."

"You have visa?"

"No, no visa required, Bangladesh born. Stamped on passport."

The foreigner line is occupied mostly by NRBs, Non Resident Bangladeshis, with a common smirk on their faces, a better-than-thou look, a "what in the hell is taking so long? I am too good for this" attitude. There are Chinese, Korean, and a few whites in the line, and on some faces the well worn look of "I've been through this before."

Like a rooster amongst chickens, ruffling its feathers, fluffing its chest, and beating its wings against its proud sides, these NRBs are impatiently shuffling their well heeled shoes, glad they are in this line, proud, their heads held high. These men and women and their born in the USA children have that certain sense of accomplishment. As if saying, "Look at me, I have come home with the Golden Goose, a passport from a foreign country."

Alex and Zaman stand together in this line marked Foreign Passports. Suddenly, someone yells out, "*Chootmarani,* line *kate kan? Amraa koto khoon daraai achi!* Why is the fucker cutting in front of us when we have been waiting for so long?"

This yelp undulates up and down the line like the pleats of an accordion flowing back and forth. In larger and larger circles, the yelp rings out. The pushing, the shoving begins and the security guards start shouting and walking the lines trying to keep order.

The workers push into each other, together stronger, squeezed into one gigantic, twisting common voice.

A young airport woman official in a *salwar kameez* holding a handful of foreign passports goes to the front of the line. She stands off to the side, looking furtively at the Customs officers as they look up at the passengers and match them with passports. Like a wisp of wind, she steps forward to a known official and hands him the stack of passports, smiles, and gets them stamped, cutting across all the lines. Alex chuckles. This is modernity.

Past the Customs officers' carousels, to the far left, is the merry-go-round of bags, where passengers desperately look for the conclusion of their tiresome journey. Some look more lost than their belongings.

A mountain of bags are piled up by the wall in the Custom's area. Here and there, attendants are running about pushing an empty trolley, "Saar, do you need help?" they ask with an eagerness dancing in their eyes.

The creaking baggage conveyor belt steadily disgorges the cargo: metal trunks, heavily over-tapped cardboard boxes with names and addresses written with black markers, TVs, VCRs in boxes strapped by jute rope and brown packing tape.

When the porter helping Alex finally pushes and shoves his suitcase-laden luggage cart out into the taxi area, Alex finds himself the target of every huckster. As if in a rush to get a new client, three of these touts are on him.

"Saar, taxi, Saar?"

"Hotel, Saar, you need hotel?"

"Saar, good taxi, hotel."

The police in khaki pants, ironed blue shirts and black berets are trying to keep order. Over in one corner behind the Panjabi-wearing young men donning white skull-caps are two people waiting for passengers holding cardboard signs.

Alex spots the Sheraton bus driver holding up a white sign with his name on it and Alex finally pushes his way past the hordes of taxi drivers and overeager touts who pull his push cart this way and that.

"Sir, you Alex McKensie?" he asks.

"Yes, I'm..."

"This way please."

"How much?" Alex asks the porter who pushes his cart to the Sheraton microbus.

"Saar, give me dollar, dollar, Saar."

The Sheraton bus driver quickly places Alex's luggage into the back of the van.

Alex takes out a five dollar bill and gives it to the brown khaki adorned porter. The five dollar excitement is contagious. In a frenzied pushing the other porters ask for more money from Alex.

"Move" the Sheraton bus driver snarls.

Grudgingly the porters disperse.

THE AFTERNOON SUN CUTS THROUGH a dusty, humid heavy air as Alex sits inside the white air-conditioned Sheraton microbus.

Outside the city throngs. The streets of Dhaka are teaming with life. Rickshaws are everywhere—the streets a maze of stick-like rickshaw-wallahs, sunburnt to a crisp, their sweaty cotton singlets stuck to their backs and ribs. Cars zigzag around people, children. People everywhere. Staring, scratching, talking, coughing, spitting.

Signs in Bengali and buses painted in vibrant greens and reds, overflowing with passengers, roll through streets of Dhaka made narrow by all the rickshaws and cars parked illegally on both sides.

"What is written on the back of the trucks?" Alex asks.

"*Maer dooa,* Mother's blessings!" the driver replies.

The buses are guided by the unflagging shouts of the drivers' assistants who straddle the vehicles' rear bumpers and yelp directions in their thick Dhakaia accents.

"*Chootia, shor na re!* Assholes, why don't you move!" the young bus conductor calls out to the parked rickshaws.

A large bus, its sides scarred from scrapes, is almost toppling over, with people on the roof and hanging onto the back windows. It nearly collides with an over laden truck, which is getting closer to that baby taxi, which is being overtaken by a family of four on a motorcycle, which is getting to within inches of the rickshaw.

"*Saar, Allah dibo, achaal manush, bow, bachha achee,* Allah *roste* Saar. Saar, Allah will give, I am a disabled human being, I have wife and kids. By the blessing of Allah." Another beggar chants.

Alex hands a dollar to the blind woman. Immediately, the van is mobbed by a crowd of begging hands poking through every window. A woman with a little baby on her lap stretches out her hands. Little boys come up wearing only shorts, little girls in dirty frocks.

"*Oi, jaah,* go away," the driver tries to shoo off the crowd, unsuccessfully.

Horns.

Smoke.

Noxious diesel fumes.

—❧—

THE VAN ENTERS THE GROUNDS of the Sheraton. An hour trip now stretched out in traffic to two.

Alex steps out of the hotel microbus, tired and happy.

"Saar, I am Jalal," salaams the bell boy as he quickly gets Alex's bags down from the bus.

Alex strides into the reception area of the Hotel Sheraton, its walls paneled in Mahogany with brightly polished brass inlays. After registering at the desk, Jalal escorts Alex down the polished marbled hallway lit up by bright overhead lights to the elevator.

"Room sir?"

"733."

Jalal pushes the cart with Alex's bags into the elevator. Alex follows. Jalal hits the button and the doors close and Alex feels he is being transported in time. It was here, inside this hotel that the foreign journalists were held on the night of the March 25th, 1971 massacres.

"So much took place here," Alex says looking at the elevator buttons going all the way up to the eleventh floor. He thinks about what clandestine political meetings took place here in 1971.

"What Saar?" the porter asks.

"Oh, nothing."

"Saar, you need anything, please ask for me. Jalal."

"A shower. Some food."

"Saar, just dial room service. The Bithika restaurant is open on the ground floor, Saar. We can get food to your room right away."

Alex follows Jalal to his room. Jalal puts away Alex's bags in a corner of the room and Alex tips him a five dollar bill.

"Thank you, Saar, thank you."

The plush room has large windows overlooking the back of the Hotel. Alex pushes away the thick curtains. Far below are tiny bamboo and burlap shacks of a slum that stretches to the edge of a pond. The sun, just disappearing, leaves a painted sky of gold, pink, orange and purple before becoming a melancholy blue, then turning to deeper tones of dusk over Dhaka.

Memories rush through Alex's brain, from childhood to today. Incidents, tears, humiliation—all revealing, like lines of light invading a dark space, a painful place. The sketchy silhouettes, the unanswered questions, the deep shadows cast on his life by his birth in the 1972 war-ravaged country of Bangladesh.

He looks at the clock. 6:00 P.M.

4:00 A.M. Los Angeles.

He picks up the phone, asks the operator to place a call to Sangeeta.

A few minutes later the phone rings.

"Sangeeta, Sangeeta, can you hear me?"

"Yes Alex. How are you?"

"Tired. Just got here."

"How was your flight?"

"Good. Bit bumpy over the Bay of Bengal."

"How do you like Dhaka?"

"Like you told me. Very crowded, very colorful. In some ways similar to downtown LA!"

"Interesting. Did you talk to Mom and Dad?"

"No, not yet, can you call them?"

"I will, honey, but please call and let them know you are fine. Did you eat anything?"

"No! Had lunch on the plane. I will go down to the restaurant in a bit. I love you, Sangeeta. Miss you."

"Me too, Alex. Get some rest."

Putting the phone down, Alex sits down on the bed, the tension growing in his neck, moving down between his shoulder blades. Digging his toe into his shoe, he wishes he could dig into the enigma of his birth.

Slowly, he takes his shoe off.

The phone rings, dispersing Alex's thoughts.

"Alex. Good morning, son," Jack says, his voice groggy, sleepy. "Oh, I should say good evening. What time is it there?"

"Six in the evening."

"How was your flight? Everything alright?"

"Flight was good, bit bumpy, everything is fine. Don't worry Dad."

"How is Dhaka?"

"Very interesting place, Dad."

"Your bags get there?"

"Yes."

"Be careful Alex. Talk to Laura, she is worried about you."

"Bye Dad."

A transcontinental silence.

"Hi Alex," Laura says, her voice soft, sleepy.

"Hi Mom."

"How was your flight?"

"It was good."

"Are you OK Alex?

"Mom, I'm fine. Don't worry; everything is great."

"How is Dhaka?"

"Colorful. Crowded. Humid."

"Call us everyday Alex!"

"I will."

"Alex, take care of yourself."

"I will. Love you Mom."

Alex gazes out the window. Before him the sprawling city, a city shrouded with the enigma of his birth.

As darkness descends over the horizon ever so slowly, small specks of nomadic yellow lights twinkle on like stars appearing from light years away on a canvas of darkness, bejeweling the heaving humanity. Lights hazy in the dusty dampness that hangs heavy in the *bosti* air, the city wrapped in a brown chador on a shivering street dweller on a cold night.

꩜

Mother Teresa's

"If you judge people you have no time to love them."
— Mother Teresa

Islampur, Old Town Dhaka, September 1997

"SAAR, NO CHANGE," THE CAB driver says to Alex, holding the five-hundred Taka note.

"It's OK," Alex replies.

"Thank you Saar." The cab driver flashes a twice-what-he-had-haggled-for smile.

Alex and his guide Kashem slide from the taxi's worn vinyl seats into a river of pedestrians.

"Bangla Bazaar is the start of Old Town Dhaka. Taxis don't want to go farther. Too much traffic. We have to find a rickshaw," Kashem says as they stand in the shade of a lowered plastic awning with empty bags for sale hanging all around them.

Alex's guide from the Sheraton is a stout, short man wearing black cotton pants and a light brown cotton half-sleeve shirt. Kashem scratches his thick beard, removes a handkerchief from his pocket and wipes the sweat off his brow as he looks for a rickshaw.

Against a backdrop of dark Southwest monsoon clouds looming on the morning horizon, meticulously hand painted rickshaws line the streets. The sticky air is dense with dust, smoke, the smell of cigarettes, the smell of ripe tropical fruits displayed on so many carts and baskets, the pulsating, hypnotic rhythms of the street punctuated by truck horns, rickshaw bells, shouts and yells.

As far as the eye can see, and in every shade of loud, shirts, children's clothes, frocks, jackets, athletic wear are displayed by the bazaar merchants under identical blue plastic awnings. Bamboo poles frame the sidewalk storefronts creating a continuous strip of scalloped shadow and light along the uneven brick sidewalk.

"Clothes cheap here, Saar," Kashem says.

"How come?"

"Rejected export garments from all the garment factories are sold to the local public here."

"What's wrong with them?"

"Some wrong labels Saar. Small is Large, XL is Medium," Kashem explains.

The sweat from Alex's brow gets into his eyes, and through his blurred vision, his eyes stinging, he wipes his face on the sleeve of his shirt, looks at the colorful mistagged clothes.

"*Oi Jaiba?* Will you go?" Kashem calls out to several empty parked rickshaws.

"Where?" the rickshaw-wallah asks.

"Islampur," Kashem says.

"Na, Saar," is the answer, repeated emphatically over and over again with shaking heads.

"Paper Saar," hawks a young street vendor with an armful of newspapers, noticing Alex's obvious foreignness, dreaming of a fast sale.

"Whew, hot," Alex says as he wipes beads of sweat off of his face on the shoulder of his shirt. He hands the young newspaper-wallah boy a note.

"Saar, paper, Saar," the boy says handing Alex a paper.

"Naah, you keep it," Alex replies, leaving the boy with a puzzled expression on his face.

Most of the people wear *lungis*, cotton pants, short sleeve shirts. On the sidewalk Alex and his guide pause for a moment. But only for a moment as the waves of pedestrians threaten to trample them, pushing and shoving them out of the way.

"What now?" Alex asks.

"Saar, just a minute," Kashem says as he walks to the corner to a blue carriage with a brown canvas top drawn by two thin horses that swat off with their flapping ears a cloud of buzzing flies.

"How far?" Kashem asks

"To Jagannath College." The conductor, a young teenage boy who smells of sweat and cigarettes, tanned black by the sun, hangs on to the side of the carriage, calls out to the passing pedestrians, "Old Town, Old Town, Jagannath, Jagannath."

"How much?" Kashem asks.

"Ten Takas," the boy replies, flashing his cigarette smoke stained teeth.

"OK."

Kashem and Alex get into the carriage.

"Here's thirty," Kashem says, "An extra seat. One bench for us."

"OK," the boy replies, then continues calling for customers till the carriage is full. A total of eight passengers. Content, the young boy hangs on the side and with a "Hut, hut" they are off.

The sound of plodding hoofs, the clacking of the wooden tires. Alex feels he is being carried back to the age of the Nawabs, when Old Dhaka was built, some of it dating back well before the British to the time of the Mughals.

Alex searches the store signs for English.

"Malitola lane," he reads, finally spotting a solitary store signboard in English. "Ratan Steel Corporation," on a small wholesale store full of metal rods and wrought iron parts, next to a store selling huge metal safes.

"A lot of iron and raw leather here," Alex says, turning to Kashem.

"Wholesale, Saar."

A woman balances an infant on her hip with one hand, as she pulls the end of her *áchol* over her head with the other and scampers across the street. She looks, stops, maneuvers deftly avoiding traffic. Alex swallows as he imagines the footsteps of his mother on these crowded streets. 1972. Images of his mother twenty-five years ago, pregnant and desperate flash in his mind. He turns around to look at the woman as she disappears into the crowd on the other side.

As they plod and weave into the heart of Old Town Dhaka, the traffic is mostly rickshaws, the buses and trucks far and in between.

"This place always so crowded?" Alex asks.

"Yes Saar."

"Even back in '72?"

"Yes. Old Town Dhaka before the British period."

The plodding, the creaking of the carriage marks a transformation, a narrowing of roads, a crowding of humans. In the ten minute ride they pass the old court house and water tank, then finally Jagannath College.

"We get off," Kashem says.

Alex zig zags across the street behind Kashem, dodging rickshaws, almost getting run over.

"Wow! Pyramids of books here," Alex says looking at the bookstores, the textbooks piled high on the sidewalks in front.

"Yes. Bangla Bazaar, garments. Books here. Iron and leather stores on Malitola lane."

"Seems like there are lots of pockets of specialty stores in Dhaka?" Alex asks.

"Yes. Old town is like that. Everyone comes to these stores from far."

Alleys, narrow streets, a shrunk, cramped world surrounds Alex as he walks briskly, trying to keep up with Kashem, fighting against a tide of pedestrians flitting by like lost souls in search of an address, seemingly ever so afraid of being crushed by the eager seekers right on their heels. The heavy humid air is a liquid brush, melding the world around Alex into an infusion of sounds and sights.

Colorfully displayed bright orange betel nuts in their hull, green bite-sized berry-like amlokhis, guavas. Pineapples sit in large bamboo baskets of many street-vendor-wallahs lining the alleys, crowding the side walk.

To the left, in a corner of the street, is a flat cart of a papaya-juice-wallah. The orangy-yellow thick slices of the papaya are cut and stacked on the red plastic tablecloths and glasses of papaya juice sit awaiting thirsty customers.

Next to the papaya-wallah is the amra-wallah. It is amra season and the fist-sized green-apple like fruit with a fibery core is cut up into open flower patterns. The fruit is deftly cut up into thin slices and sold with red pepper and salt sprinkled on it.

Standing by a flat rickshaw mounted with a metal rolling press, the sugar-cane-juice-wallah shaves off the skin of a sugar cane with a special shaver. The shavings pile up as he skims off the bark from all of its length but a few inches at one end, holding the sugar cane truncheon of sweetness ready to be pressed into juice.

From the Sheraton to the taxi, to the horse-drawn carriage, to being on foot. Like the means of transportation, time peels away like the shavings, the layers of a sugar cane, bearing a core sweetness, a core of history on the narrow Islampur road.

An antique world, held almost unchanged by the decades, modernity blocked by overbuilt narrow streets, holding its many secrets close like the closed in alleys.

"Rickshaw Islampur?" Kashem calls out to a passing empty rickshaw-wallah.

"No saar, *jamu na*. I won't go," the rickshaw-wallah says.

"*Kaan?* Why?" Kashem asks, standing on a corner as crowds slide, bump and rush past him.

"Police barricades," the rickshaw-wallah points to a traffic cop in front of a barbed wire barricade. "They won't let us go into Islampur here. Only traffic allowed is that coming out of Islampur."

The Old Town Dhaka sun beats through a haze upon the sweltering of this maze of streets and brick buildings centuries old. Wrought iron balconies, heavy with clothes hung to dry, reach into a dense, dark sky of tangled wires, a sky of many lives twisted together in small spaces.

Kashem turns to Alex. "Only way walking." Alex nods, follows the guide, trying not to lose track of him in the dense maze of humanity on Islampur Road.

"Saar!" the guide turns and calls out to Alex. Alex jumps aside just in time to avoid getting hit by the trailing left rear wheel of a rickshaw. Sweating as they walk into the heart of old town Dhaka, traversing serpentine jostled narrow alleys, Alex looks up through towering buildings leaning in at the top to a squeezed sky. They cut past the trampling torrent of pedestrians to the front of a shuttered store wallpapered with the faces of political candidates, unsmiling faces of unknown leaders above the insignias of the popular political parties. Symbols of the boat, the plough, blades of rice.

"Mother Teresa's?" Kashem asks poking his head into a leather store. The shopkeeper, hunched on a stool stares back blankly at him. "Sister's *ateemkhaana,* orphanage?"

"Just down the road, on the left," the man replies through red *paan*-stained teeth.

A mouth-watering aroma permeates through the mundane, the dust and the acrid smoke, distinctly different.

"What is that smell?" Alex asks.

"Islampur Biryani. Famous Saar. Very tasty," Kashem says as he passes the small restaurant inlaid into the mosaic of the many steel, and leather shops lining the street. "These are some of the oldest parts of town," Kashem says as they wind on through picturesque narrow alleys bordered by great sepia-colored walls.

The only traffic is rickshaws, weaving by the pedestrians with the clanking of bells, tassels dangling from the handlebars.

Finally, they reach a large blue metal gate with pointed spikes welded on top.

Alex reads the sign, written both in English and Bengali,

"Missionaries of Charity, Mother Teresa's-
Shishu Bhavan, 26 Islampur Road"

Alex knocks. It's hard to see beyond the towering gate. Kashem stands beside him, while Alex impatiently knocks again.

A small latched peep hole opens, and a voice asks, *"Kee chan?* What do you want?"

"Saar has come from USA. We want to talk to Head Sister," Kashem says in Bengali.

The woman peers inquiringly at Alex, then back at Kashem.

Hesitatingly, she opens a small side gate and the two men slip into the compound. Quickly she closes the gate, leads them down the long concrete driveway. In front of Alex looms a three-story building with overhanging verandas covered in wrought iron grating.

Gazing at this building, Alex feels an overpowering mix of emotions: of his past, of his birth, of his identity. Like the crowds that were on his heels on the street, the questions, the enigma of his birth come crashing over him like a wave.

It is just before noon. Women sweeping the driveway look curiously at him.

The wooden windows and iron grills are all painted in a warm apple green, the replastered cement walls in a light purple. As they walk farther down the driveway a couple of women in cotton saris are busy cleaning and working around this shaded cemented courtyard.

Alex looks at the eyes of the women looking at him.

More eyes peer at Alex and Kashem as they stand on the courtyard. In front of them is the entrance to the building and also the stairwell. On a small platform built of stone and concrete stands a statuette of Mother Mary with a pink garland around her neck, a yellow rose bush in a pot to the right of her. Alex stops, looks at her in a moment of silence. He bites his lower lip, curls his hand into a tight fist, thanks God for his life.

The Head Sister comes down the stairs. Of medium build, she wears a white cotton sari with a thin blue border. A white scarf covers her head. Through thick glasses, she looks them up and down, a scrutinizing sternness in her gaze.

"Good morning," she says, greeting Alex and Kashem in an official English tone.

"Good Morning, sister," Alex says. Wiping beads of sweat off of his forehead, thinking back to his birth, he imagines his mother twenty-five years ago. His Ma, in a much smaller Mother Teresa's, on a desperate day in 1972 greeting the Sister. What had his mother said? Who had accompanied her? Had she really come here? Or was he brought here by someone else? Questions flood Alex's mind. He exhales a long breath that fills a gap large as two decades.

"I am Sister Madeline," the Sister says. "Can I help you?"

"Sister, I am Alex. Alex Salim McKensie. I was adopted from here, twenty-five years ago." Alex adds. "I have always wanted to visit. It has taken me twenty-five years to come back here."

"Welcome," Sister Madeline says. Through her stern gaze, a kindness shows in her face, a softness sculpting the edges of her lips and cheeks. She pauses, looks at Alex and then at Kashem.

"I am with him," Kashem explains.

Sister Madeline gestures to one of the women who brings out three plastic chairs and places them on the cemented landing of the building.

"Please sit," Sister Madeline says.

Kashem sits down, his hands lie heavy on his lap. He looks at Alex gazing first at the building then at the Sister's face and then back at him.

"I was adopted through this orphanage in '72 Sister," Alex says. "Words can't express my gratitude. Thank you."

Sister Madeline looks at Alex, and her face brightens as she says, "Thank Mother Teresa."

"Yes, of course," Alex says. A few small, inquisitive children peek out from the shadows of the long corridor behind them.

"Where do you live?" Sister Madeline asks.

"Los Angeles."

"Far away."

"Yes."

Alex brings out his adoption information written on a small index card. "Sister Madeline, I have some information I hope to verify," Alex says, holding his breath. He hands the sister the card. "Sister I hope to find out if you have any more information in your birth register. Could I please check this against it?" In a tremulous voice Alex adds. "I just want to verify this."

With her hands resting on her knees, her head bent down low, she examines the card. After a long moment, where Alex finds himself suspended, Sister Madeline hands the card back to Alex. Looking at him and then Kashem with understanding eyes, she states in a firm, official tone, "No, sorry. The birth register is confidential. What is written is written."

Alex exhales a long held weary breath. Clasping the plastic handles of the chairs hard, he looks at the Sister.

"Sister, I have come all the way from America. I was adopted through this orphanage in 1972. I have a right to know," Alex says, his voice shaking.

Sister Madeline mulls over something in her mind then states, "The birth register is a confidential book. It's sealed. I'm sorry."

Alex grips the plastic handle of the chair tighter. Behind him a long dark cement corridor of no certain color stretches into a flood of light at the very far end. He hears the scattered sounds of children. A heaviness descends on the shade of the building, making the humid air even heavier, even more stifling. Alex's grip on the chair tightens, his palms now red.

Across the small space between him and the Sister, Alex thinks back. He imagines the open, lined pages of a green Orphanage register. A page where twenty-five years ago his mother etched with a fountain pen her name and address. What exactly had the Sister said then, in '72?

Had the Sister said to his mother, "Everything will be fine."

Had the Sister said, "Adoptee parents from Canada, USA and other countries will be good parents."

He digs his toe into his shoe. A long minute passes.

"You are welcome to look around, Alex," Sister Madeline finally says. "Some of our children come back to visit. We welcome all of our children."

Alex is quiet. He refocuses on what the Sister was saying and finally says, "Yes, I would like that."

"Call Sister Angelica," Sister Madeline orders a woman sweeping the veranda behind them.

As they sit, Sister Angelica, a short stocky woman, also in a blue sari comes and stands by Sister Madeline.

"Yes, Sister?" Sister Angelica asks, her hands clasped together, hanging low over her blue apron.

"Sister this is Alex. He was adopted from here in '72. Could you escort them around the *Shishu Bhaban?*"

"Of course," Sister Angelica says.

Sister Madeline gets up and looking at Alex says, "You are not the first to come and ask to look at the register. We have children who come from Sweden, Canada, Australia. All over the world. We just can't open a sealed register."

Alex feels a wrenching in his chest as he gets up and follows Sister Angelica down the long hallway.

I'll wait over here," Kashem says as he touches a pack of cigarettes in his pocket.

"Sister is there anyone here today who was here in 1972?" Alex asks as they walk towards one of the rooms.

"No."

"And how long have you been here?"

"Seventeen years."

"Long time."

"Yes. And you live in America?"

"Yes. In L.A."

"Follow me Alex," Sister Angelica says.

To the right, along the long narrow corridors of purple and green, Alex follows the Sister past the clatter and clamor of children into a large room. From outside where a large cooking facility lies, sunlight pours in through open doors. The room is filled with cots, and eight or nine children in shorts play. A few malnourished children lay on the cots with intravenous tubes running into their veins.

"These children are not for adoption. This child," Sister Angelica points, "was brought in off the street begging with his mother." A plastic tube with a yellow medicine dripping through it is taped to his forehead. "They are poor malnourished children we are helping." These children, playing with each other, seem to form one larger being, a group existence, feeding on each other's eyes of want into a larger want. In the far corner another sister, also clad in a white sari, sits on a cot talking to a mother and child and writing down the details of the child's sickness in her notebook.

Alex pats the back of a young boy who smiles, while other children mill around him. The children giggle, shyly blinking at Alex as he pats them. Their mothers stand by them. Their ages range from two to ten.

Following Sister Angelica, Alex walks out of the room into the long hallway and past another closed room, towards the stairs.

"What's in this room?" Alex asks.

"Unmarried pregnant young women. Women who have nowhere to go. We take care of them. And when their babies are born they will be up for adoption."

Alex pauses, thinks about this answer. His gaze lingers on the door and he hears the muffled sounds of young women from inside. Alex touches the card in his pocket. A mother's name. An address.

Inside a womb of burning emotions, Alex is trembling.

Where was I born? Could it be here?

Ascending the stairs behind the sister Alex looks up. At the top of the stairs is a picture of Christ with his right hand held up. On the first landing, Alex stops, his hands gripping the banister. Looking down at the mosaiced stairs, he wonders if his mother stepped here, carrying him so many years ago.

From behind the closed door a voice echoes up the stairwell. A whimpering, crying voice.

April '72. His mother. Shaking. Hot. Her feet weak. Her knees buckling as she sits on her small cot. Puts down her things on the bed. She lays down, feeling the baby kick and move. Alone, an outcast of society. Desperate, seeking shelter.

"Alex," Sister Angelica says, as he stands mesmerized.

"Alex?"

"Yes," Alex replies, and follows Sister Angelica slowly up the stairs to the second floor.

Here they enter another large room dedicated to mentally disabled children. It is noon. Lunch time for the children. In a corner kitchen, a woman wearing a skirt and apron is cooking. Three young teenage helpers are busy mixing the rice and *daal* in plastic bowls and feeding the five children gathered around them. There are a dozen white metal cots filling the room, a few occupied by children from four to ten years old in checkered dresses, shorts and shirts.

Alex looks into the corner kitchen. On the floor is a mortar and pestle for grinding spices. Inside Alex a terrible mortar grinds his emotions against the pestle of his heart.

"The mentally disabled children here are the last to get adopted," Sister Angelica says. "Very few people want to adopt them."

Alex again follows Sister Angelica out into the long hallway. There is a large bulletin board on the wall, plastered with the pictures of children, their names written below in block-letters.

At the top, hand-written in large letters is the sign, "Love begins at home." In the upper left corner is a large picture of Mother Mary. Below it is a caption, 'See your Mother,' and below in Bengali, "*Dheko tomar Ma.*"

Alex reaches up and touches the hand-scripted 'Mother.' In the middle of the board is a picture of Mother Teresa, a divine peace on her face. The bright pictures, a jigsaw puzzle of smiling faces that fade into a collage of sadness and of inspired hope, seeking a life beyond a cot.

Past the bulletin board, they walk down a long hallway and at the end make a right turn into another large room where about twenty children, ages three to seven, are up for adoption. The girls are in light cotton pink chemises and the boys in checkered shorts.

Hanging on the wall is a black chalk board. In white chalk is written,

"C-Cat

D-Dog

T-Tiger"

Sitting on little stools, they look up, mouths full of rice and *daal* and garbanzo beans.

They stare at Alex, their eyes blinking bright with curiosity. A little girl, maybe three, looks up with big dark eyes beneath long lashes, her eyes sparkling with half-awe-struck curiosity, a lean nose, shoulder length hair, silky black and straight.

Alex gently brushes his fingertips against her hair and says, "*Tomar nam kee?* What is your name?" in a few words of Bengali he has picked up.

Shy, her fragile hands clasp the hem of her pink cotton chemise. She whispers her name, beaming. A smile spreads across her face on her thin lips, a want for love rising from deep in her eyes.

Alex waits while the children finish eating their lunch.

He then reads aloud the words on the blackboard with the children, sings rhymes. He claps hands amid giggles and laughter.

"You will grow up to live wonderful lives, become scientists, doctors, artists," Alex says in an uplifting tone.

The little girl looks up at Alex with an irascible sweet appeal without a name, her light brown skin on her long collarbones trembles as Alex touches her forehead and face. And these touches make his insides tremble. In her eyes is a reflection of him. He imagines himself as a child standing next to her. Awaiting attention. Craving a little love.

In the darkness of the room, lit only by sunlight pouring through grated windows patterned in stars, her face dwindles and sparkles, sparkles and dwindles; she laughs quietly, as if sound itself is so precious that it would break the magic of the moment. The lingering look held in those brown eyes, the shared warm smile fills Alex's heart, bridging an immutable gap of wants. Alex reluctantly waves goodbye to these children.

He follows the Sister as they walk up the stairs to the third floor, where they enter another large room with tiny newborns in bright, apple green cane bassinets. Iridescent dreams hang in the shape of floating toys over the bassinets. Little bears, little dolls hover over the unfocused eyes of these newborns.

Sister Angelica looks at each newborn, attending to each one's needs with a gentle touch. She stops to change a cloth diaper.

Alex slowly walks to the window and peers through gaps in the wrought iron grill. Below in the courtyard a few children run and play. Alex looks through iron twinkles of stars, twinkles of hope.

Having completed the tour, he walks down the stairs, down to the ground floor with Sister Angelica. A collage of smiling faces floats in his eyes as he walks out into the mid-afternoon sun.

"Thank you sister," Alex says. "I will come again."

"You are welcome Alex. God bless," Sister Angelica says in parting.

Alex steps back out through the iron gate into the human crush.

"Watch out!" Kashem shouts as a rickshaw barely misses Alex. He notices Alex's exhausted face, keeps pointing the way, and says, "We need to find a taxi. Get back to the hotel."

Alex wants to focus amid the rickshaws, interspersed by honking trucks, baby taxis. All around him, up Islampur road to the corner where the road bends and the barricade starts, the Old City crawls with people, all reduced by the leaning towers of brick and mortar into a moving mass. Hurrying, rushing in the humid, hot mid-day sun, closely guarding some plan, their precious reason for living another day. Closely guarded secrets of self propagation impaled on the cross of self-preservation.

There is an intensity on everyone's faces. A destination is drawn in the wrinkles and lines.

Alex thumbs the small index card with a name and address in his jeans' pocket. In his palm he curls the card. And on his lips appears a thin sad smile, a reflected smile from the lips of that one little girl with eyes wide as the Padma.

Silently They Come

Liberation War Museum, Segunbagicha, Dhaka, September, 1997

*I*N A PLAY OF THE breeze, Nahar swings on a Banyan tree, her white sari *āchol* fluttering, her long black hair blowing. Laughing, giggling, she says, "Nazmul Bhai, how are you? Rafique and you laughed at me when I wanted to fight for my country. Today, you are the *Bir*. Hero. And I am the *Birongana*. Did we not pay the highest price for my country?"

Nahar steps off the swing. Her face reddens, her eyes aflame in bitterness. "You jeered at me because I was a woman."

"No, no, not that, Nahar," Nazmul says, his voice apologetic.

"'In the procession, tear gas. Once you swallow some gas you will be choking and running all the way to Sheetalpur!' You don't remember Nazmul?" Nahar says, her voice piercing through the malaise that now fills the room. "Everyone knows you are a *Bir*, a freedom fighter. But Nazmul Bhai, what about us? Where is our honor as a *Birongana*?"

As Nahar's laughter fades away, echoing ironically in Nazmul's ears, Professor Rahman scratches his day-old salt-and-pepper stubble, sits behind the desk, peers through his thick eye glasses

395

·at Nazmul.

Rahman looks spent; deep tense lines furrow his forehead. Tentatively clasping an empty tea cup in his hand, he says in a dejected tone, "Remember in 1971 I went to Norshindi Town for medicine? Nothing. No flu syrup, not even Detol. No sugar. No soybean oil. Only thing I could scrounge up then was some mustard oil, kerosene, and salt."

Professor Rahman takes off his dark rimmed glasses. With the edge of his Panjabi he slowly cleans each thick lens. "So this is 1997. Today Selina is still sick, only sicker. Tia is unmarried. Babul is unemployed. And Moina cannot complete her higher education for lack of money." Rahman's voice rises in anger. "What difference! And this the promise? Freedom? Selina, Tia, Moina, Babul still cry for justice!"

Rahman disappears into a dark, deep silhouette and out of the shadows Jahanara and Mustafa appear. Jahanara chewing betel nut, her lips stained red, asks, "Baba Nazmul. Have you seen Rafique? How is Rafique?" Her voice falls away, and Mustafa, white bearded, white skull cap, sits down gripping the long pipe of his unlit hookah, and asks, "Nazmul, where have you been all these years? So many years we have waited for you and Rafique, looking tirelessly down the trail."

Mustafa stares at the hookha, his voice bristling with bitterness, and asks, "What did you fight for, why did you join the *Mukti Jhuddho?* How could a free country's people vote for Neezam?"

Rintu puts a cigarette out on a teacup, chuckles, "How are you Nazmul Bhai? Got any exploding pineapples today?" He curls his right hand into a fist, slams it with a bang on the wooden desk.

In a grinding, hoarse voice, rising in anger he says, "And now, now Nazmul Bhai, after all these years, my parents try to raise the issue of my murder again. Try to bring the murderers to justice after two decades. My father and my mother protested passionately. Strongly protested. But they have been blacklisted. They have a right to speak out and not be prosecuted as anti-patriotic elements. My parents are now charged with raising unrest, agitation. Dividing the whole nation. No justice, Nazmul Bhai. None! My parents are now

In this star filled night, your memories I reminisce in sorrow.
Nazmul gets up and walks towards the door. Stops. He walks back. Sits down, lays his head down on top of his unfinished manuscript. *Should have said something. Could've said something to Alex this afternoon—he left with such sadness in his eyes. What was the use of this discussion if I am not willing to say anything?*

Nazmul slowly releases the curled fingers of his right hand. He opens the locked bottom drawer, takes out an old faded album. Just a few days ago he had brought it here. For twenty-six years it had gathered dust in his home. And for twenty-six years he had debated whether to donate it to the museum collection. An album that belonged to a *Birongana,* an album he had brought for her as an anniversary gift in 1971.

Nazmul opens the album and looks at a photograph, a black and white of him and Rafique standing on the grass in front of Ahsanullah Hall in early 1971, in bell-bottom pants, long-sleeve cotton shirts hanging out over the pants, sandals. Both of them smiling, a pack of cigarettes in the front pocket of Rafique as he brandishes a wrist watch, his hands on his hip, his stance wide.

Nazmul runs his fingers through his hair flecked with gray. He uncrosses his legs slowly, leans against the chair, pushing it to the wall. With his arms crossed behind his head, he looks up at the ceiling, his eyes glazed, filled with conflicting emotions, his face tight in the vice grip of a crushing dilemma. He picks up his pen, flicks it on the manuscript. *With ink and paper I have extracted so many articles out of my mind, but today after twenty-six years, my ink of truth has run dry, unable to extract justice for the martyred of 1971.*

Last time Nazmul had seen Rafique, he was scaling the wall on the back of Dr. Samad's in Kalabagan. Running in the alley behind. Scaling wall after wall. Running. Escaping.

This evening the wall of phantoms of 1971 form an unscalable wall around Nazmul, a wall of injustice.

Nazmul flips the album to another page. A black and white weathered photograph of Nahar, sitting in front of the Chowdhury pond. The last time Nazmul saw Nahar at the *Birongana* house from where she disappeared without a trace into a *kalbaishaki* storm.

Nazmul holds on to the photograph of Nahar Sultana looking with longing eyes at a sky filled with promises.

"Nahar," Nazmul murmurs, touching the photograph with his trembling fingertips. "Desperately I searched everywhere for you. In vain. And today. Today your son has come looking for you. All these years I didn't believe Rafique went to Sheetalpur after escaping from Dacca."

Nazmul puts down the picture, murmurs to himself.

"That smile, Rafique's mischievous smile on Alex's lips. After these decades, that long unheard voice echoes in my ears. Same age, same stance, the look of Rafique."

After twenty-six long years, Rafique reappears.

Rebirth

February 15, 2000, California

*A*LEX LOOKS UP. THE DOMED OR light above the door comes on. The wall-clock clicks into 5:30 A.M exactly. He sits stiffly on the edge of a plastic chair in the harshly lit, well-polished white Hospital hallway. Two weeks before her due date Sangeeta has been rushed into the operating room. The baby is breached with the umbilical cord wrapped around its neck.

Dr. Beecher stops on her way into the delivery room. In her soft, reassuring voice she says, "Alex, when it's time, we will have you come in." Touching him lightly on the shoulder, she adds, "Don't worry, she's in good hands."

Alex runs his fingers through his matted hair. Sangeeta's water broke at 2:30 A.M. Three long hours ago. His eyes narrow, pulling the lines taut across his forehead as he watches the OR light. He brings his forehead down, his hands join in prayer, a prayer for Sangeeta, a prayer for the baby.

"Curl up like a 'C', there, a bit more," Alex hears the anesthetist say from just inside the operating room. Sangeeta lays curled up on a bed inside the door.

Then a little minute later, "There, bit more, bit more...great."

Alex twitches. His body tenses. He feels the needle going into

401

his own spine. Perspiration beads on his forehead. Was Sangeeta OK? The baby?

The sound of footsteps echoes down the hallway, as anxious parents rush to a bedside. Alex wishes Laura and Jack were here beside him. Not expecting the baby to come so soon, they are away vacationing in the lush San Yenez Valley in Santa Barbara. He has already called them and they are on their way.

And Sangeeta's parents? For three years now, they are absent in Sangeeta's life.

One of the nurses peeks out of the swinging doors of the OR and says, "You can come in now." Alex gets up, struggling to get his footing and he struggles to put on the offered scrubs. Alex's fingers are shaking. The nurse tightens the strings on the back of the surgical mask.

"Thanks," Alex says, clearing his dry throat. "Thank you."

"Everything will be fine," the nurse says reassuringly.

Halfway through the OR door Alex remembers the camera he has left on the chair. He turns back, picks it up, grips it tightly, enters the operating room.

There is a small white cloth canopy covering Sangeeta's chest and blocking her view of the Cesarean operation. Sangeeta cannot see the incision, and Alex cannot see her face.

Dr. Sanchez and Dr. Beecher are bent over the preliminary incision in Sangeeta's lower abdomen. Alex tries not to focus on the blood being sucked out by the attending nurse through a vacuum plastic tube with the yellow fatty tissue exposed underneath. The insistent throbbing, thumping beats of all the operating room machinery, each with its own low distinct rhythm, fills Alex's mind.

He walks over to Sangeeta. A nervous smile on his lips. Sits down on a stool next to her.

She grins weakly, numbed by the epidural. A clear oxygen tube rests just below her nose. Alex rubs her cold palms trying to warm them, silently praying for the baby. Minutes pass. Sangeeta's grin quickly gives way to fear, as anxiety washes over her pale face. Alex crosses and uncrosses his legs, bites his lower lip and squeezes Sangeeta's palms to reassure her.

Then things happen quickly. A rush of activity. Dr. Beecher's voice. Quick succession of orders.

Alex hears a slap, a squawk and a shrill cry.

The baby is rushed to the awaiting incubator, and the pediatrician and two assisting nurses clean him, sucking out the blood and mucus from his mouth and nose through a vacuum tube, then giving him oxygen.

Alex is called. He walks over, his heart beating hard against his ribs, he looks at his little son, looks over each and every finger, counts the toes.

A miracle.

His son.

As he stands over the incubator, looking at the naked baby, Alex is given a pair of surgical scissors.

"You can cut through the umbilical cord just above the plastic clip," the pediatrician instructs Alex.

A ceremonial act, Alex has to work at cutting the thick membranous cord. He squeezes, releases and squeezes again.

The moment, ever so precious, a birth, stirs the phantoms of Alex's own soul. He exhales out a world of worries. An immense crushing weight is suddenly lifted. On his lips appears a thin smile, a reflected smile from the lips of that one little girl, the little girl at Mother Teresa's with eyes wide as the Padma.

Stabilized, now tightly wrapped in a white swaddling cloth with blue and pink stripes, his head covered in a matching cap, the baby is handed to Sangeeta. With Sangeeta smiling, Alex takes a picture as the baby opens his eyes, seeming to look at his mother, impervious to the whole new world around him.

Alex leans over the little newborn, kisses him on the forehead.

"Welcome, little Frank. Welcome," he whispers.

—❧—

SANGEETA, RECLINING ON HER ANGLED hospital bed, holds the baby to her breast. As the baby sucks on her nipple for nourishment, as she breathes deeply, a tremor runs through her exhausted body. After the feeding, she holds little Frank, close to her. Sangeeta smells the sweet innocence of his skin, caresses the miniature purple cheeks. The baby, eyes now closed, yawns contentedly in Sangeeta's bosom.

Alex sits beside her on the bed, silently watching.

The baby lets out a small squawk, a petulant whimper. In her newborn son, Frank S. McKensie, Sangeeta now has a new family. Someone whose palm is about the size of her finger owns her now.

Sangeeta's eyes are red and puffy, her hair disheveled. Alex helps her tie a band around her hair. He smiles, stands back and takes a few more pictures of mother and baby.

"He looks like you Alex."

Alex leans over and kisses baby Frank, coos at him, then kisses Sangeeta. At the sound of Alex's voice, the baby lets out a cry. Startled Alex looks at Sangeeta.

"He wants you to hold him, Alex," Sangeeta whispers.

"Really?"

"Yes, he knows your voice. You sang to him in my belly every night. "

"My babbling?"

Sangeeta gently hands the baby to him. The baby quiets as Alex holds him like a precious parcel in his arms, soothing him, walking about the room.

"Whaampae, thaampae, maashaae, maashaae," Alex sings his lullaby softly to the baby, walking to the window. He looks out over the parking lot of the hospital as a thin line of gray breaks the darkness of the eastern sky.

"Look how quiet he is now that you are holding him." Sangeeta says laying in bed.

"Yes," Alex says. He touches a curl on the baby's head.

A tiny song beats in Alex's heart, the song of contentment beats to the rhythm of his heart, and in the song is an almost imperceptible riff of joy, answers to questions haunting him, exorcising the phantoms of his soul.

404

For a long moment Alex is quiet. A smile appears on his lips.

"What is it, Alex?" Sangeeta asks as she looks up from bed.

Alex smiles warmly, holding little Frank tightly in his arms, walks over to her. He puts the baby in the bassinet, leans over and kisses her lightly on the cheeks, on the forehead, then on the lips.

The phone ringing pierces the silence of the room.

"Hi Mom. Yes, everything is fine, Sangeeta and the baby are both doing fine. See you soon... Yes, yes, don't worry, everything is fine...The baby is doing great Mom. How long before you get here? An hour. OK. That's great. No. No. Don't rush. Everything is fine. Bye."

"Knock, knock, can we come in?" Laura says.

"Mom, Dad," Alex says as he runs to the door and wraps his arms around them.

"Congratulations," Laura says as she kisses him on the cheeks, embracing him tightly, as tears flow from her eyes.

"Congratulations." Jack, leaning on a silver-handled dark wooden cane, fills the room with his happy, expansive voice.

"Sweetheart how are you?" Laura says as she runs to Sangeeta's side, bending over and kissing her on the forehead. Laura's eyes widen. Happiness lights up the time-traced lines of her face as she looks adoringly at her handsome newborn grandson sleeping peacefully in the bassinet.

"Jack let's wash our hands," Laura says.

The sun now cuts through the morning mist, the sky opalescent, the haze of winter and the rain drops on the green grass below glisten like a million diamonds, shimmering a bit ephemeral.

Alex slowly walks over to the bassinet and gently lifts up his infant son, and as Jack looks on, Alex holds up the baby.

Laura kisses and cuddles little Frank. He coos, makes a series of gurgling sounds and opens his eyes in response to all the attention.

"Little Frank is looking at Laura," Jack says in pride.

"He looks just like you," Laura says to Sangeeta.

"Has your chin and nose," Jack says to Alex, adulation sparkling in his blue eyes.

"And Sangeeta's eyes, her forehead," Laura adds.

Turning to Alex, Laura says, "Alex, you look tired. Why don't you go home and grab a shower and some sleep? Jack and I can stay here with Sangeeta and little Frank."

"Yes, get some rest," Jack says as he rubs Alex's back.

"Okay, Mom, Dad" Alex says, suddenly exhausted. He caresses a stray wisp of dark black hair on Frank's forehead. "Be back in a few. Sangeeta, you need anything?"

"No, get some rest. You need it Alex," Sangeeta says, her voice barely audible. Alex bends down and kisses her pale cheek, giving her hand a gentle squeeze. Sangeeta squeezes back.

Laura walks towards a first slice of sunlight coming in through the thick glass glistening with morning dew, the baby sleeping in her warm embrace. Through the window Laura can see the first signs of traffic in the hospital parking lot below, the marigolds in the surrounding flower beds brighter, more vibrant than she remembers.

"Welcome, Frank S. McKensie," she whispers—one lingering tear drop stranded on her trembling cheek.

❧

Phantoms of the Soul

ंद ंद ंद

February 15, 2000, California

THE FEBRUARY AFTERNOON SUN FLOODS into the living room, filling the home with a welcome warmth, dissolving a long night's exhaustion still clinging to Alex. The rain that hung over the grass like a silver net has magically evaporated, leaving a nourished, rejuvenated earth.

After a long shower, still in his bathrobe, Alex takes a sip on his favorite vanilla flavored coffee, the liquid invigorating, his fingers eagerly absorbing the warmth from the coffee cup. He is aware of the faint smell of the Valentine roses he had bought for Sangeeta the day before. Through the French doors, he looks down at the trail Sangeeta and he walk to the beach as it twists far below to the silver sheen of the Pacific.

On a cerulean canvas a white sail, a speck, appears on the horizon.

A new beginning.

Alex wonders if he has ever seen anything so beautiful before.

He turns, his fingers still wrapped around the coffee cup. He looks into the eyes of his brother Frank in the photograph hanging on the living room wall. Alex walks closer. A bright red marine flag with the globe, anchor and eagle insignia hangs behind. A flag Frank died for.

For a long moment Alex feels a closeness, a bond. Instinctively, he puts down the coffee cup and salutes Frank. Frank stands tall, looks at Alex with a glint of mischievousness in the corner of his blue eyes, a warm, contagious smile on his lips. Alex smiles back.

Still in his bathrobe, he opens the front door and gets the mail. Standing on the landing with the mail clutched in his hand, the flyers, the bills, he stops. He stares intently at a large air mail envelope, white edged in a border of alternating blue and red. His eyes lock on the address on the upper left hand corner.

Nazmul Islam,
232 First Lane, Kalabagan,
Dhaka-1205, Bangladesh.

He reads again, Nazmul Islam. Thousands of tiny wires pull taut inside him.

Suddenly aware of the cold outside, Alex closes the front door. As he walks back to the living room he holds the slightly dog-eared ends like a fragile crystal, any sudden movement sure to crumble it.

In the light of the French doors, he tears open the edge of the envelope. With two fingers he extracts a paper. A hand-written letter in dark blue ballpoint ink on clean lined pages. An envelope is there as well—a small yellowish card, faded, its flap open.

Gripping the card in one hand, and the letter in the other, like a lifeline he is afraid to let go of, risking the loss of something he has waited for all his life, his eyes focus on Nazmul's handwriting.

"Dear Alex,

Hope you are doing well. Meeting with you and the emails we have exchanged over the years have made me wrestle with myself about writing this letter. Many a sleepless night I thought about writing you, about sending you this photograph. She was a friend of mine..."

Alex stops reading.

He turns the small card over.

February 15, 1971.

The ink from a fountain pen, black now blued. The writing in a cursive hand now almost indescript. The moisture stains dissolving memories into the fabric of time.

Alex opens the flap. The tiniest trace of dried tropical flowers, of a place distant, a clinging past, tenacious in its hold of time.

He turns the envelope over and over again. He gazes at the outside. Unable to take out the contents, unable to break the seal of decades. Alex struggles with a sacred silence in the folds of the envelope. Whispers and tears braided in the creases.

The messenger appears.
Tenuous, faded. For so long,

The Silent and the Lost.

૱

Afterwords

❧ ❧ ❧

A BOOK, A LIFE

DACCA, EAST PAKISTAN, 1971

Around midnight, March 25, 1971, my brief happy life, as I had known it, came to an abrupt halt.

"The Pakistani tanks are flying down Mirpur road at sixty miles per hour!" screamed our neighbor over the fence. Tracers tore the night sky into white shreds. Crushed in the talons of the Governor of East Pakistan, Tikka Khan, Dacca lay burning. Time stood still.

Instead of curling up with Steinbeck, I found myself curled up in a fetal position under my bed. I was eleven, a student at St. Gregory's High School, living at First Lane, Kalabagan, Dacca. Our house was a stone's throw from Mirpur Road, less than a mile from *Bangabandhu* Sheikh Mujibur Rahman's house, and only few miles from Dacca University.

About an hour later, bursts of machine gun fire from the vicinity of *Bangabandhu's* residence filled the air.

Yahya Khan condemned *Bangabandhu* of treason, had him arrested at his Dhanmondi residence, sent him to West Pakistan. This as Bhutto claimed Pakistan was saved. Pakistan saved, I think

411

not. Pakistan destroyed, yes.

General Yahya Khan's blitzkrieg erupted around us, and in one fell swoop, we the believers were condemned by the West Pakistani Junta into a land of infidels. We the Muslims became a land of *Kafirs*.

March 25. March 26. For two long days we heard gunfire, we heard rumbling of heavy military trucks and tanks on Mirpur road. We ate little, cooked nothing, and prayed we would not hear the screech of an army truck stopping by our gate. Our lives turned upside down, we cringed in fear.

The morning of March 27. The curfew was lifted.

A flood gate opened. A mass exodus ensued out of Dacca—now a death trap—to the villages. Other than a few private cars, the streets of Dacca were deserted. No rickshaws. No buses. No trucks. A ribbon of dust clung to the roads leading out of Dacca. Walking, bags in tow, determined to escape death, driven by terror, the Daccaites trudged out of a burnt city.

My brother and a relative got on a motorcycle and headed South out of Dacca to Demra on the banks of the Buriganga to reconnoiter out an escape route. On a stretch of road that was dug up a few days before to form a blockade, they approached a four jeep military checkpoint. Too close to turn around and sure to be shot if they ran, they stopped. By the checkpoint, a rickshaw-wallah lay bleeding, shot to death only a few minutes ago. The rickshaw-wallah had finished filling a hole and cried out, "Joy Bangla."

Standing on the tar, filling the holes, my brother counted the minutes till the road was repaired, counted the minutes till they were going to be lined up, shot. A communiqué came over their wireless. The soldiers piled into the jeeps, and left in a hurry. Miraculously, breathing in a new God-given life, my brother and our relative returned.

Unsure of a safe escape route, we waited two more days.

March 29th. Our family and my Uncles' families piled into our red Toyota and another car. We joined thousands fleeing Dacca headed for the villages for safety, taking a circuitous southern route.

The northern route led through the cantonment barricades and sure death.

At Demra, we managed to cross the Buriganga on country boats. But in this mayhem, with no ferries, the cars had to be driven back home. Another dangerous trip.

After a frantic search my father finally found a truck driver willing to drive us towards Khirati, our village home. At the end of the metalled road we all climbed down from the truck and had to take rickshaws to the town of Monohardi. From Monohardi to Khirati, our village home, exhausted and relieved, we walked the last few miles and crossed a rickety bamboo balustrade bridge. Like our precarious footing on the single bamboo *sheko* bridge, our journey, a most dangerous one, luckily ended safely in our village home.

Khirati had been mostly deserted for many years. The sole occupant was my aging grandmother. My grandfather, Shaib Ali, had passed away when my father was young.

Nestled in the variegated brush strokes of nature, life in Khirati for the first month was uneventful. Behind the house was a large piece of ground that had not been tilled for decades, a quiet pasture for cows. Compost had piled up. With time on my hands, out there I decided to grow a field of *data saag*, a tall leafy Bangladeshi variety of spinach.

But with no cows, I pushed and our servant pulled the plough— farming under the shade of jack fruit and mango trees in the middle of a war. In the next two months I grew the most vibrant and healthy *data saag*. On a Thursday we harvested the *saag* and bundled it and I sold my first crop at Khirati bazaar. The bazaar was buzzing with news about army incursions into the villages.

This was 1971: few foreign journalists, cameras. Far in between the voices who reported on the horror of what Yahya Khan had unleashed in East Pakistan. Most of the foreign press was confined to Hotel Intercontinental in the heart of Dacca. For the killers, the sparseness of the news media was their clandestine cover. Into the lush green, into the heartland went the murderers, and given a license to kill, they massacred en masse.

A few months later, the West Pakistani army set up camp in Monohardi. Across the shrunken river, our village, Khirati, was no

413

longer safe. With some foreign press back in the city, Dacca, in the international spotlight, now became safer than the killing fields of the countryside. Four months after escaping from a burnt city, we headed back into the killer's lair, back to our house in Kalabagan.

We walked under the trained machine guns and checkpoints of the army. Into the innumerable rivers, rivulets and ponds of Bangladesh, rows of people were lined up and shot to float away and never to be seen. No body, no body count. The Land of Rivers became the land of the Graveless Genocide, the disposal of bodies more efficient than the Nazis.

Vividly I remember the trip back to Dacca. We had to cross the muddy Buriganga coming into the city. At the river, a soldier with a machine gun, perched atop sandbags, looked down at us. I looked up into the glint of the sun on the dark polished barrel. My knees were weak, my throat parched, a rancid smell breezed off the river.

As we crossed the Buriganga, the waves from our launch lapped over bloated bodies that bobbed up and down with the waves amidst the water hyacinth. There was this single light purple flower, the last farewell on a watery grave, nodding its head—a last tribute to the martyrs, a last salute to the uncounted many.

We entered a transformed city. In every eye was fear. Death prowled the streets in the form of the Army and informants. Every day the tension grew. Fear gripped the city, gripped every heart with the terror of the dreaded knock on the door. In August there was a palpable, visible tension in the air with the surge of the *Mukti Bahini* bombs exploding almost every night in different parts of the city.

On a tense, tenebrous night in August, a group of Razakars and West Pakistani Army surrounded our house. They came with trucks to loot and plunder.

They locked us into a corner room. Paralyzed, we sat while they ransacked our house, interrogated my brother and father at gun-point. In that one interminable hour in that room, with every ticking moment, the walls seemed to be closing in, suffocating the life out of us. What were they doing to my father and brother? Sitting on the bed next to my mother, sweat on my brow, I listened to hear the muffled sounds of an interrogation in the other room. But I could not hear the questions. I sat silently, prayed.

I breathed one of the longest hours of my life, wondering if they were going to kill us. At first, they threatened to take my father away, but after ransacking our home, after they had loaded so much loot, luckily they did not take him. Thank God! If they had taken my father, that would have been the last we would have seen of him.

We lived in terror every day, wondered into every night if the army was going to return. Each day brought more bad news of indiscriminate killings, disappearances. In this taut tension we counted our days to early December.

December. The final stages of the war started. Our house was in the direct line of strafing and bombing runs by the Indian Air Force over Tejgaon Airport. Crouched inside a trench in our back yard, I looked up in awe as the swept-back Indian MIG's made mincemeat of the outdated World War II Pakistani F86 Sabre jets. It was like watching a Harley bear down on a moped. I could taste freedom coming on the wings of those Mig's. It felt close and good.

As the bombings and shelling escalated, again we had to run and hide for our lives. While bombs fell, we ran to take shelter in a warehouse in Old Town Dacca. For a week we had little food or water and no power.

On December 14th, West Pakistani soldiers on loud speakers screamed in the streets to get ready for the last battle. That night, I snuck up onto the roof of the warehouse. I ducked as bullets whizzed by overhead. Zzwisssshhh. Zzwissssshh.

December 16th. Freedom. After nine long months of living, breathing hell, we emerged waving the flag of a free Bangladesh. After nine torturous months, freedom.

In 1972, I penned "Memoirs of a Child," my recollection of the nine months of hell, and was awarded a Shankar Prize by Prime Minister Indira Gandhi in 1973 in New Delhi. In 1974 I received a scholarship from Phillips Academy, Andover, and I left for America.

PHILLIPS ACADEMY, ANDOVER, AMERICA 1974-1977

A hand reached down. Holding on to the rope with one hand, I reached up, grabbed that friendly hand with my other as he pulled me up on top of the rock formation. Jet lagged, having just traveled across the planet, I stood gasping in the crisp Fall air. And this was orientation, my first day at Andover. Rock climbing. Canoeing.

Walking back to Smith House in the Flagstaff cluster where I started my life at Andover, crimson maple leaves floated from a New England sky, crinkled underfoot.

The stark difference in weather between the penetrating heavy humidity of Bangladesh contrasted with the cold crisp air of northern Massachusetts. But as the years unfolded, my young thirst for knowledge braided them together with the threads of history—Bangladeshi and American.

In the afternoons, exhausted after running intervals at the gym, I headed to the Commons room of Smith House for an hour of relaxation, a little break before Calculus. But my hour of *Three Stooges* was interrupted.

I found myself in the middle of the verbal crossfire over Vietnam between two of my house mates. On one side, the son of a South Vietnamese, and on the other the son of an American military officer, both whose fathers were involved in the fighting in Vietnam.

Guys, I just wanted to see Moe poke Larry and Curly in the eye! Here was the Vietnam war and South East Asian policy debates played out in the common room. I listened. I learned.

These wonderful years, the Camelot of my life, learning came as an interaction at Andover, as a process of discussion and dialogue. For me it was finding the context for Bangladesh in the global scheme of things, seeing where I had been in an entirely new light.

In my Junior year, for my American History term paper I wrote about America's involvement in the Bangladesh War of Independence. In the cold embrace of a New England winter, the fire in the hearth of history was Nixon and Kissinger's South East Asian policies. Bangladesh was a paradigm in a Petri dish, a pawn of the Super powers on the chess board of global foreign policy in 1971.

At the Boston Public Library, on microfiche in the New York

Times back-issues, I discovered Nixon and Kissinger's role in covertly providing arms as "spare parts" to West Pakistan, breaking embargoes on arms shipments to Pakistan. Despite US Consul General Archer Blood's famous Blood Telegram from Dacca depicting the ongoing massacre in East Pakistan, protesting America's "moral bankruptcy," Washington supported Islamabad because of Pakistan's Chinese connection.

Nixon's green light to Yahya's actions in East Pakistan made Yahya merciless. And drunk on Nixon-Kissinger support, Yahya Khan, the dictator, felt invincible.

Here was the world of the Super powers. The world of China, Russia, India.

And in 1971 all roads had led to Dacca.

A place I had been.

Sino-Russian conflict over Bangladesh?

Was this a possibility? Could it be?

Russian nuclear sub trailing the USS Enterprise in the Bay of Bengal?

Shades of cold World War III?

I was amazed.

DACHAU, GERMANY 1977

After my graduation from Andover where I had spent three years immersed in German, I went on a low budget Eurail-pass backpacking trip to Germany. Bavaria was wonderful and warm in the summer of '77. Backpack in tow, from Munich I took a train to Dachau.

During 1971, I remembered the recurring comparisons of Tikka Khan and Yahya Khan with Hitler's atrocities.

At the Nazi concentration camp of Dachau, Germany, I looked up and saw welded on top of the gate, *"Arbeit macht frei.* Work makes free!" The sheer irony, the hypocrisy of these words tore through me. I looked at the gas kilns, plates to pull out gold teeth and put them in, the small vents in the "washing chambers" for gas to be let in. The eerie similarities between the Holocaust and the Genocide in Bangladesh, similarities in the styles and techniques of torture became abundantly clear.

In numerous writings and descriptions by the lucky who survived the MP Hostels, Physical Instruction College and Cantonment torture, I remember hearing "worse than Hitler" repeated in 1972. The cantonments of Dacca and Dachau bore a very stark resemblance, not so much in appearance, but in the techniques and psychology of torture.

After being captured in Northern Africa, Yahya Khan was imprisoned in Mussolini's POW camp in Italy and learned firsthand the techniques of the Third Reich. Yahya Khan and Tikka Khan had closely followed in the footsteps of Hitler and Himmler. "Arbeit macht frei!" Work makes you free, yes, sure, while you burn in the gas kilns of Auschwitz and Dachau, or was it the Cantonment of Dacca and the Prison camps of Jessore or Khulna.

Dacca '71 and Dachau '45 became one.

OCCIDENTAL COLLEGE, CALIFORNIA 1980

It was Spring, barely. And I was a Junior at Occidental College in Glendale, California. I was a Physics major and Bill Robin my buddy, a Geophysics major, was jumping up and down to go see Mt. St. Helen's erupt.

After reading Robert M. Pirsig's *Zen and the Art of Motorcycle Maintenance: An Inquiry into Values*, I was convinced that the single most important experience without which my education would remain shamefully incomplete was that of hopping on my RD400 Yamaha pocket rocket two-stroke thumper and go on a 2,400 mile trip with Bill dozing off on the passenger seat.

So we don't have any money. So what. No problem. Had a pocket rocket. I had rebuilt the bike at the Ayatollah house, so called by us because this was during the hostage crisis time of Carter. Our rendition of *Animal House*. The place was a zoo, with six student hippies living in it. We all felt we were hippie hostages in that animal house! I once had the engine of my motorcycle in my second floor bedroom. I knew how to take that engine apart and put it back together with one hand tied behind my back.

It was the April of 1980. The road called.

Scrounge up $200 and we were off, duffle bag tied to the front of the bike, two pants and two jackets on for some warmth. Off we went on that thumping, thrumming bike all the way to Washington state to see an ice-clad volcano erupt.

A journey of discovery in more ways than one.

VIETNAM IN CRESCENT CITY.

Almost two days into the trip, late at night, the front tire of my bike crunched into the parking lot of an all-night Denny's at Crescent City in Northern California, just below the Oregon line. I shivered off the bike, exhausted and shaking in the frigid air.

At the counter, Bill and I held on to our coffee cups to warm our frozen hands. Across from us were two long-haired bikers. We got to talking. The two bikers, burly, wearing denim jackets with large club emblems sewn on the back, said they had a camp just outside of town. They rode out on their Harleys. I followed on my two-stroke.

They turned off the road onto a gravel road, then a dirt road into an abandoned barn, a huge bonfire in front. Around the bonfire we met a crowd of bikers. A rowdy crowd. We ended up being in the middle of about a dozen bikers, most of them Vietnam vets. We partied into the wee hours of the morning.

"College students?"

"Yes."

"Where to?"

"Mt. St. Helen's"

"Ice covered volcano, man. Let's drink to that!"

"Blow baby, blow!"

And if we at Occidental College or at the 'Ayatollah' house thought we were wild, if at the ATO fraternity, the parties were getting out of hand, these bikers were in need of help. The psychiatric variety.

They hooted, hollered. Smoked. Drank.

No Toto, we were not in Kansas anymore. These Vets were off the deep end. They started telling stories, and I listened. Our trip in 1980 to Mt. St. Helen's turned into a trip back to the Vietnam of the '60s.

Some of these guys had gone out of their minds in Vietnam and coming back Stateside, out of Vet hospitals, never quite got back into mainstream American society. Deep in post Vietnam trauma, a deep dark chasm. By this barn these men were still very much reliving their nightmares. And Bill and I thought trying to drive a kidney killing RD400 2400 miles on a journey to see Mt. St. Helen's blow was crazy.

These were all men in their mid to late thirties living a strange life: on the road, on their bikes. Refugees on Main Street, refugees of Vietnam, looking for their minds.

The unrelinquishing grip of Vietnam, its trauma, held these men together in a common camaraderie by this bonfire in Crescent City. In their eyes reflected the pain of a war of no heroes, a war of buddies lost, bodies torn apart, limbs left in the quagmires of South East Asia.

BANGLADESH REVISITED, 1997

In the year 1997, I traveled back and forth to Bangladesh over half a dozen times. During these travels, a quarter century after its birth, the thought of writing a book on the history of Bangladesh, its political and sociological evolution, crossed my mind.

The mercurial moment of possibilities, dreams of a new nation, that dawned on December 16th, 1971 were vastly forgotten, as was the history of where we had been. The aspirations of many remained unattained, atrophied in the light of assassinations and corruption. The Graveless Genocide had become the forgotten Genocide. The undocumented Genocide.

While the plight of the *Bironganas* became pallid, while the *Brionganas* became the pariahs of society, their dreams for a life ephemeral, their pain, sufferings interminable, many of the perpetrators of the very heinous crimes of '71, the ubiquitous Razakars usurped power in Bangladesh. Political polemics drowned the cries for justice. Feral and fervent were the attacks on these women by their own people, in villages, towns and cities. The atmosphere inimical towards protests against the killers of 1971.

As I tried to write this book, as discarded pages piled by my feet, I grappled with a way to tell the story of a people, a country, a pivotal time. Barbara DeMarco-Barett, my Creative Writing Professor at the University of California, Irvine, suggested, and I tried, using every literary technique I had at my fingertips—poems, letters, vignettes, multiple points of view—to write a series of stories, composites, with a common thread, constantly striving to drive the story further, the emotions deeper into the nine months of '71 and its far reaching implications decades later.

Sometimes it takes a lifetime to appreciate a moment. And 1971 is full of such moments. Forty years after the birth of Bangladesh, as I pen my last words of this novel, the fearful costs of '71 have taken on meanings I never envisioned back then.

THE CATCH 22 OF BODY COUNTS

Under trained guns of the Pakistani army, in the ferry trying to get across the bloody muddy Buriganga in '71, I watched bloated bodies bobbing in the water.

Did anyone count those bodies?

No.

Do those human beings not count?

Vanquished dreams, decimated families. Uncounted dead, unwreathed but in the sway of the purple hyacinth on so many rivers. So many, many uncounted dead.

Endless debates have raged about the number killed in 1971. These debates are mendacious, deceitful, drawing attention away from the real issue: murder, rape, genocide. While people debate numbers, we forget the very genocide itself; the debates a cover up over the scathing, salient truth.

R.J. Rummel stated in *Death By Government*, "Consolidating both ranges, I give a final estimate of Pakistan's democide to be 300,000 to 3,000,000, or a prudent 1,500,000." Other authors like Anthony Mascarenhas and Donald W. Beachler have estimated the figure to be between 1 and 3 million civilians killed by the Pakistan Army.

Also we need to recognize the dead of 1971 includes uncounted hundreds of thousands of refugees who died enroute to the border and from dysentery, cholera, typhoid and numerous other diseases plaguing the overcrowded, squalid camps.

One rape is one too many. One child killed, one starving refugee is one too many. One is where our awareness starts. And when we let one become a callous, uncounted death, we create an atmosphere where Genocide can explode and obliterate a people. And in these festering atmospheres, ethnic cleansing, targeted mass killings thrive. Today, only with the awareness that one is too many, can ethnic cleansing and genocides be stopped before they start, before the machetes drip in blood, before the bloated bodies fill the rivers.

The tear stained *āchols* of Nahar Sultanas drape across the face of this planet, today even more than yesterday. Bullet blurs of speed, the Alex Salim McKensies, the war babies of the world search for answers on the sinuous paths traversing terra firma, the ground beneath their feet blurry, their very birth an anguished enigma. Their stories are not indigenous to Bangladesh, sadly they cross the barriers of time and borders and cut across all civilizations.

Words spoken, words read, are breaths brought back alive. With clenched hands, head bowed on the good earth, I pray to have breathed new life into long silenced voices. My hope is that you make these words your own, that you breathe life into their stories, that the interminable anguish of the silent and the lost of Bangladesh finds voice in places distant and near.

Bangladesh's Graveless Genocide is one of the most underwritten tragedies in the history of mankind. In the memory of this world, it is important to remember the silent and the lost of 1971. Their sacrifices, their lives. Flowers that never bloomed. Smiles never to brighten the earth.

Acknowledgements
※   ※   ※

The fabric of this novel is woven with the threads of war, the sad vicissitudes of many—the Martyrs, the *Bironganas*, the *Mukti Juddhas*, the wounded—who have been for so long silent and lost. A million salaams to the martyrs who gave their lives, for the *Bironganas*, for the wounded and the freedom fighters who fought with nothing against odds seemingly insurmountable and won.

Without the encouragement of Brother James, Headmaster of St. Gregory's High School, and my father, Mr. M.A. Majid, my writing life would not have taken root and flourished. Encouragement that led me to write in 1972 'Memoirs of a Child,' and in 1973 meet and receive a Shankar Award from the Prime Minister of India, Mrs. Indira Priyadarshini Gandhi. I saluted her and as she smiled I expressed my deep gratitude to her for her seminal role in liberating Bangladesh.

"Writing is the act of burning through the fog of your mind," said Natalie Goldberg, and on that note many thanks to my editor, Debra Cross. Her patient, detailed editing has made this work possible, as she has assisted me in burning through the fog of my own mind, in reaching for the texture of time, and in the details seeking the truth, the beat, the rhythm of the story.

As I penned this novel, my moral compass was given direction by two books recording the facts and capturing the sweep of heart-breaking emotions of the 1971 Bangladesh War of Independence. They are:

Ekattorer Dingulee, Days of '71, by Jahanara Imam, and
Ami Birongona Bolchhi, I, the Heroine, Speak by Nilima Ibrahim.

Compellingly captured in these two books are the excruciating details about the *Bironganas*, the *Mukti Bahini* and everyone else whose lives were wrapped up in the macabre nightmare of the nine months of 1971.

Ekattorer Dingulee, Days of '71, is written in the form of a diary where day by day events unfold around Jahanara Imam and her family in the center of Dhaka. Her detailed account of her son Rumi, who joined the *Mukti Bahini,* his stories and life on the run as a guerrilla, as well as everyday events around her are poignantly etched in her monumental book. I have walked with Rumi on muddy roads towards Agartala, I have cried with Jahanara Imam listening to that song on *Swadhin Bangla Betar Kendro*, lamenting the loss of a son, a loss only a mother can feel.

Originality has a flavor all its own. And that is what I found in Nilima Ibrahim's interviews as a social worker with seven *Birongana's* in *Ami Birongona Bolchhi*. Nilima Ibrahim was a Bangladeshi educator, littérateur and social worker. Written in the first person, these heart wrenching stories tell what each of these women went through in 1971 and equally important the tragic aftermath of war, the social castigation that these *Bironganas* faced in a liberated Bangladesh in 1972. And it is her interviews as a social worker that make this book an outstanding source.

The aftermath of war, its long lasting scars, are encapsulated by none better than the lives led by war babies. Ryan Badal Good, his life in Canada and his return to Bangladesh as depicted in *War Babies*, a documentary directed by Raymonde Provencher, released in 2002 from Canada was instrumental in the writing of this book. Ryan's life gave me direction, gave me definition. War babies, regardless of race and color—black, brown, white, from every corner of terra firma—paint a picture of the ravages of war on this planet. And their stories are sadly as valid today as they were yesterday.

Tales of Millions, by Rafiqul Islam, is an invaluable historical compendium of 1971 particularly in detailing the military and guerrilla operations, the arms used, the type of mines detonated, and the intricacies of war field operations.

Professor Nur Ullah of East Pakistan Engineering University taped from his residence just across the open field the Jagannath Hall massacre described in *Dacca or Dachau*. A heroic effort, the only video documentary of the murders in progress at Dhaka University, it serves today as it did in 1972 to inspire me to write, to put into words the tragedies of '71 on the grounds of Dhaka University.

The chapter *While My Guitar Gently Weeps*, was based on the DVD as well as the website for *The Concert for Bangla Desh*. Always, heartfelt acknowledgements to Ravi Shankar and George Harrison and everyone involved in the most magnanimous musical event in the history of Bangladesh, the most significant in its birth.

The Vanderbilt University News Archives were used extensively to research the national news sections that are described in *Tears in the Heart* and *One World*.

The chapters, *Intelligentsia Genocide* and *On Wings of Freedom*, are based on Hamida Rahman's article, *"Katasurer Baddhabhumi"* (*The Mass Grave at Katasur*), where she describes her visit to Rayerbazar.

On the cover of the book, the unknown photographer who took the picture of the *Mukti Bahini* soldiers in the water remains anonymous. In future revisions, I hope to find and give my salaams to that person.

I deeply appreciate Dina Patel and Myra Hissami's meticulous and artistic efforts that have made the cover design of this book possible.

The Bangladeshi imprint of the book cover is based on a painting by Samiran Chawdhury and printed with the help of Najmul Khan and the design group at Twister Media.

For their insightful critique of the book, I am grateful to Roger Chasin, Robin and Syeda Khundkar, Virendra Mahajan, Mofidul Hoque, Nawaz Ahmad, and Akku Chowdhury.

I am indebted to Md. Habibullah, retired Assistant Registrar of Dhaka University, for recounting his family's survival on the Dhaka University campus on March 25, 1971.

Discussions with my brother, Kaisar Majid, and his recounting of his motorcycle ride to Demra on March 27th refocused my memories of those dark nights and days.

I retraced the steps of my characters in Bangladesh with the help of Md. Fazlul Haque whose keen sense of place and people is surpassed by none. He was able to find locals who were at Rayerbazaar just after the liberation of Bangladesh, dig around the back of the Halls of Dhaka University, find professors who were on campus just before March 25, 1971, smooth the way through Mother Teresa's. For the pounding on the pavement research assistance, second to none, thank you!

I must not forget Dr. Nizamuddin Ahmed, former Dean of Faculty, BUET for being so cordial on my visit there and describing the campus of EPUET in 1971 and also his experiences at the guerrilla training camp in India.

My wife's insightful critique and editing were invaluable in the writing of this book. For her reading, re-reading, and editing every single draft of the novel, many thanks Zeba.

And finally, without the smiling enthusiasm of my infant son, Zarrar, first avidly typing away on his keyboard while sitting on my lap and then with keen eyes and bated breath, waiting for the printer to instantaneously spit out paper, I would not have been able to get to printing this last line in such focused fashion.

Glossary

achar—*n.* Pickle, usually spicy, made from a variety of vegetables and fruits. The name is used in Bangladesh and in most regions of India.

áchol—*n.* End of the sari, can be intricate in design, draped over the head.

aka-dooka—*n.* A hop-skotch type of game played by children on markings on the ground.

aktara—*n.* one string musical instrument carried by wandering bards of Bangladesh, used in folk and philosophical songs.

almira—*n.* armoire; a usually tall cupboard or wardrobe.

alna—*n.* a rack or stand usually of wood for clothes.

amlokhi—*n.* sub-tropical green bite-sized berry-like tart fruit.

amrool—*n.* sub-tropical fruit; bell-shaped edible berry sometimes called a Java apple.

Anarkali churidar—*n.* Frilly, princess like dress, worn on top of the *churidar* pajama. Refers to the famous lovelorn dancer Anarkali of Akbar's court; usually made of chiffon or muslin. *Churidars* are tightly fitting trousers that can be worn by both men and women. They are wide at the top and quite narrow at the ankle.

attem—*n.* orphan.

bachaow—*v.* help, save me, cry for help.

bandar—*n.* monkey.

bari—*n.* house.

Baul—*n.* wandering bard, musician.

Beti—*n.* endearing term for daughter.

Bhabi—*n.* sister-in-law, also endearing term for calling married women.

Bhaijan—*n.* endearing term for brother.

Bhai—*n.* brother. Also commonly used endearingly after the name of elders.

bhat—*n.* cooked rice.

Bir—*n.* hero.

biri—*n.* A small hand-rolled cigarette manufactured in Bangladesh, India and other southeast Asian countries. Also called *bidi*, the cigarettes are made from tobacco wrapped in tendu or temburni leaf, sometimes tied on one or both ends with a string.

borooi—*n.* sub-tropical green plum-like fruit with hard seed core, indigenous to Bengal and the Indian sub-continent.

bosti—*n.* slum.

Bou Maa—*n.* endearing term for daughter-in-law.

Boudi—*n.* elder brother's wife, Hindu term. Also used in an endearing way to call married women.

Chacha—*n.* uncle.

Chachi—*n.* aunt.

chalta—*n.* fist-sized to grape-fruit sized tree-fruit, fibrous and layered, tart and acidic.

chaltar achar—*n.* Pickle made from *chalta* (see definition above.)

chanachur—*n.* Mixture of spicy dried ingredients, which may include fried lentils, peanuts, chickpea flour noodles, corn, vegetable oil, chickpeas, flaked rice, fried onion and curry leaves. Also known as Bombay mix.

chira—*n.* flattened rice, similar to puffed rice.

chitoi pithas—*n.* *Pitha* is a type of cake or bread common in Bangladesh and India, usually sweet. *Chitoi pitha* is a very tasty and popular winter snack in Bangladesh.

chootia—*n.* swear word, asshole.

chotpoti—*n.* chick peas in tamarind sauce.

daal—*n.* lentil soup.

daow—*n.* curved machete.

Devi—*n.* Hindu goddess.

dhenki—*n.* The *dhenki* is a foot-operated rice mill made of a log of wood fixed to a pivot, used for husking rice and for pounding rice to a fine powder. Usually it was worked by village women, two at a time, who push on one end of the log with their feet, raising the pestle on the other end. They let go, the pestle on the other end of the log falls on the rice husks in a small wooden bowl dug into the floor, separating the husk from the rice. The *dhenki* is now antiquated with electric mills abounding in Bangladesh.

dost—*n.* friend.

dupatta—*n.* A long, multi-purpose scarf usually worn in a 'v' over the chest that is essential to many South Asian women's suits and matches the woman's garments. Also a sign of modesty.

durwan—*n.* doorkeeper, guard.

Eid—*n.* Short for either *Eid ul-Fitr* or *Eid al-Adha,* two of the most auspicious and celebrated days of Islam. A day marked by special morning prayer, followed by a sumptuous meal and celebrations.

Eid Mubarak—*n.* A traditional Muslim greeting used on the festivals of *Eid ul-Adha* and *Eid ul-Fitr.* Literally translated into English it means, "blessed festival," or "may you enjoy a blessed festival."

Falgun—*n.* Bengali month marking the arrival of spring, usually starts around February 13th.

foochka—*n.* Also known as *pani puri* is a popular street snack in Bangladesh and India. It is comprised of a round, hollow *puri* shell, fried crisp and filled with a watery mixture of tamarind, chili and potato.

gamcha—*n.* Literally translated is a "sweat body wipe." *Gamcha* is a traditional Bangladeshi and Indian towel made up of thin coarse cotton fabric. Although it is normally used for drying one's body after bathing, *gamcha* serves other purposes also. It forms an important item of men's clothing, especially for the laborers of the Indian society. One often sees laborers, construction workers and farmers carrying a *gamcha* on their shoulders.

garam masala—*n.* *Garam* is the Indian word for "warm" or "hot." Containing up to twelve spices, it is a blend of dry-roasted, ground spices from the colder climes of northern India, adding a sense of "warmth" to the palate and to the spirit. There are almost as many variations of *garam masala* as there are Indian cooks. The mixture can include black pepper, cinnamon, cloves, coriander, cumin, cardamom, dried chiles, fennel, mace and nutmeg as well as other spices.

ghat—*n.* A broad flight of cemented steps leading down to the bank of a river or pond in Bangladesh and India.

gram—*n.* village.

haramir baccha—*n.* bastard's son.

haramzada—*n.* bastard.

Hawaldar—*n.* military rank. Examples: Company Quartermaster *Hawaldar* and Regimental Quartermaster *Hawaldar*.

hookah—*n.* Also known as a water pipe, is a single or multi-stemmed instrument for smoking. The smoke is cooled and filtered by passing it through water. One form, using a coconut as a base to hold the water, is very popular with farmers in Bangladesh.

Jai Namaaz—*n.* Muslim prayer mat.

jallad—*n.* butcher.

Jamindar—*n.* landlord.

janaza—*n.* funeral.

jawan—*n.* soldier.

kaash phool—*n.* grass native to South Asia. It is a perennial grass, growing up to three meters in height, with spreading roots. Has beautiful white feathery plume-like flowers, often adorning river and wetland banks with a swath of white.

kajol—*n.* An ancient eye liner, used by women to apply a black lining around the eye.

kalbaishaki—*n.* sudden Bengali spring storm.

kalshi—*n.* earthen pot used to carry water.

kameez—*n.* long tunic worn by many people from the Indian subcontinent (usually with a *salwar* or *churidar*); long top. The *kameez* is usually cut straight and flat. The neckline, sleeves and bottom edge are often decorated with embroidery or lace.

kashondi—*n.* fiery chile mustard relish popular in Bengal.

Kathol—*n.* Jack fruit, the largest tree fruit grown. Sometimes weighing over a hundred pounds. The many seeds inside are covered in a sweet edible yellow fibre. A much relished fruit during the monsoons of Bangladesh.

khadi—*n.* Bangladeshi and Indian hand-woven cotton cloth. Also a symbol of patriotism often associated with Mahatma Gandhi.

Khallama—*n.* aunt.

Khandan—*n.* lineage, heritage.

khichri—*n.* a dish made from rice and lentils.

Khoda Hafez—*v.* God Bless you.

koi bajhee—*n.* variety of carp fried in oil, battered in spices.

korma—*n.* sweet curry, yogurt based.

kurta—*n.* A traditional item of clothing worn by both men and women in the sub-continent; a loose shirt falling either just above or somewhere below the knees of the wearer.

lail—*n.* Narrow raised dirt path between fields, used to walk on and demark fields.

langol—*n.* hand held angled wooden plough pulled by cattle. A metal blade is attached at the tip of the wood cutting into the earth as cattle pull it along the rows.

lassi—*n.* yogurt drink.

lehenga choli—*n.* *Choli* is a short-sleeved blouse or bodice, often exposing part of the midriff, worn by women in the Indian sub-continent. The ensemble still comprises a customary long skirt, the *choli* and the *dupatta*. The *dupatta* is currently made of silk, linen or chiffon.

lungi—*n.* Also known as a sarong, is a traditional skirt-like garment worn around the waist by men in the subcontinent and Asia. It is particularly popular in regions where the heat and humidity create an unpleasant climate for trousers.

machranga—*n.* kingfisher.

mahallah—*n.* neighborhood, section of town.

makaal faal—*n.* fake fruit; term used to mean imposter.

matla—*n.* flat wide bamboo hat worn by farmers.

Meemshaib—*n.* respectful term for madame, lady.

mela—*n.* fair, festive gathering.

mehndi—*n.* henna.

435

Milad—*n.* a Muslim prayer meeting.

misriv—*n.* cupboard.

mooa—*n.* made by mixing puffed-rice with molasses as a binder and forming it into a ball. Eaten as a sweet.

moola—*n.* Daikon, long white Asian radish.

muezzin—*n.* The official of a mosque who calls from the minaret the faithful to prayer five times a day.

Mukti Bahini—*n.* freedom fighters; guerrillas of the 1971 Bangladesh War of Independence.

Mukti—*n.* freedom; also freedom fighter.

Mukti Fauj—*n.* Freedom fighter, was the first term used to refer to the Bangladeshi guerrillas before *Mukti Bahini* became popular.

Mukti Juddha—*n.* Freedom fighter; guerrilla of the 1971 Bangladesh War of Independence.

muri—*n.* puffed rice.

naala—*n.* open road-side drain.

naan—*n.* flat, leavened bread of northwest India, made of white flour and baked in a *tandoor*.

napeet—*n.* barber.

naru—*n.* coconut snowballs, a Bengali dessert.

neem—*n.* medicinal tree with bitter tasting leaves and branches. Branches used for toothbrush, and extract used as organic pesticide.

paan—*n.* betel leaf; chewed with other ingredients in the Indian subcontinent.

para—*n.* Place, meaning a small section of a city or town or village that is a neighborhood by itself.

pitha—*n.* A type of cake or bread made from rice flour common in Bangladesh and India.

pilau—*n.* Bangladeshi, Indian and Middle Eastern form of fried rice; a dish in which rice is cooked in a seasoned broth. In some cases, the rice attains its brown color by being stirred with bits of burned onion, as well as a mix of spices.

puris—*n.* stuffed deep-fried bread. Can be stuffed with lentil and little spices.

pukur—*n.* pond.

puthi—*n*. A small fresh-water fish, usually swims at the edge of lakes and ponds close to the surface.

rakhashi—*n*. witch, daemon.

Riaspora—*n*. the returning Diaspora. Term created by author.

roti—*n*. daily bread handmade of finely milled whole wheat flour and water.

rupkotha—*n*. fairly tales.

salwar kameez—*n*. The *salwar* is a loosely-fitting pajama-like pant. The *kameez* is a long shirt of tunic length which hits at the middle of the thigh, but traditionally, it would come down to the top of the knee.

Shaakha Pola—*n*. Red (*pola*) and white (*shaakha*) colored bangles symbolise marriage in Hinduism.

Shadhinata—*n*. freedom.

Shaliks—*n*. A very common bird in the myna family in Bangladesh with a striking bright yellow beak. It is about the size of an American robin with colors ranging from brown on the lower breast to deep shiny black on the head and neck.

sheko—*n*. Bamboo balustrade, bridge, usually one or two bamboo wide used for foot crossings. They can be precarious, as the ropes tying the bamboos together can break underfoot.

shemai—*n*. sweet vermicelli.

sherwani—*n*. men's overcoat, long, usually reaching to the knees.

shindoor—*n*. Hindu red dot or line on the forehead, a sign of being married.

shootki—*n*. dried fish curry, usually small fish, very pungent.

Surah—*n*. verse from the Koran usually uttered in prayer.

taaks—*n*. hillocks.

tabiz—*n*. good-luck charm, or verse from the Koran, written on a piece of paper, folded and put inside a small copper capsule worn around the neck on a string.

tabla—*n*. Indian sub-continental drum. A pair of percussive drums which can vary in their size and timbre. Derived from the arabic word for drum, *tabl*.

tangra macher dopeaza—*n*. fish curry made from a small fresh-water fish.

teeps—*n.* dot on forehead.

tookai—*n.* street urchin, young child living on the street, trash-digging for discarded items to scrounge out a living.

ABU ZUBAIR was born in Dhaka, Bangladesh. He attended St. Gregory's High School in Dhaka and came to the United States on a scholarship to Phillips Academy, Andover, Massachusetts in 1974. Zubair holds degrees in Engineering from Boston University.

He lives in Southern California.

The Silent and the Lost is his debut novel.

Praise for *The Silent and the Lost*

"Saga of Liberation" - India Post
Prem Kishore
A searing account...Zubair is a consummate master spinning between two time zones shifting between periods and situations as he explores the grim past, constructing frameworks of memory versus history, flashbacks of pain and loss, destruction and hope.

San Francisco Review of Books
"Vivid characterizations and searing descriptions of wartime violence arouse sympathy for the freedom fighters, as do the hardships inflicted upon them by the eventually defeated Pakistani (West Pakistan) national forces.
...compelling romantic epic dramatizes the price paid for freedom while weaving a remarkable lesson in later twentieth century history."

Midwest Book Review
"dancing between a story of war and a story of romance, "The Silent and the Lost" is a unique and very highly recommended read"

The Daily Star
Nameera Ahmed
"**a compelling heart-rendering read** which develops striking imagery in itself... biting portrayal... an evocative tapestry of deep emotional scars, broken lives that brings to life characters that will linger long after the book is read...touches the soul."

"Incredible novel"
Patricia Blomeley-Maddigan
"Facts of history wound up in a story bound to reach the heart of readers...will change the reader forever....scenes and chapters [are] filled with such love, beauty, and grace...subtle experiences of spirituality expressed about the characters."